ASSASSINATION! JULY 14

Assassination! July 14

Ben Abro

With a historical essay by
James D. Le Sueur

University of Nebraska Press
Lincoln and London

© 1963 by Ben Abro
Historical essay © 2001 by James D. Le Sueur
All rights reserved
Manufactured in the United States of America

♾

Library of Congress Cataloging-in-Publication Data
Abro, Ben.
Assassination! July 14 / Ben Abro; with a historical essay by James D. Le Sueur.
p. cm.
ISBN 0-8032-5939-5 (pbk.: alk. paper)
1. Gaulle, Charles de, 1890–1970—Assassination attempts—Fiction.   2. Attempted
assassination—Fiction.   3. Intelligence officers—Fiction.   4. British—France—Fiction.
5. France—Fiction.   I. Le Sueur, James D.   II. Title.
PR6051.B76A96   2001
823'.914—dc21
00-064778

Contents

Illustrations

1. The Beginning

ONE

Baraka

The sun shone down upon Montceau for the visit of President de Gaulle. Banners of welcome stretched across the main street. With the stalls of a traveling fair beneath, they gave a holiday atmosphere to the small country town. But the motorcycle escort that guided the president's Citroën to the rostrum in the main square was there for protection rather than ceremony.

It was two years since de Gaulle had been solemnly sentenced to death by the Secret Army Organization (OAS). There had been many attempts to carry it out. Some had failed by a matter of inches. Others had been abandoned before the police had discovered them. But the precautions had not ceased. Each proposal of de Gaulle's to visit a particular region of France involved several months of preparation and the transport of as many thousand members of the police force.

Thus for the minister of national security and his subordinate Morin there was nothing new in the scene below them. They stood at a window of the Town Hall, watching de Gaulle leave the Citroën and, at the mayor's invitation, climb up the steps onto the rostrum.

It was the mayor who spoke first. In the absence of a microphone, he addressed the crowd with tremendous effort, attempting almost literally to throw his voice as far as those at the back. It was an effort wasted on Morin, who had heard the speech a hundred times before.

He thought instead of the men he had placed at every point affording cover for an ambush along the road the motorcade would take to the next town. Every farmhouse, every tumbledown hut, every clump of trees, was being guarded. Helicopters patrolled above to warn of a possible air attack.

Morin had nearly forty men in the crowd below. There were more still on the rooftops overlooking the square. And against the individual who was prepared to sacrifice his life to kill de Gaulle, Morin had a squad of men prepared to go to the same extreme to save him. These were the eight personal bodyguards, the "gorillas," who were standing beside the president on the rostrum.

At the slightest sign of danger, it was the duty of three of them to hurl de Gaulle to the ground and to wrap themselves around him. The other five fired five hundred rounds a day in training. They could hit a man between the eyes at sixty feet with either hand. A suicide attempt would be destroyed almost before it could begin.

But there was a further protection of a different kind. It was provided by de Gaulle himself.

"I have *baraka*," he had once said. No one knew exactly what *baraka* was. It was thought to be a mystical protection claimed by some primitive tribes. But it meant that de Gaulle believed the bombs and the bullets of the OAS would bounce off him when they came, as ineffectually as a paper death sentence.

Morin had taken care of the natural side of security, de Gaulle of the supernatural. It was impossible for the OAS to kill the man they hated.

And yet . . .

TWO

Canine Kamikazes

Reluctantly the mayor was bringing his speech to a close within the limits set for him by the organizers of the tour.

De Gaulle stepped forward as the mayor finished and extended his arms in front of him as if to embrace this crowd of a thousand people. There was a pause: for a moment de Gaulle seemed overcome with emotion. "Dear citizens of Montceau," he began with great feeling. Morin looked at the crowd. Women were crying and everyone was gazing at de Gaulle with great concentration. Only the plainclothesmen stood out because their attention was elsewhere. But there was nothing to attract their suspicion.

Morin looked at his watch. De Gaulle would be speaking for another four minutes. With his elbows on the windowsill, Morin leaned farther out to catch the sun. He noticed three Alsatian dogs behind the crowd. They had just turned into the square from the main street, and they were coming at a walk toward the crowd.

Each dog had a box tied around its neck: a box that hung like the little brandy-barrels on the Swiss St. Bernards. Morin remembered the idea from his boyhood. A Great Dane that, seen through children's eyes, would look as large as a horse would sit beside a poster proclaiming his measurements, and you would be invited by the poster and the gypsy owner to place a coin in just such a box around his neck, and then to stroke him, if you were brave enough.

De Gaulle would speak for three more minutes. Morin's head was in the sun and he was beginning to dream a little. He looked again toward the oncoming dogs that were now about a hundred and fifty yards beyond the farthest person in the crowd. They've chosen a perfect day for making money, he thought, with everyone gathered in the town square.

There was nobody with the dogs. But then, Morin thought, if the owners were gypsies they'd realize it would be best for them not to intrude. The dogs could do it better by themselves; they seemed to know what they were about. The dogs indeed looked extremely well trained.

They had been advancing at a steady speed, three abreast, and had halved the distance that a moment before had separated them from Morin.

"Beautiful animals," Morin could not help exclaiming to himself. In those inevitable moments of fantasy, like now, when he was not a senior police official but the mysterious and infinitely enviable owner of a country house with rambling grounds—*rambling* was a word that indicated something vague and vast, but nonetheless real; it therefore occurred frequently in Morin's dreams—in these "rambling" grounds a brown-and-black Alsatian was always at his side. Early on autumn mornings, as he walked in track suit and basketball shoes, the Alsatian would be with him; after lunch they would play on the lawn, and in the evening they would be together as Morin sipped cognac in front of a "rambling" fire.

At this point, his fantasies pulled at him so sharply that he woke from the almost hypnotic state which the three advancing Alsatians had induced in him. He jerked his head out of the sun and became once more Morin the professional. A glance at the crowd told him that nothing had changed, though he noticed one man holding a small unlit cigar to his mouth. An odd smoke for a country man, though perhaps he was the tobacconist.

De Gaulle was bringing his speech to a close with the assurance that the country people's claims would be listened to. "But," said de Gaulle, "though your demands will be noted and attended to, you must realize that, things being what they are and in the critical period for our country through which we are passing, any exaggerated claims risk the destruction of that national unity and cooperation upon which the maintenance of our republic depends so much." Morin registered this familiar conditional, and thought that some of the crowd had noticed it too.

But in a moment there would be applause, and de Gaulle would wade through the crowd, pulling himself from handshake to handshake toward his car. The descent into the crowd was the climax, dear to de Gaulle, that cost the security men so much in anxiety. De Gaulle would quickly leave his bodyguards behind, and it was up to the men placed in the crowd and to the rooftop watchers to ensure that nothing happened.

De Gaulle paused before his last words. "Montcelliens, Montcelliennes, do not betray the trust you gave me in May, 1958. Vive Montceau! Vive la France!" His arms fell to his sides; he made his way down the steps of the platform.

In one movement the crowd, the watchers on the roof and the security men in the square leaned forward, the first to be among those who had shaken the hand of General de Gaulle, the second and third as professionals whose duty it was to miss nothing.

The three Alsatians had reached the very edge of the crowd. Morin could see the white plate bearing the request for money on the front of the box that each dog carried. But why, he wondered, didn't they wait until the crowd dispersed, instead of forcing their way through so purposefully at a time when no one would notice them? For surely it could not be that they wanted *not* to be noticed. Morin was puzzled and felt strangely uneasy.

De Gaulle had by this time penetrated a yard or so into the crowd. Then Morin noticed a very curious thing. The man in the middle of the crowd with the small cigar seemed not to be drawing, but to be blowing on it. Morin looked again. There was no doubt; the man's cheeks were puffed and red; and he was giving no indication of a wish to shake the hand of de Gaulle. The three Alsatians had disappeared.

Morin moved away from the window and hesitated. He knew nothing, but his uneasiness was so strong that he had to do something. He excused himself to the minister. He half ran to the head of the stairs, then in a kind of a panic he tumbled down them. He knew he could not reach the man with the cigar in time. He ran across the gravel of the square to the back of the crowd where he had seen the dogs disappear.

He found two dogs still on the outside searching vainly for a way in. The third Morin caught sight of two or three rows in front of him. He pushed his way through to find himself in the third row and the object of some unpleasant remarks. He caught the Alsatian by its collar, and began to pull it with him out of the crowd. "Help me get him out," he said to a peasant beside him in a voice whose tone showed that he wasn't asking a favor. Together they brought the dog out. The man moved to return to the crowd.

"Hold the other two fast," Morin ordered him, and he looked down at the dog he was holding. "I am dumb—thank you," said the inscription nailed to the box. Nevertheless, Morin asked the Alsatian a question, with his arm around him and in quite a different tone from the one he had just been using.

"Now what's it all about?" he asked, speaking perhaps more to himself than to the dog. He had forgotten the man with the cigar, who now stood at the edge of the crowd watching Morin and the dog. The man brought the still unlit and indeed unlightable cigar to his lips and blew, just as Morin had seen him do from the Town Hall window. But this time Morin was not watching. He had noticed a short string hanging from one corner of the box fastened round the dog's neck. Attached to the end of the string was a piece of wood the size of an acorn.

Morin was about to reach for it when the Alsatian forestalled him. It caught the wooden acorn in its teeth and tugged sharply to one side. Morin recognized the action of a grenade thrower. But he was unable to profit from his discovery. The box was breaking. The sound and the sight of an explosion came slowly toward him, to split his ears and his eyes as it had done the box.

2. Max

THREE

Mr. Palk

That it was almost lunchtime Mr. Palk could tell not so much from the emptiness of his stomach as from the feeling, born of long practice, that the two hands of the office clock were about to join over the figure twelve. He realized that, after several years in the office, he'd come to have a better feeling for the clock than for his own stomach. Mr. Palk looked up and saw that Mr. Cornwall knew about the clock too; he watched him complete his schedule of current order balances with an air of pride and enthusiasm that was only understandable to those who knew him when they knew also that he would be obliged to stop his work in a very short number of seconds.

Mr. Cornwall had once confided to Mr. Palk that he could never really enjoy his lunch hour unless he'd done a good morning's work. These last-minute efforts in self-deception with which most mornings and some afternoons were concluded were sometimes so successful that twelve o'clock and the general movement following would bring a sharp "Dammit!" from Mr. Cornwall's lips. And if you interrupted this concentration upon concentration with a remark or a question, as Mr. Palk had once been unable to prevent himself doing, by asking, of all things, "What do you make the time, old man?" you would receive only the raising of a hypocritical hand for an answer, its palm turned toward you like a policeman's: "Do not disturb," it would read.

Apart from these moments in which he was not to be approached, Cornwall was a pleasant enough person. Mr. Palk admired the device by which he made office work bearable and even fulfilling. He might have deprived him of it, with a few simple questions and observations, but he had no wish at the moment to be the sole support of Mr. Cornwall once he had kicked away his crutch.

Mr. Palk looked dreamily at the clock and played a game. The little hour hand was lying under the larger minute hand, her head on the white between the one and two of the figure twelve. The rest of her lay on the clock face, white like a sheet. The one and the two of the figure twelve were where the pillow ballooned out on either side of her head as it rested there after the chase of the last hour. For a few moments she was completely covered by the large minute hand. Then the minute hand moved away, and Mr. Palk got up and walked over to behind Mr. Cornwall.

"Well," he said, "that looks a fine job of work you've done there this morning, old man. You're miles ahead of me."

Mr. Cornwall was pleased and even stayed a moment longer at his desk to tidy up. He detached the day's ticket from the book of canteen vouchers that he kept in the top drawer of his desk.

"You won't be needing that today," Mr. Palk pointed out. "Remember?"

"Of course," exclaimed Mr. Cornwall, annoyed at his forgetfulness. "Dr. Soper said he'd be speaking today, didn't he? But I didn't bring any sandwiches."

"Never mind," said Mr. Palk kindly, "I've got more than enough for myself."

With lunch thus assured for both of them, they left the small room where they worked together.

If there was a single general question that Mr. Palk asked himself of his colleagues in the office, it was to wonder what device they had like Mr. Cornwall's last-minute concentration that allowed them to get through their office routine. With the typists it was undoubtedly sex in its most general sense, and the interminable fund of conversation it permitted, stimulated by the constantly renewed university material passing through the office on executive training courses. With the men it was more difficult to say. Perhaps some had a club to look forward to in the evening or at the weekend; but most simply felt that office work was a respectable means of earning bread for the family.

Had the others been asked Mr. Palk's question about Mr. Palk himself, they would probably have laughed and said triumphantly, "I know, it's his asthma! It's because he goes down with it every now and then that he's able to take it here."

Mr. Palk's asthma was indeed proverbial. It had begun soon after he joined the firm two years before, and it kept him away from the office at irregular intervals. It had endeared him to the typists, who were rather thrilled at first to be asking him personal questions about his health. But Mr. Palk was not a glamorous figure. The initial thrill had soon gone. There was left an almost maternal affection for the old fellow and his Affliction. It had even aroused the jealousy of his less fortunate male colleagues, who, in their irritation over office routine, had no such complaint to fall back on.

True, they had often wondered how a man of Mr. Palk's age, who was stricken with asthma into the bargain, had ever managed to find a place in their office at all. There were even some who had whispered of a certain complicity between Mr. Palk and Mr. Salmon.

But there was no doubting Mr. Palk's word. After his first attack, he had returned with a full and authoritative medical report stating that, despite treatment, the asthmatic attacks would almost certainly recur over the years to come. And the forecast had been fully borne out. Mr. Salmon, head of the London office of ERA Export Limited (ERA for England, Rhodesia and America), had debated with himself after examination of the report, and had decided, in view of the high standard of Mr. Palk's work and of the difficulty he would have without degrees in finding another job, to exercise his mercy.

So Mr. Palk had stayed on. And many people with no previous knowledge of asthma began to consider him as typically asthmatic. His occasional cough and heavy breathing were remarked on, of course, but so also were his rather lifeless walk and the small particles of dead skin from the scalp that would bespatter from time to time the collar of a suit which appeared to have been woven from cardboard. But this is not to say that Mr. Palk was in any way a repulsive-looking person. He was simply the man in the office who suffered from asthma and he was never regarded as anything else.

Mr. Palk followed Mr. Cornwall into the corridor. A porter stood halfway along, at the entrance to the board room, a finger to his lips, enjoining silence: the directors were in conference. The typists flew by like so many birds, to stop, chattering, outside the washrooms. Mr. Palk and Mr. Cornwall followed at a more sedate pace with their colleagues. The conversation among the secretaries, they found, concerned the likelihood of such and such a menu. The knowledge that the issue would be decided beyond recall in a short while and independently of what decision they might reach seemed only to intensify their interest in the conversation.

"Time for a holiday, Mr. Palk?" asked one typist, giggling. "How long's it been now—nearly two months without a break, hasn't it?"

"Two months too long," said Mr. Palk, joining in the banter.

In the men's cloakroom, Mr. Palk and Mr. Cornwall straightened their white collars in the mirror. After a wash and a brush-up, they went back down the corridor to the lift, Mr. Palk carrying his small packet of cheese sandwiches. The porter was still in attendance. As Mr. Palk and Mr. Cornwall came level, the porter, at a signal, no doubt, from the interior,

halted with one arm the pedestrian traffic in the corridor and opened the
door of the board room. Seven directors came out, still clearly in the throes
of discussion, seemingly unaware of their surroundings, as if content to leave
the driving to an invisible chauffeur. The porter, in fact, quickly assumed
this function by calling out, "This way, gentlemen, if you please." Mr. Palk
realized that he was addressing those directors from the Rhodesian and
American branches who were unfamiliar with the corridors of the London
office. He noticed Mr. Salmon among them, beckoning his companion.

"What are Nchangas, Cornwall?" he asked, as if the detail had for a
moment slipped his mind.

"Up ninepence, sir," replied Mr. Cornwall promptly.

As the directors disappeared, one of them, from the New York office,
turned and smiled pleasantly back at Mr. Palk. Mr. Cornwall and his
colleague took the lift down to the street, and reached Tower Hill after
a brisk five-minute walk.

Several speakers were already on their boxes, having attracted the curiosity of a circle of office workers. They gesticulated against a background
of bombed brick wharfs, the river Thames and the Tower of London. The
largest crowd was gathered round a strongly built, grey-haired man, whose
priestly clothes were partly covered by a brown leather jacket. It was Dr.
Soper of the Methodist Mission.

"I'd like to speak to you today . . ." he began, and within a minute he
had been interrupted by the first question and its extensions, to which the
rest of the meeting would be devoted.

Mr. Palk and Mr. Cornwall moved into the middle of the crowd and
began to eat the sandwiches. Neither had ever asked Dr. Soper a question.
Still less had they ever heckled him. Those who did were put firmly in their
places. Mr. Cornwall shook his head.

"I like to see a religious man preaching pacifism," he said to Mr. Palk.
"After all, that's the real Christian attitude, isn't it? It's a fine ideal. But, in
practice, well, I don't know if people are made like that . . ."

Mr. Cornwall's thoughts died away to become private to himself.

After a glance at their watches, Mr. Palk and Mr. Cornwall left before
the meeting ended.

"I never tire of hearing him," said Mr. Cornwall. "He's an interesting
fellow."

"Indeed his is," agreed Mr. Palk.

They walked back to the office in silence. Their discussion of Dr. Soper's
opinions never went any further.

Before he sat down, Mr. Palk went to the window and opened it wide.

He enjoyed fresh air, or the best substitute for it that the City of London could provide. Stuffiness, he told Mr. Cornwall, only aroused his asthma. He looked down at Mincing Lane; the pavements were clearing after the lunch break and the traffic continued unrelenting as ever. Mr. Palk stood for some moments in the warm July air before returning to his desk, where he worked on details of a special shipment to Rhodesia until the end of the afternoon.

Nobody in the office seemed to live in the same suburb. Perhaps some of the typists traveled part of the way home together, but Mr. Palk would always find himself alone the moment he stepped out of Plantation House onto the pavement of Mincing Lane. The separation between office and home life was complete. He knew that Mr. Cornwall was lodged by the Essex County Council in a house on Canvey Island, and would spend nearly three hours a day traveling. But if incidents of home life on Canvey Island were occasionally evoked by Mr. Cornwall and were duly replied to by Mr. Palk in the form of similar extracts from events in Wimbledon Park, no invitation was ever extended or even hinted at by either. The office dance, held annually in November, was not by itself sufficient to bridge the gap. Besides, wives were not encouraged and therefore rarely came.

So Mr. Palk would travel home alone. He bought an evening paper with the three pennies he would place specially for that purpose in his pocket before leaving the office. He glanced at the headlines: OAS ASSASSINATION ATTEMPT FAILS. Then he put the newspaper under his arm and went down the steps into the Bank Underground station. With a smile he flashed his green season ticket to yet another West Indian official of London Transport. He smiled because he liked to be known to such people as ticket collectors and newspaper sellers. A month before, when this particular West Indian had come on duty, Mr. Palk had purposely mislaid his season ticket. He had left his name and address and insisted on paying the day's fare. He had returned the following morning with the ticket, which he and the West Indian had admired together as if it had been a rare stamp. They now greeted each other with the utmost cordiality.

The escalator bore Mr. Palk to the Monument. He gave the column on de Gaulle's narrow escape his full attention. He was reading the lower half of the page when his teeth could be seen pressing hard for a moment against his lower lip. Then his face resumed its normal expression.

Mr. Palk did not feel fully settled until comfortably wedged in the last carriage but one of a homebound District Line train. As usual, he recognized most of those in his carriage, but though they had traveled home together regularly for several years, they still observed the customary silence. The train had never been known to crash, and nothing similar ever occurred to serve as a pretext to conversation. Indeed, it was one of the pleasures of the journey to watch a regular undergoing the torture of talking in front of the others to a person either ignorant or careless of convention.

Twenty-five minutes later Mr. Palk was walking along the quiet roads of Wimbledon Park. The shops were closed; it was only on Saturdays that he saw them open. He turned into Vineyard Hill Road. The name was odd, for no one related the road to the plot of earth in which grapes are grown. But it commemorated the men who on odd occasions in the past had attempted to introduce the vine to England. The pressure of the climate or that of the local housing authority had in each case forced them to yield. The vineyard hill had been covered over, with a street name above to remember it by.

Two men from the same City train were ahead of Mr. Palk. Two more, he knew, without even looking, were behind him. One by one they disappeared into their houses. It was so ordinary as to be almost sinister. Three-quarters of the way up the road, Mr. Palk unlatched the wooden gate of Memoriam, where he lived as one of the two lodgers taken in by Mrs. King after her husband's death. He let himself in with his own key and stopped as usual to examine the mail that lay on the chest of drawers in the hall.

There were two letters for him. One concerned insurance, the other— Mr. Palk looked up, and heard Mrs. King preparing to leave the kitchen. He went quietly and quickly up the stairs to his room before Mrs. King could catch him for conversation. With a knife he slit open the envelope from Paris bearing the urgent red band of express post.

FOUR

Max Palk

Mr. Palk reappeared fifteen minutes later at the head of the stairs, a melancholy figure. In one hand he carried a small suitcase held together by a strap around its middle; the other clutched the envelope containing his hastily written excuses and the news of the onset of another bout of asthma. He stood on the faded flower carpet, his mock-tortoiseshell glasses halfway down his nose after his exertions in coughing and breathing.

Mrs. King had left her kitchen and stood at the bottom of the stairs, her head on one side and her hands on her hips.

"I know the signs, Mr. Palk," she said ominously. "Am I right?"

"I'm afraid you are, Mrs. King," admitted Mr. Palk. "I felt it coming on in the office, even before lunch. Then, after lunch, I went and opened the window. But with Mr. Cornwall there, I can't have it my way all the time, you know. We sat there the whole afternoon with the windows shut. I think it was the train that finished me off, all those people, in July, every day . . ."

Mr. Palk passed a weary hand in front of his face, as if to clear the air of the heavy gas that was blocking his lungs.

Mrs. King's hands left her hips. She was slipping from the knowing and efficient to the maternal and providing. She sucked her teeth.

"I don't know, Mr. Palk," she said. "I really don't. It never seems to get any better. Isn't there anything they can do about it?"

"If there was, Mrs. King, you know I'd get it," said Mr. Palk.

He began a gesture with his free hand, but he abandoned it almost immediately. For a man in his condition, even this degree of conversation was wearing.

"Believe me," he added, "St. Anne's is no pleasure when you're there in the state I am."

He coughed and, with his hand on the banister, took his first steps down the stairs.

"Why do you go so far?" asked Mrs. King. "Why not try some place nearer home? I'm sure it doesn't do you any good to travel all that way."

Mr. Palk shrugged his shoulders.

"St. Anne's is the only place where I'm able to breathe, Mrs. King, I'm afraid. Besides, I'm known there now after all these years. It's difficult to change."

"I suppose so," said Mrs. King. "Let me get you a little something before you go. A boiled egg, some baked beans on toast, perhaps?"

"Really, Mrs. King, I'm very much obliged to you," said Mr. Palk. "But my train leaves at 7:15 and I'll have to be off."

"Like that, Mr. Palk? You haven't even a clean shirt to change into. Here," she said, "at least I can do your old case."

And she passed her shammy leather over the battered suitcase.

"Thank you, Mrs. King, and be sure I'll bring you something back."

Mr. Palk was at the door.

"Well, Mrs. King," he said, "you know where to find me, at the Pickles' Boarding House, St. Anne's, the usual address."

"I really am sorry, Mr. Palk," said Mrs. King with feeling. "At least I hope you'll be better when you're back."

Mr. Palk nodded his agreement and his glasses fell a little farther forward. But he didn't seem very convinced.

Not surprising, poor man, thought Mrs. King as she watched him swing the front gate shut, too tired to close it properly as he usually did. He comes back better, but that never stops him from going down with it again.

Mrs. King closed the door on Mr. Palk as he turned down toward the station, and went back to her kitchen.

The man who walked swiftly out of the Knightsbridge Tube station bore little resemblance to the Mr. Palk who had shuffled miserably from Memoriam half an hour previously. But if the manner was different, the clothes and the suitcase were unmistakably the same.

The man walked almost in a circle, along Knightsbridge, right at the Post Office into Wilton Crescent and right again into the Mews behind. Halfway along the row of garages, he drew a ring of small keys from his pocket. When the doors swung open, the long low hood of the Mark X gleamed under the old-fashioned lights that illuminated the Mews.

Max Palk took the great Jaguar out slowly onto the road. The car was relatively new. It was not often that he had had occasion to drive it. He liked its size and strength. He had never been able to bear two-seaters. He stopped at the lights in front of the French Embassy. It was the tail-end of the rush hour. He wound down the window beside him. The air came in, and with it the syrupy sound of his tires on the road.

Behind him, along the Cromwell Road, a car was flashing its lights. Max Palk saw a Sunbeam Alpine in the reflector. He let it come alongside and he looked at the young man in the driving seat, whose almost invisible chin was close to the wheel as he strained to overtake. It was extraordinary how cars and their owners went together. Here was a young man who must have blushed with pride and confusion when the salesman had said, "This car, sir, is you." It was as if the young man had looked with the eyes of Max Palk first at himself and then at the car and reached the hundred-percent-correct conclusion that each was made for the other: and what a couple that made, thought Max Palk as he pushed the Jaguar forward to leave the Sunbeam swerving violently in his wake.

Four miles beyond London Airport, he slowed to turn into the long drive of the West London Flying Club. He watched the figure of the jaguar on the point of the hood describe a regularly held curve from the gate to the parking lot that would have done credit to a compass.

"I'd like everything ready in an hour, Haines, if that suits you," he said to the mechanic.

"Right you are, sir."

The man set off toward the small hangar which housed the Piper Comanche. Max Palk went to the bar and ordered a glass of bitter lemon. He took it with him to the telephone booth, where he made two calls, both in the form of telegrams. He sent the first to the country house near Château-Chinon, his immediate destination. He wired the second to Morin's widow. It was she who had summoned him to France in the express letter he had received that evening.

He thought of her as he cruised south at 200 m.p.h. Morin's death might have left her a widow, but she would refuse to let widowhood become her profession. Her reactions had been practical. One had been the express letter. Max Palk would discover the others when, as he had suggested in the telegram, she came down from Paris to meet him at Château-Chinon.

He enjoyed flying by night. The hum of the single engine was a soothing background. He looked over at the ground beneath him. It was nine o'clock and dark, but there were few lights below. He was passing over the cemeteries of retirement of coastal England, where *Greystones* meant *Gravestones*, and *Mon Repos* was to be taken literally.

He flew almost carelessly, in his shirtsleeves. Within a few minutes he was over Normandy. He had managed to leave England with no more difficulty than usual. The doctor would forward his letter of confirmation, just as the landlady of the boarding house would post on to France any mail that was sent to him at St. Anne's. Both were absolutely trustworthy.

He passed Paris to the west and flew low over the scattered lights of the French countryside into Burgundy. The radio forecast good news the next day for Lancashire's asthma colony; bracing sea-front winds and unaccustomed low temperatures. He shivered in his seat and peered in front of him to determine his bearings from the lights of the two towns ahead. One was Château-Chinon. He banked the Piper Comanche sharply to the west and began to lose height. A moment later he caught sight of the searchlight he had been looking for, pointing straight upward from one side of a field.

FIVE

Max and Silesia

Max circled over one of the most enviable properties in Burgundy. He would have been proud to have shown it to Charles the Bold, especially at night. But there was a chance that Charles had already seen it. It was a manor house of the late fifteenth century, restored according to the twentieth. It stood on a hill with woods and fields beneath.

Max dropped to treetop height. His runway was a field like the others, only rather smoother. Bucking a little on its brakes, the Piper came to a halt after a run of scarcely more than three hundred yards. Max had made another of his unorthodox entries into France. The following morning he would put things right at the local police station, where he and a bottle of whisky were always welcome.

Max unfastened his seatbelts and stepped out of the door onto the wing. He waited there, with one hand resting for support on the fuselage, while the peasant woman below came hurrying across the grass. "Mister Max!" she cried. Max jumped down. As she steadied him, the woman kissed him welcome on both cheeks. Max returned her greeting with equal warmth.

"So you're home again, Mister Max," she said, as if Max's presence were not by itself sufficient proof.

"Yes," Max confirmed, "home again."

The woman nodded.

"But," said Max, shaking his head, "I'm afraid it's simply for tonight. Tomorrow morning I must be off early."

The sadness the woman felt on hearing the news was overcome only by her curiosity.

"With the lady who's just arrived?" she suggested.

"What lady?" asked Max.

"Well," began the woman, plunging into the luxury of a long explanation, "she came only a moment ago, about a minute before I left to meet you. It was a chauffeur who'd driven her. We saw him drop her at the gate. She had no bags or anything. She was in an awful hurry. Then she told us you'd be expecting her. But, of course, we couldn't just believe her like that. And I thought I'd better let you know that she was there. So, while my husband gave her a drink, I slipped out the back, saying I was going to milk the cows. Naturally I'd done that hours before. But how was she to know, a Parisian?"

Max feigned by his respectful silence to admire the perspicacity of the farmer's wife. Her eyes meanwhile flitted shiftily about the field. Her air of intrigue was, for Max, a clear sign that there was nothing for him to be intrigued about.

"So don't tell me," he said, cutting her short. "Her name was Madame Morin."

"Wrong!" declared the woman triumphantly. "It was . . . Wait! Did you say her name was Morin?"

"I did."

"But wasn't Morin the name of the man who got blown up with the dogs at Montceau this morning?"

"It was," answered Max.

"So she must be . . ."

"She is," Max confirmed with simplicity.

In silence they walked across the field toward the house.

"How terrible for her," said the farmer's wife at last.

"So we'll help her," Max suggested as he glanced into a stable occupied by a purebred Charolais bull. "We won't just feel sorry for her."

"All the same," said the woman, "it was dreadful what they did, using dogs to carry explosives. I must say I don't feel any pity for the man they caught."

"Whom did they catch?" asked Max quickly.

"Who do you expect?" replied the woman wearily. "Another deserter from the Legion. He'd been controlling the dogs with a special whistle that humans can't hear."

"I wonder who thought that one up," said Max admiringly. "But it was bad luck to have killed someone in the police force. They'll be reminding him of it so much during questioning that I don't suppose he'll be fit to stand trial for a long time."

"Serve him right," declared the woman with conviction. "They said on the radio that he wasn't sorry for what he'd done. He wasn't even sorry he'd failed. He just promised his friends would make a better job of it next time."

"As they probably will," said Max. "They're very determined."

"But just a minute," said the woman, perplexed. " 'Morin' wasn't the name the lady told us. It was something else. 'Jacobs,' I think . . ."

"That's right," said Max. "Jacobs is her maiden name. She uses it for her medical work."

"She wasn't being a doctor with us, though," retorted the farmer's wife.

"Maybe not," Max agreed. "She was just refusing to be a widow."

"I don't think it shows much for a marriage," answered the woman, unconvinced, "if the wife's so quick to change her name."

Max gave up any attempt to make her see differently.

"All I can say," he declared finally, "is that they were very happy until this morning."

He bent down to offer a piece of rock salt to the goat that was tethered in the courtyard.

"Did you know him as well?" asked the farmer's wife.

"Through her," Max explained as he stood up. "They got married in '39, just before the war. Then they came over to England. Morin was in the Free French under de Gaulle, like almost everybody else in the French administration today. I worked with them for a while."

"So that's how you got to know him," declared the woman.

"And not only him," Max corrected. "Others too."

"My, my," breathed the farmer's wife, a little bemused.

They walked up to the house. Its walls were overgrown with vines. Max had three rooms and a bath on the second floor. The couple occupied the rest of the house all the year round. It was an arrangement that fully suited both sides. The woman's hand was on the kitchen door. Her tone changed as she left politics aside for hospitality.

"What can I get you to eat, Mister Max?"

They passed into the kitchen which, except for the wooden table and chairs in the center, had been equipped entirely, and wholesale, by Westinghouse. And on one of the chairs, with a glass of wine on the table before her, sat . . .

"Silesia!!"

"Max!"

They hugged on the porch, half in delight, half in despair. And when Silesia held Max at arm's length a moment later, her eyes were shining moist in the evening light. The farmer's wife gave her a commiserating look intended to show that she "knew." Then with a movement of her head she dispatched her husband to the cellar to fetch the bottle of Beaujolais that was the traditional mark of Max's return.

Silesia was unreservedly included in the homely scene that followed. The warmth of the wine and of the country meal that went with it soon revived her spirits. She and Max did honor to the farmer by more than sharing his plate of hare. The old man gave them a knowing wink, which they rightly took to mean that the hare had been shot out of season. This topic was one of the several to which the conversation had scarcely time to do justice. And Max finished the meal with some goat cheese that he ate with sugar, without having heard from the old couple half of what had happened since he had last been with them.

Some time later Max brought the conversation to a halt by calling for silence. "Listen!" He had caught on the radio the pleasant and cultured tones of the man under whom he had worked with Morin in England during the war. He was now the minister of national security; tonight he was making a declaration to the press. Max hadn't seen him for some time, even when his work for Morin had brought him to France. He leaned back and turned the radio up higher. The declaration began with a tribute to Morin. The minister passed on to condemn "the cowardice and blindness of those egoists whose perverted sense of patriotism is drawing such ignominious publicity onto the French state throughout the world." This latest act of cowardice, he decided, would only serve to confirm the French people in their intention to rid their country of "this rot and gangrene that is the OAS."

"Fine words!" exclaimed the farmer's wife.

"Maybe," said Silesia. "But he means them more than most of the government."

The country woman shrugged. It would, she felt, be impolite to argue with Silesia. Instead she simply sighed, as did her husband with her.

"What a country you've come back to indeed, Mister Max."

Next morning with Silesia beside him and a packed lunch of cold duck and pâté on the back seat, Max eased the heavy Facel Vega out of the garage and headed for the National Six.

With its eleven individual dials, the wood-framed dashboard made the Facel seem more complex to handle than the Piper. Quite apart from the high speeds at which the car could be safely and relentlessly driven, Max had had its weight in mind when he bought it. Yet he still wore a diagonal safety belt, loosely, so as not to crease his light Italian suit. Not only were the office clothes and dandruff left behind in Château-Chinon, but the glasses through which Max scanned the road ahead bore little resemblance to the old pair in mock tortoiseshell. These were gold-framed and rimless.

The lenses, T-coated in Western Germany, were entirely transparent and unreflecting.

Max had known Silesia in the early thirties when she had been a medical student in Vienna. Then, after the Nazis had come to power, he had helped her escape from Berlin.

He drove carefully, without haste. The gentle rhythm of the car, together with the presence of Silesia, brought him gradually back, almost to childhood days. He began to feel as if he were caught in the center of a Sophie Tucker record, as if he were being slowly paralyzed by the incoming spirals of sadness and nostalgia. The farther he retreated in time, the less he advanced in space, until the Facel was being overtaken by everything except bicycles. It was Silesia's look of alarm that brought him back to the present. He stretched in his seat and asked wistfully:

"Well, Silesia, what have you got for me to do?"

"I want you to trip the OAS up. I want to see them fall flat on their faces."

"I see," said Max. "But why should I do that? To avenge Morin?"

"No, no," Silesia insisted. "Not for that. It's more because if the OAS ever succeeded in killing de Gaulle and taking the country over, I'd feel that what Morin had done would be made absolutely useless."

"You mean, then," said Max, "that you want to see the OAS defeated in order to give sense to Morin's otherwise senseless death?"

Silesia nodded her agreement.

"But that's not the whole reason, is it?" asked Max. "After all, if Morin had been with the OAS and not with de Gaulle, you wouldn't be wanting now to continue his work, would you?"

"Of course not, Max," Silesia assured him. "If I want to see the end of the OAS, it's not only because it's what Morin wanted, it's also because it's what I believe is right."

"Good," said Max. "But do you realize that, in fighting the OAS, you're also helping to keep de Gaulle in power?"

"I know," admitted Silesia, aware she was caught in a difficult position. "But it's the lesser of two evils."

"Hmm," said Max doubtfully.

"But listen, Max," Silesia pleaded. "If the OAS take over, there'll be torture every day, in every prison, in every police station . . ."

"Hasn't there been already?" Max interrupted.

"But there'd be more," Silesia insisted, "much more. There'd be films censored, books burned and hundreds banned . . ."

"Aren't there now?" asked Max softly.

"There'd be . . ."

"Restrictions on the trade unions," Max anticipated. "There'd be a Parliament of police, there'd be treaties with Spain and Portugal. But Silesia, for heaven's sake," he exclaimed, past himself, "don't you ever read the papers? All that is happening at this very moment! And here you are, asking me to save the life of the man responsible!"

There was silence in the car as they were shunted in heavy traffic down the main street of Sens. Max took the long stretch of motorway that followed at high speed. They came into Paris by the Porte d'Orléans.

"Police, police," Max muttered to himself as he glanced at the pavements on either side. "Police everywhere."

Twice in ten minutes they were forced to a halt at the side of the road to let past a convoy of armored police cars led by motards with screaming lights and sirens attached to the handlebars of their motorcycles.

Max continued his way past the garish neon of Segalot's furniture store to the stone lion of Denfert-Rochereau. Soon he had pulled up beneath Silesia's flat in the rue Notre-Dame-des-Champs. He switched off the engine, pulled up the handbrake and told Silesia what he thought.

"All right," he admitted ruefully. "De Gaulle isn't exactly the same as the OAS. He's the lesser evil, as you said. They may have characteristics in common, but they've got a different personal style. And of the two, well, I prefer de Gaulle."

"So you'll do what I ask?" broke in Silesia excitedly.

"Well," said Max resignedly, "if the OAS have got to get rid of de Gaulle to come to power, then, whether we like it or not, it's de Gaulle we've got to save to prevent them."

Once they had understood each other, the atmosphere became easier. Silesia was made happier, and so, too, at the sight of her, was Max.

"But now, how am I going to do it?" he asked.

"Look, Max," said Silesia, her hand on his arm. "You know a lot of people. You know the people you can trust and those you can't. You can fight the OAS a hundred times better than a government that's half working for it anyway. And," she added, reserving the best for the last, "I've arranged for you to meet the Minister in his office tomorrow morning. He'd be very happy for you to help."

"How's he been?" asked Max in surprise.

"Wonderful!" exclaimed Silesia, with a flap of her hand. "It was his chauffeur who took me down to you last night. He's been arranging things for me, and so tastefully. He'll even be giving a little speech in memory of Morin at the prefecture tomorrow afternoon. I'll be meeting you both there after you've had your chat. Max," she said, tightening the pressure of her hand on his arm, "I'm sure he'll be able to get you started on something."

After he had left Silesia at her flat, Max drove on to his own apartment in the place des Vosges. He was feeling uneasy about the whole business. He was sure that he would not be allowed to share government secrets, as Silesia expected. He had no official position, not even his association with Morin had been official, and his personal friendship with the Minister was not by itself going to be a sufficient credential. Even the fact that he found some assorted foodstuffs waiting for him, ordered by Silesia from Goldenberg's Delicatessen in the rue des Rosiers, was hardly enough to lighten his spirits.

SIX

The Minister

"Maxie!" exclaimed the Minister as he rose from his desk and came toward Max to take his hand in a two-fisted grip.

Max looked around at the office with its official portraits and paper-covered desk.

"The politician!" he replied, half jokingly and half deprecatingly. "And what a bureau-cat!" he said in English as he bent down to stroke the animal that was curled up in the visitor's chair. The cat was not amused. But Max was accustomed to having his puns ignored.

"Off you get," he said in its ear, and lowered the still-inanimate cat onto the carpet.

"So you've seen Silesia?" the Minister asked.

Max nodded.

"Of course," said the Minister, waving his pen, "I've been doing what I can, but in situations like these, first you don't know whether it's decent to intervene, and then if you decide to, what can you do?"

Max nodded understandingly.

"So I've been compromising," the Minister went on, "by keeping as much out of the way as possible and arranging things for her from a distance."

"She's very grateful to you," Max told him.

The center telephone rang on the Minister's desk. "Yes . . . yes . . . yes . . . right!" Max heard the Minister answer in quick succession before replacing the receiver. The official nature of the interruption made it easier for Max and the Minister to pass to a more businesslike topic.

"Well, Max, there are two main items I can tell you of," began the Minister, leaning forward over his desk and studying the glasses he held in his hands. "But first let me give you an introduction to show you how I see things."

Max raised a hand in surprise as if to say, "Go ahead!" The Minister was being unusually pompous. Or perhaps, thought Max, he was only being ministerial. The development was a pity, but only to be expected.

"The OAS," declared the Minister, with no concern for Max's private thoughts, "is a Fascist organization that came into existence, as you know, about three years ago, when it was realized that de Gaulle was prepared to withdraw France from Algeria. But it failed to stop things from going the way de Gaulle wanted. Algeria became independent. But the OAS did not disband, for all that. If it was too late to retrieve Algeria, they thought that there was still plenty to be done in France—the traitor de Gaulle to be got rid of and his government to be taken over."

"So?" said Max impatiently.

"So," the Minister went on, "how does the OAS go about it?"

The Minister had not asked the question for Max to answer it. It was purely rhetorical.

"The OAS," answered the Minister, "has no popular support, but there are plenty of people in high places behind it. So if it can't get into power through a general election, it can at least do so by a coup d'état. But for a coup d'état to be successful, de Gaulle must go. And because he can't be persuaded to go, he has to be forced. The OAS condemns him to death for treason. And the attempts to carry it out follow quickly. So far," and the Minister stressed these two words heavily, "so far, all the attempts have failed. But there's no reason to suppose that they will continue to do so."

The Minister paused for effect. Max looked down at the cat by his feet. The Minister had known Max for twenty years, but his manner on this occasion was curiously indirect. Max wondered if he was being so long-winded simply because he had nothing to say.

"What are these two things you had to tell me?" asked Max too eagerly.

The Minister raised a restraining hand.

"Suppose one day the OAS does succeed?" he said, as if the idea had only just occurred to him. "What happens?"

It was another rhetorical question.

"So, what happens?" asked Max to hurry him on.

The Minister glanced sharply at Max for this attempt to make conversation out of a monologue.

"I'm sorry," said Max.

Generously the Minister forgave him with a half smile and a nod of the head.

"What happens?" asked the Minister again. "De Gaulle is blown to pieces in his car or at some official get-together. For a few moments there is pandemonium. Nobody knows what to do—except, of course, the men who organized the assassination. These men arrive—the generals with their regiments, Soustelle and Boudin from exile. De Gaulle's succession is assured. The trade unions and Communist Party are outlawed with the help of the police. Two days after the assassination France is a fully Fascist state."

The Minister sat back a moment, to consider his conclusion.

"But that's not all," he warned Max, leaning forward over his desk. "With the armed forces behind them, who'll ever be able to get rid of them? Other countries won't intervene. World War Two, after all, didn't start because the Allies were horrified by Germany's concentration camps. Soustelle will have Britain in the Common Market. He's said so. He'll insist on a common European nuclear force and not on an independent French one. He's said that too. It'll be much better than de Gaulle; it'll be perfect, in fact, for everyone but the French."

The Minister stopped.

"You're coming to the first item?" Max prompted.

The Minister's head fell ominously to indicate that he was.

"All that," he said, "may be under way by the end of this week."

"And how?" asked Max.

"There's to be a final assassination attempt on de Gaulle this Saturday, the fourteenth of July."

"How do you know?" asked Max.

"Mittelbach, the legionary we caught after Morin's death, has talked a little. We've kept it from the press. Only Morris, the prefect of police, and a squad of his men know of it. That will be all we need on the day to catch them in the act."

"Did Mittelbach say how they'd do it?" asked Max.

"He didn't," the Minister admitted, "and that's what we are trying to get out of him. The strange thing is that he doesn't seem to feel he's given anything away in warning us of the fourteenth of July."

"Then it's because he knows they've got something like the dogs at Montceau," said Max, "something you'll only be able to stop by an accident."

"That's what we thought, too," said the Minister. "We are doubling the men on everything we usually cover. We are even going to provide air protection."

"So there's not much I can do," Max concluded.

"Well," said the Minister awkwardly, "with that side of things, I'm afraid there isn't. We are able to see to it best."

He paused and his awkwardness increased.

"I've only just realized that I've got very little, in fact, for you to work on. All I can do is to give you a general picture, but as for giving you something to do, I'm afraid I can't."

It was what Max had suspected all the time.

"In any case," he said, waving the Minister's apology aside, "let's hear the second point."

"That's just it," said the Minister. "All I can tell you about it is that I can tell you nothing. At the moment," he continued, his manner changing and becoming confidential, "Morris and I have a member of the government under suspicion. I can't give you his name. We've got no concrete proof on him, though he's never tried to hide the direction in which his sympathies lie. But even if I told you, you see, it wouldn't do any good. We've got the man so closely watched that now he couldn't do anything."

Nevertheless, Max went quickly in mind through the members of the French government. But it was no use—it might have been any one of them. He switched to another topic.

"Hasn't there been any news of Soustelle?" he asked.

The cat at his feet stirred mysteriously, until the Minister cried, "Ssh!" and explained to Max that the name he had just spoken was not only that of one of the heads of the OAS, but also that of the cat. The two men smiled— Soustelle was known publicly by the nickname of "The Big Tomcat."

"Soustelle," said Max sadly. "Once he was on the opposite side and we used to know him so well. . . . To think he's now working with a man like Boudin."

"It's a tremendous change," the Minister agreed, "though for him, of course, it's not been one for the worse."

"I wonder if it would be possible to persuade him to think otherwise," thought Max aloud. "I should like to see him again anyway. And then perhaps I could try. Where is he?"

"He was seen the night of the assassination attempt in Pontarlier, only a few kilometers from the Swiss border," said the Minister. "It was only to be expected," he added. "It was all part of the plan. The deserters from the Foreign Legion look after the execution, and Soustelle comes in from Switzerland to put this Minister we suspect, or else himself, into power. But the execution fails, and Soustelle hops back across the border again to prepare the next attempt."

"Why did the news come so late?" asked Max. "Was it your own censorship?"

"No, no," said the Minister. "Someone in Pontarlier saw Soustelle at the lights in a Peugeot 404. He recognized him from the papers, but didn't tell the police till this morning. Scared to do it earlier, probably, until Soustelle was well away. We had the Swiss agree to refuse him the right to cross their frontier," the Minister went on. "And the witness saw him making for Strasbourg and the north. That means Belgium. We've asked the authorities there to cooperate too, but the OAS are much better developed in Belgium than in Switzerland—friends among the police and so on—so we are not counting on them to turn him back. In fact, any minute we're expecting to receive confirmation that Soustelle's settled in Belgium."

"Well, today is Sunday," said Max in conclusion, "which gives us the week to find out what they are going to do on Saturday and then to stop it. And Mittelbach knows you're going to take precautions. But he doesn't seem to care."

"Which suggests," said the Minister, "that things are going to be difficult."

"I'm afraid so," said Max.

He got up.

"Yes," said the Minister, looking at his watch, "it's time we were off, to get this business over. Well," he added, his awkwardness returning, "I hope I do something that Morin would have liked."

"I don't envy you," said Max, "it's almost an impossible thing to do well. As for me," he continued, following the Minister into the corridor, "I don't know what to do. There's no one I can usefully go and see for the moment. I'll be spending the rest of the day with Silesia, and maybe we'll think of something. Otherwise . . ." He shrugged his shoulders, leaving the sentence uncompleted.

They waited for an elderly man to come up the stairs.

"Of course," said Max, after a while, "I suppose there's always one thing I could do . . ."

"What's that?" asked the Minister.

"Go to Belgium and find Soustelle," answered Max with embarrassment, for he was aware that his plan sounded a little hollow.

"Hmm," said the Minister doubtfully, as they walked down the thickly carpeted stairs. "We've been wondering," he went on, "just how much this government man we're suspecting suspects *us*. If he's smart, then perhaps the next one to go will be the prefect of police or me. I've had two extra motards, in addition to the two I normally have, to escort my car, just in case. So you needn't worry," he laughed at Max.

At the foot of the staircase they were met by a younger official with an envelope. They stopped as the Minister broke its seal and withdrew the contents. He turned to Max.

"Soustelle's been seen in Brussels."

They walked along a corridor to a second flight of stairs that led down to the main entrance of the ministry. Two motards were by the door. As they saw the Minister, they turned and went down the steps into the courtyard beyond. There they let the chauffeur know that the Minister was coming and kicked their machines into life.

The second pair of motards, who were to ride behind the car, waited for Max and the Minister to pass in front of them out of the door. But the Minister, drawing Max aside, signaled to them with a nod of his head to wait for him outside.

"I forgot," the Minister said to Max, "for the fourteenth we mustn't overlook the weather, if . . ."

As the Minister prepared to complete his sentence, a young man in an upper room of a building across the road from the entrance to the big enclosed courtyard of the ministry saw the doors open and leaned on the trigger of a light mortar. The first two motards were on their motorcycles and the chauffeur was standing by the door of the car, ready to open it for the Minister, when the shell was lobbed over the wall of the courtyard. The young man saw not the Minister and Max, but the second pair of motards emerge from the doorway onto the steps at which the shell had been so expertly aimed. If a mistake had been made, it was too late to correct it. The shell, clearly visible to the young man, was coming to the end of the arc it had so gracefully described, when the two motards stepped unknowingly into its path.

The breath was blown from Max's body as the Minister was thrown violently against him and they pitched together to the floor. Splinters of wood and glass were falling as Max covered his head with his arms and kept absolutely still. Dust, into which the stone and building materials had disintegrated, filled his lungs when he tried to snatch his first breath. When the noise of the explosion had died away, Max got to his feet to drag the unconscious Minister to one side.

With a feeling of utter hopelessness, Max waited against the wall, the Minister at his feet, for the men with the submachine guns who would come up the shattered steps to finish off the attack.

SEVEN

The Forgotten Forecast

But the men did not come. Max heard instead the first sirens wailing in the distance. He bent down to attend to the Minister; he unbuttoned his jacket and guessed that he had not been seriously hurt. He signaled to the members of the staff who had found cover under the staircase to take care of him. Then he walked weakly to the main entrance, where the great doors had been torn from their hinges, and leaned against the solid stone wall.

The center of the flight of steps into the courtyard looked as if it had been mined from beneath. It was almost entirely destroyed. Farther down, at the foot of the steps, the chauffeur lay on the ground. Max looked more closely, and felt, as usual, sick at seeing the results of an explosion. The man had been decapitated, probably by a razor-sharp fragment of stone that had been blown toward him at a speed greater than that of a bullet. Death must have been instantaneous and painless. He had slipped to the ground without losing his cap. The head lay only a few inches from the body, and the gravel of the courtyard between was red with the blood that now trickled only slowly from the veins of the severed neck.

It would be left to the police with their microscopes to find motards three and four. Three men destroyed, perhaps three widows and several more orphans created. Behind the chauffeur, the Citroën lay lopisdedly, its two nearside tires punctured. The windows were shattered, the coachwork was dented and scarred. In front, some twenty yards away, motards one and two were getting painfully to their knees. Their helmets, boots and thick uniforms had kept them from serious damage. Their motorcycles had been thrown from their stands. The engines were still running, making the only sound in the stillness that followed the explosion.

The first police car, its siren on and the emergency yellow light on its roof turning, burst through the gate into the courtyard. The men jumped out before the car had stopped, but then they hesitated, for there were no wounded, only dead to be taken away. Soon the courtyard was full of police.

Max went back inside the building, feeling sick and a little dizzy. He found the Minister lying in the porter's lodge, still unconscious. A police doctor was attending him. Already on the telephone was the young official who had handed them the dispatch concerning Soustelle. He glanced from the Minister to Max.

"That was some luck you just had, sir," he said, one hand clamped over the telephone receiver. "If it'd been you who'd gone out next, instead of those two motards, in the usual way, then . . ."

He broke off to answer the call. Max heard him tell Morris that the Minister would be unable to attend the service at the prefecture for reasons of which Monsieur le Préfet was doubtless already aware. The voice at the other end was replaced by one that Max, even in his bemused state, did not fail to recognize.

"It's Madame Morin," said the official, passing Max the receiver.

"You okay, Max?" asked Silesia in concern.

Max mumbled a reply.

"You don't sound too good," was Silesia's diagnosis. "Get back home, have a sleep and take care of yourself."

Max nodded.

"Do you hear me, Max?"

Max managed to tell her that he did.

"Then I'll come by your place when I can," Silesia told him. "And take care of yourself," she repeated before ringing off.

It was pleasant to be thus ordered to rest. Max let himself feel to the full the effects of shock and concussion, as any doctor would have demanded of him in the circumstances. He refused police offers to drive him home and had the official order him a taxi instead. Wearing a borrowed raincoat over his tattered clothes and peering through glasses that were less transparent though not cracked, Max left the ministry by a side exit, since the center steps were no longer in service. He walked across the courtyard, which was being subjected to a series of highly technical examinations by various squads of police specialists; and because the courtyard was closed to anyone but them, he found his taxi waiting for him outside the main gate.

Back in the place des Vosges, he drank a glass of hot lemon tea and went to bed. He slept peacefully until late in the afternoon. He awoke with a start and without a trace of the uncomfortable sensations that had followed the explosion. It was only minutes before he was expecting Silesia. He got up and took a shower. Dust and tiny particles of glass and stone had been blown into his skin and scalp, so that it was a painful task extracting them with hot water and brush. As a precaution he splashed a mild antiseptic on his face and neck after drying. With a chopped-chicken-liver sandwich in one hand and glass of Vichy water in the other, Max sat down in the living room, wearing a new set of clothes.

When Silesia arrived, she was exhausted.

"Oy vey!" she exclaimed, as she fell back into the sofa and passed a hand over her brow. "Max, I've been everywhere!"

She got up again to take off her coat, which Max collected and hung in the bedroom. When he came back, Silesia explained herself.

"After the service, I went home to change. I couldn't stand being in those formal clothes any longer. Then I went to see the Minister. He's in the hospital. He looks miserable, but he's all right really. That's what I told him. 'There's nothing wrong with you,' I said, 'though you're worse off than Max maybe.' Then I had an idea. 'So why,' I asked, 'don't you take a couple of days' rest in that nice place you have in Switzerland?' 'Hmm,' he said, 'I've got business here.' 'What's two days?' I said. So gradually he accepts. I gave him a sedative and then came a car to take him away."

She paused.

"And you, Max?" she asked.

"I've been to sleep, and there's nothing wrong with me," he told her. "But," he added sadly, "the Minister didn't have much to say."

"Never mind," said Silesia. "Remember it's still only the beginning."

They continued the conversation over an early supper at Polidor's, a restaurant in the Latin Quarter off the boulevard St-Michel. After her busy day, Silesia had been reluctant to leave the sofa and go out again, but Max had offered to drive her there and treat her as his guest. Silesia was won over.

They took a table by the wall and selected a meal from the menu. The restaurant was quiet and correct in a provincial way. In addition, it was Sunday. The manners and clothes of the customers were fittingly subdued. There were history professors from the Sorbonne, with their wives and without their briefcases. One of their younger colleagues had come with his family. And there were students who sat opposite respectable girlfriends.

"But what did the Minister say?" asked Silesia as they began their tomato salad.

Max went over the conversation of the morning.

"So you see," he told Silesia, "it's as I said, there's not very much—an attempt planned for the fourteenth and a member of the government under suspicion."

"But Max!" exclaimed Silesia, "if the Minister said that a member of the government knew he was under suspicion, surely what happened this morning proves the man's in the oas. Obvious, no? So we go to Morris and have him arrested."

"Wait yet!" said Max, holding up his knife and fork. "I told you, Morris is in on the secret as well as the Minister. It's even his special branch who are keeping a watch on the man. Of course," Max conceded generously to Silesia, his point having been made, "I could go and offer Morris my opinion that the man should be arrested. But that's not going to persuade him to do anything he's not doing already. They made that deduction as fast as you did, and once they've done that, it's hopeless for anyone who isn't a top government official to intervene. Perhaps they're holding him at this very moment. At any rate, they'll be watching him too closely for him to be able to do anything."

"So what are you going to do?" asked Silesia.

"That's just it," Max confessed. "There's plenty for the government people to work on, but for me there's nothing. Perhaps I'll just think for a bit, and if nothing turns up that way I'll go and see Soustelle."

"To talk him round!" exclaimed Silesia. "Soustelle!"

It was a well-earned rebuff. Max looked crestfallen. Silesia took pity on him.

"Max," she said softly, "all the same, let's be serious. Have you been over everything the Minister told you?"

"I have," said Max wretchedly.

"And there's nothing to begin on?"

Max shook his head.

"Nothing," he confirmed.

"Well," said Silesia mysteriously, "maybe if you keep thinking, something will turn up later. As I said, we're only at the beginning."

So they put the events of the morning aside and, with the carelessness of a cholesterol nonconformist, Max even finished the meal with a bowl of sweetened fresh cream.

"Right, Max," said Silesia as they waited for the bill, "we've had our meal, let's get back to work."

"It's not so much that I'm sure there's nothing for me in what the Minister had to say," Max began. "It's more that I feel I haven't remembered everything he said."

"So," said Silesia encouragingly, "there is something already!"

Max paid the bill and moved to get up from the table. But he hesitated when he saw that Silesia was remaining in her seat.

"Max," she said, "don't go thinking I'm psychic or something. But look. You say you may have forgotten something. Now, what's the most likely cause of your forgetting a thing the Minister said to you? Isn't it the explosion? So think: what did he say just before?"

As she spoke, Silesia's words became superfluous. The last moments of his morning with the Minister were coming back to him—the walk along the corridor, down the stairs, the news flash on Soustelle, the second pair of motards, the Minister taking him aside and saying . . . and saying . . . what? The words seemed to have been blasted by the explosion from Max's memory. Silesia was listening intently.

"He said—" began Max slowly "—of course!"

Max paused, to enjoy his discovery a little longer before surrendering it to Silesia.

"He said that we mustn't overlook the weather for the fourteenth."

Silesia's face fell.

"That doesn't seem to mean much, if anything at all," she said disappointedly.

"But it must," Max insisted. "He took me aside to say it."

"So what do you think it means?" asked Silesia.

"How do I know?" Max exclaimed. "The Minister was knocked out before he could get started. And now you've sent him off to Switzerland. Thanks!"

"Okay," said Silesia, ignoring the sarcasm. "But wait, if you go along to the prefecture tomorrow morning, you can ask Morris about it. They are working together, so he'll be sure to know."

"And if he doesn't?" asked Max.

Silesia shrugged her shoulders.

"I can't say," she said unashamedly. "But that's what you've come here for."

After dropping Silesia, Max returned home by the boulevard St-Michel. There he was forced to slow down behind a marching crowd of students. They had poured onto the road from the nearby Sorbonne. They waved banners and chanted slogans against the OAS. Max could make out their cries after a moment. "OAS—assassins! OAS—ss!"

Suddenly they turned and took to their heels.

"Police! Police!"

Max stopped the car out of prudence and watched from behind the windshield. And there they were The police surged from behind, their truncheons held high under the street lights—truncheons that were matured, according to the newspapers, in barrels of vinegar for just such purposes as this. They brought them down viciously on the heads and shoulders in front of them. Most of the students escaped. But, among those who could not keep up, were girls whose high heels made cripples of them on the cobbles, and others who were encumbered by the banners and leaflets they were carrying. Where they were struck, they fell. And the police who followed clubbed them repeatedly as they lay sprawled in the roadway. The government forces retreated. The crowd reorganized itself around its injured.

Max was about to drive away when he heard his offside door being opened. He leaned over and realized that it was a student pulling himself to his feet by the door handle. His hair was matted with blood. Somewhere his scalp had been split open. He got into the car. Max drove him to the nearest chemist's.

"Salauds!" shouted the student through the open window as they passed a batch of police.

"You think so?" one of them shouted back. "Then come here and say so."

"I shouldn't take him up on it," Max advised.

"But they're salauds all the same," said the student. "They love to beat us up, as much as they love to leave the OAS alone."

EIGHT

The Prefect

Preceded by a phalanx of motards the official car swept through the gate into the courtyard of the prefecture. Morris sat deep in the back seat, chuckling over a point in *The Age of Responsibility*, a work written by his hero Papon.

With two burly men by his side, the prefect of police walked from his car to the lift that took him direct to his office. He glanced with surprise at the first visitor's card of the morning.

"Show him in right away," he told his secretary.

"Pleased to see you, Max," he said. "But why so early? What's the matter?"

"It's about the fourteenth," said Max.

"Yes?" asked Morris politely.

Max looked down into the courtyard of the prefecture.

"By the way," he remarked, "your boys were certainly on form last night."

"On form?" Morris frowned.

"At the demonstration," Max prompted him. "With the students."

"Oh yes!" Morris exclaimed. "Well," he said with a touch of pride, "the government's orders were carried out. They weren't able to hold a proper meeting."

Morris looked up.

"You weren't there, were you?" he asked.

Max nodded.

"It was illegal!" Morris exclaimed. "But listen, Max," he added confidentially, "you shouldn't have gone there like that. You should have come to me first for a press badge, so that—" the prefect seemed ill at ease as he searched for a paraphrase "—so that the men could have seen who you were and so that there wouldn't have been any trouble."

"I forgot, I completely forgot," said Max. "But as it happened, I was all right. There were quite a lot of people, though, who weren't."

Morris brushed the observation aside with a little philosophy.

"Well, Max, what can you expect? The government gives us a job to do and we see that we get it done. And where there are crowds together, you'll always get people who lose their heads."

"I thought I saw a whole force lose its head," said Max.

"There are some who exaggerate," Morris admitted. "But, Max, you must remember, policemen aren't choirboys."

Morris glanced quickly around his office. He suddenly lost his composure and his manner changed to that of a cornered man.

"Don't you see," he whispered desperately, "I can't hold my boys back. Some of them were trained by men who've since been convicted of belonging to the OAS. They're the backbone of the police force. Once you let them out of the trucks, there's nothing I can do except pray that nobody gets killed. Of course," he corrected himself hastily, "I'm talking about demonstrations by Frenchmen. With the Algerians it's different. The boys can knock off a hundred and sixty of them in one evening, right here in Paris, and there'll be no public protest. Once they've tasted stuff like that they don't like going long without it. And if you try to make them, they get restless in the barracks."

He shook his head.

"It's an impossible situation."

He swiveled his chair round and took a newspaper at random from the pile that had been put on his desk as a kind of office breakfast. He turned to the back page, flattening the paper with his hands.

"Look at these pictures," he said, holding the paper up for Max to see. "Do you think I like them?"

He looked closer at the paper and seemed shocked by what he saw.

"And they're not the worst either," said Max.

"You were there, weren't you?" said Morris.

He looked contrite.

"I should have been there as well, I suppose, instead of . . . well, instead of reading about it all in the papers next morning, like everyone else."

"Never mind," said Max briskly. "All that's for next time, not for now."

Morris put the paper back on the pile. He shook his head. Then he pressed a button for his secretary to come and take the newspapers away.

"Now what was it you wanted to tell me?" he asked.

"It was about the fourteenth, Saturday," said Max.

"Ah yes, the fourteenth," said the prefect, soothed from his recent feelings of guilt by this swift immersion in official matters. "What about the fourteenth?"

"Well," said Max, "I've heard all about it from the Minister."

The prefect seemed a little sorry that the secret had been shared.

"But there's one thing," Max went on, "that I'm not clear about."

"Which is?" broke in Morris, following carefully.

"A remark he made to me just before the explosion."

"Oh?" Morris sounded interested.

"He said he'd forgotten to tell me that the weather for the fourteenth had to be looked into."

With an impatient wave of the hand, Morris asked Max to explain himself.

"The remark seems important to me," said Max. "But I can't think what the Minister meant by it."

"Maxie, Maxie," said Morris wearily. "Did the Minister say how or why it ought to be looked into?"

"He didn't," Max admitted. "But the point is, he hadn't time. And now he's in Switzerland, and he won't be back for two or three days."

"Yes, yes," said Morris intolerantly. "We've had a call from his secretary. He hopes to be back the day after tomorrow, in good time for the fourteenth."

"But can't you see," asked Max, "that that is precisely why I'm here now?—to find out if this weather business meant anything to you, and thus save myself the trouble of going all the way to Switzerland to see him?"

Morris became conciliatory, without, however, abandoning his position.

"I'm sorry, Max, I'm sorry," he said. "But let's suppose the Minister had said this to me. I'd have waited for him to explain what he meant, as you were doing, I suppose. By itself it means nothing."

"Why doesn't it?" asked Max.

"Because," explained Morris, "weather conditions are perhaps the first thing we take into account in setting up security arrangements for anything so big as a fourteenth of July parade."

"That had also occurred to me," said Max irritably. "The point, though, is whether this remark of the Minister's rings a bell anywhere for you, whether it reminds you of anything, that, like him, you'd forgotten."

Morris was willing to see if it did. As Max walked slowly up and down the room, beneath the portrait of de Gaulle, who posed against a bookcase as if it were part of his uniform, Morris enumerated on his fingers all that weather could mean to a security official.

"First, we'll suppose it rains. There'll be a smaller crowd, but submachine guns can be concealed under raincoats, or bombs inside a coat over the arm. Then, we thought that this year, if the sky is overcast, we'll use radar to spot anyone who tries to bomb or machine-gun from a plane. They've had reconnaissance flights over the prisons where we're holding the generals, you know . . ."

"Yes, of course I know," said Max, turning round. "But the Minister meant something other than that. He must have done. He was thinking of something unforeseeable, something like the dogs at Montceau."

"Well, if it's unforeseeable," said Morris, "we won't foresee it. We'll simply cover every method known to us to reduce the risk of something like that happening to a minimum."

The conversation was clearly getting nowhere.

"Look, Max," said the prefect. "It's simple. There are two things we can do. Either we leave it at this, which would satisfy me, if it wouldn't you."

"Of course," said Max, "otherwise why would the Minister have said it?"

"Or," continued Morris, "you give the Minister a ring. But I wouldn't advise that. You can't trust the telephone these days. The best is that I send a dispatch rider."

"No," said Max, "in that case I'll go myself. It would be quicker, and I'd rather hear about it first hand."

"Go, go with my blessing, if you want to," said Morris, "and give the Minister my regards, but . . ."

"What's your explanation, then?" asked Max.

"I don't think an explanation's necessary," Morris answered confidently. "Perhaps he'd just forgotten to tell *you* about taking the weather into account, but he hadn't forgotten to tell *us*."

When Max reported back to Silesia, he could tell her only that he was going to Switzerland to see the Minister. There he would try to find out what the Minister had meant to say before he had been cut short by the explosion.

"It's funny," she said disbelievingly, "a bright man like you going all the way to Switzerland to talk about the weather."

"Wait!" Max warned her. "You don't know everything."

"So you're not going to talk about the weather."

"Hmm." Max was doubtful. "Yes and no," he said. "You see, I thought of something as I was coming from the prefecture."

Silesia nodded importantly.

"And," Max went on, "it's something that's already been mentioned."

Silesia frowned and looked to one side as she tried to think what it could be.

"And mentioned," said Max, "by you!"

"By me, Max?"

NINE

The Sentence That Never Was

Max entered Switzerland on the same road from Pontarlier by which Soustelle had left it three days before. At the frontier, suddenly remembering, he posted off in an envelope a picture postcard of St. Anne's, selected from the wide range of views he had at his disposal. The landlady of the boardinghouse would forward it to Mrs. King, thus ensuring that it received its proper postmark. Then he set off on the final lap of his journey.

He drove alongside Lake Leman toward Geneva, well prepared for his first visit to the Minister's Swiss home. He knew from the address exactly where it was, and even the type of house it was—one of those large white villas built on the hills above the lake, ideal for convalescents of all kinds. Max glanced at the lake, only the edge of which was still caught by the light of the setting sun. He would be just in time for the private talk with the Minister which he needed before the inevitable guests arrived for dinner.

On reaching the side road he was looking for, he turned and climbed into the hills. The villas, set back from the road, were quiet and sumptuous. As he came out of a sharp bend, Max, who was driving at a speed a little above walking pace, braked hard nonetheless, and backed round the corner out of sight—out of sight of the villa that a moment later he was examining carefully through binoculars from between two rhododendron bushes.

But the Minister, unfortunately, was not alone. Max saw the French windows of the drawing room open and three men come out into the garden, followed by a woman in a white apron. Max recognized the Minister in the middle, but the two men with him he had never seen before. The woman, who began to clean the top of a garden table, was clearly the maid. Max looked anxiously at his watch. It seemed as if the pre-dinner aperitifs had already begun. But to Max's relief, the men walked past the table and the maid went on to clean the rest of the garden furniture.

Max could see the gestures of the men, but could not hear their voices as they talked for some minutes on the lawn overlooking the lake. Then they shook hands, and the Minister, confiding his guests to the maid, walked back into the drawing room, and closed the French windows behind him. Max heard a car starting up in the drive, and a moment later the Minister appeared alone in a room on the second floor.

Max waited a little while longer, hesitating before making his next move. The Minister might be alone, but that did not mean that Max could reach him without being seen by a third party. He took another look through the binoculars. The Minister had left the bedroom, to reappear at the French windows. He stepped into the garden, accompanied by a dog. At a rose bed, they stopped for the Minister to admire the flowers. They then walked round to the front drive, where they opened a gate, leaving the garden and Max's field of vision.

Max got back inside the car and, releasing the hand brake, rolled slowly down toward the villa. At the corner he saw the Minister walking with his back to him on the near-side pavement. The dog was somewhere farther on. Max started the engine. The Minister had not heard. Max came abreast of him and braked, leaning over as he did so to open the door.

"Maxie!" cried the Minister. "Here in Switzerland! I can hardly believe it."

"Can we go to a café?" asked Max. "You see," he explained dramatically, "I'd like to talk to you alone if possible."

The Minister shrugged his shoulders.

"You don't mind if the dog listens in, do you?" he asked.

Max shook his head, and the Minister called down the pavement.

"He'd do anything for a ride," he explained as the dog jumped into the back seat. "He hates walking."

The Minister swung the door shut and Max turned the car back to the lake.

"It's serious, is it?" asked the Minister gravely. "Well, I wish it wasn't; I like being a convalescent."

"How are you feeling?" Max asked.

"Fine," said the Minister. "The doctor says I'll be back in Paris tomorrow."

The prospect did not seem to please him. There was a pause, during which he glanced at the villas on either side.

"Some beautiful places here," he said appreciatively. "Mind you, mine's not so bad, but I always seem to forget it when I see what these others have got. By the way," he asked after a moment, "have you heard how that attempt on me was done?"

"It was a mortar from a balcony," Max told him, as they reached the lake. "The flat belonged to a family on holiday; according to the concierge, a young man had been there all last week, told her he was a relative, and showed her the keys, so she had no reason to be suspicious."

"I don't suppose they found the man?" the Minister asked.

"He got away before anyone knew what had happened," Max told him.

They drew up at the first lakeside roadhouse. Max led the Minister to the back of the café, where they settled deep in the comfortable chairs and ordered drinks, plus a bowl of Bovril for the dog.

"Well, Max," said the Minister, looking at his watch, "glad as I am to see you, I've got people coming for dinner in half an hour's time. You're invited, of course, but I'm afraid half an hour's all we've got to ourselves."

"We'll just have to make it enough, then," said Max.

"But what's the big secret, Max?" asked the Minister. "Why did you have to see me by myself?" The Minister found it difficult to believe that anything could be so important as to warrant such caution.

"If I hadn't come out for a walk," he asked, "what would you have done?"

"I don't know," Max confessed. "I'd have vaulted the wall or something."

The Minister shook his finger.

"The dog wouldn't have liked that," he said.

"He'd have been jealous?"

The Minister nodded.

"It's something he's never been able to do," he explained.

They sipped the drinks that each had ordered for the other.

"Come on, Max," said the Minister a little impatiently. "Let's hear it."

"Well," began Max cautiously, "it's about this suspected minister."

"You mean to tell me that the attempt to get rid of me is a proof that our suspicions were correct?" exclaimed the Minister. "For God's sake, we all realized that the moment we got up from the ground."

"The attempt on you has something to do with it," Max admitted. "But not in the way you've just said."

"How then?" asked the Minister.

"I'll tell you," said Max. "But first let me say that I think I know which member of the government is implicated."

The Minister held up a hand.

"And I in my turn must warn you, Max," he said conscientiously, "that even if you get the name right I will be unable either to confirm or deny it, I'm sorry—" here the Minister shook his head: it was clearly a case of force majeure "—but what I said in the office about keeping it a secret must still hold."

"But you'll let me go on?" Max asked.

"Of course, of course," said the Minister. "There's no harm in that."

"Then I'll start at the beginning," said Max. "After the explosion, I went through all that had happened up till, and including, my first conversation with you. And it seemed, as you'd said, that there was nothing there for me at all."

The Minister nodded to show that he was following. His face at this point registered a depth of respect that was almost disrespectful. "But that evening," Max went on, "I felt sure I'd forgotten something you'd said to me. And it was Silesia who made me remember it."

The Minister looked puzzled.

"It was the remark you made just before the explosion," Max told him. "You know, the one about not overlooking the weather for the fourteenth."

"Yes," said the Minister uncomprehendingly, "now that you remind me of it, I remember having said it too. But so what?"

"I couldn't think what you meant by it," said Max simply.

"But that's hardly surprising," protested the Minister, "considering that I was knocked unconscious before I could say another word. Nonsense!" he exclaimed, looking out to the lake in irritation.

"What did you mean, though?" Max insisted.

"But, Max, what an absurd question, for Heaven's sake! We hadn't mentioned taking the weather into account for the fourteenth in our conversation, so," he concluded, as if explaining himself to a child, "when I remember it at the last moment, I draw you aside and tell you. What could be simpler!"

"But surely," Max persisted, "you were aware that I knew weather was basic to security for the fourteenth?"

"Perhaps," admitted the Minister. "But it was nonetheless true that we had not spoken of it in our conversation."

"But why tell me of it?" asked Max. "What aspect of it was there that you thought it important to tell me about?"

The Minister waved a hand.

"I would have gone on to mention the weapons under the raincoats, the bad visibility in case of air attack, and so on," said the Minister. "You know the sort of thing."

"And that's the point," Max emphasized, "I do know all that sort of thing. I was sure your remark led to something important that I knew nothing about and that you considered worth telling me. So I went to Morris and asked him what he thought of it."

"And?"

"Morris explained to me the different precautions taken by the police in different types of weather," said Max, "just as you are doing now. And it was obvious with him that we were not getting anywhere. So I came here to you."

"And you find," anticipated the Minister, "that you don't get any further with me than you did with Morris?"

"That's right," agreed Max.

"Of course it is!" the Minister exclaimed. "Because my remark concealed nothing unusual at all."

"But that's just what is unusual about it," Max pointed out.

The Minister this time had not followed.

"It was Silesia who first said that your remark seemed to mean nothing," Max explained. "And it was only later that I realized that of all the meanings I had thought it might have, it hadn't occurred to me that it might actually mean nothing."

The Minister's composure had not altered.

"But to say nothing means something," said Max, who was close to his conclusion. "When someone speaks simply in order to speak, he almost invariably makes a remark on the weather. And that," said Max, leaning forward, "is what you did. You adapted a commonplace remark on the weather to the conversation we had just been having, so that you could send out the two motards to 'save' you from a prearranged death."

The Minister was shaking his head.

"Incredible," he said. "Maxie, you're wonderful. And where does the cat come in?"

The dog beside them growled.

"So, Maxie," said a third voice softly, and Max turned to see Soustelle standing quietly at the door behind a pair of dark glasses.

3. The Villains

TEN

Boudin Beards a Barbouze

Max got to his feet.

"Jacques!" he exclaimed.

Soustelle was escorted by two bodyguards in dark suits. He smiled at Max, then raised a reverent hand in greeting and said:

"Hail, my beloved son."

"Hail, my respected father," said Max in reply.

The two bodyguards exchanged glances. The Minister gave an embarrassed laugh and waved his hand impatiently.

"Come on, you two," he said, "this is not the time to start playing at cowboys and Aztecs."

"No Aztec was ever more serious," countered Soustelle. "But never mind," he added, drawing up a chair.

"Well, Max," the Minister began conversationally, "how do you feel now?"

"Glad at least to have been right," Max replied.

The Minister threw back his chair.

"Why, you slanderous . . ." he exclaimed, fighting for his words in fury at this insult. "Yes," he said suddenly, through approaching tears, "yes, I must confess . . . Well, Max," he said, as he laughed uproariously, sitting down again, "I think we can concede you that one all right. Not that I mean to belittle your efforts."

"Poor Max," said Soustelle. "As usual your method was good, only an accident could upset it."

"How did the accident happen?" asked Max.

"Absolute chance," said Soustelle. "Absolute chance that I happened to be passing on this road, absolute chance that I happened to be thinking of you as I was doing so. When I saw the Facel outside, with the 58 numberplate from Château-Chinon, the two things clicked. Even then it wasn't till two or three miles farther on that I realized it clearly enough to think of turning back."

"And then?" asked the Minister, who was also interested.

"We drove slowly past the café," Soustelle went on, "and I saw you two in the back. Knowing Max, I was sure that my interruption would tell him nothing he didn't know already."

"How was it you were thinking of me at this time?" asked Max.

"Ah," said Soustelle coyly. "Who knows?"

"You do," said Max.

"Yes, of course," Soustelle admitted. "We were tuned into the BBC and Bud Flanagan was singing his song about London. I was all nostalgia, just a person who had once seen Flanagan sing that song and who would never forget it. Then noticing your car brought me back to Switzerland and 1962. I had traveled twenty years in a second."

The Minister coughed, and the bodyguards, still standing, were becoming restless.

"Yes, it is extraordinary," the Minister politely observed, "how the past is present and the present past."

The conversation lulled. The bodyguards asked permission to withdraw and went out to sit in the car.

"My word," the Minister declared, "I do feel good. You've no idea, Max, how unpleasant it was talking with you at cross-purposes in my office like that. It was so stilted. At least now we know what we are saying to each other."

Then he ducked and began weaving, boxer-style, behind his aperitif.

"Okay," he said to Max, throwing the words across the table with his chin, "are you coming quietly or do we have to make you?"

His eyes suddenly gleamed dark behind his imaginary gloves.

"We need some help this side, Max," he said. "What about it?"

"That was a dirty foul, Minister," said Max.

"And that's enough," said Soustelle.

They were about to return to normal conversation when one of the bodyguards came in from the car.

"Well, Anton?" asked Soustelle impatiently. "What's the matter?"

"It was just that I thought we shouldn't be around in public too long," said the young man, "especially in the Minister's company."

"You're right, Anton," declared Soustelle. "I'd quite forgotten, these last few minutes, that this country considers me undesirable."

Bills paid, they made their way out to the waiting Mercedes.

"You don't mind letting Anton follow us in the Facel, do you, Max?" asked Soustelle.

"Not at all," said Max.

"He's always wanted to drive one," Soustelle explained.

They sat three together in the back seat while the other bodyguard drove them back slowly in the dusk to the house.

"Only people like us," said the Minister, "who really enjoy each other's company, make the best enemies."

"Enemies nonetheless," said Max, with the righteousness of a detective superintendent.

"Understanding ones, though," the Minister answered.

They sat back silent in the seat, and through the windows they watched the end of the day. The car suddenly turned and climbed steeply away from the lake toward the villa. Soustelle began musing aloud.

"To think," he said, "we might be taking Max up to some hilltop temple to be sacrificed. All five of us would wash in a trough of holy water. The Minister would watch a moving star. We would lay Max down on his back on a lightly arched stone altar. As we held him down, the Minister would make a sign when the star approached another, and I would take my flint knife, cut into Max's chest and extract his heart, holding it up to the sky so that the world might keep on moving."

There was silence again. The car was close to the villa.

"But no," said Soustelle, after a while, shaking his head, "we wouldn't do that. Max is too sensitive. He doesn't like physical pain."

"It's for the fourteenth, like I said, Max," the Minister began briskly, cutting across Soustelle's divagations. "Since you won't help, and we can't trust you to keep secrets to yourself, I'm afraid we'll have to hand you over into Anton's keeping. You will stay with him till the fourteenth at least. I will be back in Paris tomorrow myself, and if all goes well, as it should, then Jacques here will follow me on the fourteenth. By that time, you will be able to go free, since things will have gone too far to be in your control, but not, I hope, too far to be still within ours."

The car drew up in the drive. Anton, who had passed them on the way, was there waiting.

But beside the Facel was another car with a Belgian numberplate that had not been at the lakeside café nor in the drive when Max had explored the villa through the binoculars.

Soustelle spoke quietly to Max as they stood by the Mercedes and prepared to go into the house. He nodded toward the unknown car.

"I'll soon be introducing you to the real head," he said. "Someone you've never met."

"Boudin?" asked Max.

"Correct," said Soustelle. "You'll see, he's a little different from me. A little . . . well, you'll see."

The front door was open and they walked through into the hall, the Minster just behind them. Ahead, a short and bulbous man stepped out from the lounge and came toward them.

"Who's that you've got there?" he asked Soustelle and the Minister not unpleasantly.

"Mister Boudin," said Soustelle, "allow me to present you Max Palk—a friend of mine."

Boudin held out his hand.

"A friend of yours?" he asked. "Pleased to meet you, Mister Palk. For a moment, I thought . . ."

"Well, as a matter of fact," Soustelle began, clearly used to having to deal with Boudin's rather slower understanding, "when I say he's a friend of mine, I don't mean it in a party sense. It's even for that reason that we're only partial friends. But I won't say more about that. It might only bore you and embarrass and sadden Max and myself."

Soustelle bowed his head and turned away. But Boudin threw his hands violently in the air.

"And you brought him here?"

"He did and he didn't," answered the Minister enigmatically.

Boudin gestured short-temperedly.

"These damned evasive answers! Did he or didn't he?"

"He brought him here from the lake," replied the Minister. "But Max had already got that far by himself."

"To see the lake, I suppose?" asked Boudin heavily.

"A little remark I made in Paris had aroused his suspicions," said the Minister.

"So he knows all about it," said Boudin, staring at Max with growing hostility.

Soustelle was returning from a spell of nostalgia for his lost friendship with Max.

"There's quite a lot he doesn't know," he said.

"But a hell of a lot he does all the same, I'll bet, the little . . ." Boudin checked himself, only to be seized by a strange kind of agitation.

His confident manner disappeared. It was with fear that he raised a hand and pointed toward Max.

"A Bearded One!" he exclaimed.

Max, who had shaved that morning, remained silent. Soustelle and the Minister looked at each other and shook their heads sadly.

"A Bearded One!" repeated Boudin regardless. "One of de Gaulle's secret agents!"

"Max a secret agent now!" the Minister echoed with amusement.

"And a secret agent of de Gaulle!" Soustelle exclaimed.

"They're everywhere I go," said Boudin in a low and desperate voice. "In every country. I'm photographed one day in Piccadilly Circus, and the next day they're onto me. They know my disguises, they know my contacts and now here's one about to have dinner with me!"

"This is the French politician in exile for you," the Minister whispered confidentially to Max. "He's on one of the ways into paranoia."

"Mister Boudin," announced the Minister in a pained but patient voice. "We'd never have brought Max here if we'd had any idea you'd be so uncivilized about it."

"Civilized—uncivilized!" cried Boudin. "You talk like that when our best men are kidnapped abroad and brought back to the French police, though the government's too cowardly to admit it."

He paused for a moment, his heavy eye upon Max.

"They may be cowardly, they may be treacherous," he said, "but they're clever, damned clever. And now they're here!" he shouted, pointing down at his feet.

"He knows the Bearded Ones never in fact have beards," said the Minister in Max's ear. "So he gets round to suspecting quite a lot of people."

"And when he does meet someone with a beard?" asked Max.

"Don't ask!"

It was Soustelle who this time turned to Boudin.

"Max is a friend of ours," he said, joining himself to the Minister. "We may have gone different ways since 1940, but . . . we're still friends."

Soustelle had finished his sentence lamely, a weakness from which Boudin was quick to profit.

"You don't know what you're talking about," he declared. "I saw from this man's face straightaway what he was. I want him dealt with exactly as we dealt with the others."

Soustelle winced.

"Don't worry," Boudin reassured him, "we'll do it quicker this time."

But it was not that which had made Soustelle wince.

"Yes," confirmed Boudin, "we'll have him shot in the cellar."

He turned to Max.

"Does anyone know you're here?"

"Morin's wife and the prefect of police," answered Max, innocently.

"Is he telling the truth?" Boudin asked the others.

"Well," said the Minister, "he doesn't usually lie."

"That's easily settled then," Boudin concluded. "The Minster has only to give them both a story when he gets back tomorrow."

He was pleased to have dealt with the problem so quickly. But it was clear to him that Soustelle and the Minister did not agree.

"What's the matter with you two?" he asked.

Soustelle and the Minister exchanged glances. For a moment there was silence.

"Well," began the Minister, edging toward the dining room where the table had been laid. "A condemned man deserves a last supper. Let's eat first before we decide anything. Besides, we know Max. He's not one of those tiresome and fantastic people who's going to jump up suddenly when we make a conveniently silly mistake and knock us all out."

The Minister's voice carried a little more authority with it than had Soustelle's. But although the Minister by this time had reached the dining room door, Boudin remained in the hall.

"If he doesn't do that," he asked ironically, "then what does he do?"

"It's not easy to say," the Minister told him.

"So how am I ever to know?" Boudin protested with reason.

"That's just it," the Minister awkwardly confessed, stopping his advance into the dining room.

"And that's just what I wanted to hear," said Boudin, who had obtained satisfaction. "Anton!" he called, beckoning to one of Soustelle's bodyguards who at that moment was passing from the kitchen to the dining room with a soup tureen. "Go and get one of the men to take our guest here down to the cellar. Tell him to hurry."

Anton laid the bowl of soup on the hall table and turned to execute his orders. Boudin, with no further obstacle between himself and his supper, moved into the dining room and pushed one corner of a long serviette aggressively inside his collar.

"Just a minute!" Soustelle shouted.

Anton stopped and looked from Boudin to Soustelle for his next set of instructions.

"I've got an idea," said Soustelle.

Boudin testily motioned for Anton to bring in the soup from the hall.

"Ideas," he muttered, "you've always got ideas."

"It's an idea for a sort of compromise," Soustelle went on.

"Compromise!" cried Boudin. "But there's no compromise between life and death!"

With a nod, Max hastened for once to agree with Boudin.

"I don't mean we're going to find a state for Max halfway between life and death," said Soustelle, shaking his head anxiously. "What I mean is that we should find a way to decide whether he ought to live or die."

"Yes," the Minister agreed. "We don't want Max to sabotage the fourteenth any more then you do," he explained to Boudin. "But we want him to live."

Soustelle quieted them all with a soothing movement of his hand.

"Why not let Max himself have a say?" he suggested. "Punishment should always be decided on jointly, by the victim and the victors. So I propose we give Max, provided he agrees, that is, a little test. If he passes, then he's guarded in the attic by Anton till the fourteenth. If he fails, then he's taken down to the cellar and . . ." An embarrassed stammer served to complete Soustelle's description of the alternative.

Boudin's hand was on the soup ladle.

"But I'm not going to put off my dinner just for that," he objected, as he sat down at the table.

"That's no argument," the Minister countered. "We only have to have a test that can be continued through dinner."

"Such as?" asked Boudin, as he helped himself to soup.

"Something in Max's style," said the Minister, "to give you an idea of what I was trying to tell you."

"Too hot and no salt again!" cried Boudin over the soup. "If only that maid of yours would give even five minutes' thought a day to her cooking."

"It's these legionaries we've got here," the Minister explained. "They give her a full time."

"Yes," said Boudin, blushing a little.

His own amorous exploits in that direction hadn't met with much success. The Minister and Soustelle judged the moment ripe to seat themselves surreptitiously at the table. Only Max remained standing.

"Well," asked Boudin, "what kind of test have you got in mind? Almost anything would be worth taking my attention off this food," he explained as if to excuse himself.

The tension lessened. At a nod from the Minister, Max, too, took a seat. He was helped to the soup. Forewarned, he salted it. Soustelle and the Minister set themselves to thinking, while Boudin sucked noisily at his soup spoon. Nothing was said. Soustelle's eyes roamed around the room. Along one wall there was a bookcase. He concentrated his gaze upon it.

"I've got it!" he exclaimed after a moment. "Perfect!"

He went over and returned with a tome in blue and white. He laid it to the left of his place on the table. Boudin leaned over in curiosity, pronouncing the words on the cover out loud.

"*Oxford Dictionary of Quotations*, second edition," he said.

"That's right," agreed Soustelle triumphantly.

"You're going to test him on that?" asked Boudin, his anger returning.

"Well, yes," said Soustelle, "if it's all right by Max."

"How do we know he's never studied it?" asked Boudin.

"Who ever studies a dictionary of quotations?" scoffed the Minister.

Boudin grumbled his final agreement. The idea of a mental contest had begun to intrigue him.

"Well, even if he has studied it, it's not going to do him any good," he declared with relish, and reached for the volume.

ELEVEN

The Oxford Dictionary of Quotations, second edition

"No," said Soustelle firmly, "I'll begin."

"Then I retain the right to take up the questioning whenever I think fit," said Boudin.

Soustelle paid no attention. With his left hand he was already turning the pages of the thick dictionary.

"But just a minute," Boudin shouted. "We haven't settled the conditions."

"So we haven't," said the Minister dryly.

He had been giving thought to this point for the last five minutes.

"We say," he declared, "that Max must get twelve or more right out of twenty to win."

"Fifteen," Boudin promptly countered.

"Fifteen," agreed the Minister, "provided that Max is allowed to ask us three questions on each one."

"One question," said Boudin, bringing his hand down hard on the table.

Soustelle and the Minister said nothing.

"I'm not having any alternative," said Boudin firmly. "Except the one you're aware of."

For Max, there could be no hesitation.

"Let's go," he said.

Soustelle and the Minister looked anxiously at each other.

"Good," said Boudin. "Anton," he called, "we'll have the fish now."

The soup plates were cleared and an almond-coated trout was placed before each diner. Boudin poured himself a glass of white wine, which he drained immediately and filled again from the bottle that his hand had not left. He sat back. He was clearly one of those for whom the adjective *full* could not be properly applied to the first glass, but only to those that followed. Picking up his knife and fork, he began to dismember his trout. The first mouthful tasted good. Only Max's presence, which he had welcomed at the time of the soup, was there to mar it. He realized suddenly how scandalous the situation was. He, Boudin . . .

"Come on, come on," he said irritably to Soustelle. "We haven't got all night."

"I'm just looking through," said Soustelle.

Boudin's hand clenched hard over his knife handle.

"Ha!" said Soustelle.

Everyone stopped eating.

"Here's an appropriate one to start off with," said Soustelle. "Who said," and in silence he spoke the words, " 'You ain't heard nothin' yet, folks'?"

Boudin was mystified.

"Al Jolson," answered Max. "In *The Jazz Singer*, the first talking film."

Boudin looked from Soustelle to Max and back again.

"He saw it!" he shouted. "He could see from across the table where the book was open."

Soustelle shrugged his shoulders. "If you say so," he said. Boudin got up from the table and came back with a newspaper which he folded and propped up against a candlestick in front of the dictionary.

"Carry on," he said curtly.

Soustelle opened the book at random and ran his eye over each page, pausing from time to time to take mouthfuls of trout.

"Who said," he began slowly, " 'Cheer up, the worst is yet to come'?"

Boudin laughed loudly.

"Another appropriate one," he said.

Max drank a little mineral water. His expression of doubt was genuine.

"An English music-hall artist?" he asked.

Soustelle shook his head.

"You've had your question, Palk," said Boudin swiftly.

"I'll guess then," said Max, "and try . . . Kipling?"

"I'm afraid not," said Soustelle softly. "It's not someone I've heard of either. His name is Philander Chase Johnson and he wrote it in *Everybody's* in 1920."

Max thought he saw alarm in the look the Minister gave Soustelle. But Soustelle was unruffled. Max's mistakes were being as carefully planned as his successes.

"One right out of two," announced Boudin, the self-appointed scorer. He was beginning to enjoy himself.

"As a special concession," he said largely, "I'll let you have two questions instead of one."

There were no thanks to be given, but Max was glad of the advantage all the same. They waited for Soustelle to swallow his last piece of trout. Max could hear the pages being turned behind the newspaper.

"Fetch in the next course," ordered Boudin, and he leaned forward to catch the third question.

"Who remarked of someone," asked Soustelle, "that he 'deserved to be preached to death by wild curates'?"

"It certainly sounds typical of one person that comes to mind," said Max, careful not to appear too knowledgeable.

"Was he an Anglican minister?" asked Max.

"He was," said Soustelle.

"And that's your first question gone, Palk," said Boudin, breaking in.

"Was it Sydney Smith?" asked Max.

"It was," Soustelle answered.

Boudin helped himself to a thick tournedos Rossini. The Minister seemed less anxious. Soustelle laughed over his next question.

"Let's hear it then," said the Minister.

"Who said," began Soustelle, lulled by the repetition of these two introductory words into using a nursery rhyme voice, "who said, in answer to a lady who had told him that a landscape reminded her of his work, 'Yes madam, Nature is creeping up'?"

"Obviously a painter," said Max, "and perhaps someone who could speak as well as he could paint. Did he live at the time of Oscar Wilde? Did he even have any connection with Wilde?"

Soustelle nodded.

"Two separate questions there, Palk," said Boudin with his mouth full.

"Then it was Whistler," Max concluded.

Max was right, though Soustelle contrived to make it as little obvious as possible. And the Minister filled in the awkward gap to the next question by some makeshift conversation about the food. Boudin was already a little flushed from the strong red wine. Anton had been relieved of his serving duties. Boudin passed the vegetables to Max without so much as a sidelong glance.

"Here's a good one on professional critics," announced Soustelle.

A great many pages had been turned. Max thought of authors at the beginning of the alphabet. Soustelle read out the following verse:

'Who killed John Keats?'
'I,' says the Quarterly,

So Savage and Tartarly;
'"Twas one of my feats.'

"Very good," the Minister commented.

"Was the man who wrote it a poet?" asked Max.

After a nod from Soustelle, he went on to his second question.

"Did he live at the same time as Keats as well as after him?"

Again an assenting nod.

"Byron," Max softly stated.

"Another right! the little rat!" Boudin exclaimed, unable to contain himself. "Step up the questions."

This was precisely what Soustelle was intending to do. He looked over the folded newspaper at Max and asked, "Who said, 'Examinations are formidable even to the best prepared, for the greatest fool may ask more than the wisest man can answer'?"

"Someone in the eighteenth or nineteenth century?" asked Max.

"Yes," said Soustelle.

"A university don?" asked Max.

"No idea," Soustelle confessed. "I'm seeing the name for the first time."

It was clearly not in Soustelle's plans for Max to get this one right.

"Not Sydney Smith again, I suppose?" he asked tentatively.

Soustelle shook his head.

"The name is Charles Caleb Colton."

"That's better," said Boudin. "What does that make it now? Four right out of six. That's below what he needs to win. Let's have the next."

"Which isn't a bad one," said Soustelle, by way of introduction. "Who said, 'I should like to see, and this will be the last and most ardent of my desires, I should like to see the last king strangled with the guts of the last priest'?"

"I don't like that bit about the priest," said Boudin.

"But it suggests," said Max, taking up where Boudin had left off, "that it was said in a Catholic country, probably France and before the Revolution."

"Correct," said Soustelle.

"Voltaire's the obvious person," Max went on. "But it's a bit too strong and straightforward for him. It's the sort of thing he'd have welcomed but not said himself."

"Again right," said Soustelle.

But he pushed the book along to Boudin, and they whispered.

"What's the matter?" asked the Minister.

"We're just deciding what to do," Soustelle explained. "Max got everything right, except the name of the man. It was a Will published by Voltaire and the man's name was Messelier."

"Count it as right," said the Minister. "We can't be bothered with halves and things."

"Just what do you think you're doing?" said Boudin, coming back brutally.

"Look," said the Minister, brandishing knife and fork in Boudin's direction, "we give him this one and he's got five right out of seven, which is still less than what he needs to win."

Boudin made a calculation on the tablecloth.

"Five out of seven gives him . . . 14.29 out of twenty," he said aloud. "Okay, he can have it," he added ungenerously. "Now let's get on with it."

He helped himself to some young French beans.

"Number eight coming up," said Soustelle, running through the pages. "Who wrote, 'But, good gracious, you've got to educate him first. You can't expect a boy to be vicious till he's been to a good school'?"

"Somebody of this century?" asked Max, watching Soustelle. "Or at the end of the last?" he added, correcting himself.

"That's right," said Soustelle, aware that Max was in difficulty. "But the name you must give is a one-word pseudonym, not the name down on the man's birth certificate."

"Saki," said Max.

"You just gave it away," said Boudin in disgust.

"He didn't," said Max. "I've never read Saki in my life. It was the only pseudonym I could think of that fitted."

Boudin sat back uncomfortably in his chair. He suspected treachery.

"Ah yes," said Soustelle, appreciatively, as he fell upon his ninth quotation. "Who was it who said, 'I beseech you, in the bowels of Christ, think it possible you may be mistaken'?"

"There's only one century that that could have been said in," said Max, careful not to give the answer immediately.

"That's right," said Soustelle, "the seventeenth."

"But he hadn't said it," shouted Boudin. "It's you who've just told him. He might have said something else."

"He might have," said the Minister with special emphasis.

"Of course he might have," Boudin agreed.

The Minister smiled.

"I knew it was Cromwell all the time," said Max, coming in with an explanation. "I just asked the question about the century to make sure."

But there were too many explanations for Boudin's liking.

"Extraordinary thing, this *Dictionary of Quotations*," said the Minister, speaking quickly to distract Boudin's attention. "You find a concentration in a couple of lines of points of view it would take volumes to describe. It makes you think it would be more worth your while composing quotations."

The device had served its purpose and Soustelle found his next quotation without an interruption from Boudin.

"Number ten," he announced. "Who said, or rather, who wrote, 'Scratch the Christian and you find the pagan—spoiled'?"

"A Christian, I hope," said Boudin.

Soustelle coughed.

"I'm afraid not," he said.

"Not a Christian?" echoed Boudin incredulously.

"Not even a Catholic," Soustelle pointed out apologetically.

"Zangwill," said Max quietly.

"Give it here," shouted Boudin. "Give me that book."

TWELVE

How Odd of God

Soustelle pushed the dictionary round to Boudin. The newspaper and the candlestick followed. Boudin arranged them carefully between himself and Max. In the excitement he had forgotten about his food and drink. The serious half of Max's trial by ordeal was about to begin.

"Eight out of ten," muttered Boudin, giving Soustelle an unfriendly look.

To fortify himself for the questions to come, he poured another glass of wine and emptied the silver dish of beans that had been left to keep hot over the table-burner. The rest of the company were quiet.

"My God, that's good," Boudin exclaimed, laughing to himself.

He looked at Max and said, "Here's something to pay you back for the last one.

How odd
Of God
To choose
The Jews.

"Isn't it good?" Boudin laughed again.

"I can't tell you who wrote it, but I can give you the answer," said Max.

Oh no
It's not,
He knows
What's what.

Boudin lost countenance.

"All the same, you didn't get it," he said, recovering. "The name is Ewer. That still gives you only eight right and now it's out of eleven. Just let me find another like that one," he added, and he searched through the pages.

Max took the opportunity to finish off the little food he had taken.

"Here's something from a poet," said Boudin meditatively. The very idea of poetry was enough to change his manner.

"Who, speaking of Oxford, said, 'Ye sacred Nurseries of blooming Youth'?"

"Wordsworth," Max answered promptly.

"How did you know that?" asked Boudin in astonishment.

"I just thought of a poet you might like and thought of Wordsworth," Max told him.

Boudin did not answer, not knowing whether to take the intention behind Max's accuracy of method as flattering or abusive.

"Cheese!" he shouted into the kitchen.

The second bodyguard appeared, took the plates away and brought in the cheese board. Max beckoned to him and ordered more salad instead. It was too hot and heavy an evening for cheese. Max helped himself from the wooden salad bowl.

After scraping his camembert, Boudin was ready to resume the questioning. But he, too, was undergoing the fascination of the dictionary, and it was a little while before he found the thirteenth quotation.

"Please don't get your fingers all over it," said the Minister coldly.

"They're wiped," said Boudin, without looking up. "And here's my question," he went on. "Another good one, by a man who knew what he was talking about. 'The people have nothing to do with the laws but to obey them.'"

"It could have been a hundred people," said Max, beginning to feel uneasy as Boudin asked another he knew he did not know.

"Well," said Boudin, "there's only one name here, and that's all I want."

"English?" asked Max.

Boudin nodded.

"Is it some medieval doctor of the Church?" asked Max.

"It isn't," said Boudin.

"Then it's not the man I'm thinking of," said Max. "I'll hear it from you."

"It was said by Bishop Samuel Horsely," Boudin informed him, "in a speech to the House of Lords at the end of the eighteenth century."

"And I'm sure it went down very well," said Max. "Let's have the next."

Max may have sounded confident, but he didn't feel it inside. In spite of the lightness of the meal, he was forced at this point to mop his forehead with his serviette.

"Just a minute," said Boudin. "You've got nine right out of thirteen.

You've got to get five or more out of the next seven to avoid going down to the cellar. Hey," he said suddenly to Soustelle, "wasn't it you who called de Gaulle's France 'A dictatorship tempered by anarchy'?"

"I think it was," said Soustelle.

"Here's a man who said practically the same thing about Louis XIV," Boudin told him.

"Whose originality are you doubting," asked Soustelle, "de Gaulle's or mine?"

"Yours, of course," answered Boudin flatly.

"I've never heard it said before," said Soustelle mildly.

"Well, it has been, and better," said Boudin. "Who said about pre-Revolutionary France that it was 'A despotism tempered by epigrams'?"

"A historian of the nineteenth century?" asked Max, feeling this time on safer ground.

"Yes," said Boudin.

"English?"

"Yes."

"Macaulay wrote a history of England," said Max slowly, looking at the Minister, whose expression suddenly changed. "So it must be . . . Carlyle."

From Boudin's expression it was obvious that Carlyle it was. He resorted once more to the tablecloth.

"You needn't count," said Max. "I've got ten out of fourteen."

Very few pages were turned over behind the newspaper. Max thought, somewhere near to the letter *C*. As Boudin looked up, Max could see that something had come over his features that indicated the presence before him of another piece of poetry. Sure enough it was.

"Who begins and entitles a poem with the line 'I love all beauteous things'?"

"Bridges."

Once again the reply was instantaneous.

"By the same method," said Max, smiling at Boudin and anticipating his question.

A great many pages were furiously turned.

"What an ugly word *beauteous* is," commented the Minister during the interval.

Boudin had stopped.

"Who said," he asked, " 'The heart has its reasons which reason knows nothing of'?"

There was a general relaxation.

"A Frenchman?" asked Max.

"Of the seventeenth century?" he asked again.

"Pascal."

Boudin did not seem sorry to let him have it.

"At least you know some philosophy," he said, almost good-humoredly. "Let's try you now on this one. 'A man is in general better pleased when he has a good dinner upon his table, than when his wife talks Greek.'"

"That's true," said the Minister shaking his head, "though whether it ought to be is another matter."

"Is it Johnson?" asked Max.

Boudin was forced to admit that it was; he had not been doing as well as he'd expected. Max felt a definite relief. There was a lull during which the Minister reached for the fruit on the sideboard. Boudin chose a peach, as Max had half expected he would do, and he did not manage to eat it cleanly.

"These are your last three questions coming up, Palk," said Boudin. "And you've got to get at least two of them right. Your first is 'To God I speak Spanish, to women Italian, to men French, and to my horse—German,'"

"It sounds almost medieval," Max began. "But it doesn't seem something that a man of the Church would have said. Though who else was in a position to say it? An ambassador?"

Boudin shook his head.

"A king perhaps?" asked Max.

Boudin conceded the point with a curt nod.

"A king who could have said that must have been king of several . . . of course," said Max, interrupting his own sentence, "it could have been only one man—the Holy Roman Emperor Charles V."

Boudin was already turning the paper in search of his last quotation but one. Suddenly he alighted on something in a manner that for a moment or two made Max prepare for another line of poetry. But Boudin's expression wasn't quite the same. It managed somehow to be more profound, even gentle.

"I am a man, I count nothing human indifferent to me," Boudin quoted.

"I thought for a moment it was something you'd said yourself," Max answered quickly. "You see," he explained, "it's what the humanist says, but not the human being."

Boudin, for whom indeed humanism had ever been a holy word, stared uncomprehendingly at Max.

"I don't care what you think of these quotations," he shouted suddenly. "Give me the man's name and be done with it."

But Max had no idea who had said it. He thought of the cellar, and as he did so his fruit knife slipped, to fall, fortunately, on a fingernail.

"One of T. S. Eliot's more philosophical lines?" he asked.

Boudin looked breathlessly over the newspaper.

"No," he said.

"A pre-Christian maybe?"

"Yes," said Boudin, almost hoarse in his anxiety.

But Max needed more than a *yes* to one of his questions to get the author's name.

"Cicero," he said, from no knowledge except that of general impression.

"Equal," announced the Minister with a sigh. "It all depends on this last one. You might as well know, Max," he added without waiting for Boudin to supply the information, "that it wasn't Cicero, but Terence."

"Yes," echoed Boudin dreamily, "it all depends on this last one. And I promise you, Palk," he declared harshly, "that you won't get it. Hear that? I promise you."

Max wondered and was afraid at the reason behind such confidence. Boudin, two dripping peach stones on his plate, was grotesquely sinister. Max was already in a position he had not counted on and now Boudin had revealed that he had been saving something special for the end. For the first time, Max saw the alternative of the cellar in its real light.

The newspaper shield was carefully adjusted. Boudin deliberately turned over so many pages that Max was thrown off the scent. The newspaper was placed so high and Boudin was bent so low that only that part of his head to which the hairline had not yet receded was visible. The delay seemed unnecessarily long, seeing that Boudin clearly had this move all prepared. But as his victim, and indeed, the audience of two, were becoming more and more nervous, Boudin was savoring certain victory. At length he looked up at Max.

"And here's the question, Palk," he said.

He spoke the word *question* with a brutal whoosh of saliva and air.

"Absence makes the heart grow fonder."

It sounded strangely soft and out of context after what had preceded. To Max and the others it seemed unreal. Something was wrong. Yet Boudin's expression had not changed, apart from the attempts he was making to suppress sudden surges of happy excitement.

Max repeated the quotation. It was so much a part of the English language that those who used it did not attach it to any particular author. Such things sometimes happened to Shakespeare. But surely Boudin wouldn't stake everything on a person so obvious as Shakespeare? Or perhaps, thought Max, he would, simply because it was the last thing an opponent would have suspected. He decided therefore to try it. But Boudin shook his head almost before the name Shakespeare was out of his mouth.

"You still have another question, Palk," Boudin was saying invitingly, making it clear at the same time that he considered he was giving nothing away. "Why don't you use it?"

Max looked at Soustelle, who seemed at as great a loss as he was himself. The Minister, on the other hand, was shaking his head when Boudin wasn't looking and moving his fruit knife backward and forward horizontally. He seemed to be saying "No," but "no" to what?

"Palk," announced Boudin happily, "I'm afraid you're caught."

Under such a stimulus Max thought of a possible name.

"Is it a poet of the sixteenth century, by any chance?" he asked.

Back went the Minister's head, his eyes closed in a silent gesture of despair. Max did not need Boudin to tell him that his guess had been hopelessly inaccurate.

"You've had your two questions, Palk," said Boudin. "And now let's hear the name."

With the sudden increase in tension, Max burst through the clouds into the light. The Minister's mysterious signal became clear and he himself might all the time have been dreaming.

"It's a proverb," he said.

Boudin was badly hit. But the blow had not been fatal. Within a moment, he had recovered.

"No, and no, and no!" he exclaimed in exultation, slamming the dictionary shut. "It's *anonymous!*"

He was so happy as to be almost delirious. It had indeed been a smart move. He got up from his chair, his serviette still inside his collar. He grabbed Max's arm and called loudly for Anton. And with that, Max was hustled out of the room toward the door by the kitchen that led down to the cellar.

THIRTEEN

Famous Last Words

Soustelle followed, talking anxiously at Boudin's shoulder, for the cellar steps could not accommodate the passage of two men abreast. The Minister was left alone at the dinner table, the book of quotations in front of him.

"But all the same," Soustelle was saying, "a proverb's anonymous."

"Maybe," said Boudin, "but the dictionary lists them under separate headings."

Max was first into the cellar, with Anton's gun in his back. Ropes, hooks, bare tables, strange cupboards, a single tap over an old zinc bath—the cellar furniture was conventional. Max moistened all over in horror. Boudin, though, was returning to such surroundings with satisfaction.

"It's here that the parachute boys we have upstairs do their workouts," he explained, treating Max more as a visitor than as a victim.

Soustelle stayed at the bottom of the steps, wringing his hands so that he appeared to be retreating even though he was standing still. It was all his fault, he was thinking, for having come upon Max with his bodyguards. It was true that their friendship was less than it had been, but for it to have come to this . . .

Boudin was placing Max against each of the heavily pitted walls in turn. He stepped back to consider each position thoughtfully.

"That'll do fine," he said, as they came back to the first wall. "Anton, fetch The Limper, you know—the one who likes to watch these things."

Anton disappeared up stairs. Boudin searched for a suitable material with which to blindfold the victim, tugging deep in thought on his serviette as he did so—until the serviette came away and Boudin realized that it provided him with the very thing he had been looking for. With the serviette over his face Max was smelling the meal he had just eaten. It reminded him, if he needed reminding, that he was to be machine-gunned at point-blank range in the stomach, just after he had eaten.

The door at the top of the steps opened and Max's nausea gave way to his original feeling of terror. But those around him were silent. It was the Minister who was slowly descending the stairs. He held the book open in front of him. At the sound of his voice, Max pulled down his blindfold. The Minister stopped on the third step and looked down upon Boudin. His manner was that of a fearsome preacher.

"Max has lost within the rules we all agreed to in the beginning," said the Minister. "But your last move was not within the rules so much as not against them."

Boudin quailed.

"So I think there is room," pursued the Minister, "for one more try under those same conditions. More important even," he added, "is that I have not yet chosen a single quotation. What I propose is for me to select a question that you two will ratify before I submit it to Max."

Boudin shifted uneasily. He was extremely loth to risk his victory.

"Come on," said the Minister mockingly. "Don't you know this?

We were brothers all
In honour, as in one community,
Scholars and gentlemen.

"Your own Wordsworth said it. And," asked the Minster, indicating with a wave of the hand the equipment around them, "did he live in a cellar?"

"All right then," said Boudin at last. "What's your quotation?"

"I'll show you," said the Minister, "if you will replace Max's blindfold."

"Ah!" exclaimed Boudin, grateful to the Minister for having reminded him of so elementary a precaution.

The Minister stepped down and the dictionary was passed from one to another.

"Hmm," said Soustelle, now a different man. "Difficult!"

"He hasn't got much, this fellow," Max heard Boudin say, still suspiciously. "Only three quotes."

So Boudin was prepared to accept the quotation. The dictionary was returned to the Minister.

"I'll read it then," he announced.

But after the first few words, he took his eyes off the text and recited the rest from memory.

"Two things fill the mind with ever-increasing wonder and awe, the more often and the more intensely the mind of thought is drawn to them: the starry heavens above me and the moral law within me."

As Max listened, he understood why Soustelle had sounded so uncon-cerned a moment ago.

"A German philosopher?" he asked. "Would it be Kant?"

Boudin was silent. But he made a final desperate effort.

"Give us where it comes from," he said, knowing already, however, that all was lost.

"The first sentence of the conclusion to the *Critique of Practical Reason*."

Anton, who had been called minutes before by Boudin for quite another purpose, took Max's arm and led him up the stairs to the attic.

FOURTEEN

Tuesday, July the Tenth

The room had a skylight and a sloping ceiling. There was a washbasin in one corner. It was pleasantly furnished in a strong shade of red. The walls had been painted white. There was a chair but Max preferred to sit on the bed with his back against the wall when he wasn't at the table reading.

The first evening Max began to pick out the different sounds made by the closing of each of the doors below. They seemed to come to him through the walls of the house, since the door to his own room was too thick to allow the sounds to pass freely. Because of this, he never knew how many men there were in the house. The number seemed to be continually changing. Sometimes he counted only two, which he supposed to be Soustelle and the Minister, Boudin having already left. At other times he seemed to hear four or five and even more. The noise of washing-up and cooking would come to him through the skylight from the kitchen two floors below. The Minister appeared to have only one maid. Evidently he did not wish to increase the number of those in whom he had to have absolute trust. Through the open skylight, Max would also catch over the following three days the sounds of the cars that came and went on the gravel drive. But he couldn't see them. The first evening he stood on the chair and looked through the skylight, scarcely wide enough for his head, at the road and the lake and the mountains opposite that composed the view from the back of the house. But Max was unmoved, and he never felt the need to get onto the chair again.

Built into the middle of the door of his room was a small metal grille that worked like a Venetian blind—only, the cord by which it could be opened and closed lay on the other side. At the moment it was closed. Max imagined that Anton would be on the floor beneath it, preparing to go to sleep on the cushions he had seen him collecting from the different rooms as they came up the stairs. Before taking Max into his custody, Anton had hesitated between a pistol and a submachine gun.

"Above all, beware of noise," Boudin had said to him. Anton had chosen the heavily silenced pistol.

Max knocked gently on the door, gently in case Anton was already asleep. Bu the shutters slid open.

"What the hell do you want?" asked Anton belligerently.

"A couple of books from downstairs. Doesn't matter which." Max added, "Let Soustelle choose, and bring up some paper, too, if you would, please."

Anton went down the stairs with bad grace. Max did not urgently need the books he had asked for, nor even the paper, but he wanted to have them around.

There was nothing that Max could do while Anton was absent. It was impossible to tamper with the lock, for example, even if Max had known how to. The keyhole had been filled in on his side.

The times when he had the slightest chance of escaping were when Anton opened the door or took him down to the second floor to the lavatory. But Anton covered him with great concentration. He was large, much larger than Max, and seemed relatively agile; even supposing he failed to fire at the first sign of trouble, the noise of the fighting would certainly bring Anton's friends from downstairs on the scene.

Anton was back with the books. He unlocked the door and drew the bolt. Max stayed sitting on the bed. It was a safety arrangement they had reached almost immediately. Anton, keeping Max covered all the time, laid the books on the chair and retreated backward to the door.

"Thank you and good night," said Max.

There was nothing to be gained by being unpleasant to Anton. Sympathy, on the other hand, might get him a little farther.

But so far Anton had failed each time to return the politeness that Max offered him. At first Max knew that Anton was unaware of refusing anything, but even at the end of this first evening, he could see that the young fascist was becoming irritated by the knowledge of his own unpleasantness and his ignorance of or lack of belief in his reasons for it. Max guessed that the strain that this produced would be resolved in one of two ways. Either Anton would decide to become more and more hostile or there would be a period of silence during which he would be trying to persuade himself to be pleasant. In this he would have to be helped by Max. But Anton swung the door to viciously, swearing under his breath, and it was the first guess that had proved correct.

Max picked up the books from the chair. He smiled as he recognized *Happiness Is a Warm Puppy*. Underneath was the unabridged American edition of Louis Nizer's *My Life in Court*. Giving mental thanks to Soustelle, Max settled down to read the first case, the long account of the defense of Quentin Reynolds.

The following morning, Tuesday, July the tenth, Max was still asleep when Anton came in with the breakfast of white coffee and buttered bread. Max woke as the door slammed shut. He washed and ate his breakfast.

Anton came in again when he had finished, to take Max to the lavatory and the tray to the kitchen.

"I'll give you a good reference," said Max on the way back, "any time you apply to be a full-time maid."

"I didn't join the OAS to bring you your breakfast and take you to the lavatory," Anton replied quickly.

"Then what did you join it for?" asked Max.

But the question did not draw Anton into the room. Instead Anton blew scornfully down his nose and, turning his back, pulled the door shut. Max shrugged his shoulders and sat down at the table.

Halfway through the morning, Anton brought in a fruit juice. Max tasted it before Anton left the room.

"It's too sweet," said Max, handing the glass back to Anton. "Bring up something that tastes a little less like syrup."

Anton hesitated.

"You heard what I said, didn't you?" asked Max. "Go down and change it."

"I will not," answered Anton, setting the glass on the table.

"You will not?" echoed Max disbelievingly. "And why not?"

For a reply Anton would have liked to have slammed the door in Max's face.

"That has nothing to do with you," he said.

"Why not?" asked Max again.

"Because we're not here for that," said Anton reluctantly, regretting that he had ever resorted to speech.

"Then what are we here for?" asked Max.

"You're here to stay and I'm here to guard you, if you want to know," answered Anton.

"That's what I was afraid of," said Max. "If you're going to refuse to carry out the orders I give you, like changing my fruit juice, then you're going to have very little to do out there all by yourself. Instead, why not try something like bringing me round to your way of thinking?"

"To the OAS, you mean?" asked Anton contemptuously. "And how would I do that?"

"I don't know," Max admitted. "If I did, I'd be on your side already. You could try talking to me, for instance."

Anton snorted and turned to the door. He'd had enough.

"So the idea doesn't appeal to you?" Max called to him. "Why not, afraid it mightn't work?"

"Perhaps," said Anton, over his shoulder, with heavy sarcasm.

"And you'd be right," Max told him. "You wouldn't have the time, because I have decided that I must be out of here by midday, Friday the thirteenth. Now there's something to occupy yourself with on your side of the door."

Anton left the room quietly. Max returned to the table, where he continued to work for the rest of the morning. At one o'clock, Anton came back with Max's lunch. He looked nervous.

"What's the matter, Anton?" Max asked. "Are you worried about what I said to you this morning?"

Anton shook his head, but his manner remained the same.

"Because if you are," continued Max, "you needn't be. I don't carry a gun. You saw that when you searched me. If I leave here by Friday, as I intend to, it will be with your consent and cooperation."

"Huh," said Anton, "I'd like to see that."

"You may yet, Anton, you may yet."

Anton was relieved to discover that his prisoner's method did not include the secret exits and strange weapons that he had spent an anxious morning thinking of. And Max smiled, as he saw Anton's readiness to accept an assurance that was itself part of the method by which he would make his escape. Anton saw the smile and did not understand it.

"Espèce de con," he said with great feeling.

So Max was being taken seriously. It was exactly what he wanted.

"You're a miserable person, Anton," he said. "In fact you're one of the most miserable men it's been my misfortune to be guarded by."

"Ta gueule, con," said Anton viciously.

Anton had only to laugh and tell Max to try something else. But his reaction had been quite different.

"Yes," said Max reflectively, as if he were turning a specimen of misery over in his hands, "one of the most miserable . . ."

"Tu la fermeras, ta gueule, non?"

Max got slowly to his feet. His manner was melodramatic, but not for one moment did he consider changing it.

"Anton," he said, emphasizing each word, "you are weak."

Anton this time did not reply.

"Yes, Anton, you are weak because you're afraid to talk to me. And you're afraid to talk to me because there are weaknesses within you that you don't want brought out into the light."

Anton was too unused to such conversation to be annoyed. He shrugged his shoulders.

"What weaknesses?" he asked.

"That's what we'll soon be finding out," said Max. "But there's one I have spotted already. You tried a moment ago to hide it by swearing. You were afraid I would show you that you don't believe in your own decisions."

"What do you mean?" asked Anton.

"I mean," said Max, "that you do things, like joining the OAS, but you don't *decide* to do them."

"What do I do then?" asked Anton.

"You join, not out of an absolute decision, but from a half conviction that the OAS is right. The whole of your subsequent career in the OAS is an attempt to convince yourself that the conviction was absolute. That is why you so strongly resent being assigned to the job of guarding me. Someone wholly given to the OAS would regret such a job and wish he had been given something more positive. But you feel that the job is given you because somehow your half decision has been recognized for what it was. You feel you've been seen where you thought you were safely concealed. You've been given a job only half inside the OAS because you only half decided to join it."

Max paused. Anton still pointed his revolver at Max as steadily as before. That he stood there and listened was all that Max needed—for as long as he did so, it meant that he thought there was something true in what Max was saying. And, in the circumstances, Anton was the only judge whose opinion counted. Max smiled.

"Am I right?" he asked.

"What does it matter whether you are or not?" Anton answered.

"This morning," said Max in conclusion, "you were annoyed by my reference to your job as being that of a maid, because it reminded you of the weakness I've just mentioned. And my remark at the end, in which I told you of my intention to leave you on Friday, strengthened the reminder, because you recognized it as the remark of someone who seemed absolutely decided. I think the feeling's spreading. Perhaps you even take the fact that I'm not carrying a gun as a suggestion that you're unable to use your own."

"I can use my gun perfectly well," shouted Anton excitedly. "And any time you give me the opportunity I will prove it to you. Besides," he added, "I joined the OAS out of conviction and I know what conviction."

"Well?" said Max expectantly.

"I wanted to be among those who would save France," said Anton.

"Save France from what?" asked Max.

"From communism and dishonor," Anton replied.

"Let's take communism first," said Max. "What do you object to in it?"

"It's evil," said Anton, "and I hate it."

"Perhaps," Max answered, "but this doesn't get us very far. It tells us something about you, but nothing at all about communism. Now let's have a precise and intelligible objection."

"Communism is international," said Anton.

"What do you dislike about internationalism?"

"It doesn't respect national sovereignty," replied Anton.

"Is that what you mean by honor, too?" asked Max.

"Yes," Anton told him. "A nation that is its own master is an honorable one."

"Do you think therefore that each state should try to become its own master?"

"Of course," said Anton.

"And that Vercingetorix was right in trying to rid France of the Romans?"

"Of course," said Anton again.

"Why, then, do you refuse to the Algerians the right to become their own masters?"

"Times and situations change," said Anton, shrugging his shoulders.

"Perhaps," said Max, "but your principles shouldn't. You affirm for one case what you deny for another."

The exchange came to a stop. Anton fumbled for a reply.

"Algeria is not a nation," he said.

"But neither was Vercingetorix," Max answered. "By your reasoning no nation could ever come to exist."

And thus they talked into the late afternoon. They had begun with Max sitting back on the bed and Anton standing, keeping him covered with the gun. But the end of the conversation found Max on his feet, pacing up and down the room, and Anton shriveled into silence and immobility on the chair. The gun lay idle on his lap. Max had promised to do nothing but speak. He would not rush for the door or assault Anton. And he had kept his promise with a vengeance. The intellectual foundations of Anton's fascism had been cut to pieces with a speed and decisiveness that left the victim with nothing to say. Anton listlessly picked up his gun and walked numbly out of the door.

Max lay back on the bed with his hands behind his head. Like a general he mapped out the plan of the campaign to follow.

He had to be out by Friday lunchtime at the latest. Everything else would be subordinated to that. Anton therefore was to be allowed no quarter, though he could avoid further pressure simply by keeping his mouth shut.

Perhaps he had already determined to do this. But he had taken Max too seriously already to find such a resolution easy to carry through. Max knew what lay in store for Anton once he opened his mouth. Anton did not and this ignorance would make any decision of his to remain silent very vulnerable indeed. Max had only to tell Anton why he wasn't talking, for the boy to talk instinctively to deny it.

By constantly maintaining the pressure Max reckoned that three days would be sufficient. A hardened legionary in his late thirties would have required a good deal longer, and might even have proved impossible, in which case Max would have resorted to another method. Anton, however, was typical of the younger and less experienced section of the OAS; his attachment to the organization and the semblance of coherence it gave to his person might have seemed solid enough to the average observer, but to Max they were very frail because he knew that secretly they were frail to Anton.

FIFTEEN

Wednesday, July the Eleventh

Though Max had read late into the evening, he was up waiting for Anton when he came in with the breakfast.

"Thank you," said Max as usual, but there was no reply.

"So you're not talking?" Max shook his head. "A little ray of sunshine. What a wonderful person for a man who sees nobody else to meet first thing in the morning."

Anton walked sullenly to the door.

"You know," said Max, "losing your political beliefs is not half so serious as losing your sense of humor."

The door slammed shut. But the breakfast things had to be cleared away and Max had to be escorted to the lavatory. This, too, was accomplished in silence.

"For Christ's sake," said Max in exasperation, "you're so heavy and melodramatic about it all. Lighten up a little."

Anton shrugged his shoulders.

"That's it," said Max, encouragingly, "that's already a little better. But you're afraid to talk," he went on, "because you're afraid of a repeat of yesterday afternoon."

"I'm not," said Anton. "Besides," he added defiantly, "they were only words."

"Which you are criticizing to me now by using more words," said Max.

"I can't do anything else," said Anton.

"That's where you're wrong," said Max. "You could have kept quiet. You cannot prove by words that words are useless, any more than I can prove by words that words are a kind of action. In each case the proof is in something other than words—silence in the first case, a transformed person in the second."

"I should have said nothing," said Anton. "I meant to."

"Perhaps you did," said Max, "but it is as if you didn't. Now that you've spoken you'd better forget you meant to keep quiet and think only of speaking as well as possible."

"I hate your bloody words," Anton said suddenly. "You talk and you talk and you get nothing done."

"But if that were true," said Max, "it would be odd for you to have such a violent dislike for words. You're not such an active and busy man that you hate things simply for the reason that they don't allow you to get anything done, are you?"

"You go on and on," said Anton, trying hard to control his temper.

"And you become more and more angry," said Max. "That's surely a sign that things *are* being done. It is that which makes you angry. Yesterday afternoon, for example, while I was speaking you knew something was happening. It only became words for you when the words stopped and you went outside. It was precisely because you didn't want the words to go deeper that you meant not to speak today. But remember what I said to you yesterday about decisions—you're a person who finds them difficult to abide by, especially when they're your own. So you talked."

"Espèce de vieux con," Anton blurted out.

"Your actions have proved," said Max, ignoring the interruption, "by the only kind of proof that to say 'words are useless' is false. It is also a lie, for you wish it to be false, in order to escape the consequences of it being true."

Anton still held the pistol aimed at Max's chest. He had not wavered all the time that Max had been talking.

"So once again," said Max in conclusion, "you chose the way out of the weak."

"Salaud," shouted Anton, "you deserve to be shot."

The gun steadied in his hand but nothing happened.

"You can't even decide to shoot me," said Max.

Anton had reached the state in which he felt independent from Max only by doing the opposite of everything Max said. He now realized this. He didn't pull the trigger. He even lowered the gun. Then he walked out of the room.

Even though things had gone to plan, Max was sweating a little as he sat down at the table. Anton had broken his silence but he had said very little. He had to be brought to say a good deal more if Max was ever to pursue the conversation beyond the point at which it had been left the previous afternoon. To achieve this, a different subject of conversation had to be found, one that would allow Anton to talk without inhibitions of any kind, and even, if possible, with friendliness. Once such an atmosphere had been built up, Anton would find it difficult to revert to this morning's attitude when Max switched the conversation back to the only topic that mattered.

Max let a quarter of an hour go by before getting up from the table and knocking on the door. There was no reply. He knocked again and called, "Anton."

The grille came up and Anton could be seen behind it, his eyes full of suspicion.

"Would you open the door?" asked Max. "You see, I can't talk to you through the grille."

"Talk to me about what?" asked Anton.

Max shrugged his shoulders almost sheepishly.

"I don't know really," he said. "I just wanted to talk. I just wanted to talk to someone." He paused and looked at Anton. "Would you mind coming in . . . and . . . talking to me?"

"You mean you're lonely?" asked Anton.

Max shook his head.

"No more than you out there, I suppose. But I don't see why we can't make a kind of truce. You see," he said, glancing over his shoulder as if at all the hours of conversation that lay behind them, "words can be pleasant just as much as unpleasant."

And so could Max, though Anton did not know it. The boy hesitated, and then with the beginnings of a smile, he asked:

"Will you promise like you did yesterday afternoon not to try anything?"

Max nodded.

"I promise," he said. "I promise not to try anything."

"Okay," said Anton.

Max turned away from the grille. He heard Anton put the pistol off safety. The door opened and Anton came in watchfully, keeping Max covered and at a safe distance from him.

"You take the chair," said Max, who was lying back on the bed.

Anton was Max's guest. The situation was difficult because there was nothing in the way of food or drink that Max could offer. He sat up and unlaced his shoes. As he did so, he began a monologue that was designed for Anton to enter little by little.

"You know," he said, "I don't much mind being in a place like this. I'm well looked after, I've all the time to myself I want. But that's just it. It gets to be too much. Of course, I know we've been talking a little the last couple of days. But that isn't quite what I felt I was missing. It's difficult for us to do any better, I suppose. After all, I'm a good bit older than you for a start. How old would you be, if you don't mind my asking?" he asked, looking up at Anton for the first time. "Around twenty?"

"Twenty-one," said Anton.

"There you are," said Max. "Twenty-one. And then I'm a working man. You're a kind of student, I suppose?"

"A kind of," said Anton with a grin. "I was in a radio engineering school in Paris."

"You were?"

"Yes, they threw me out."

"On account of . . . ?"

"All this," answered Anton, shrugging his shoulders to indicate the house they were in and the organization that ran it.

"I see," said Max, nodding. "In Paris, you say? But you don't come from Paris originally, do you?"

"As a matter of fact," said Anton, "I . . ."

"Don't tell me," Max interrupted. "Let me guess. You're from the east somewhere, Strasbourg maybe."

"And what makes you think that?" asked Anton.

"Well," explained Max confidently, "you're big, blue-eyed and fair— you're hardly the typical Frenchman. But the funny thing is, you don't have any German accent."

"That's right," said Anton. "I don't have an accent."

"Why not?" asked Max.

"Because," Anton told him, "I was born in Paris and I've lived there all my life. Only, everyone thinks I'm from Strasbourg."

"That's not surprising," said Max. "There's your name I forgot to mention. *Anton*'s German, not French. The French is *Antoine*."

"That's what's on my birth certificate," said Anton, looking down into his lap.

"How's that?" asked Max sympathetically.

"My mother," said Anton, looking up. "Or rather my father, I should say. He was a German soldier, he wasn't my mother's husband."

"And this got around?"

"Naturally," said Anton. "It began at school, when I was much blonder than I am now. One or two of the parents drew the obvious conclusions and told their kids. At first they called me Boche, and then one of the smarter boys just turned *Antoine* into *Anton*. That's how it's been ever since."

"I can understand," said Max. "It must have been an awkward situation."

"I'm not the only one around, of course," said Anton. "But you get noticed all the same."

"And when a patriotic movement like the OAS comes along," Max suggested, "you feel obliged to join it to prove to everyone that you're really French?"

"I don't know anything about that," said Anton.

"What I mean," Max explained, "is that you feel you'd like a chance to shout Boche at someone else for a change."

"Maybe," Anton admitted. "But, as I told you, I couldn't really say. There are other things besides that, I can tell you."

Max nodded quickly and smiled to show how he and Anton understood that nothing polemical was to be brought up that morning. There were obvious openings for anyone who wished to cure Anton of his attachment to the OAS. But this was not Max's intention, even if, in other circumstances, it might have been. Instead he had three days in which to leave Anton's custody. If Anton could be helped in the process, all well and good, but that was a side that wasn't essential.

Anton was smiling. He was ready to speak and he needed no prompting. Max looked at him for a moment almost distractedly. Then he suppressed a feeling of pity and sat up as bright as before.

"It's good to hear something about you," he said. "Tell me, does your legal father live with you?"

Anton nodded.

"And how do you get on together?"

"Not badly," Anton answered. "It was even he who told me about the German soldier business. It had never worried him. He's a pretty quiet and peaceful fellow."

"Does he share your views?" asked Max.

Anton shook his head.

"He's a Communist," he said. "But that doesn't mean much. Everyone round us votes Communist out of habit. I keep my opinions to myself, anyway, so we don't get any arguments at home.

"Does he know where you are right now?"

"He doesn't," Anton admitted. "But I think my mother has some idea."

"Doesn't she let on?" asked Max.

"He's got too much to worry about already," Anton said. "He works twelve hours a day in a pork meat factory—so he doesn't see my mother much anyway. And when he does, he's too tired to pay attention to her. He's in the refrigerator and salting departments mainly. The salt's made holes in his hands. It stopped hurting years ago, but the holes are always getting bigger."

"He doesn't wear gloves because they don't let him work so fast, is that right?" asked Max. "Yes, I know the sort of thing. And what about the radio school?" he added.

"Oh, that," said Anton carelessly. "Well, the work was boring for one thing. And then I preferred painting slogans on walls and handing out leaflets to any of the things the other students did, like going to the cinema. I felt I was doing something. They expelled me because of that and also because my work was bad—naturally."

Anton had been left without employment or ambition. He had gravitated as a full-time member into the OAS, which provided him with a little of both.

His conversation became more and more voluble. He seemed indebted to Max for granting him this reprieve. He prayed that it might be final, but Max had decided it would last till lunch and no longer. They shook hands at the end of the morning. Max was pleasant but firm. Anton noticed it and suddenly remembered the situation he was in. It was as if during the last two or three hours he had been in a cinema.

When he came to clear away after lunch, Anton tried hard to steer the conversation back to the pleasanter topics of the morning. But if it lay with him to determine whether or not in the first place there should be any conversation at all, he was quite unable to control the conversation once it had started.

Max had already stacked his things neatly on the tray. Anton had only to take it down to the kitchen. But he stayed a moment, awkwardly standing.

"The view from the window is beautiful," Anton said at last. "Have you seen it?"

"I have," said Max. "It is beautiful, but on the other hand it is not."

"What do you mean?" asked Anton.

"In the conventional sense, of course, it is beautiful," Max explained, "because *beautiful* is the name you give to a view of mountains and lakes, just like a sky without clouds is called blue. It is so conventional that beauty has become part of the view itself—like the rocks of the mountains or the water of the lake. In other words, you were stating a fact, you weren't describing a feeling."

Max paused. His tone was sharp.

"So you see what I mean?" he asked. "*Beauty*, as you used it just now, is not a word that refers any more to the feelings of the spectator. Anyone who believes that it does is wilfully deceiving himself."

Max's voice became sharper still and he looked hard at Anton, whose eyebrows were raised in a question.

"Yes," said Max, "wilfully. Because such a person once again refuses to accept the responsibility of having personal feelings. Instead he throws them off into the view itself. Such a person is weak. And I do not think the view is beautiful," he quickly added.

Almost automatically they resumed their positions of the previous afternoon. Max walked about the room while Anton sat still in the chair, fingering the gun on his lap. He realized that he had returned wholly into Max's orbit. That morning he felt he had left it. He did not yet see that it had been the same thing in a different, almost unrecognizable form.

Max watched Anton as he spoke. For the moment the boy was numbed into immobility, but he still held the gun and any movement from Max would bring him back to life. Anton would have been greatly relieved to have had an opportunity of using his gun and his physical strength. They spoke again until late in the afternoon.

Anton, who at all costs wanted to prevent the humiliation of the previous day, gained a little in defiance and self-confidence. He said "no" to Max for no other reason than he could not bring himself to say "yes."

Max painstakingly went over the argument by which he had shown Anton's politics to be nonsense. He repeated the points he had made, and Anton's answers to them, which Anton himself had conveniently forgotten. Realizing that he was about to be caught in a complete reenactment of the day before, Anton tried to fight his way out.

"Right or wrong. I don't care," he shouted, "but that's me."

"But it's wrong," said Max. "Don't you remember yesterday that you admitted it was wrong?"

"Yes."

"So if 'that's me,' then it's 'me wrong'?"

Anton did not answer.

"It's 'me wrong,' isn't it, Anton?"

"Okay it's 'me wrong,'" Anton shouted in Max's face as he got up from the chair. "And I couldn't care less."

He slammed the door behind him.

Max leaned back on the bad and considered that the day had gone according to plan. Anton had broken his silence. Max had reinforced his attack of the previous afternoon. Anton now realized how much his own person was vulnerable. It was this awareness that Max's plans for the following day, the last whole day that was left to them, were designed to intensify.

SIXTEEN

Thursday, July the Twelfth

Max was at the table when Anton came in next morning with the breakfast tray.

"Good morning, Anton," said Max.

Anton, who carried the gun in his free hand, mumbled something unintelligible in reply. He found it difficult to return the "good morning" because he wasn't sure how to address his prisoner. "Monsieur" was out of place, he could never find the courage to say "Monsieur Palk," and "Max" had not even occurred to him. He felt obliged to say something because he was not strong enough to bear provoking Max's dislike over so small a point. But "good morning" without a name sounded worse to him than anything else. Therefore he mumbled.

It was an uncertainty that Max had noticed from the beginning, when Anton had been disconcerted by Max's familiarity with Soustelle. So the pleasant "good morning" was not without its point. Anton was ill at ease from the first moment.

"Did you sleep well last night?" asked Max as they returned from the lavatory.

"Fairly well," Anton admitted, smiling a little uncertainly.

He wasn't sure how to reply because he didn't know what Max wanted.

"You shouldn't have," said Max abruptly.

Anton's expression changed into one of alarm. He'd realized his mistake too late.

"If you did," Max went on, "then there's something wrong. How could you possibly have spent an untroubled night after what we discussed yesterday?"

"But that's not to say I haven't been thinking about it," Anton protested, in near-desperation at seeing the morning begin so disastrously.

"Do you even remember what we said yesterday afternoon?" asked Max.

"Yes," said Anton quietly.

"Tell me then the last words you spoke," Max said.

" 'Me wrong.' "

"Correct," said Max, "but only partly so. You added something before you slammed the door. Do you remember that?"

"Yes," said Anton, "I said I couldn't care less."

"Right," said Max. "And what do you think of that?"

Anton, who still held his gun at Max, shrugged his shoulders and said hopelessly:

"I don't know."

"You've had more than twelve hours by yourself outside that door and you've got nothing to say!" exclaimed Max.

"It's not that . . ." Anton began.

"It *is* precisely," Max broke in emphatically, "everything you say it is *not*."

Ignoring Anton, Max walked for a while up and down the room. Then he turned.

"May I ask then what keeps you at your post today after all we have said these last two afternoons?"

"It's my position, even if it's wrong," said Anton defiantly.

"So you still hold to your words of yesterday afternoon? You've made great progress in the night."

"It's my position," Anton repeated.

"Your complacency is disgusting," Max insisted, "disgusting as you stand there dumbly repeating it. You cannot continue doing something you know to be wrong. If you try to, as you seem to be doing at the moment, it means either that you are not doing the job wholeheartedly or that you do not really believe it's wrong."

Max paused. He continued slowly and with great emphasis:

"You will not persist in such a compromise. I am leaving here by midday tomorrow and I will make you choose."

The reversal of roles was complete. The real gun was held by Max. Anton's hung down in his hand.

"You see what I mean?" said Max, indicating the gun that pointed toward the floor.

"That gun should either be looking straight at me like it was a moment ago, or it should be being used to defend me as I make my way past your friends out of this house."

The gun came up, pointing at Max. Anton gained confidence as Max smiled and nodded his condescending congratulations.

"That's right," said Max. "But I want your choice to be genuine. You must not just choose because I am forcing you to do so, then forget it the moment you're the other side of the door. Your choice must stand."

The gun wavered. Anton turned in desperation and rushed out of the room.

As the door banged shut, there was a metallic click and Max noticed that the bronze flaps of the small Venetian blind set in the door had opened a little.

Anton came back at one o'clock with the lunch. When Max thanked him, Anton replied:

"You're welcome."

Max was pleased to see that Anton was gaining some confidence. He looked forward to an afternoon in which some progress on Anton's part might at last be made.

But Anton did not come back as he usually did to take away the lunch tray. At first Max was unconcerned. He sat at the table and worked for a while. But so little time was left that even half an hour was precious and Max began to get anxious. He got up from the table. Anton might be downstairs with his friends. He might have succeeded in persuading one of them to take over his job. Or perhaps, thought Max, he was only having an after-dinner sleep on the cushions outside the door. Even this would be no less disastrous, for it would show how little Anton was concerned by the accumulation of arguments against him over the past two and a half days.

Max decided to check at least this possibility. He went to the door. He looked more closely at the flaps of the blind that had been slightly open as the door slammed shut that morning. There were only four flaps set into a rectangle a little broader than it was high, measuring perhaps four inches by five, cut into the thick wood of the door. The fine chain controlling the flaps dangled down the other side, as Max knew from the times he came back into the room from the lavatory. Otherwise the flaps could only be opened by an equal pressure applied simultaneously to each.

Max brought the tips of four fingers under the flaps. He pushed gently upward. Silently the flaps opened to their full. With excitement and curiosity Max watched the scene before him.

The thick feather cushions had been laid out to form a bed in the middle of the landing carpet. It was early afternoon, and the sun was still high, so that it shone through the larger skylight of the landing to make a ring of light and warmth around the center of the line of cushions. Max recognized Anton's jacket lying on the floor beside the farthest cushion. At the end nearer the door, he saw Anton's shoes. But there was no sign of Anton himself. Holding the flaps in place. Max turned away for a moment to look at his watch. Nearly an hour's possible conversation time had been lost. He turned back to the flaps. Anton was standing by the bed of cushions, with his back to the door. He had come across the carpet in his socks, which was why Max had not heard him. His movements were anxious and watchful. He was taking care to make the least possible noise.

Then he bent down and Max saw the white laundered handkerchief that Anton held in his hand. At once Max understood the reason for Anton's caution and for the odd position under the sun of the line of cushions.

Anton lay down on his front on the feather bed. For some time he lay prone, his arms stretched beyond his head, the rest of his body slowly settling into the soft cushions. Then he raised himself a little, and as he did so the cushions filled with air so that they were softer still when he let himself gently down again. His body began to move rhythmically from the middle.

Max felt his heart beat a little harder. It was something he had never seen before.

Anton had stopped. He turned over and sat up. He was facing the door, but he was thinking of something else. He did no see the open grille. He pulled his shirt out from under his trousers. Undoing the cuffs and top button, he brought the shirt over his head and laid it next to the jacket on the floor. He wore no vest. His torso, though solid, was white and blotched. The bronze medallion that he wore on a chain around his neck seemed incongruous against such a background.

Anton turned back onto his stomach. With his bare arms he gathered the cushions beneath him and pressed them against his chest. All along his body, he was trying to coax the cushions into life. His white back began to glisten where the sunlight touched it.

He rolled off the feather cushions and onto the floor. He got to his feet and went to the head of the stairs and listened. He returned to the bed, his face flushed and his movements jerky.

Before lying down he undid the clasp and top two buttons of his trousers. Then he lowered himself on his hands as if he were doing a kind of exercise. By the action of his body against the cushions the loosened trousers were slipping back over his thighs. He moved down the bed and made his way up it, wriggling as he did so. The cushions had come to life by drawing the trousers off him. With a final kick they were sent to the floor midway between the jacket and the shoes.

Only the pair of pants was left. No longer hindered by the trousers,

Anton's bare legs began to caress the cushions as his arms had done before. He rubbed his chest and his body against the soft material so that he seemed to be freely swimming over it. And all the time his middle was going up and down with the movement of a pump. His pants slipped off and down his legs as his trousers had done.

Naked except for his socks, Anton turned on his back and exposed himself, still moving gently, to the sun. He stroked himself along the insides of his thighs and between his legs. But on his back he could see that it was the sun that was warming him and his own hands that were stroking him. He turned over to the cushions and held them again with all his body. His hands came up and pressed him down from behind into the bed so that it might have been the hands of the cushions themselves that were clutching him. The muscles under his hands were taut and sweat ran down between them along the back of his thighs.

He got up and went to the banister, where he leaned over and listened. But the rest of the house was asleep after a heavy lunch. Max could see the streaks of sweat on the cushions that were drying quickly in the sun. Anton came back. He was a grotesque sight. He stood for a moment in the sun with his head back, like someone under a shower. Then he took a cushion from the near end of the line. He tossed it in his hands until it filled with air. He laid it in the middle of the bed. He unfolded the white handkerchief that he had left beside the bed and stretched it at double thickness over the top of the extra cushion. Then with his hands each side of the bed he let himself slowly down onto the handkerchief.

His body began to move softly backwards and forwards. His hands came up and down behind him, where the sweat shone under the sun, and his legs strained as they pressed and stroked themselves against the cushions. Anton seemed unable to decide where to keep his hands for the end. From behind they came to clutch the cushion beneath his chest and then they went behind again. His whole body was moving faster and faster. His muscles tightened and his head came up. He was not on the cushions but held by them. He drove hard into the bed and held it long as his head slowly fell. His body hurried in tight, almost painful motion while the cushions drew the liquid from him. His hands came up beside his head and clenched as he sobbed gently into the cushion that a moment before he had been kissing.

Max let the flaps silently downward. For a moment he had forgotten that he was a prisoner. He returned to the table armed with a new and unexpected weapon and established the plan for his next conversation with Anton.

An hour later Max went to the door and looked through the blind. Anton was asleep. Max shut the flaps tight and waited.

"Where have you been all this time?" he asked when Anton finally came into the room to clear the lunch things away.

"I've been asleep."

"But you don't usually sleep after lunch, do you?" asked Max.

"I was tired."

"And you slept for more than two hours?"

"I was very tired."

"Indeed you must have been," said Max. "But do you realize you've wasted a large part of the afternoon?"

"I suppose I have," said Anton. "I'm sorry."

"There is no doubt that you have," answered Max. "And so you should be sorry. It's not only for my benefit, you know, that we have our little discussions here as often as we can. You're also involved. In fact you're the only person really involved, though you never seem to realize it."

"I do, I do," said Anton, beginning to sound pitiable.

"All right, all right," said Max, "let's hope you're telling the truth."

He nodded toward the gun that Anton was pointing at him.

"You seem to be keeping to this morning's decision," he said, "but I wonder how long it will last."

Anton rose to the chiding tone in Max's voice.

"It'll last," he said.

"Sit down," said Max, waving to the chair.

Anton obeyed.

"Let's see where we've got to," Max began, as he walked up and down, his eyes on the floor. "Do you remember, Anton, that when we were talking about your politics you said 'that's me wrong'?"

Anton nodded.

"I told you how that was an impossible thing to say, didn't I?" Max asked. "You are a member of the OAS—that's you, as you said. Now for you to be able to say that that's you is wrong, there must be a you that is right, different from the you that is the member of the OAS. Do you agree?"

"Yes," said Anton.

"Therefore," argued Max, "it is impossible for the whole of you to be engaged in the OAS. Only a part of you can be, and that is the wrong part. Agreed?"

"Yes," said Anton again.

"But," asked Max, "do you think that if you are going to work for the OAS you must work for it one hundred percent?"

"Yes."

"Which you are not doing."

"I know."

"Do you think you should be working for the OAS at all?"

"No."

"And does that appear to you to be the reason why you're not working for it a hundred percent?"

"Yes."

"So what are you going to do about it?"

"I don't know."

There was a pause.

"Do you remember that I said that, if you think something is wrong, your thought means nothing until you do what is right?"

"Yes."

"So when you say you think your job is wrong, what ought that to mean?" asked Max.

"It means something but . . ." Anton failed to finish.

"But," Max said for him, "something you can't decide to do."

"Yes."

"Tomorrow morning you will decide and I will help you," said Max.

Anton looked up, and he did not answer.

"You haven't made a great deal of progress," Max pointed out. "You sleep all the time."

"I don't," said Anton, contradicting Max automatically.

"You weren't sleeping? Then what were you doing?"

"I was worried. I was really worried."

"Good," said Max softly. "And I believe you."

Max was sincere. But this did not stop him from moving on to what he had decided would be the point of the afternoon's conversation.

"So you admit," he began, "that you do not work for the OAS one hundred percent. But," Max exclaimed, suddenly raising both hands in the air, "are you really interested in anything? Isn't everything you do done in the same passionless way you work for the OAS?"

Anton fingered his gun anxiously.

"Well?" asked Max harshly.

"I go to the cinema sometimes . . ." Anton's voice did not drop at the end of the sentence, the better, so it seemed, for Max to cut it down.

"But you're not a fan, are you? You wouldn't want to discuss with me any film you had seen, would you?"

"I enjoy my holidays . . ." said Anton.

"Perhaps," Max objected, "but a passion for holidays isn't what I meant by a passion."

Anton looked up defiantly.

"I have a girl," he said.

"Ha!" exclaimed Max. "But why didn't you say so at once? Like that, it sounds more as if you'd just invented it on the spur of the moment."

"Well, I haven't," said Anton.

"Now that's funny," said Max, almost lightly. "You see, I would have thought that that side of your life would have been as seedy as the rest is. I wouldn't have credited you with a regular girl at all."

"I suppose you'd have credited me with something else, then?" said Anton heatedly.

Max raised his eyebrows in simulated surprise.

"Who suggested that?" he asked. "I certainly didn't. And anyway that's not what I meant. But you seem to have taken it a little too seriously."

"It's a serious matter," Anton muttered.

"Maybe," said Max. "All I meant was that I couldn't see you passionately involved with any particular girl. I saw you as seedy, the kind of person who either buys his satisfaction or else finds it by himself at home."

"Salaud!" exclaimed Anton. "You who know nothing . . ."

"So what are you getting so excited about?" asked Max. "I said it was only a guess. But if that's the way you react to it, I can't help suspecting I'm right."

"Salaud, salaud," shouted Anton.

His face was red. Max turned his back and pretended to be thinking. In fact, he was watching Anton in the mirror above the basin. Anton glanced first at him, then at the grille in the door which was tightly shut. Anton jumped up, convinced that since Max could not have seen him on the bed after lunch, the act had not in fact taken place.

"Liar, slanderer," he screamed. "You say filthy things you know nothing about."

Max turned around.

"I don't think I ever said they were filthy," he remarked.

"I can have that maid downstairs whenever I like," Anton said in a trembling voice by way of proof. "And I have her often."

"Are you telling the truth?" asked Max.

"Of course I am!"

"You don't frequent prostitutes? You don't masturbate?"

"Don't you dare say that to me. Of course I don't."

"What would happen if I found out you were lying?" asked Max.

"You never would, because I'm not."

"It's a small thing," said Max, "but a lot depends on it. It's you as much as your politics are. Are you sure you are not wrong again this time?"

"What the hell are you insinuating?" asked Anton. "I wouldn't mind betting that you yourself . . ."

"I said, 'Are you sure you're not wrong again?'" Max repeated.

"Of course I'm sure," said Anton impatiently.

He turned and left the room angrily. Max allowed him the night to think it over.

At the table Max thought ahead to the last morning that was left to them. Anton would break down because he had thrown his whole person into the denial of something that Max had in fact seen him do. To escape would be easy. The point was now to make the escape with Anton. Otherwise Max would be forced to kill him, for he could not trust him not to raise the alarm once he had gone.

SEVENTEEN

Friday, July the Thirteenth

Max was even a little nervous as he woke and prepared for the final morning. He put on a clean pair of socks that he had washed the evening before and let dry in the night. He collected all his belongings from the room and set them together in a parcel on the floor. He wanted to avoid all last-minute delays. Only the loudly ticking traveling clock he left out on the table.

It was like this that Anton found him when he came in later than usual with the breakfast. He was thrown off his balance.

"Good morning, Anton," said Max.

The reply was unintelligible.

"You look surprised," Max went on. "I suppose you'd completely forgotten that I have to be off by twelve o'clock."

"I'd not forgotten," said Anton, "but . . ."

"But you never thought it would actually happen," said Max. "I know. Well, Anton, as usual you were wrong."

Anton was behind him with the gun as they went to the lavatory.

"But you do seem to have forgotten something," said Max, "or perhaps you were not paying attention to what I was saying."

"What was that?" Anton asked.

"Just a minute," said Max.

Anton waited outside. On the way back Max told him.

"Do you remember just now that I said 'as usual you were wrong'?"

"Yes."

"And do you remember at the end of yesterday afternoon that you promised me you were not wrong?"

"Yes."

"But this morning I say 'as usual you were wrong'?"

Anton did not seem to understand.

"Think, Anton. What is the only thing that I can mean?"

"That you know . . ." began Anton dimly. "But that's impossible, it's impossible for you to have . . ."

"For me to have what, Anton?"

"To have seen me . . ." said Anton hopelessly.

"Yes," said Max. "But why was it impossible?"

"Because you had no means of doing so," said Anton, faltering. "There's the door, the blind . . ."

"But yesterday the blind was opened when you slammed the door," said Max. "And after lunch," he continued, articulating slowly and carefully, "*I saw you*. I saw you masturbate on the cushions under the landing skylight."

Anton sank onto the bed. The gun fell at his feet. Max picked it up and laid it beside the clock on the table. Anton's face was in his hands and he was crying.

Max walked up and down in front of him.

"Pull yourself together," he said. "I haven't got you into this state without showing you a way to get out of it. But it will need your cooperation, just as it needed your cooperation for me to get you where you are now."

The sobbing continued.

"Will you please pull yourself together," Max repeated. "You won't find your way out by crying. We haven't much time. In fact," he said, looking at the clock, "we have exactly forty minutes. But that time is all yours."

Max leaned down toward Anton.

"All yours," he repeated, "because if I wanted to, I could go now. Are you listening to me?" he asked. "Can you hear me?"

Anton had stopped crying and he nodded vigorously while still holding his head in his hands.

"Either you prevent me getting out of this house or you help me," said Max. "But it must be one or the other. If you do neither, I will be obliged to shoot you. I can't trust you if you stay behind."

Anton looked up.

"But I can't come with you," he said in despair.

"If you ought to, then you can," Max told him.

"But I can't," Anton insisted.

"Why can't you?" asked Max.

"Because what will they think of me, the people down there?" asked Anton, raising his hands.

"What people downstairs?" asked Max. "People proud to be in the OAS? But they've got nothing to do with it. So at least be honest about it and choose one way or another."

"But they're my friends," said Anton through his hands. "I can't do that."

"For three days," said Max sharply, "I have been showing you they are not your friends, because you've got no good reason to be with them."

There was a pause.

"You're not getting any stronger," said Max ominously. "You seem much the same as before. But this time it matters. Ten minutes have gone by. We have thirty more to go."

Anton raised his head and made an effort.

"But a traitor?" he asked.

"You don't betray people you know to be wrong." Max insisted. "If you were once friends, you regret having to turn and fight against them, but you do it for reasons that you know to be right, and that you want them to see as right. You're not remorseful. You don't want to go back. If you do, then you're a traitor to both sides and to everything, which is worst of all."

"That's what I am at the moment," said Anton.

"I'm afraid so," Max told him. "But being aware of it is not by itself enough to get you out of it."

"What must I do then?" asked Anton.

"You must do something by yourself," said Max. "I've shown you the two things you can do, and what will happen if you do neither. I can't do any more than that, because the whole point is that these are things for you, and for nobody else, to do."

"I could stay," said Anton, suddenly becoming confident.

"You could," said Max, "but *stay* is not the right word. You must prevent me leaving. That means we will fight for the gun or the table, and if you reach it first, you will shoot me."

"I couldn't," said Anton, and he sank on the bed again.

He brightened suddenly.

"Perhaps I could let you bind and gag me," he suggested.

"I'm hopeless at tying people up," said Max. "You'd get out too soon and you'd give the alarm. Worst of all, you would be despised by all sides. Can't you see," he asked bitterly, "that that kind of suggestion is precisely the sort of thing I don't want?"

"Another ten minutes have passed," he added. "Twenty left. I'll give you five minutes in which I won't speak."

Max sat at the table with his back to Anton. There was no noise except for the heavy irregular breathing from the bed, and the ticking of the clock.

"I don't know, I don't know," Anton moaned, as he rocked backward and forward on the bed with his head in his hands.

Max said nothing and stayed at the table. As he listened, he wished he had known nothing of what Anton had done the previous afternoon. It had provided him with a weapon that he realized he had not needed. He had used what he had seen to break Anton and to make his escape. Though this had been necessary, it had been accomplished too thoroughly. Anton had been broken beyond the point at which he could be helped.

"I just don't know," Anton said again.

He was asking Max to speak. He himself had nothing more to say. Max felt remorse as he realized the mistake he had made.

"Listen," said Max, getting up, "I know you a hundred times better than any one of your so-called friends downstairs. I know you without knowing any details of your life as they probably do. I don't care if you have masturbated a million times, I don't care if you masturbated yesterday. I only want you to cease being the weak person that you are, and I will go so far as to push you into fighting me to succeed. At the moment you are despicable. You're worth only what you can become. Your weakness will disappear the moment you pick up that gun to shoot or to defend me. Then you will be an Anton I can fight or admire. But at the moment, I can only put you to sleep. Do you see?"

Anton nodded.

"Then please do either one or the other," Max urged. "You have ten more minutes left in which to choose. If you decide to prevent my escaping, I shall try to kill you, but if you decide to come with me I will help you."

Anton nodded again. Max walked up and down the room in front of him, while Anton watched.

"You're thinking that so long as I'm here, walking in front of you, talking to you, everything's all right," said Max. "But they have not just been words I have been speaking. I meant everything I said. You must understand that," he insisted. "*Please* wake up and realize that just because I'm not shooting you at this very moment, that's no reason why I shouldn't be doing so in less than five minutes' time."

Max's voice had risen to a controlled shout. Anton cried into his hands. Max bent over him.

"Anton, Anton, please wake up."

But Anton's head fell even a little lower. He had finally become absolutely nothing. Max walked sadly away. He went to the table where he picked up the clock. Two minutes of the morning were left. He turned to Anton and said:

"Anton, I will shoot you in two minutes' time."

Anton seemed not to hear. It was hardly worth waiting for the two minutes to pass. But Max decided to, just in case. As he examined the gun, it occurred to him that in Anton there was nothing left to kill. He clicked back the safety catch and said:

"One minute."

Anton fell back onto the bed, his head wrapped in his arms, crying silently into the material of his jacket. Anton had collapsed. It seemed that Max's bullet would change nothing. Max put the clock in his parcel of things on the floor. Then with a knee and an arm on the bed, he knelt over Anton.

"I'm not sorry to do this, Anton," he said. "I only wanted you to be somebody stronger."

Anton did not seem to feel the cold nose of the pistol as Max placed it carefully on his neck at the base of the skull. Max pressed the trigger and with a soft "phfft" the bullet passed through the barrel into Anton's brain.

EIGHTEEN

Max Escapes by the Back

After he had taken the keys to the Facel from Anton's jacket pocket, Max stepped out softly onto the landing carpet. He locked the door and drew the bolt, slipping the key into his pocket. At the top of the stairs he stopped and listened. It sounded as if there was some kind of party being held on the ground floor. There must have been fifteen or twenty people down there.

My God, thought Max as he lifted the small parcel of things up under his arm and gripped tighter the pistol that he carried in his free hand. He began slowly to descend the stairs to the second floor. The boards creaked a little and the carpet was thin; clearly an economy had been made in building and in furnishing this less frequented part of the house. But there was no one to hear him on the second floor, where Max found to his relief that the boards were firm and the carpet thicker.

The noise from downstairs increased. Max pushed open the door of one of the rooms on the second floor and went to the window. It gave onto the garden and the ground was soft, but Max had no head for heights. The rooms all had high ceilings; it was at least a thirty-foot drop from the window. If he tried to jump, he would either injure himself or attract attention—and he suspected he would do both. He opened the window and looked out. In the drive three men were admiring the Facel. But they couldn't get in, because Anton had locked it. The walls of the house were smooth, the pipes had been built in; there was no chance of climbing down.

He closed the window and returned to the landing of the second floor, aware that he was a little relieved. With great caution he advanced down the stairs to the first floor.

Here again there seemed to be nobody about. But all the doors were closed. Max went up to one and slowly turned the handle, pulling hard toward him at the same time so that there would be no noise. The door was locked. Max tried another. It was also locked.

With one hand on the banister to take part of his weight, he put a foot onto the first stair down to the ground floor. It made no noise. He went down another. The men below had not come here to guard him. Right now they were waiting for their lunch, and, when they had finished that, they'd be waiting for the phone call from Paris to tell them all was clear. None of them even knew who Max was, but if they saw him with a gun in his hand coming quietly down the stairs, they would not be slow to draw the obvious conclusion.

The stairs were straight. At the bottom a corridor crossed them at a right angle. Max, on the fifth step down, could not yet see to either side, but the noise was coming from the left end of the corridor. The voices were very close to him. He distinguished five or six against a background of a good many more. It sounded like a crowded café. There was only one woman's voice, which he supposed to be that of the maid. He had almost reached the bottom of the stairs when his leg was touched from behind. It was the cat. Max watched incredulously as the animal went silently to the bottom stair, turned into the corridor and disappeared. For him it would not be as simple.

He was one step from the bottom. Ready at the slightest danger to run back the way he had come, he leaned forward to see what was at the right end of the corridor. It was another door. He knew that the room behind it gave onto the garden. Much more cautiously he leaned forward the other way to see what was going on to the left.

"Last round!" he heard the maid proclaiming. He could see the end of the hall. Chairs and tables had been brought in. The men were sitting round their glasses. The maid came into sight, the same one that Max had seen through the binoculars four days before, but this time playing quite a different role. Her thin dress was tied tightly round her waist, and on her high heels she swung her hips from table to table, pouring from her bottle into the glasses of the men and replying in provocative fashion to their gestures and remarks. She was about to pass out of Max's sight when a man suddenly appeared and caught her round the waist.

"Eh, eh," she shouted, but she let herself be half carried to the corridor. Max ducked quickly back and prepared to run up the stairs. But the two had stopped at the entrance to the corridor, and the man had the girl up against the wall. Her dress rustled against his uniform and Max heard her whisper endearments. Then she freed herself and said:

"Cheri, let's work up a little appetite for lunch."

"Okay," said the man, in a hoarse red-wine voice. "Go in and get ready. I'll follow in twenty-five minutes."

"Oh, but cheri," said the girl, and Max heard her kissing him again, "we won't have long enough. Am I worth only a quarter of an hour?"

"You are, for what I want to do with you," said the man coarsely. "If you want it, that's how you'll have to have it. It's all the time I've got."

The girl, who obviously knew that the man's coarseness was not superficial but who for her pleasure preferred to pretend that it was, kissed him and said:

"I know you're only joking. I'll wait for you all the same."

"Give me a drink of that first," said the man, and Max heard him drain the contents of the bottle. Then the girl came down the corridor. Max was still only three-quarters of the way up the stairs when the girl passed the bottom. But she did not look up. She went into the room at the right end of the corridor, without shutting the door behind her. Max came down again to the foot of the stairs. He leaned forward and looked. The girl was drawing the curtains. Max drew back as she came to close the door. He looked at his watch. He decided to give her eight minutes.

He stood on the stairs feeling extraordinarily vulnerable both from above and below. If someone came along the corridor as one of the doors opened above he would be trapped, and the gun would not help him get out of it. He could have gone into the girl's room immediately, but almost certainly she would have screamed before he could kill her. Besides, he did not like the idea of shooting her or anyone else if he could help it. So he waited.

Five minutes had passed and Max was beginning to hope that he would be able to give the girl all the time he had planned when he heard a lock turning above him and then a door beginning to open. Two men came out onto the landing and walked toward the head of the stairs. Max had no alternative.

He turned into the corridor and went up to the door of the room. Quickly he opened the door, and without letting any more of his body pass through he reached out with his hand flat against the wall, found the light, and switched it off. At first the darkness was complete; neither he nor the girl would be seeing anything very clearly for several minutes. The rest of his body came into the room, and he closed the door behind him. He locked it and transferred the key to his pocket. Then he thickened his throat.

"I couldn't wait," he announced hoarsely.

The girl was already in bed. As Max had suspected, she could not have been wearing any underclothes. She had kicked off her shoes, pulled her dress over her head and got under the sheets, where she now lay, moving a little, as she waited for him.

"What did you turn the light off for?" asked the girl.

"Makes a change," said Max, "all that light blinds you."

The girl started to hum softly to herself. Max undressed quickly.

"I couldn't have waited either," said the girl.

Max kept his socks on.

"At least it's good to get out of the uniform," he said.

"Is that all?" asked the girl, beginning to giggle.

"It isn't," said Max, huskily, "and I'm coming for the rest."

With his arms held out in front of him, Max groped his way toward the bed. He stumbled over her shoes but supported himself on the back of a chair. Under his hands he felt the thin cotton dress that the girl had thrown over it. There was nothing now between him and the bed. Max was alarmed to discover that his sight was returning. He could see the wide white bed in front of him. In the hot weather it only had a pair of sheets. Max reached out a hand over the end of the bed. The sheets were soft and supple. The girl was in between, humming a tune that Max liked and holding the top sheet taut, as she rubbed her breasts and stomach against it.

"I'm waiting for you, Jojo my big legionnaire . . ." she sang. "Jojo is strong, Jojo is brave, Jojo is—ow!" she exclaimed, as Max pinched her toe.

He was up on the bed beside her covering her with the sheet. Then he joined her underneath it. It was dark again. Max looked at his luminous watch.

"That's new," said the girl, "where did you get it?"

"The boys gave it to me so's I wouldn't be late."

"Were you late last time, then?" asked the girl.

Max, though anxious to cut verbal preliminaries to a minimum, could not help remarking to himself that she was a nice bit of flesh, vigorous, strong and smooth.

"Yes," said Max, "I've only got ten minutes."

Beside him he could feel the girl's bottom, which with a slow circular motion was polishing the underneath sheet.

"Ten minutes!" she exclaimed, "and I so wanted you to do everything to me."

She took Max's hand from between her legs and brought it to her breasts.

"We can try," said Max, into her stomach.

He made his way up, past her breasts and over her shoulder, to press his face into the sheet beside her head.

"Yes," said the girl, and she threw back the sheet. It was as if the light had been turned on. Max thought quickly. Then he put his mouth to the girl's ear.

"On va à l'usine de gaz?" he asked.

Fortunately his knowledge of working-class French and of the customs that went with it was considerable. The girl quivered with pleasure.

"Saleté," she said.

Obediently, she turned over onto her stomach. With his arms underneath her, cupping her breasts in his hands, Max mounted her. She opened her legs wide for him.

"Having the light off made a change," said the girl, giggling again, "but this doesn't."

Max's sudden inspiration had not been misplaced.

"Oo-o-oh," she said. "Your watch is all cold."

"It may be," said Max, thus reminded of the short time he had at his disposal. "But I'm hot where it matters."

And Max tried hard to finish quickly. Stifled by the feelings they were giving each other, both had stopped talking. Besides, the girl's mouth was over Max's hand. Her lips and her tongue slipped over the fingers and palm that were wet with her own saliva. She made a noise like a baby whose bottle had been withdrawn. Underneath Max she moved with ease and passion over the sheets. In such conditions Max had no difficulty at all in completing the act within the time limit he had set himself.

The girl's movements gradually became slower. Max lay beside her gently stroking her back. Her eyes were closed. Max leaned down and pulled the sheet back over her. He got out of the bed and dressed hurriedly.

He passed the bed again to go to the window. The girl had not yet stopped moving, but she seemed asleep, satisfied after her feed. Max bent over and kissed her, for the first time, on her cheek.

"You're a good girl," he said.

She smiled. Her arms came up from under the sheets.

"Jojo," she said, in her sleep.

"He'll be here in a couple of minutes," said Max softly.

The girl nodded, and her arms went back to her sides.

Behind the curtains, the window was wide open. There was no one in the garden. Max dropped onto the soft earth of a flowerbed and crept round by the wall to the drive. The Facel was unguarded, but it stood out in the drive, in full view of the men in the hall. With a final glance around him Max ran toward the car. He had already opened the door when he heard the first shouts. Starting the car immediately in first gear, he had turned out of the front gate before the bullets could reach him.

4. THE SETBACK

NINETEEN

Max Must See the Prefect

As Max raced toward the frontier, he kept glancing in the reflector. There had been only one other car in the drive with the Facel—an old Peugeot. For a while, at least, they might try to chase him. Max drove at the limit of safety as he sought to gain sufficient lead on his possible pursuers to avoid being overtaken at the frontier.

Along the straightest section of the lakeside road, he caught sight of the Peugeot far behind, being driven no doubt at a speed far beyond its theoretical maximum.

It decided Max not to swap his Facel for something less distinctive. He could not afford the delay necessary for an exchange. Besides, he needed a fast car to reach Paris in time to see the prefect. The risk of being ambushed on one of the several roads he might take to the capital was too small to count.

As Max drove away from the frontier into France, the Peugeot was nowhere to be seen. He traveled on through the Jura Mountains. As he came out of a series of bends, Max caught a glimpse of Besançon beneath him, in a loop of the river Doubs. He drove past the citadel and the seminary, through the town by the main street and out across the bridge on the road to Chaumont.

The hills and the bends became less frequent, and Max was able to keep the accelerator close to the floor for long intervals. It was the afternoon of the thirteenth. Morris, who so far knew nothing of what was planned for the following day, had to be warned. Max might have telephoned from the frontier, but the risk of the call being tapped at the prefecture was too great. If he could have been sure of catching Morris at home that evening, he would have waited and telephoned him there. It would be safer—but there it was, he could not be sure of finding him in. Max would try therefore to meet Morris before he left the prefecture. He hoped that the business of routine preparations for the parade would keep Morris at his desk until late.

Max slowed to follow a truck up a hill. He never honked at trucks. Once, the Facel before this one had broken down miles from anywhere. Max had looked under the hood for the second time (the first time had been in the showroom). Then a truck driver had stopped, pushed back his cap and said, "There's your trouble." With his two fingers he had solved it. Max honked twice as he passed the truck down the other side of the hill.

In the villa they would have battered down the door to find Anton shot on the bed. They would be standing round the body, trying to discover a link between the tears and the bullet hole in the back of the head. One would suggest suicide. Another would point out that it was impossible. Anton must somehow have let go of the gun and consented to his own execution. Max had left them a problem.

He slowed as he passed through a village. The younger children were leaving school. They wore blue and gray smocks and carried satchels on their backs. One of them turned as he heard the car approaching. He smiled and waved once, then went to join the others as if nothing had happened.

Max had taken possession of the gun at ten minutes to eleven. He had given Anton forty minutes of time that he could have spent usefully, only to shoot him. It was a pity, but it was worth the try.

Paris was no more than a hundred kilometers away. Max had to see Morris to tell him what he knew and to give him time to organize a counterattack. But he realized that nothing really effective could be done until it was known how the assassination was to be carried out. And no amount of thinking over the past four days had allowed Max to discover this.

In fact, what had worried him most about Soustelle, the Minister and Boudin was their confidence. There seemed no doubt that this time was it. They had considered themselves as good as in the Élysée already. Yet they had given no hint of how this was to be accomplished. All that Max knew was that, as sure as the fact that tomorrow's parade would take place, de Gaulle would be assassinated. And not since his second interview with the Minister had he had any idea how this was to be accomplished. He was driving to meet Morris with only the hope that a second interview with the prefect would prove more fruitful.

Max entered Paris on the National 19, past the factories along the river— factories built like prisons, with high brick walls and solid gray gates. Max swerved to avoid the men as they came out onto the road on their bicycles and motor scooters. But most went away along the pavement, to the homes that their factory hired out to them. Supper and two hours' desultory viewing would follow a working day that for some had begun at five o'clock in the morning.

Max wound down the window beside him. When it was closed, everything outside was like a film: the people made no noise and they were seen in slow motion. Max felt he had arrived. The tires beat hard on the cobbles, the cyclists beside him were real people going home from work, and it seemed possible to have an accident, as it had not done when the window was up.

Max double-parked in the square in front of Notre-Dame and, keeping his eyes to the ground to avoid seeing any policeman who might be signaling to him his traffic offense, he walked quickly under the main gate of the prefecture. He was stopped by two police with submachine guns and told that all the offices were closed.

"I must see the prefect," he explained.

The two men looked at each other. One of them grinned.

"Yes," he said. "But the point is, must the prefect see you?"

He put out his hand for Max's papers. After looking them through, they handed them back without a word and waved him on.

Everything in the courtyard of the prefecture that evening was concerned in one way or the other with preparing for the parade of the following day. The black coaches in which the police would be transported early in the morning to the Champs-Élysées were in position. Men in overalls were hosing down the small radio cars that would control the traffic and pass first down the Champs-Élysées, several hundred yards in front of the parade proper. Max stepped aside to avoid one of the last truckloads of silver crowd-barriers as it passed out of the main gate. In one corner, a group of motards sat talking on their machines.

Max looked up and saw that the light was on in Morris's study. He quickened his pace across the courtyard, afraid that at this last moment he might miss him. He passed under an arch and pushed on the door that led to the prefect's office and its immediately dependent departments. But the door was closed. Max rang the bell.

Almost immediately an official came down the square staircase and opened the door. Max recognized him as one of Morris's many secretaries. He nodded toward the man and stepped inside.

"Good afternoon," said the official.

Max looked up and realized at once that a barrier was being put up to prevent him going any farther, though the way to the staircase was free.

"Good afternoon," he said.

The man smiled politely.

"A friend of yours has instructed me to tell you," he said, "that if you insist on seeing the prefect, the life of Madame Morin might be seriously endangered."

They stood for a moment on the carpet together. Then the official asked pleasantly:

"Would you care to go up right away, or will you leave it?"

"I'll leave it," said Max, and stepped back into the courtyard.

TWENTY

The Telephone Call

Outside the prefecture, Max backed the Facel into an official parking space and sighed. He remained sitting in the car. He had not been sure how the OAS would react to his escape. He had even hoped that the men in the villa might withhold the news for fear of reprisals from their superiors. But clearly they had got in touch with their Paris headquarters. They knew that Max would be most likely to go to Morris. Why then hadn't they got rid of the prefect himself? The answer was obvious. Apart from the extreme difficulty of such an operation, Morris's death would not have prevented Max from contacting any other member of the government. Holding Silesia, on the other hand, was an effective weapon against whatever Max might do. So before he could go any further, Max had to find Silesia.

But the OAS had any number of hiding places in and around Paris at their disposal. A meticulous and pedestrian search was out of the question. Max was not a policeman. Even less did he have the police force behind him. There was, in fact, no one whose help he could enlist without letting it be known and thus risking Silesia's life. He would have to find her by himself.

At first the task seemed hopeless. But a man whose only resource was himself was forced to be unorthodox. It was this which enabled him to succeed where a giant search party would have failed. Max began to think along lines that he had formulated and used several times with success in the past: if a man can get you into a situation, he can also get you out of it. To do this, of course, such a man needs a special kind of help. Exactly what kind was the only problem left to answer, once Max had brought the principle to bear on any situation.

In this case the man in question was the official who had passed on the message a moment ago in the prefecture. Max could have followed him home. But he could not be sure which of the many exits of the prefecture the official would use. And the idea of having at the end to extract the information by torture and threats was not attractive. Such methods were in any case uncertain and slow. Silesia had to be found that evening, and perhaps the official might yield to an approach of a different kind.

Max sat in the car a little longer, slowly cleaning his glasses. Then he got out and walked to the nearest café.

He collected three telephone coins from the waiter and went downstairs to the booth. To confirm that she had in fact been taken away, he first called Silesia. There was no answer, and his coin was returned. Max telephoned her concierge and was not surprised to hear that a note had been left for him earlier that afternoon by a gentleman who had come to drive Silesia to stay with relatives in the country over the weekend. He made a third call to his own concierge to learn that a similar note was waiting for him there. The oas had been very anxious to ensure that Max received their warning.

Max was aware that if he had come across one of the notes instead of meeting the official, the problem of finding Silesia would have been many times more difficult. But, he reassured himself, it was his own determination to see the prefect before doing anything else that had made the problem easier. So he did not consider himself lucky.

As Max lifted the receiver off its hook and dialed the prefecture, he cleared his throat in order to adopt a new voice. He began to assume Soustelle's manner and accent. It was unlikely, he calculated, that a mere secretary in the prefecture would be more than vaguely acquainted with one of his leaders in the oas. There was a chance that Max might succeed and no risk to Silesia if he didn't.

That Max would be speaking to the secretary he had met on the stairs just before, he had no doubt. Even if he was not alone on duty, the man would surely make it his business to answer all the calls, just as he had been ready for Max when he had rung the bell below.

"Put me through to the prefect's office, would you, please?"

His first words had been in the voice he had wanted. He heard the operator make the connection and the phone began to ring a second time.

"The prefect's secretary speaking."

The voice was the same as that of half an hour ago, though the tone was neutral, ready to slip into something more positive, depending on the caller.

"This is Jacques Soustelle," said Max sharply. "I want to . . ."

"But, sir," the official interrupted, overcoming the hesitation he felt at criticizing a superior, "should you be telephoning me here, sir?"

Max's assumed identity had been at least temporarily accepted. Surprise was far stronger in the man's reaction than suspicion.

"And why shouldn't I be?" asked Max, as curtly as he had introduced himself.

"Well, sir, the call might be being tapped."

"For Christ's sake!" Max exclaimed. "Who do you think you're speaking to? It's not them, it's us who are doing the tapping."

There was a grumble from the other end.

"Well, isn't it?" repeated Max.

"I suppose so, yes, sir," said the man. "It was just the rule not to phone, and . . ."

"It was, but it isn't now," Max corrected. "Forget the rules and listen to me. Did he come?"

"Who? Palk?"

"But who else should I mean?"

"He did, sir, yes." The official was glad to perform the simple task of providing information. "In fact he came about half an hour ago. I gave him the message and he said he'd leave it. I saw him walk out. I think it settled him."

"Settled him!" echoed Max, and gave a Soustelle sigh. "I should live so long!"

"You don't think so?" asked the official anxiously.

"Hmmm," went Max. "Maybe, maybe not." Then, suddenly conspiratorial, he added quickly, "But do you think he has any idea where we're keeping the Morin woman?"

The official whistled.

"None at all, I should say."

"Which is hardly surprising, considering . . ." said Max.

"I should think not, sir," the man agreed.

"Ye-e-s," said Max slowly and thoughtfully.

There followed an embarrassing pause.

"Look," said Max urgently, "I don't want to talk to you any longer on the phone, but there are one or two things I'd like to make sure of about Morris's arrangements for tomorrow . . ."

"Certainly, sir."

"But the point is," cut in Max, "not now, not over the phone. Can I meet you there instead?"

"Meet me?" asked the man in surprise.

"Yes," said Max, "I'll be going there myself anyway."

"But meet you where?" the official insisted.

Max ground his teeth in exasperation.

"Can't you think? Do I have to say it?" he exclaimed. "Where we've got the Morin woman, of course."

"At the Red Cross, you mean?"

"Idiot!" said Max. "Idiot!" he repeated, compressing all Soustelle's scorn into a fierce whisper. "Anyone around you might have heard. I expected you'd be up on these things without all this prompting."

"I'm sorry, sir," said the man. "There's no one here in the office, by the way. But I just thought your suggestion a little impracticable. Besides, I won't be off duty until another hour at least."

"Perhaps you're right, then," Max agreed. "We can leave it altogether. I would have liked the information, but it was only to fill in a couple of details. My main concern was Palk."

"Well, you needn't worry about him, sir," said the official.

"You did well," said Max.

"Thank you, sir, and . . . may tomorrow see us triumph," he finished with a brave flourish.

TWENTY-ONE

The Red Cross

Max picked up the telephone directory. What kind of connection the OAS could have with the Red Cross he had no idea. That Silesia, as a doctor, might be connected with it, he could understand. But that did not explain where the OAS came in. Three hospitals were marked in the directory, as well as the administrative center off the Champs-Élysées. Perhaps the connection was there—a building completely taken over by the OAS from which they could assassinate de Gaulle in tomorrow's parade. But why the Red Cross building should have been chosen rather than another was a mystery.

Max decided to telephone the hospitals first. They were the least likely hiding places, and the easiest to check. Silesia might have been drugged as a pretext for having her admitted to a hospital to recover. Perhaps there was a doctor inside to carry out the threat if he was told that Max had tried to see Morris. It was possible, but somehow not in the usual OAS style. They had a vast number of other facilities, which made the hospital idea seem unnecessarily complex and melodramatic.

Max was onto the first hospital. The receptionist had not been there during the day, he had just come on night duty. But would he look all the same at the list of patients admitted that afternoon? He would. Max waited as he heard metal drawers being pulled open and pushed shut, and later the steps of the man as he shuffled back. No woman by the name of Morin had been admitted. There had been five new patients that afternoon, of whom only one had been a woman. She was seventy-five, she'd been knocked down in the road and she'd died an hour after arrival. Max cut the man's explanations short and put down the receiver. Silesia could not have been there. The OAS could not avoid registering her, though they might do so under a false name.

Max dialed the number of the second hospital. There were few problems that could not be partly or even wholly solved by judicious use of the telephone. This time a woman answered. The register was once again consulted. One woman had been admitted that afternoon, but not under the name of Morin. "Could you describe her to me?" asked Max. But again, she was just beginning night duty. Max held on as she opened a door and called out. She came back to the phone followed by the man who had been on duty that afternoon. Max repeated his question to him, and added:

"It's quite possible that she gave you a false name. You see, she has bouts of amnesia. She forgets things."

"But we have her identity card made out in the name she gave us," said the man. "And she came to have a baby."

Max dialed the third hospital, a small home for convalescents, where no one had been taken in during the day.

Three of his numbers in the book had been eliminated. Max hesitated before trying the fourth. The administrative center would be no more than a set of offices, extending over one or two floors. There might be a night porter for the building, but hardly one for the Red Cross itself—especially over the weekend of the fourteenth, a national holiday. There seemed little point in telephoning. But again there was no reason not to try. Max dialed the number carefully and waited. As he did so he prepared a suitably harmless question. But the number rang and rang and there was no answer.

Max hung up and climbed the stairs to the café floor. The ringing of the telephone in the Red Cross offices might have scared a whole squad of the OAS into silence, or it might have passed innocently over the rows of covered typewriters. But from the information Max had at his disposal Silesia could be nowhere else. He would have to go and look at those offices for himself. This would mean breaking into a building off the crowded Champs-Élysées at night.

"Ach!" he exclaimed in exasperation.

Something was wrong, and he knew it; he had a strong feeling of being completely out of place. But he could not think of a better place to be. This one was forced upon him. Shaking his head, he walked back to the car and drove without enthusiasm toward the Champs-Élysées.

The long covered rostrum beneath the obelisk on the place de la Concorde was already in place. It faced up the Champs-Élysées to the Étoile, and it was from there that the president would take the salute at the parade next morning. As he drove up the avenue on the fast outer lane, Max saw the crowd barriers on each side reflecting the lights hanging between the trees. Everything was ready.

The first queues were forming outside the cinemas. Max looked to either side, pleased to be distracted for a moment from the job in hand. There was no one outside *Lolita*. It was hardly surprising, thought Max, since it was a brilliant film that the critics had murdered with complacency the day of its release. Farther up, he saw that *Last Year at Marienbad* had drawn its inevitable crowd.

"For the goyim," he said with understanding, and with one hand, he flapped the sight away.

Halfway up the Champs-Élysées, he turned left under the TWA building into the avenue George V. He drove slowly along and found a parking space a minute's walk from the street for which he was looking. He turned off the engine and reached for the briefcase on the back seat. It would be the least suspicious way for him to carry Anton's pistol.

He packed it away with misgivings. He always felt weaker with a gun.

Max left the car and within a few minutes had reached the rue Quentin Bauchart, whose far end joined the Champs-Élysées. He walked slowly down toward the Red Cross building. The street was without cafés or restaurants. There were few people about. A policeman walked in front of him, but too quickly to be patrolling. So Max had the street virtually to himself. The buildings on either side were given over entirely to offices. There were no lights on anywhere.

Max counted down the street ahead of him. The Red Cross was just past the next lamppost on the other side. He walked down a little farther and looked up. On the fourth floor of Number Seventeen he saw the only light in the street.

"It just had to be," he said to himself.

He crossed the road. Quietly and close to the wall he went nearer. The entrance was at the farther end of the building. Max was walking close to its dark gray stone. He did not look up or around him. He glanced at the names of the companies inscribed on either side of the door. They confirmed, if confirmation was needed, that the fourth floor was occupied by the Red Cross.

Max uttered some words to himself designed to help him through the next few minutes and unzipped the briefcase. He made sure the pistol was there and left the briefcase open.

He put his hands tentatively on the door. To his horror it moved slowly away from him and swung fully open onto the dark interior of the building. It had been ajar all the time. He felt for a moment as if he had been put up against a wall of light to be shot. He stepped quickly inside, pulling the door back to its original position.

He started forward on tiptoe but found he made more noise than if he walked normally. The carpets were thick and the building was so insulated

against sound that Max could hear nothing of the city outside. Before
putting his foot on the first stair, Max looked up. He could not even see the
banisters that led from the first floor to the second. For a moment he felt,
and managed to suppress, an impulse to sabotage his expedition by walking
straight up the stairs. He put a foot silently on the first step. The carpet was
firmly fitted. There was no slip or noise from the rods that held it in.

Perhaps there was a man on guard at the fourth floor, to welcome fellow
troops as they came unobtrusively in twos and threes through the open door
below. In that case, Max would be at an advantage. But, on the other hand,
there was no reason why the whole building should not at this moment be
waiting for him.

He had reached the first floor. Again he could see almost nothing of the
stairs in front of him. He felt each step firmly before putting his weight on
it. There was still no sound in the building. He rested awhile on the second
floor. Going upstairs in such a way was exhausting.

He crept up to the third floor, stopping on each step to listen. The heavy
building was strangely calm. The doors that Max passed on each landing
were so thick that an army might have been behind them without Max
hearing. He had reached the third floor.

He withdrew the pistol from the briefcase. He was beginning to pant
from a combination of fear and fatigue. Trying to breathe as quietly as he
could, he made his way up the stairs to the last floor. Still he heard and
saw nothing. At the turn in the stairs he faced the landing. He stopped and
listened, holding his pistol in front of him like a torch. After a moment he
found no reason not to continue.

He had just stepped onto the landing when he heard the lock of the
door in front of him turning. He began to run back down the stairs. But
the door had opened; a man was standing there with a light behind him.
Max felt himself being forced to stop his movement of retreat and to turn
his head slowly to look at the man in the doorway. His pistol followed, but
he did not fire.

"What are you doing here?" asked the man in a tone that carried a
weapon behind it.

Max was relieved that the man was prepared to talk even that much
before opening fire. He himself was unable for a moment to find his voice.

"I came for some information from the Red Cross," he said.

Terror had brought his foreign accent to the surface.

"Why didn't you turn the lights on?" asked the man.

Max gestured hopelessly. He did not know what to do with his pistol.
So far, it had not been seen.

"Not surprising," the man continued. "You foreigners always come here and see nothing."

It was the voice of an elderly man. Max saw him reach for the light switch and hid his pistol behind his back. The man was wearing a uniform—but not a soldier's. It was the blue suit of a porter, with a firm's initials woven into his lapels. A bunch of keys rattled in his hand.

"Well, now you can see your way, what are you waiting for?" asked the man, not unpleasantly.

Max took a step toward him and at the same time tried to slip the pistol inside his jacket. But it missed his pocket. Max clapped his other hand to his chest, just in time to prevent the pistol slipping through to the floor. The man, who was coming down the stairs toward him, noticed the gesture.

"What's the matter with you?" he asked.

"My heart," said Max, "it's getting at me again."

"Well," said the man, "you've come to the right place. There's the door in front of you."

They passed each other on the stairs without incident. Max called "Thank you" to the man and, after transferring the pistol to the briefcase, he walked through the door of the Red Cross office. Except for a man and a girl at the reception desk it was empty.

"Yes, sir?" asked the girl.

"I phoned about half an hour ago," said Max.

"And you didn't get a reply?" the girl anticipated. "I'm sorry, it was before we took over. There's always someone here the evening before national holidays, parades and so on, because that always means work for us."

"Yes, of course," said Max. "I hadn't realized. It was about a friend of mine who's been hospitalized by the Red Cross. I wonder if you could tell me which hospital she'd be in?"

"We don't deal with that here," the girl said. "You must phone our three hospitals in Paris."

And she showed him their numbers.

TWENTY-TWO

Max Goes Underground

With a docile "good night" to the porter, Max went out into the street. He felt completely at a loss. He had drained the telephone directory of all information it could give him. He was left with two words, *Red Cross*, and he had no idea what they referred to. It was clear that they had nothing to do, directly at least, with the international health organization of that name. Perhaps the words were in code, in which case Max would be unable to break them. The official he had spoken to would no longer be at the prefecture, and besides, Max was not eager to risk a second call.

He walked slowly down to the Champs-Élysées. The air was thick and warm, softening the brightness of the lights. Long American cars raced silently toward the Étoile. At the traffic lights they stopped and swayed on their brakes like boats at anchor. It was a summer's evening on the Champs-Élysées and it was there when Max cared to look at it, as he did now because he could get no further with the problem.

He passed the rue Pierre Charron, with the flashing green sign of the Sexy nightclub. The Paris office of Gala Films was, appropriately, at the top of the same building.

Max stopped by a newsstand and ran his eye quickly over the headlines. But he didn't buy a paper. He turned and walked back up the Champs-Élysées. Fouquet's, a restaurant he had no intention of ever visiting, was draped in red. There were emblems on the terrace hangings and on the curtains inside, but there was no cross. And on the other side of the avenue, a chemist's was still open, with an illuminated green cross above his door.

Max could spend all night interpreting everything he saw in terms of *Red Cross*. At the next newsstand he bought the tourist's weekly guide to Paris. Perhaps there was a restaurant he had never heard of, perhaps there was a film or a play called *Red Cross*. He flipped through the index. Nothing. He left the magazine on a bench and walked on. There was nothing that gave

him a lead on the words *Red Cross*. Yet all the time he knew that there had
to be something that the words would fit like a key in a lock, something
that would be so much simpler than all the instruments he was fumbling
with at the moment. He tried to put himself in the position of someone
who knew the answer and was watching his efforts at finding it, telling him,
"But it's so obvious." This only made his search more confused.

He stood looking into the window of an airline's office. Cutout models
of the company's planes pointed skyward on their stands. Max began
mechanically to count the seats. It helped to clear his mind. He felt relaxed
enough to look for the associations that the words *Red Cross* evoked for him.
In English, he thought of Charing Cross and King's Cross, the London
railway stations that he knew so well. This accounted for *Cross* but it left
the *Red* out. Then he had a mental picture of four people being tortured
on a burning cross, in the Middle Ages perhaps, but he wasn't sure. He
realized he had thought of this after seeing, in the Renault show window,
a car turning slowly under the lights. He tried the words in French: *Croix
Rouge*—what did that remind him of? He could think only of a decoration
for bravery awarded in the Russian Army.

He turned away from the window and continued his walk. A station,
a torture and a medal—he hadn't found very much. Besides, it was what
the words meant in France in the present situation that mattered, not what
they reminded him of. It was absurd to think he could reach one through
the other.

He stopped and stood with his hands in his pockets, looking across the
road. Under the gates of the National City Bank on the other side, an old
blind man was selling lottery tickets. Behind Max, the crowd was passing,
speaking in different languages. He began to realize why he had stopped
walking. One of those three associations had worked.

Without waiting for the lights to change he ran across the avenue through
the moving cars. There were the steps down to the Métro, and there, behind,
some people were gathered round the map of the Underground network.
Max waited for the people to go away. He went up, feeling excited almost
beyond control. The brightly colored map was in front of him. He had it all
to himself. When he had first seen it as a boy, he had wanted to take it home
and hang it up above his bed. It was just the sort of picture a child would
like. The lines ran in red, yellow, blue, green and brown across Paris. A
large circle showed Max where he was. The stations had odd and attractive
names, like Michel-Ange Auteuil, Stalingrad and Sèvres-Babylone. Here
and there the names had been crossed out in black. Pasted on to the top
left-hand corner of the map was a short list of about six closed stations—

stations closed because they had been built too near each other and were used by too few people. Max looked at the list and saw immediately as if it were his own name, in the middle of many unknown others, the words *Croix Rouge*.

He knew he had been right. He half ran back to the car. There was no time to be lost. He put the briefcase on the seat beside him. There was no doubt that he would need it this time, but his new confidence made it feel less incongruous. He drove into the Latin Quarter. It had been absurd of him to have thought even for one moment that the OAS could have been working through the Red Cross organization—whereas he could scarcely think of all the possibilities that the possession of a disused Métro station afforded. Why was the name the same? The Red Cross headquarters must have been in this part of the Latin Quarter when the line had been constructed, and the station must have been called after it. Then the headquarters had been transferred to the Champs-Élysées, and the station name had stayed.

Max drove slowly along the road between Sèvres-Babylone and Mabillon that followed exactly the line underground. Halfway, several roads met at a small square. Max saw from the blue street signs on the houses around that its name was Red Cross Square. The entrance to the Métro was on one side. The area was quiet and unfrequented. Max parked in a side street. He came back to the square, approaching the Métro from behind.

A map like the one he had looked at on the Champs-Élysées a few minutes before was there, framed in green-painted wrought iron. Max walked round it to the steps. They were open, but the doors at the bottom were covered over by a grille locked and chained in the middle. The OAS would have the keys and they would go in that way at night. The people in the flats around the square, if they noticed them, would suppose that they had come to carry out repairs. They would not be suspicious, even when the men carried large bags of tools. Repairs on the Underground were always undertaken at night.

The men underneath would be expecting reinforcements. It was dangerous for Max to linger there. He would have to find his way in underground. He walked on to Sèvres-Babylone, the next station along the line. Inside, as he looked at a Métro station for the first time from such an angle, Max noticed that there was plenty of room, especially along the corridors. Several hundred men could be lodged there without difficulty.

Max went down the steps and handed in his ticket to the woman at the barrier to be punched. Some people said "thank you," and others didn't, but Max had never known of a ticket-puncher who seemed to be concerned.

He walked a little way along the platform and leaned out over the edge.

The tunnel curved so that he could not see all the way to Red Cross. It was lit by unshaded bulbs hung on both sides every fifty yards. It was so clear that a rat could not have moved there unnoticed.

A train came in the other side. As it moved out, Max watched how it swept like a searchlight the tunnel walls and the giant soda-water advertisements splayed along them. He had already decided not to walk through the tunnel. The OAS acted on the assumption that no one knew of their hideout—for what otherwise could be the point of a hideout? But they had to guard against accidents in the form of railway workers who came along the lines at night for repairs. So Max expected that there would be at least one man on the platform at Red Cross whose job it was to look regularly both ways along the tunnel. The last thing he would be suspecting was a jump directly onto the platform itself.

He went to the far end of the platform, the end that would be farthest from the driver and guard, who rode together in the front of the train. The platform was filling up. Usually the trains ran at two- or three-minute intervals. This one had been a long time coming. The more people in the carriages the better. If Max was to pass Red Cross several times this evening, he did not want to be recognized on his fourth or fifth run by an OAS lookout hidden on the station.

With his briefcase and the evening newspaper, *Le Monde*, under his arm. Max felt he looked every bit like a businessman returning home. If only he was, he thought. The station was one of the older ones, with white-tiled walls, giving it a public-lavatory aspect that contrasted oddly with the large multicoloured signs and posters.

Max stepped back as he saw the train come curling into the station. He got into the last of its four carriages. He stayed standing by the doors. He had not used the Métro often. He needed to familiarize himself with it as much as with the disused station. There was some impatient buzzing at the doors as the guard hurried the last people into the train. Then the doors banged shut and were held there by pressure. Max remembered that London Transport had used trains like this about ten years ago. On the London ones, you could pull open the doors in the tunnel, and this was what Max needed now. The train was drawing out of the station. Max felt a little self-conscious as he tried to pull the doors apart. It was impossible.

He leaned back against the side—to hear a moment later the pressure being released. Max gripped the door handles and pulled. They came apart easily.

But the train was going too quickly for a jump—at twenty or twenty-five miles an hour. Compared with the London underground, this was not fast, but in Paris the stations were much closer to each other. Max stood by the window, careful not to cloud the glass with his breath.

The train was straightening out. Stations were not built on a bend if it could be helped. Red Cross would be just ahead. The train was braking. It braked down to no more than ten miles an hour. Then it rumbled past the platform of the empty station and out, gathering speed, into the tunnel again.

Max leaned back. In the light from the train he had seen an empty, unlit platform. The door of the stationmaster's office, halfway along, had been wide open. The platform and the white-tiled walls had looked gray with dust. The spaces reserved for posters had been empty, or perhaps dust had covered over their colors. But Max had seen twice, in white on a blue background, the name of the station: Red Cross. The speed of the train had been perfect for a jump, but Max was worried by the empty and open platform that would give him no chance to avoid detection. He had noticed that the driver at the front of the train began to accelerate out of the station some time before the back carriage left it. For him to jump at the train's slowest speed, that is to say, the moment he saw the platform, would mean landing by the exit where he expected the OAS to be. He could, on the other hand, delay the jump till the end of the platform, but then the train's speed would make it dangerous. Neither alternative was attractive.

The train slowed to come into Mabillon, the station that was on the other side of Red Cross from Sèvres-Babylone.

Max got out and changed platforms by the corridors that passed underneath. He went again to the back of the train. Some fifteen to twenty people got in with him. For the jump he needed to be alone and in the last carriage, so that no one lower down the train would see him on the platform after he landed. He also needed the rest of the train to shield him from observers on the disused platform. In an hour or so he counted on there being less people.

The train slowed shortly after leaving the station, just as it had done from the opposite direction. Max had resumed his position by the doors. They were passing Red Cross. It was covered by the same dust and seemed as dead as the other platform had been. But on it were heaped great concrete slabs like paving stones, piled irregularly on top of each other. Wooden posts had been thrown carelessly over them. The train accelerated and the station disappeared.

Max knew immediately that it would be from this side that he would jump. For at one point, the concrete had almost reached the platform edge. If he could fall behind it, it would be a perfect position from which to begin his exploration of the station. He would jump when the train was going most slowly, exactly as he had planned. The exits where he expected the OAS to be were, on both platforms, at the other end of the station from which he would jump. For an observer at either exit he would be invisible from one side because shielded by the train, and from the other, he would be difficult to see at the far end of the platform beyond the pile of concrete and wood.

He was back at Sèvres-Babylone. He ran quickly under the line to the other platform, just in time to squeeze past the thick automatic door that closed the station off when a train came in. Max stood on the other side of the carriage, the side from which he would be able to see the platform he had chosen for his jump. Once more Max passed slowly through the deserted station. He concentrated his attention on the exit and saw that the automatic door had been dismantled. The post was still there, but the space was free. Max could make out the stairs that led from the empty ticket-puncher's box to the corridors above. But he could see no one, nor any trace of the people he was looking for.

He stood waiting for a train to take him back. The concrete and wood could not have been brought there by the OAS. They must have found it when they arrived, and no doubt they considered themselves lucky. It formed a ready-made barricade in case of emergency. It would also serve Max as cover.

Max got in. He counted seven people in the carriage with him. Already the number was thinning. The train pulled out of the station and Max tested himself. "Now," he said, under his breath, and an instant later the acceleration stopped and the train ran on its momentum before the brakes were applied. Max was learning quickly.

The moment his carriage entered the station his eyes were on the spot where he would jump. It was a small patch scattered with concrete chips and thick with dust. It was some two yards deep and some three or four yards long. Provided his timing was right, he would have some space in which to roll over if he needed it. And when he got to his feet, he should find himself looking from behind the concrete at the exits on both platforms at the other end of the station.

The train quickly left Red Cross behind. Max found himself hot from anticipation of the jump that he had experienced almost as the real thing. Again he had seen no trace of anybody on the platform. There was no reason, after all, for them to be there; it was much safer in the corridors. But where was the man guarding the platform? It worried Max that he had seen no sign of him.

He changed trains. On the return journey he tested himself again at predicting the driver's movements. He was becoming more and more accurate.

At Mabillon he walked thoughtfully down to a point that would be level with the last doors of the last carriage. He put the newspaper inside the briefcase. He made sure at the same time that the pistol was still there. Five people were waiting with him: they alone were too many, and there were four more on the train when it came in. Max hung back and stayed on the platform as the train pulled out.

Not a minute had gone by before its place was taken by another. The back carriage contained only one person, a middle-aged man, sitting facing the front of the train. It was the empty, or at least inattentive, carriage that Max needed.

But as he stepped into the train he was followed by a man who leapt through the doors only a moment before they closed. Max watched him anxiously. The man wore the uniform of a trainee fireman. He seemed unable to decide whether to sit or to stand. But unless he sat Max could not be sure that he wouldn't turn round unexpectedly. And he had to sit facing the front of the train for Max to have the back of the carriage to himself.

The train had started and the last carriage was passing the end of the station. The young fireman moved from one side to the other. At length he made his way to a group of seats. The train was about to reach its maximum acceleration. Then the fireman stopped. It seemed as if he was wavering in his decision to sit. The brakes were applied. The fireman, aided by the alteration in the train's speed, slumped in one movement into the seat, his back to Max.

"Gott sei Dank!" murmured Max in relief.

TWENTY-THREE

Jacobs among the Jackboots

Quietly he unzipped his briefcase. He reached inside and withdrew the pistol wrapped in the newspaper. He laid the briefcase on a seat. There was no point in taking it with him. He returned to the doors and lifted back the catch that held them together. Then he pulled, and they came apart easily. The train slackened its speed until it seemed to Max to have almost stopped. He strained to look ahead and caught a glimpse of the carriage in front entering the station. He pulled the doors wider, and when he saw the space of dusty platform, he jumped.

He had allowed for impetus, but, though he landed on his feet, he was forced over and fell with his left arm and shoulder on the concrete. The station was surprisingly solid after all the theoretical consideration he had been giving it. When he looked up he saw the back lights of the train disappearing at the end of the platform. He flexed his left arm. It was bruised but not broken.

He was crouching behind the pile of concrete blocks. He held the pistol ready. The station was as quiet as it had seemed from the train. There was the noise of the trains along the line, and even vibration from their movement. Max wondered for a moment if he hadn't been wrong. Then he corrected himself. It was certain that the OAS were there. They had to be. Max stayed where he was, not daring to go forward until he received some sign that all was safe. The stillness of the station was not by itself enough.

A train was approaching from the other direction. Max felt the noise and the vibration as if he had been on the line itself. The train passed by him into the tunnel. Max looked down the platform toward the exit. Nothing moved. Shrugging his shoulders, he shifted into a more comfortable position.

Suddenly there was a light from the other end, a torch light. It was moving forward from the ticket-puncher's box at the height of a man's stomach. It seemed to be propelling itself. It moved to the steps down into the tunnel. Then it switched off. Max could see the outline of a man against the lights of the tunnel. The man was looking up and down the tracks. He came back onto the platform and walked toward Max, his torch hanging downwards.

Max, at the very end of the station, watched him coming. The man was only a silhouette walking on the edge of the platform. He was twenty yards away when Max saw that he was a paratrooper with blackened hands and face and that he carried his submachine gun tucked under his arm. He came on toward Max, who pressed his face into the concrete to blot out the bad dream. The paratrooper came to a stop three yards away and stayed there, looking down the tunnel. He paid no attention to the platform. But Max was quite certain that he could feel movements in the station like movements in his own body. The man would have turned and fired before Max could have raised himself high enough above the concrete blocks to shoot. The paratrooper turned and walked back down the platform.

Max realized how wise he had been not to try coming along the tunnel. The paratrooper patrolled a little more on his short beat up and down in front of the exit. He went back to the ticket-puncher's box. Moments later Max heard another train coming. The paratrooper's reactions were faster. He'd probably been down there several days already. Max turned his face away as the train passed. He could not afford at this point to be seen by the driver or the guard. Whether any passengers caught sight of him or not was of less importance. He looked over the concrete blocks. The paratrooper, or rather the torch—for the man was invisible except against the tunnel lights—had reappeared.

His guard duty was simple. As each train went by, he had to avoid being seen even by the passengers. After the train had passed or after two trains had passed simultaneously, as had been the case when Max jumped, he was to check that the tunnels were clear.

The paratrooper announced the passage of another train by getting into the box, where he was invisible to Max even though he could now see more clearly. And, Max thought, if he could not see the man, then there was no reason why the man should see him. Besides, the paratrooper had seemed to be paying no attention to the platform.

The train came in beside Max. As soon as the front carriage had passed him, he moved quickly forward and inward, close to the tiled walls of the station to a point behind a lower set of concrete blocks. He was lying on his stomach. He had moved a quarter of the way down to the paratrooper.

Max lifted himself on his hands and looked down the station toward the exit. Five seconds or so after the last carriage had passed his end of the platform, the paratrooper stood up and left the box. He walked to the platform edge and leaned over. Max saw the outline of the beret and of the machine gun that swung from his shoulder. All was clear, and the paratrooper came up the platform to inspect the tunnel at Max's end. Max lay in a shallow gutter that ran along the base of the station wall. He kept his head down and his arms by his sides, the hands hidden, so that the white parts of his body did not stand out against the dull gray of the wall and the concrete blocks. The paratrooper wore boots, but he walked like a cat, without making a sound. Almost painfully, because he needed to be so careful, Max turned his head to see where the man was. He was inspecting the tunnel from the far end of the platform. He seemed satisfied and started on his way back. It was at this point, when he had made sure that both tunnels were clear, that Max was afraid the paratrooper's gaze might stray off the tracks onto the platform. But the silhouette came level and passed him, silently as it had done on the way up.

Max watched him continue his beat down to the end of the platform. As he did so, he realized that he had no choice but to kill the man. On this occasion there was hardly the time or the opportunity to argue it out. But even if the pistol was accurate at a distance, Max did not trust his aim. He would not be allowed a second shot if the first was not fatal. So he would have to kill the paratrooper at point-blank range, preferably as a train was passing.

He had to wait nearly five minutes for the next one. As before, the man warned him it was coming by moving into his box some time before Max heard it himself. This was a proficiency that had come from habit. But the same habit had bred a certain blindness. The man had never thought that a jump would be made directly onto the platform. And for this failure to think, Max was certain that the paratrooper would die—so certain, indeed, that he saw it as suicide. As Max watched the man settle deep behind the door of the ticket-puncher's box, he saw him also as the most useful instrument in his own execution. Max did not kill people until they were already dead.

"The Lord bless thee and keep thee," he said softly, even as he looked.

The train came in from the other side. When the front carriage had passed, Max sprang to his feet and, at a crouching run along the wall, reached the last barrier but one of the concrete blocks. As the train accelerated out of the station he dropped down into a kind of trough, shielded this time both from the exit and from the platform edge. The door of the ticket-puncher's box swung open as expected. Max felt secure if uncomfortable in his concrete pen. He watched the routine inspection of the tunnels. On the paratrooper's way back, there was a noise from the tracks. The man flashed his powerful torch under the overhanging edge of the platform. A rat must have moved. He switched his torch off and continued his patrol back to the exit.

He was a very quiet man. He did not smoke, or hum, or whistle to himself. Max could see nothing of his features, which, like his hands, were daubed in black. When his head was at a certain angle, Max could see the lights reflected in his eyes.

"The Lord bless thee and keep thee," Max repeated in a whisper. "The Lord make His face to shine upon thee, and be gracious unto thee."

The dead man returned to his box after more than five minutes. The trains were already running at longer intervals. The last pile of concrete blocks was only fifteen yards in front. The train came in from the other side. Max ran and dropped behind the final piece of cover. He was more exposed than previously. He needed another train immediately to keep the man in the box.

But no train came. The paratrooper glanced down the tunnel by the exit and came up the platform toward Max. He passed as he had passed the other times. On the way back, he stopped close to Max on the platform edge. Max heard a boot stubbing against the platform and, farther away, the sound of things falling lightly on the tracks. He turned his head slowly and silently. He saw that the man, with his weight on one foot, was idly swinging his free leg and knocking the concrete chips over the edge of the platform. The paratrooper was bored. He was amusing himself. He moved on down to the exit. Six minutes passed before he went into the box for the last time.

Max listened for the train and heard it coming from behind him. The noise it made suddenly increased when it broke out from the tunnel into the station. Max released the safety catch on his pistol and raised himself on one knee. As soon as the front carriage had passed him, he ran across the empty platform to the box, his pistol swinging in his right hand.

He steadied himself when he had reached it. The last carriage was being pulled quickly out of the station. Max leaned over the door of the box. The paratrooper's elbows were on his knees, his head was in his hands. He was looking down at his feet, tired of his monotonous guard duty. He had realized nothing. In the noise of the disappearing train Max shot him from six inches in the back of the neck. It was his second execution of the day.

"The Lord be gracious unto thee," he said, still in a whisper. "The Lord turn His face unto thee and give thee peace."

The man fell forward, pushing the door of the box open. Max caught him and dragged him out with considerable effort onto the platform. He got down onto the tracks. With his legs on two sleepers, he pulled the man from the platform onto his shoulders. His legs shaking under the weight, he crossed the rails to the other side. There he jumped up onto the platform and pulled the corpse toward the stationmaster's office.

Max stripped the body of its camouflage uniform. He put it on over his suit and set the beret at the correct angle on his head. He dragged the paratrooper into the office and wedged him under the desk in what was the darkest part of the station.

Now to find Silesia. Taking the dead man's torch and machine gun, Max crossed the tracks to the other platform. He stood with his torch dimmed at the foot of the stairway to the corridors. Slowly he began to go up the steps, keeping the torch pointed downward. At the turn of the stairway the edge of the beam caught something jutting over. Max had his machine gun ready. It was another machine gun. There was a whole stock of them, but the men behind were asleep, sleeping in preparation for the next day. There were three of them, each covered by a blanket. Max flashed the torch quickly: there were groans, but no one woke. He walked on between the piles of ammunition.

He stepped over a fourth man, who was awake and who asked, "What's up?" Max waved the torch for answer and passed on. There were no other lights. Perhaps only the guard was allowed to have one. Max realized that he was far from the center as yet. That would be in the old ticket hall, behind the doors that led up into the street.

He came in silence and darkness to a junction of two corridors. He shone the torch down one of them and caught a glimpse of a long and crowded dormitory. Two or three hundred men were sleeping there. Max turned the torch onto the other corridor, but it had been filled in after only ten yards. It was being used as another arms depot.

Max was beginning to wonder what he should do next, when he heard a muffled exclamation from between the stacks of ammunition. Guided by his torch, he took a few steps forward in the direction of the noise—and there was Silesia. She was bound and gagged and lying on a bed of grenades, her head pillowed on the magazine of a machine gun. Max bent over her and pulled the piece of cloth out of her mouth.

"Noo?" he inquired anxiously.

"Don't ask!" was Silesia's weary reply.

There were a few tense moments as he wrestled with the knots that held her.

"Am I stiff!" she went on after Max had pulled her to her feet. "What a night! I thought I'd never get to sleep."

"Sha . . ." Max whispered. "Hold on."

With one hand on Silesia's and the other round the torch, he led her back the way he had come. The machine gun swung by its strap from his shoulder. He shone the torch almost directly on each man as he remembered where he was. He provoked restlessness and even hostile remarks from those who were awake, but with the light in their eyes, they could see neither him nor Silesia.

They reached the top of the steps and went down together. A train went by as they got to the bottom. They needed another to pass almost immediately in the opposite direction for them to be sure the tunnel would be clear for the five to ten minutes they would need to reach the next station on foot. They still could not afford to be seen by the driver or the guard; they had not the time for the explanations that bureaucracy would find necessary.

While they waited, Silesia stretched her arms and legs. Max took off his beret and uniform and left them, together with the machine gun, by the body of the paratrooper in the stationmaster's office. He came back to Silesia and they sat on the bottom step, glancing up behind them every now and then, but with increasing frequency as the minutes passed. No second train came by. Even if it came now, they could not move, because it would by then be time for another in the first direction. It was like waiting for two drops of water to fall from a tap at the same time.

"A quarter of an hour gone already!" exclaimed Max, shaking his head. He still had his pistol, but he wished he had not got rid of the machine gun so quickly. Then Silesia nudged him and cocked her head.

"I hear something," she said. But which side? Both sides!

Two trains passed within a few seconds of each other. Max and Silesia climbed down into the tunnel to Mabillon and walked as fast as they could along the strip of gravel that lay between the tracks and the wall. They were astonished, after the darkness of Red Cross, at the brightness of the tunnel lights. At the bend Max saw that there was no train in the station ahead, though there were passengers on both platforms. They came to within twenty yards of the station and stopped.

But no passenger had noticed them or even looked in their direction. The stationmaster's office was closed. He had long since been off duty. The only officials were the women ticket-punchers. They would have to be disregarded.

"Run," cried Max.

They came up onto the platform. Few people seemed to have noticed. Max was halfway up the exit steps, pulling Silesia by the hand, before even the ticket-puncher could shrilly protest. But by herself she was powerless, and no passenger was willing to sacrifice his ticket by taking the exit stairs and catching up with the fleeing couple.

They didn't stop running until they reached the Facel. Silesia sat back in the front seat and expelled all the air from her body with a long, "Oy! Never again!" Max was still trembling from the excitement and the effort. The keys slipped the first time he tried to put them in. Then they were off in their comfortable seats, moving fast.

TWENTY-FOUR

The Prefect Loses Some Sleep

With Silesia beside him in the Facel, Max felt able to begin controlling a situation that up till then had been controlling him. The Métro had been the turning point. It was just past midnight as Max drove toward the Champs-Élysées. He had the next stage of the operation clear in his mind.

"You feeling okay?" he asked Silesia.

"So-so," she said, shrugging her shoulders. "Tired mostly."

"But you're well enough to fetch Morris for me?"

"Yes, of course, if it's important."

"Well, I can promise you it is," Max assured her. "But before we go into that, I'm going to fix us up with a hotel room. We can hardly go back to our flats."

He stopped the car near a café, then went inside and phoned.

"The George V? I'd like two adjoining . . ."

"I'm very sorry, sir," the desk interrupted, "but we're full up."

Max, however, did not ring off.

"Get Henri for me, will you?" he asked.

He waited, listening to the special confusion of sounds that characterize a busy hotel reception desk. Henri suddenly broke in; it was a cheerful voice, even at this time of night.

"Henri!" Max exclaimed. "You know who this is?"

He did not wait for an answer.

"Tell me, Henri," he said, "how are things? The wife? Hmm! The children? Well, now! And the boy? Marvelous; and yourself, Henri, how are you keeping? So. Listen. Could you do a favor for your old friend Max? Two adjoining rooms with a bath for tonight? Okay? Give me half an hour."

He joined Silesia in the car.

"That's the hotel settled," he told her. "Now to get Morris."

"But why now?" asked Silesia. "Why didn't you go before?"

"Because if I had done," said Max, "they would have taken it out on you. That's what they were holding you for, to stop me getting in touch with Morris or with anybody else."

Silesia nodded thoughtfully. She was beginning to understand.

"So that's what I was doing down there," she said. "But if you hadn't been able to find me . . . ?"

Max gestured to say that he didn't know what he'd have done.

"I might have risked it," he said, "and gone to Morris anyway. But I found you, so I didn't. Don't you prefer it that way?"

"Naturally, Max," said Silesia quickly. "I was only asking."

"Here we are then," said Max, as he brought the Facel to a stop some two streets away from the prefect's flat. "This is where I drop you."

Silesia didn't move.

"Can't you drop me at the door, Max? What's two more streets for a car like yours?"

"A lot," answered Max. "Enough to ruin everything. Because it's my car, the car anybody who's keeping Morris under observation is watching out for."

"But how can you be sure there's anybody?" exclaimed Silesia.

"Because," Max explained patiently, "when they told me what would happen to you if I tried to see Morris, that had to mean they were watching Morris to check if I tried to see him. So, not only is his telephone being tapped, but they must have him covered from the street as well."

"Well, Max, I hope you're right," said Silesia. "I don't want to have to walk all that way for nothing."

Silesia had never been one to enjoy physical exercise.

"Now," began Max, looking at her intently, "when you get there this is what you do."

Silesia listened carefully.

"And you, Max?" she asked when he had finished.

"Don't worry about me," he said. "I'll be waiting for you at the hotel."

Silesia set off toward the prefect's flat, armed with Max's memorized instructions that were like so many invisible weapons. The street looked normal enough to her as she came into it several minutes later. Surreptitiously she glanced at the parked cars as she passed, but not one concealed the watcher Max had warned her of.

The building where the prefect lived was set back from the road. There was a noise in the shadows outside the porter's lodge as Silesia was about to open the door. In spite of Max's instructions, she turned and looked. It was a girl and a boy kissing. The girl was straining upward, supported by the boy's hand concealed in her clothing. The hand reappeared hastily when the boy saw Silesia. The girl glanced over her shoulder and tried to see who it was at the door. Then she shrugged and turned back to the boy.

Silesia took the lift to the top floor. But she hesitated before ringing the bell. If I get him up, she thought, he'll turn the light on and then the men down in the street will see something's wrong. She was still considering what to do next when the door of the lift opened behind her.

"Oh!"

Silesia and the prefect's daughter recognized each other simultaneously.

"Oh!" exclaimed the girl again.

"Don't worry, darling," said Silesia. "It's not about that that I've come to see your father. So you have a key on you?"

"Yes, here," said the girl in relief, holding up the key for Silesia to see.

"Don't turn on any lights," Silesia told her as they went into the flat.

Only too ready to do anything she was asked, the prefect's daughter led Silesia to the door of her father's bedroom before slipping off to her own.

Silesia opened the door onto the heavy and irregular breathing of a man whose sleeping was done for him by pills. The breathing shuddered and stopped, to be replaced by a most convincing kind of groan.

"Morris! Listen. It's Silesia."

"Sha . . . you'll wake the wife."

"Morris!"

"For God's sake, Silesia, what's up?"

"Get your clothes," Silesia whispered fiercely. "Get up. Get awake. We're going out."

"Now listen to me, Silesia," Morris protested. "I've just taken my pills. I'm in no mood to go on one of your hysterical wild-goose chases."

Silesia was by now both anxious and annoyed.

"Morris!" she insisted. "Listen, Morris! This is important. I've come from Max and he's got work for you."

At this she poked at the prefect.

"For *you*," she continued, "because you happen to be prefect of police in this city."

Morris tried a last hopeless objection.

"But you can't have come from Max. The Minister told us Max was back in London."

"Well he's not!" whispered Silesia triumphantly. "He's waiting for you in a hotel."

Gracelessly the prefect swung his pajama'd legs out of bed and reached for the benzedrine bottle.

"You won't need that with what Max has to tell you," said Silesia with a hint of self-satisfaction.

While Morris dressed, Silesia shifted the net curtain slightly and glanced down into the street. There, in a car parked under a lamppost farther up, were the men Max had predicted.

"Here," said Silesia to the prefect. "Tell me what you see."

Morris approached the window in stockinged feet.

"Where?"

"There," Silesia pointed.

"A Volkswagen," said Morris, in a voice that was still far from clear. "A nice German car. So?"

"But the two men inside?" Silesia insisted.

"The two men?" Morris repeated, without understanding.

"Never mind," said Silesia. "Now get your shoes on."

Morris sat back on the bed and fumbled between his legs for his shoes. As he tied his laces he looked up at Silesia and frowned.

"What were they doing," he asked, "Those two .men down there just now?"

"They're still there," said Silesia. "So don't think they've gone."

"But what are they doing?"

"They're waiting for you," Silesia told him.

Morris assimilated the information as he put on his jacket.

"Got your car keys?" asked Silesia.

"But you said they're waiting for me," Morris objected.

"So?"

"I won't need them."

As he spoke, the uneasiness in Morris's mind became certainty, and then he did not need Silesia to tell him that he hadn't been understanding the situation correctly at all.

"Waiting for me!" he exclaimed at last. "So it's like that they're waiting for me! My telephone's tapped, I can't move out of my house, I can't do anything!"

"And the radio telephone in your car," asked Silesia sarcastically, "is that being tapped?"

"You're all prepared, aren't you?" said Morris, a little unsteadily.

"I've got Max's instructions."

"Where?" Morris asked.

"Here," said Silesia, with a finger on her forehead.

Morris stopped the car, with its lights dimmed, at the foot of the ramp that led up from the garage into the street. It was from here, while he was no longer underground nor yet fully occupied in driving, that he could give (Max's) orders over the telephone. He cut the radio contact. Silesia huddled down in her seat. The back of the Citroën dipped suddenly as Morris accelerated up the ramp and spun the car with a scream of tires into the street. The Volkswagen never got closer than two hundred yards. Morris passed through the gates of the prefecture. The Volkswagen realized the trap too late. As it turned, twenty motards, their front wheels lifting from the acceleration, leapt toward the escaping car like so many black grasshoppers and shot its tires to pieces. The Volkswagen finished against a wall, and the line that the OAS had had on Morris's activities went dead.

Silesia and the prefect continued their journey to the George V.

"Max," said Morris, drying his palms on a crumpled monogrammed handkerchief, "I don't mind admitting it, you've got me frightened."

Silesia had retired to the adjoining room. Max and Morris sat talking across the low table, in tones that were urgent but hushed.

"Being chased across Paris after midnight," Morris went on, "like a criminal, when it's the city I'm prefect of police of . . ." he shook his head, unable to continue. "If it hadn't been for that car behind us just now, Max, I don't think I'd have believed you. The Minister, the Métro—it's incredible."

"Perhaps," said Max, "but we still don't know everything."

"That's it," said Morris, becoming even more dispirited. "It makes you wonder what they've got up their sleeve for tomorrow—for today, rather."

The fourteenth had started two hours before.

"Well," Max announced, "we've got tonight to find out."

Morris left his chair and went to the window.

"If their attempt succeeds," he said, "I'll probably be liquidated as an undesirable member of Soustelle's France."

"He won't liquidate you," Max told him. "He'll give you plenty of warning and you'll be able to get away in good time."

"All the same," said Morris, looking down into the street.

"Come on," said Max, disregarding the prefect's misery. "We've got work to do."

Morris turned in despair from the window.

"But, Max, what about those men in the Métro?"

"We'll begin there," said Max. "I feel sure for a start that the OAS are not at Red Cross because they've got nowhere else to stay. They are there because they're going to use the Métro."

"How?" asked Morris. "By walking through the tunnels?"

"That would be impossible," Max told him. "They'd be seen by the trains. And what do you think they'd do when they came to the stations? No," he said, "they can only be using a train."

"They must have some accomplices in the Métro," said Morris.

"There's no doubt that they have," said Max, correcting the prefect's observation into something more emphatic. "That's how they got down there in the first place."

"If, as you said, there were two or three hundred of them," Morris admitted, "that's just about what one train would hold. But what do they do then? Drive under the Champs-Élysées and lay dynamite for when de Gaulle comes by?"

Max made no attempt to conceal his astonishment.

"Come on!" he said to Morris. "You must wake up! *They* can sleep tonight because they have everything ready. But *you*'ve got work for every minute till the parade begins. The OAS are a fighting organization. They'd only need ten men at the most to dynamite de Gaulle. Those three hundred are there for another purpose."

Morris kept silent under the rebuke.

"All right," he said at last. "The OAS will take a train from Red Cross. But when and where will they drive it?"

"First," said Max, "for the time. The parade begins at eleven and de Gaulle will be taking the salute in public for about three-quarters of an hour. The men at Red Cross won't begin to move until a few minutes before, or even after, the assassination. Otherwise, if they start too early, they might raise the alarm and sabotage the plan."

"But why shouldn't they carry out the assassination themselves?" asked Morris. "Not with dynamite, but by some other means?"

"How could they?" asked Max. "They'd never get through the barriers of police and soldiers, even three hundred of them."

Morris was left thinking. Max reached for the white telephone. He rang down an order for smoked-salmon sandwiches and coffee, then turned toward Morris.

"Is there anything you'd care for?" he asked.

The prefect hesitated for a moment.

"That sounded very pleasant to me," he said.

"Sandwiches for four, please," said Max and replaced the receiver. "It's always best to order double," he explained. "There's nothing better than smoked salmon on a hot night."

Morris was coming to life.

"Of course!" he said, in a tone that announced a discovery. "It's as if I've only just realized what it's all about. They are not going to kill de Gaulle and leave it at that. They are serious people, as you said. They want to do more than kill a president, they want to take over a state. Those men—they'll be used for capturing targets like the radio."

"That's more like it," said Max encouragingly.

"But they won't need three hundred for the radio," continued Morris. "I had only ten men guarding it."

"That's just what I thought," said Max. "Obviously they'll split their forces up. Let's say they drop fifty men off at the station nearest the radio on the Champs-Élysées. That will leave them with two hundred or two hundred and fifty."

"The other places in the area they should be trying for," Morris suggested, "are the Élysée and the prime minister's palace, Matignon."

"Both only a hundred yards from the Champs-Élysées," Max added. "We'll suppose they need seventy-five each for those. That leaves them with a hundred, if our guesses are correct."

"And they'll be the hundred most difficult to place," said Morris. "Because so far we've left out the assassination itself. If they are not going to carry it out themselves, then surely they will arrive to back up those who do."

"Now that's just where I have my doubts," Max began.

There was a knock on the door, a soft knock, careful to avoid disturbing those asleep in nearby rooms. Max and Morris remained silent as the white-jacked waiter entered with his tray. He served with an easy efficiency that made command or suggestion unnecessary. He laid the silver dish of salmon sandwiches on the table between Morris and Max and poured a cup of coffee for each. Max nodded his thanks as the waiter left the room, lifted the lid off the dish, and served Morris and then himself.

"If I were head of the OAS," he went on, "the last place I would want my troops would be where the assassination is to be carried out. As soon as de Gaulle is dead," he explained, "there will be a general paralysis while people realize what has happened and hesitate before using any initiative. To put before their eyes a hundred men who have come to support those who killed de Gaulle might well push them into a counterattack. Much better to leave them with nothing to fight and with increasing doubts as to their loyalty to de Gaulle once he's dead. Then, when they learn some time later that the radio and the public buildings have been taken over, they'll hardly be in a position to reply."

Morris waved a salmon sandwich.

"Maybe they'll compromise," he suggested. "They could turn up to show their force but not to use it. Anyway," he went on, returning with confidence to the side of things he knew best, "it's not important. We may have guessed wrongly how they'll use their men, but we can be almost certain that around eleven o'clock they'll be coming up under the Champs-Élysées in the Métro. We'll have all the stations they can get off at cleared of passengers. I'll put plenty of my own men in the tunnels and at the exits. I won't take any chances. But I don't want there to be a scandal. And if I can prevent any of this getting past the people immediately concerned and out to the public, I will."

Max took the opportunity while Morris talked to reach for the food and coffee.

"In that case," said Max, sipping sparingly from his cup, "the best thing would be to get them now at Red Cross while they're sleeping."

"But I want all those associated with the plot to show their hand," Morris exclaimed in officialese. "And the only way to do that is to let their operation go to the limit of safety."

Max shrugged his shoulders.

"As you like," he said. "I'll be pleased to leave that side of things to you. It's a separate problem from the one we haven't dealt with yet—the assassination itself."

Morris seemed almost to have forgotten the sandwich he held close to his mouth. He had suddenly lost his appetite. The expression of catastrophe returned. As he had been talking of his plans to capture the OAS troops, the assassination had failed. Now, it might already have taken place.

"Dogs, guided missiles, who knows?" he asked. "Who can foresee?"

"But the OAS aren't magicians," Max objected. "They haven't thought of something that in principle we can't think of too."

"We've got nothing to start from, though," said Morris. "Nothing's happened since we last spoke."

"That simply is not true," Max exclaimed.

Morris seemed unwilling to ask why and kept his eyes off Max.

"It's not true," Max went on, "because when I came to see you the first time we had no idea that the Minister was a member of the OAS."

"So?"

"The result," Max explained, "is that every event with which the Minister was associated becomes different and new once it no longer means what we thought it to mean at the time."

"That sounds correct to me," said Morris, regaining a more creditable position. "But what does it give us?"

"It's a possible beginning," said Max.

"Perhaps," Morris admitted.

They drank their coffee in silence. Then Morris frowned and set his cup on the table.

"But just take, for example, that mortar shell the morning of Morin's funeral."

"Let's take it," agreed Max. "It's what I was thinking of particularly."

"Well, to me," Morris began, "the whole incident is easily explained in the light of what we know now, without, however, telling us anything new."

"How do you explain it, then?" asked Max.

"You know the story of the suspected member of the government that he put around," said Morris. "It was aimed at drawing suspicion away from himself."

"But," Max interrupted, "whoever suspected him in the first place?"

"Let me finish," said Morris, raising one hand. "The Minister goes one step further. The suspected man knows he's being watched and will try to get rid of the people watching him—the Minister, me and so on. By the way, all that time we were checking an innocent man. Just this afternoon, the Minister was telling me . . ."

"Never mind that now," said Max.

"Then comes the concluding piece," Morris went on, "the faked assassination attempt on himself. No one could suspect him after that."

Max spun his empty glass in irritation.

"It also allows him," Morris continued, ignoring Max, "to take a couple of days' convalescence in Switzerland. There, he fixes up the last details with Soustelle, whom he's given everybody to believe is in Belgium. Perfect!"

"I'm sorry," said Max. "But I can't understand why he should go to such lengths, killing three people and getting hurt himself, simply in order to remove a suspicion that was never there."

"Perhaps he thought it was," Morris argued. "*He* knew he was in the OAS and he couldn't help feeling that others did also. Such fears are common enough."

"Maybe," said Max. "But the Minister is an uncommonly intelligent person; and anything he organized would first have been ratified by Soustelle, who is even more intelligent. Simply out of respect for them, I think we ought to suppose they meant something more by that faked assassination than we so far have discovered."

Morris gestured as if to say, "What?" He had given his opinion, and now he remained silent. Max poured himself some Vichy water and looked at his watch.

"It's three o'clock," he told Morris. "I like my sleep and you have plenty of work to do. So let's not waste more time on this than is necessary."

Max had spoken to urge the prefect to think. For a moment he himself had come to a standstill. But Morris, aware he was being pressed, spoke to relieve the pressure rather than to contribute something new.

"I suppose you saw the chauffeur?" he asked, saying the first thing that came into his head. "He was completely decapitated."

"Yes," said Max, "I saw him."

Then Max sat up. He always talked as if he knew what was coming. But in fact he never did. Had he done, there would have been no point in talking. Now he leaned over the table toward Morris.

"It was just that which impressed me most about the whole incident," he said. "The Minister had everything arranged with the person in the building across the street. Deliberately, he sent out those two motards to die. Perhaps he didn't intend the chauffeur's death, but he didn't do anything to prevent it. He wasn't the sort of man to have done all that simply to lay a false trail which in any case was never needed."

"I don't think he cared much about those two motards, anyway," said Morris. "He'd only had them two days. In fact, I'd transferred them to him when he first gave me the story about the suspected member of the government. It was extra protection."

"And the other two motards?" asked Max.

"Oh, that was different," said Morris, waving a hand. "They'd been with him some time already, a year or more. Their real names, I think, are Pilou and Bernard. But they are known as Al and Jo."

"And what happened to them?" asked Max.

"Nothing," Morris laughed. "What would you expect? They're the toughest men we've had—as tough as their motorcycles. When we got into the courtyard, you know, they were already on their feet, and their machines hadn't stopped running."

"Yes, yes," said Max impatiently. "But what I mean is, where are they now? Are they back riding with the Minister?"

"As a matter of fact, they aren't," Morris told him. "When the Minister went to Switzerland for his 'convalescence,' I gave them the transfer they'd been asking for. It's quite an honor."

The prefect rose suddenly to his feet, his hand to his mouth.

"My God," he said. "I've only just realized . . . my God . . ." he repeated, "my God . . ."

"Realized that you transferred them to ride beside de Gaulle in the parade?" asked Max, smiling.

Morris sank back into his seat and nodded.

Max was the first to break the silence.

"Well!" he said. "We've made some progress this evening. And the Minister hasn't been wasting his time."

"It's a nightmare," was all Morris could say.

He shook his head. But the nightmare wouldn't go.

"Max," he said desperately, "it's not going to be easy. At best there'll be a tremendous scandal, at the worst de Gaulle will be assassinated. Can you imagine it? Those motards will just have to ride up to the car and shoot, in front of all the newsreel cameras. It'll be a public execution."

"Of course," said Max, "they might get killed themselves afterward."

"Who by?" asked Morris. "It's as you said. People will stop the motards from killing, but they don't do anything once they've killed."

"You could arrest them tonight," Max suggested.

"Yes," said Morris, leaving his seat and walking to and fro across the room. "But that would be the scandal. There'd be protests from the Minister. He'd accuse us of calling his loyalty and honor in question. And if the matter got as far as de Gaulle, he'd never believe a word and he'd have the motards ride with him. In fact, the big problem is to know what to do with the Minister. He can't be arrested right now, and he knows it. He'll take every opportunity to act the innocent man."

"So," Max concluded, "you're going to let the two motards ride?"

Morris brought out his handkerchief.

"I can't do that either," he declared wretchedly. "It'd be even worse."

"What situations you civil servants get yourselves into!" Max exclaimed. "Think, if you only paid more attention to de Gaulle's policy than to his person, these assassination attempts wouldn't worry you so much."

The prefect shifted uncomfortably.

"But never mind all that now," said Max, brushing the topic aside. His attention was already fixed on something else ahead. He motioned Morris to sit down.

"I've got an idea that'll appeal to de Gaulle, if it won't to you," he began. "But it should fit your requirements all the same."

Morris prepared himself reluctantly to hear what Max had to say.

"Now, Al and Jo can do the job either during the ride up the Champs-Élysées and back or while de Gaulle's taking the salute on the rostrum. But they're most likely to do it on the Champs-Élysées. They'll be only a few yards from de Gaulle, with nothing between them and the open car. They'll be able to draw and shoot without even changing position, and long before any security man realizes what they're doing. Now, to stop them there, I think we'll . . ."

"Let's see to the details later," Morris interrupted. "But what about the rostrum, in case they try something there?"

Max leaned back.

"In that case," he said with a smile, "we've got them, we've got them all. And," he added with a finger raised toward Morris, "with the minimum of scandal!"

5. THE ASSASSINATION

TWENTY-FIVE

Breakfast on the Fourteenth

The sun was already hot when at eight o'clock that morning a black chauffeur-driven Citroën drew up quietly beneath the Minister's apartment on the luxurious avenue Foch. A young girl stepped out with a long and slender cardboard box under her arm. The façade of the building in front of her was a brilliant white, cut across here and there by green strands of ivy. Above, the sky was blue. It was a summer's day to make your mouth water.

The girl pressed the button that opened the door in the middle of the high, overgrown wall. When she had closed it behind her, she might have thought herself in a country house. There was even a man wearing the trousers of a morning suit conscientiously weeding a corner of the garden. It was a house to the Minister's taste.

The glass doors of the building opened automatically before the girl reached them. She actually went back to make sure she had not been mistaken. A silent lift bore her to the top floor, which was occupied, together with the extensive roof, by the Minister. The girl stepped out of the lift onto a landing flooded by daylight. Rearranging the box under her arm, she rang the bell set in the solid oak frame of the door. It was butler who opened to her. Behind him stretched an apartment that was fully in keeping with the building outside.

"Madam wishes . . . ?" asked the butler.

"To see the Minister," the girl replied promptly.

The butler shook his head.

"I'm afraid that's impossible," he said. "The Minister's still asleep."

"Then can I leave this with you?" asked the girl, presenting the cardboard box.

In these days of plastic bombs, the butler was justifiably suspicious. He cocked his head.

"May I know what it contains?" he asked.

"Certainly," said the girl. "It's a uniform. Here, you can see for yourself."

She lifted one corner of the box for the butler to catch a glimpse of brown material. But this did not satisfy him.

"Would you open it so that I can make sure?" he asked.

The girl obliged by undoing the string and removing the lid. The butler inserted a hand, probed around and finally withdrew it, satisfied.

"So it's a uniform," he agreed. "But the Minister's already got one."

"I know he has," said the girl, as she re-tied the string round the box. "But this one is for him to wear instead."

"Why should he change?" objected the butler.

"It's all explained in this," the girl answered, handing over an envelope.

"Who's it from?" asked the butler.

"From Madame de Gaulle," replied the girl.

"And you?"

"I'm her secretary," said the girl. "I typed it out this morning. There's her signature at the bottom."

"Well," said the butler, puzzled, as he accepted the envelope and the cardboard box, "I suppose there's no harm in a uniform."

"It's all rather confidential," the girl added before she left. "If the Minister has any queries, tell him to phone me at the Élysées. Otherwise Madame will be expecting him to wear the uniform."

"I'll do that," said the butler automatically.

He closed the door behind the girl. He had understood very little of what she had said. Perhaps the Minister would find the contents of the envelope clearer.

The Minister woke, stretched and stepped out of bed into a bathroom sumptuously sculptured in Amtico, a marble substitute that he preferred to the real thing. It was, indeed, so effective that there was no point at which it could be said exactly that the bathroom ended and the rest of the room began. The Minister was feeling in splendid physical condition. His eyes shone back at him in the mirror after eight hours of undisturbed sleep. His hair was thick and silver-gray. His body, clad in light-blue pajamas, showed no unpleasant signs of middle age. He was the envy of his contemporaries, and even of the younger generation.

But as from today, he thought, he'd be something rather more than that. He turned on the shower. He hated the hypocrisy of the fourteenth of July. It commemorated the Revolution, the Revolution with a capital *R*, to which the country turned its thoughts yearly, as to a venerable relic that it never wanted to see rise again. There was indeed nothing more absent from the fourteenth of July than the spirit of revolution. It was merely a day on which the common people were permitted to enjoy themselves while the ruling classes watched carefully over them. The Minister was determined that this should change. It was not for nothing that the fourteenth of July had been chosen for the execution of King Charles de Gaulle.

So the Minister felt he had history behind him as he rinsed himself with a final burst of cold water. He reached for a warm towel. He was eager for breakfast. He shaved briskly, then wrapped himself in a bathrobe, thick and white like the coat of a polar bear. Feeling light and refreshed, he walked to the hall, singing something he remembered from *The Pajama Game*: "This is my once-a-year day, my once-a-year day."

He picked up a pair of sunglasses from a table and called down a corridor to the kitchen.

"I'd like breakfast on the roof today if you don't mind. The weather's so good."

"I thought you might, sir," the butler answered. "The cereal's already there, I'll bring the rest up in a moment."

The Minister marveled at the coolness with which the butler was controlling his excitement. He called once more, and a dog came bounding out from the kitchen—bounding even though it was only a wire-haired dachshund. The Minister picked it up, carried it out onto the balcony and from there up the steps to the roof. He set the dog down in a garden built specially for it.

Had the Minister not been wearing sunglasses, the brightness would have been dazzling. Seen in the sun, and from above, Paris was white like some city of the south. The Minister drew up a chair and sat down to his breakfast. He quickly disposed of a small glass of orange juice, before pouring milk over his cornflakes and sprinkling the mixture with Bemax. He disliked French breakfasts. De Gaulle believed in them and expected his people to follow him, ministers especially. But it was like the headmaster insisting that the staff eat the school lunch. The Minister knew what was good for him.

The butler came up the steps with coffee and a plate of bacon and eggs.

"That looks wonderful," declared the Minister. "You know, I've got the kind of appetite people have when they go camping."

With a steady hand, the butler poured coffee and added milk. The Minister smiled and shook his head.

"I don't know how you do it," he confessed. "*Tell* me how you feel, if you can't *show* me how."

The butler's reserve broke a little.

"I'm feeling pretty good, sir," he admitted with a grin.

"And how's your brother?" asked the Minster.

"I spoke to him on the phone," said the butler. "Al's fine. So's Jo. They reckon they could do it blindfolded."

"I believe them," said the Minister. "After all, we didn't pick them for nothing. But too much confidence is a dangerous thing."

"That's what I told Al, sir," said the butler. "He just laughed and said that it all depends what you're confident about."

"Well, in a way he's right," admitted the Minister. "There'd certainly be something wrong with them if they missed at that range."

"By the way, sir," said the butler, "someone called on you this morning, a young lady from the Élysée, a secretary of Madame de Gaulle . . ."

"A secretary of whom?" exclaimed the Minister.

"A secretary of Madame de Gaulle," the butler repeated.

"And what did Madame want?" asked the Minister.

"The secretary left a box and an envelope," explained the butler.

The Minister looked up in alarm.

"She left a box?" he asked. "Have you checked to see what's inside it?"

"No need to worry, sir," the butler reassured him. "I had a look myself. It's only a uniform."

"A uniform?" frowned the Minister. "Whatever would she leave me a uniform for?"

"No idea, sir," the butler admitted. "I told her you'd already got one. But she said it was all explained in the envelope."

"Well," sighed the Minister, "you'd better get me that envelope."

The butler disappeared down the steps while the Minister gazed vaguely at the dog. His mood had been jarred by the unusual news about the uniform. It rankled him to have something that did not slip easily into the morning as he had planned it. The butler returned after a moment and it was almost with impatience that the Minister reached for the envelope he was carrying.

The letter inside was typed; it was headed "confidential" and it contained a request that struck the Minister as extremely odd.

"Just what kind of a spiel is this!" he exclaimed.

He read the remainder of the letter, stumbling as he did so, not over the form, which was clear and legible, but over the irregularity of the matter expressed.

"Listen to this!" he cried to the butler when he had finished. "She wants me to change my uniform for that one in the box."

"That's what I gathered from the secretary, sir," said the butler.

"But can you guess the reason for it?" asked the Minister.

The butler shook his head to show that he didn't know. And the Minister was shaking his head because he did know. He read excerpts from the letter as if they were written in some obscure foreign language.

"Would you be so kind . . . he's never wanted to change since 1940 and I could never succeed in persuading him to start now . . . he never seems to mind, but I've felt all his embarrassment for him . . . I would for this reason greatly appreciate it if you were to etc., etc."

The butler seemed scarcely more enlightened than he had been before the Minister started reading.

"Shall I tell you what it's about?" asked the Minister. "When de Gaulle takes the salute on the rostrum, he's going to be wearing his usual uniform, the one he's had ever since 1940. Onward to 1940! He won't wear a modern one. Typical. He's stubborn on the little things, but on the big things he's quite different. Algeria's French one year, Algerian the next. The uniform never changes."

"So his wife wants you to change instead?" suggested the butler.

"That's it. What a couple they make!" exclaimed the Minister. "She thinks he looks ridiculous. Now she wants us all to look ridiculous."

"All?" inquired the butler.

"Me, and the ministers of defense and agriculture . . ."

"Of agriculture?" asked the butler.

"He was once a major," explained the Minister, "and he likes to remember it. All the other members of the government wear suits."

"But are your uniforms so different from de Gaulle's?" asked the butler in an attempt to moderate the Minister's annoyance.

"I should say so!" declared the Minister emphatically. "Can you see me in the sort of thing he wears? That long jacket . . . those flapping trousers . . . the cut's quite different. You can imagine the style."

"So what are you going to do?" inquired the butler.

The Minister waved a hand.

"She says here it's not just 'a woman's foolish whim.' But that's precisely what it is. Does she really think we're slighting de Gaulle by wearing modern uniforms? Of course not. De Gaulle certainly doesn't. In fact, I'm sure he believes it's a way of showing he's superior to us. And why today, of all days, should she decide that we should start to change? No, I'll say I never got the message."

"But the secretary told me to ring the Élysée if there were any queries," said the butler. "If we don't ring, then they'll take it that you'll be wearing the uniform."

"She said that?" asked the Minister. "Well, we can at least check their story. Go down and give them a ring."

The butler took the breakfast tray with him.

"Hell," exclaimed the Minister to himself. "Police out on the prowl already."

Opposite him, two helicopters from the prefecture, tilted slightly forward, skimmed over the rooftops. They went on to inspect the antiaircraft guns installed on the roofs overlooking the Champs-Élysées.

"Just the same as before, sir," said the butler when he reported back. "I spoke to the secretary. She confirmed all the letter and said that Madame de Gaulle would be very much obliged if you would do as she asked."

"Thanks!" exclaimed the Minister. "Did you speak to her personally?"

"No, she was dressing," said the butler.

"I've been looking at this letter again," said the Minister. "It's her signature at the bottom all right. I was thinking it might have been one of the minister of finance's practical jokes."

"Well, sir," said the butler, shrugging his shoulders, "if you don't wear the uniform, you'll be the one who'll be out of place. So . . ."

The butler left the conclusion for the Minister to supply.

"Yes, you're right," said the Minister. "There is only one thing to do."

He stayed at his table and thought for a moment. Then his manner changed.

"But we won't begrudge it her," he said. "If we do it, we'll do it gladly. It's a trifling matter. Let's grant the president's widow her last official request. Fetch me the box!"

Back came the butler with the uniform.

"Here you are, sir!" he said. "All wrapped up, with string around it tied in a bow, like a box of chocolates."

The Minister smiled. But the chocolates had been poisoned.

TWENTY-SIX

Max Puts on His Uniform

As he had arranged with the night porter on seeing Morris out, Max was awakened four hours later on the same morning. He was alone. Silesia was still asleep in the next room. Breakfast and an envelope were on the table by his bed. The waiter was pulling the curtains.

"That's enough! That's enough!" Max exclaimed before the man could pull the cord that hung by the other window. The sharp sunlight was hurting his eyes. For a moment he regretted having gone to sleep at all. He might have felt less tired had he stayed awake. But breakfast in bed could only make things worse. He got up and went to the bathroom, where he stood for as long as he could hold his breath under a cool shower. He came back to a breakfast of strong black coffee and croissants. He had a morning in front of him that would be short, whatever happened, and very full.

With his jacket open over a clean white shirt, he went down the stairs of the George V to the taxi that was waiting for him outside. The handle of the car door was hot from the sun when he touched it.

"The prefecture," he said.

"The prefecture," echoed the taxi driver almost absentmindedly as he stretched an arm out of the window to set the meter.

Max sat back. It was cooler after the car had begun to move. Apart from the envelope he had nothing with him. Morris would have seen to the rest. The taxi was slow at first. Vehicles that were to take part in the parade were parked everywhere in the vicinity. On the road beside the Seine the traffic moved faster. Max had no more fears of being late. People were strolling and sunbathing on the river bank. The flags fluttered in the breeze as lightly as the women's dresses.

Max was dropped outside the prefecture. Two men stood on guard at the main entrance. But Max flashed the contents of the envelope—a police identity card made out in his own name—and walked straight through.

Morris had promised to keep his secretary fully occupied, but Max was taking no chances of being seen by the man he had spoken to as Soustelle the evening before. With his head down, he walked quickly across the courtyard to the police mess.

He pushed his way through a fog of cigarette smoke and blurred conversation. Policemen sat on the benches, their helmets on the tables in front of them, playing cards, reading the newspapers and talking. Max walked between them to the back of the room. For a moment he was lost. Then, through a half-open door at the end of a corridor, he caught the back view of a man in shirtsleeves, easing a leg into a knee-high boot. The man turned as Max came into the room, and he grinned, standing awkwardly with his leg only half inside his boot.

"Mister Max?" he asked, holding out his hand.

"That's me," said Max, comforted to see that his partner was exactly the kind of man he had wanted.

"Call me Coxy," said the man, grinning again.

This was odd. For it was exactly what Max had been going to do.

"Well, there you are, sir," said Coxy, pointing to a corner, "There are your things."

The ceremonial uniform of the motard had been laid out carefully on a bench. Coxy echoed Max's thoughts as he bent down to examine it.

"Let's hope it fits you, sir," he said. "It's the boots that are the worst. Even I can hardly get mine on, and they're my own. There!" he exclaimed, as he succeeded in fitting his heel into the heel of his boot. He stamped on the stone floor to prove and to settle their union.

"That's better," he said. "Once they're on you," he explained, "they're like your own skin, they're so comfortable. It's the getting them on that's the difficult part."

Max closed the door and stripped to his vest and underpants. He went to the mirror, where he put on the blue shirt and tie. Then he picked up the dark blue jacket with the red shoulder straps and silver buttons.

"Trousers first, sir," said Coxy cheerfully.

"I was just going to look at it," said Max, excusing himself. "I wasn't going to put it on."

"That's all right, sir," Coxy assured him. "Trousers go under the jacket when it's buttoned, like ordinary clothes."

Max drew on the trousers, hopping alternately on each foot. He was glad to find that they were not rough inside like most uniform material. He buckled them at the waist. They felt a good fit. He reached for the jacket.

"I can see that you've fallen for that jacket," said Coxy, grinning. "But it's the boots next, sir."

Max folded the bottom of the trouser tightly round his ankle. The boot came on easily, only to stop at the heel. Max stamped but the boot would go no further.

"Just a moment, sir," said Coxy, coming over.

He told Max to lift his leg, and he gripped the boot tightly with both hands. He pulled and twisted for a moment.

"Now stamp," he said, standing back.

Max stamped and the heel slipped through. The same method worked with the second boot.

"Just practice, sir," said Coxy. "Six years in the service I've been now. You get to know a thing or two. Good idea, wasn't it, sir," he added conversationally, "having me and you dressing together? You'd have been noticed otherwise, and it'll give you a chance to try the bike before we join up with the others."

As he walked over the stone floor in his boots, Max felt three-quarters a motard already. It was almost with a feeling of pride that he stood before the mirror watching his thumb push the silver buttons of the jacket through the holes. He flexed his arms and the jacket settled comfortably on his shoulders. He turned back to the bench. There was more to go on yet. Coxy, who was all ready, was holding it up for him.

"Here you are, sir," he said.

Max raised his arms and Coxy fitted on the broad white leather belt with the holster waist-high on the right side. A diagonal strap from the waist to the shoulder and down across the back completed the harness. Max tapped the holster.

"All ready and loaded, is it?" he asked.

Coxy nodded.

"Same with you?" Max wanted to know.

"It's all there, sir," said Coxy in a tone that suggested he felt it indecent to check details he himself had seen to.

"Then there's this, sir," said Coxy, pinning to Max's lapel the blue metal disc with the word "Police" across the middle.

Only the white crash helmet and gauntlets were left. Max tied the strap of the helmet under his chin.

"Do you know Al and Jo?" he asked.

"I should say so, sir," said Coxy chattily. "I wasn't surprised to hear about it either. They were always a talkative pair. With us at least."

"We're riding right behind them, aren't we?" asked Max a little nervously.

"No need to worry, sir," said Coxy briefly. "The revolver's all ready. At the first suspicious move, you just point it at the man's back and pull the trigger. At that range you can't miss. Besides, there's a man every ten yards down the Champs-Élysées ready to shoot if Al and Jo even move out of line. De Gaulle may believe in baraka, but we believe in taking precautions."

"I mean," Max corrected himself, "won't the very fact that we're directly behind make them suspect anything?"

"Not a chance, sir," said Coxy reassuringly. "A thing like that wouldn't put them off. They won't even notice."

Max picked up the white gauntlets.

"Besides," Coxy added, "they've had extras in parades before at the last minute."

The gauntlets were on. Max looked at himself in the mirror.

"Perfect, sir, perfect. You'd take anybody in."

Coxy frowned.

"So much of the motard is in his uniform and bike," he explained, "that I've found people never look at the man."

Max decided that Coxy had once again echoed his thoughts. He was pleased with what he saw in the mirror. He looked around. Nothing that he needed had been left behind. He stretched inside his uniform and took a few steps.

"Okay, sir?" asked Coxy.

Max nodded. Coxy opened the door.

"Well, sir," he said with a smile, "you're on."

They walked through the police mess to jeers of reluctant admiration. Coxy led the way to a garage in one wing of the prefecture. Two BMWs were propped up on their stands, their whitewalled tires gleaming and their metalwork shining black and silver. Large motorcycles are not made in France. They are imported, and expensive. To ride one confers great prestige.

"That one's yours, sir," said Coxy, pointing. "I've had a look at her myself. She shouldn't give you any trouble."

Coxy pushed his own off its stand and let it free-wheel slowly forward. Standing on one footrest, he swung the other leg over and started the engine with a kick. He braked and looked behind him. It was some time since Max had ridden a motorcycle and he could not afford to begin again with anything so spectacular. He rested a boot on the kick-starter and pumped downward once. The engine did not roar into life: indeed, its first note was almost inaudible. There was little or no vibration in the handlebars. Max swung himself into the seat and rolled the machine off its stand, bringing his feet up to engage first gear as he did so.

He followed Coxy out into the courtyard. He was much more comfortable. A moment ago, on his feet, he had felt like a knight without his horse. In front, Coxy stopped and started as he threaded his way through the vehicles and pedestrians in the courtyard. His feet never touched the ground. He made a path for Max, who was able to ride at an even speed. The men at the gate held up the traffic for them as they passed under the archway into the street. Coxy waved for Max to come up beside him.

"Okay, sir?"

"Okay," said Max.

Coxy accelerated away. Max followed, pleased to be riding a motorcycle in such weather. It was like taking a shower of cool air. He was astonished by the ease with which such a powerful machine could be controlled.

At the bridge across the Seine into the place de la Concorde the chain of police forming the traffic barrier broke to let them through. The pavements were thick with spectators pressing against the railings that had been set in place overnight. But the bridge and the square were free of all traffic. the stone of the newly cleaned buildings at the end of the square shone almost white in the sun. Max leaned his machine to one side, then to another. He stood up on the footrests and settled down again. Coxy, in front, was doing the same. They were taking the edge off their nervousness.

In front of the rostrum they turned into the Champs-Élysées. All along its length it was empty, like an airport runway. People stood a hundred deep on either side. The crowd was restless and excited, but as yet there was little noise. Max followed Coxy up the middle of the avenue. When they caught sight of the other motards parked beneath the exhibition hall at the first crossroads, Coxy slowed and Max came alongside. For a moment they rode abreast. Then Coxy's hand came off the accelerator and hung out across the road toward Max. The tips of their white gauntlets touched. They rode fast into the closed-off area outside the exhibition hall and parked.

As they got off their machines, a burly motard, his chest resplendent with decorations, waded toward them.

"So you're the two extras?" he said. "Though God knows what we needed you for. Anyway, you've arrived on time, which is something. Know your positions?"

Max and Coxy nodded.

"The speed's the usual. Fifteen kilometers an hour, no more, no less. Watch the man in front of you. That's all."

"Thank you, sir."

"And won't we just be watching them," said Coxy with relish as the captain walked away.

"Well," asked Max, "where are they?"

Coxy glanced over Max's shoulder. Whereas all the other motards were grouped together under the trees, there were two sitting on their machines who seemed to be talking as carelessly as if they were in a café.

"Al's the one with the moustache," said Coxy. "It's about the only way you can tell them apart."

"They certainly don't seem to be paying much attention to us," said Max.

"Like I told you, sir," answered Coxy.

"Which is yours and which is mine?" asked Max.

Coxy cocked his head to one side in thought.

"You'll be behind Al, sir, on the left side of the car," he said at last, "and I'll be on the right with Jo."

Max shrugged his shoulders. Between Al and Jo, there wasn't much to choose. At this point the captain called out to the men under the trees. They came sauntering over to where their motorcycles were parked. Max and Coxy got back into the saddle. As each of the engines was started, more and more of the crowd nearby turned to watch. Children tried to squeeze their faces through the railings to get a closer look. For them, and for many adults reluctant to admit it, the motards were the most exciting part of the parade.

Max shifted into position behind Al and waited for the signal to go. The captain's boot left the ground for his footrest. Behind him, forty boots followed suit. A flag flew on the captain's machine as he led his squad slowly across the empty avenue to the president's palace. Max watched the man three yards in front of him. To keep in line was for the moment his only concern. The motards drove to the main gate of the Élysée, beside the high wall round the president's garden. Above them the branches of the trees on either side of the road almost touched. Here, there were few people. It was a spacious, exclusive area, the more agreeable side of officialdom.

Meanwhile, for the first time in many years, an empty train was drawing up at Red Cross, where three hundred armed paratroopers had suddenly assembled. Earlier in the morning, Silesia and the sentry had been reported missing. Neither had been found. The commander had hesitated. But, when no police came to disturb them, he decided to say nothing to headquarters about the events of the night. Silesia, at any event, was not his concern. As for the sentry, he had probably lost his nerve at the last moment and deserted. Thus, when everything went as planned and the commander had his men on the train at exactly the scheduled time, he had no more doubts.

The train ran through several stations before it could switch onto the line that would take it under the Champs-Élysées. People on the platforms stared and shrugged their shoulders. Troops late for a parade, they seemed to be thinking, who could only get there on time by taking a Métro to themselves. It was odd, perhaps, and even irregular, but whatever it was, it had nothing to do with them. The attitude of the station-masters seemed much the same. As he passed through, the commander observed these details with satisfaction. He had predicted exactly that.

But an hour previously all the Métro stations under the Champs-Élysées had been closed to the public. Morris had conferred with the civil engineers and had decided that the OAS could come under the Champs-Élysées through two stations only, those beneath the arc de Triomphe and the place de la Concorde. Morris had three heavy machine guns and a hundred and fifty men placed on each platform. The same number of men stood ready at the stations in between. The prefect left the command, together with some instructions on tactics, to one of his subordinates. After a last inspection, he hurried to the surface to proceed to his final duties on the official rostrum.

But the commander of the paratroopers knew nothing of all this. His train passed through station after station as if it had been invisible. Every platform of uninquisitive faces that went by filled him with contempt, and with confidence that the very extraordinariness of his operation would make it succeed.

There was a crowd on the pavement opposite the gate to de Gaulle's palace, a crowd of which at least one half was composed of policemen, in plain clothes and in uniform. Those who could see through the open gates into the courtyard of the Élysée began to cheer and wave. An official signaled to the fleet of forty waiting motards. Twenty moved forward past the gate to form the front half of the escort. Al and Jo were the first men in the second half. Max and Coxy were still right behind them, their engines ready in first gear and their boots barely touching the ground. The officials stood back. Half the crowd stiffened while the other half abandoned itself to its enthusiasm. Wearing his general's uniform, de Gaulle waved from the open Citroën as it swept through the gate to insert itself in the center of the spearhead formed by the front motards. The captain rode at its tip. Simultaneously, the second group of motards fanned out to seal off the car from behind. Max had been slower than Al in getting away, but the Citroën was not traveling fast and he found his correct position after a moment.

Coxy was on the other side. The motards had enclosed de Gaulle inside a flexible suit of armor.

From the shaded road beside the wall of the palace garden, the motorcade wheeled into the Champs-Élysées. As they straightened out, Max looked up past Al at the arc de Triomphe on its hill far ahead. The noise made by the crowd drowned that of the motorcycle engines. It was because he had had this roar in his mind that Max had found the Champs-Élysées so quiet when he had come up it a quarter of an hour before. There was a confusion of colored flags being waved, not only from the pavements but from every floor of the buildings on either side. Max saw all this out of the corner of his eye. He was concentrating entirely on the broad back in front of him. Where Al's tires had been, those of Max followed an instant later. They might have been riding tandem.

A hundred feet underneath the rostrum on the place de la Concorde, Morris's men leaned out over the platform edge to watch for the train whose distant rumble they had just begun to hear. Other men crouched behind the protecting shields of the heavy machine guns. The rest held themselves in readiness.

The sound of the approaching train became louder. The watchers on the platform drew back as the front lights came suddenly into view at the bend in the tunnel. The train slowed. All the weapons on the platform were aimed and ready to fire. The first carriage came into the station almost at walking speed.

Paratroopers at the open doors had their feet out ready to step off onto the platform. When they saw the heavy machine guns pointing at them they drew quickly back. But they had nowhere to retreat to. The train could go only forward or back.

"Accelerate!" their commander screamed to the driver. For a few moments only and for just long enough to allow the front carriage to clear the platform, the driver did so. Then, in accordance with the instruction that Morris had left him, the man in the station-master's office leaned on a switch and cut off the current. The train freewheeled slowly forward to stop inside the tunnel. The back lights were only five yards from the end of the platform.

The man in the station-master's office waved and picked up the telephone: the machine guns moved forward to hold the stationary train in their sights, while at the next station along the line, men got down onto the platform on their stomachs to cover the tunnel with long-range rifles. The paratroopers were hopelessly trapped.

Max's holster was already unbuttoned. He could see that Al's was not. In fact Al was riding like any other motard. He had done nothing to suggest that he considered his assignment to accompany de Gaulle as anything but the greatest honor. Al sat so solidly in his saddle that Max, whose right hand was constantly at his hip in anticipation, found himself becoming mesmerized. He was afraid he would be too taut to move fast enough when the time came. He took each hand off the grips in turn and stretched his fingers. De Gaulle was no more than six yards away in the back of the Citroën; Max felt that he could even hear him returning the shouts of the crowd.

It came as a shock to Max when, after a minute's intense concentration, he realized that Al was breaking away to the left, following the man in front of him. They had reached the arc de Triomphe already. The Citroën went on unescorted to draw up before the tomb of the Unknown Soldier underneath the arch. Still in formation, the motards parked at the side of the square, close to the crowd.

A hundred yards away, de Gaulle was getting out of the Citroën. The distance was sufficient for Max to feel less tense. Besides, Al seemed to be sitting at attention in his saddle. Homage to the dead of France, even when rendered by de Gaulle, was still too serious an affair to be broken into by an assassination. Max risked a glance sideways to Coxy. He, too, had relaxed a little. He shook his head as if to say, "Not to worry yet, sir." Max nodded his agreement.

The prefect's subordinate stood on the end of the platform and called through a megaphone to the men in the train.

"Open the doors and come down onto the tracks one by one, unarmed. The current has been switched off, you have nothing to fear."

In the front carriage, the commander oscillated between despair and rage—rage not against the police forces on the platform but against the "politicians," Boudin, Soustelle and the Minister, who had organized the operation. Only when he had convinced himself of the worthlessness of his superiors could the idea of capitulation to government forces seem not dishonorable. A door opened and the first paratrooper jumped down swearing onto the tracks, to be followed at a regular rate by the others.

A band of ex-servicemen played mournful music as de Gaulle laid a large wreath on the tomb of the Unknown Soldier, stepped back and saluted. It was the most solemn part of the official day. France was excusing itself before its dead soldiers for holding a military parade. Under the arch, only the newsreel men were active. De Gaulle was at attention. Even the band had stopped playing. They held their instruments like rifles. Then de Gaulle turned and walked briskly back to his car.

Forty boots clicked their engines into gear and moved slowly forward behind their captain. Max looked quickly over at Coxy, whose hand slipped off the front brake to make a sharp cutting gesture. Al and Jo would come to life on the long run back down the Champs-Élysées to the rostrum. It would be for Max and Coxy to deprive them of this life. As the motards slipped into position round the Citroën Max began to realize that he could no longer tell how much of the anxiety he felt was for Al and how much was for himself. The two had become one.

TWENTY-SEVEN

Salute the Rostrum

The Minister arrived on the rostrum rather later than his colleagues. The confusion he found there was extreme. The prefect had not yet arrived. None of the ministers knew where to stand. Each nonetheless expected the other to enlighten him. But not even the minister of information could tell anybody anything. When ignorance had been proven general, they had shrugged their shoulders. Turning their backs on the parade, the ministers had formed small groups among themselves for the purposes of conversation.

The minister of finance tried, in the absence of the prefect, to assemble his colleagues into line. But if to the head of state they were obedient to the point of subservience, they were especially touchy about receiving orders from each other. They paid no attention whatever to the minister of finance.

He strolled over to meet the Minister. There, to regain some status, he began to tell a story.

"Have you heard this one?" he asked.

Once the Minister had decided to wear the old uniform, it no longer bothered him. He even felt pleased to be doing Madame de Gaulle a favor. He surveyed the scene around him with intense interest and prepared to lend a quarter of his attention in the meanwhile to what the minister of finance had to tell. But for some unaccountable reason there was a delay.

"All right, don't tell me," the Minister forestalled him. "It's another one about St. Peter at the Gates of Heaven."

"A dentist comes to St. Peter looking for work in Heaven," began the minister of finance, undaunted. "But St. Peter says, 'What would you do? Nobody's got teeth in Heaven.' Then . . ."

And then, thought the Minister, as his colleague hurriedly excused himself, the presence of the head of the country's finances was fortunately requested elsewhere. It was a story with a happy ending.

The prefect had still failed to show up. The Minister observed the activities of his colleagues and was disinclined to participate. Already he felt separated from them. He crossed the red carpet of the rostrum and leaned with both hands on the balustrade. The crowd beneath was still quiet. The Minister looked up the Champs-Élysées at the colorful but massive motorcade that was advancing slowly down toward him. It seemed to swell with the cheers it received. But for the Minister, it was a wave that was building up only the better to break.

"So it's true!"

The Minister started at this exclamation from behind. He turned to find the minister of defense standing there indignantly in his old uniform. He smiled almost playfully.

"What's so funny?" cried the minister of defense. "Do you like your new clothes?"

"I'm very happy to wear them," declared the Minister mysteriously. "There are things more important than uniforms."

"You're a disappointment to me," observed the minister of defense. "I thought I'd at least get some support from you. I've never been so humiliated in my life."

The Minister shrugged his shoulders, but said nothing.

"Maybe you're in the know a little," his colleague intimated with sudden suspicion. "You're looking rather smug."

"I promise you," said the Minister, "that I know no more about it than you do."

"Quite apart from the administrative side, I don't mind admitting I was frightened," exclaimed the minister of defense. "How was I to know that the uniform hadn't got plastic buttons that exploded when I tried to do them up?"

"How indeed," agreed the Minister.

"I was forced to make it an official matter," his colleague went on. "The Army has rules on uniforms, rules that I must abide by. I couldn't move an inch before confirming it at the highest level . . ."

"No sooner had St. Peter turned the dentist away," interrupted the minister of finance, "than there was a second knock on the door. 'Who's there?' he asked. 'A doctor,' was the answer. 'Please go away,' said St. Peter. 'No one's got bodies in Heaven.' Finally . . ."

But would it really be "finally," wondered the Minister, as his colleague ran off to pick up a thread somewhere else. he turned back to the minister of defense, who was telling him what steps he had taken to confirm the strange news he had received that morning.

"I phoned Morris. He'd heard something vague about it. In the end he thought I'd better do what Madame de Gaulle wanted. But I didn't really believe the story was true until I saw the same uniform on you just now."

The minister of agriculture suddenly appeared between his two colleagues. He wore the old uniform with an expression of pleasure that he knew he ought to hide but couldn't.

"Tell me," asked the minister of defense sharply, "did a girl come round to you early this morning with that uniform?"

The minister of agriculture beamed.

"I have a confession to make," he admitted eagerly. "She did bring me a uniform. But I got my own out of the cupboard. I'd been wanting to put it on for years, of course. Only with de Gaulle wearing his, I'd always felt I'd look a little . . ."

"Ridiculous?" suggested the minister of defense.

"That's it," said his colleague. "That's how I felt I'd always look if I ever tried to imitate him."

"Yes," commented the minister of defense. "You and I haven't at all the same problem."

"Then forget it," advised the Minister, "since you're the only person concerned by it."

The minister of defense was made to feel rather small. He retreated out of the Minster's sight.

There was still no order on the rostrum. The Minister returned to the balustrade. He glanced up against the sun at the president's car and its shining escort. It had less than halfway to go. It was enormous. It was drawing the crowd along with it. The Minister could see de Gaulle in the back of his car. But of the motards that surrounded him, it was impossible to distinguish one from the other. Helicopters hovered above. Soldiers patrolled the rooftops, next to others who swept the sky from the swivel seats of their antiaircraft guns and still more who covered the avenue below with long-range rifles. In the middle of the road in front of the Minster, a manhole was raised and quickly lowered, giving a glimpse of a helmeted head. Only seconds later, the lone motard who led the parade by several hundred yards passed over it. Every now and then, in order to adjust his distance from the motorcade, he would halt for a moment, before moving off again with his siren full on. The crowd in front of the Minister began to cheer. The motard was the motorcade in miniature.

The Minister turned from the balustrade at the sound of the prefect's voice. Morris had arrived back late from his duties underground. He carried a sheet of paper which he consulted feverishly before assigning each minister to his place in the line. But opposite the two members of the government in uniform, the prefect stopped to explain some final instruction that was greeted in one case by a blissful nod, in the other by a resigned shrug of the shoulders.

"I've just time to tell you the end," announced the minister of finance at his colleague's uniformed shoulder. "St. Peter sends the doctor away, but there's another knock soon afterward. 'Who's this?' asks St. Peter. 'A psychiatrist,' comes the answer. 'What do I want with a . . .' St. Peter begins to say, out of habit. But then he says, 'No, no, please come in.' 'Why the sudden change?' asks the psychiatrist. St. Peter explains. 'Our Father thinks he's de Gaulle.' "

The Minister laughed perfunctorily. His colleague's supply of such stories seemed endless. The Minister even suspected him of having scriptwriters.

It was time, the last time, to take his place among his colleagues. The Minister stood to the right of the spot marked for the president. He noticed that the step from which, to distinguish himself from his cabinet, de Gaulle normally took the salute, had been continued all the way along the rostrum. The Minister cocked his head. It was encouraging, he thought, to see any indication of a movement toward equality, even at this low level, even at this late stage.

"That's a nice bit of cloth," said Morris, taking the material of the Minister's sleeve between two fingers.

But the Minister refused to rise to the sarcasm.

"Yes," he agreed, "I like it too. Just for one day," he exclaimed confidentially in the prefect's ear, "I don't mind wearing it. For a favor."

"All the same," said Morris considensed, "it was an unusual business."

"Unusual, perhaps," admitted the Minister. "But understandable. After all, it's her privilege. Why shouldn't she use it?"

"Especially with the situation as it is," observed the prefect.

"Quite," agreed the Minister. "She should take every opportunity."

"By the way," said the prefect, "there's been no report yet of anything suspicious."

"That's good to hear," said the Minister enthusiastically. "You know, Morris," he added, shaking his head, "I can't understand what Max was fussing about the other day."

"Over the weather, you mean?" asked the prefect.

"Yes," said the Minister. "Extraordinary him getting an interest in a thing like that. Look what we've got today. Security's fine and there's a perfect blue sky. Not a cloud to be seen."

"Well," said Morris, "I told him there was nothing in it. But he wouldn't listen."

"And he came along to me," pursued the Minister sadly. "All that way for nothing. Poor old boy. I just packed him off on the first plane back to London. Even paid his ticket for him."

"Frankly," confided Morris in the Minister's ear, "I think he's getting a bit past it . . ."

They considered this conclusion together as they gazed for a few moments at the oncoming motorcade. Then Morris suddenly turned.

"There's something I forgot to tell you!" he exclaimed. "He wants you to . . ."

An interruption was provided by the arrival of Prime Minister Pompidou. He came panting up the steps directly behind them in a dark blue double-breasted suit, in whose coarse lines the Minister recognized the clumsy hand of many tailors of his acquaintance. Pompidou withdrew a handkerchief from his breast pocket and dabbed the perspiration from his face.

"What a life!" he exclaimed to Morris.

"I wouldn't say that," the prefect replied kindly. "After all, it's quite something to be prime minister."

"Prime minister, schmime minister!" cried Pompidou. "The Rothschilds treated me better."

He whispered something in the prefect's ear, stepped back and confirmed it with an earnest nod of the head.

"You did?" echoed Morris disbelievingly. "You actually had to brush his coat for him this morning?"

The news that the prime minister had finally consummated his relationship with the president was passed down the line. The ministers gave the man who was theoretically their superior a series of ribald looks. Pompidou grinned self-consciously back at them before taking his place.

"We've hardly a moment left," said Morris, returning to the Minister.

He was forced to raise his voice. The noise of the motorcade was beginning to drown everything.

"Left for what?" asked the Minister.

"I forgot to tell you," shouted Morris. "He wants you to salute."

"He?" inquired the Minister. "Who?"

"He," said Morris, indicating the motorcade. "He with a capital *H*."

"He wants me to what?" exclaimed the Minister, frowning so hard that it seemed to Morris he could not have heard.

"To salute," Morris shouted.

"So we all wear the old uniform," cried the Minister, striking off each item on his fingers, "we all stand on the same step and we all salute!"

The prefect nodded quickly. There was no time for discussion. This had been his intention in arriving so late on the rostrum.

"Yes," he shouted as he moved to go. "There's to be no discrimination between ministers and president, he wants you all to salute, all to look the same . . ."

"You mean that he's ordering us all to be equal?"

With an awkward movement of his head Morris admitted that he was.

"That's the last act of a dictator!" shouted the Minister in the prefect's ear.

Morris was not even sure that these were the words he had heard. For there came from the crowd a roar that seemed to engulf them like a sudden yawn. The motorcade wheeled into the place de la Concorde directly beneath the rostrum. And Morris stared down in horror as he saw Al, like a swimmer beginning a slow crawl, bring his right arm from the handlebar back to his hip.

TWENTY-EIGHT

Assassination

When Al's arm went back, Max was ready, almost too ready. His hand had reached his holster an instant before Al's had reached his. Then it had stopped, because Al's had stopped. Al did not even unbutton his holster. He patted it instead and his hand returned to the grip in front of him. It had not been the movement of a frightened man. It had not been the assassination attempt itself, abandoned at the last second through failure of nerve. It was merely a final verification that Al had accomplished with the utmost serenity. He had betrayed nothing but the quiet confidence of a professional operator.

Max set both hands thankfully on the grips. He leaned the motorcycle first right, then left, before the motorcade drew up behind the rostrum. The president's Citroën slipped through the gap in its escort left by two of the front motards and stopped beside the pavement in the center of the square. The crowd which had gathered on this side of the place de la Concorde was small by comparison with the mass of people Max had already seen. The real show would begin in a few minutes' time on the other side. Max felt he was backstage as he watched de Gaulle step out onto the pavement with scarcely any applause to accompany him.

The president's car moved forward to join the group of stationary black Citroëns that had brought the ministers. At a signal from their captain, the motards parked in a line along the length of pavement reserved to them. Max caught a final glimpse of de Gaulle walking under the sun across the twenty-five yards of pavement to the entrance of the rostrum. He was followed at a respectful distance by two men in civilian suits. The red hangings of the rostrum backing were held aside for him. He disappeared up the stairs beyond.

The motards held themselves to attention along the pavement, each man's machine parked in front of him. They and the rostrum were separated only by the breadth of empty pavement. The motards were still in formation. Between Max and Coxy stood the two men who had ridden a year with the Minister, their eyes to the front, their arms straight down by their sides.

A roar from behind indicated that de Gaulle had taken his place on the rostrum. The roar was sustained as the first column of troops passed by. Al had not moved. He gave no indication to Max that they were not to spend the next three-quarters of an hour with their backs to the parade like a group of unlucky spectators. Max was becoming as taut from waiting as he had been on the motorcycle. The line of his shoulders was not straight. His right was higher than his left. It meant that his hand was that much nearer his holster.

De Gaulle was reviewing a cross-section of the armed forces of France. With the passage of each contingent, the crowd's applause had somehow accumulated down the length of the Champs-Élysées. It suddenly burst onto the place de la Concorde as a formation of jets from the French Air Force swept overhead at treetop height to drop their sound behind them like bombs.

It was at this moment that Al turned. Max saw him out of the corner of his eye. He could even hear him because he was thinking of nothing else. Al turned right round. Max was about to follow him when he remembered that he was not on the motorcycle any more. It was no longer a question of keeping in formation. Al had disappeared. Max still did not look round. He delayed a few seconds longer before glancing sideways at his partner.

Coxy was waiting for him. Jo too had gone. He and Al had crossed five yards of the pavement already. They were walking abreast toward the entrance of the rostrum. It was time for Max and Coxy to follow them.

The captain had noticed nothing. He was standing at attention at the end of the line and, like the others, he was facing in the opposite direction. The path across the pavement from the row of motards to the rostrum was straight. It ran between the Egyptian obelisk and the playing fountain. Max felt some of the spray on his face.

Al and Jo strode purposefully onward, their arms swinging freely by their sides. Their mission was nearing completion. But they were still visible to any onlooker who might care to glance their way. Neither made a move for his gun.

Without hesitation they pushed the red backdrop of the rostrum aside and stepped out of the sun. But the curtain through which they had passed had not yet swung shut. Max and Coxy were able to slip noiselessly after them into the darkness beyond.

They saw Al and Jo as no more than outlines at the bottom of the staircase that de Gaulle had used a short time before. The only light came from the rostrum ahead. Max and Coxy drew their revolvers. A few seconds later, Al and Jo did the same. Already the order was being reversed. One behind the other, the two pairs of motards climbed the stairs. Halfway, they stopped. Then Al and Jo took two steps more. Max and Coxy stayed where they were. Ahead the curtains of the rostrum had been drawn almost shut. They framed the outline of a single man. His right arm was bent in a military salute. The cut of his uniform was loose and dated. He was standing high on some kind of platform.

Neither pair of motards questioned the identity of the outline. For Al, the stance, the dress and the style of the salute were typically those of de Gaulle. But for Max they could belong to no one but the Minister. The salute was a little halfhearted. The outline was not even standing still. It was shifting sideways across the space left between the curtains. The Minister, unused to firearms rather than doubtful of his motards' accuracy, was anxious to be as far from the victim as possible at this eleventh hour.

He did not know that the curtain was open only on him. Nor did he know that, over the phone to the prefecture and in the early hours of the morning, Madame de Gaulle had hesitated a long time before giving Morris her consent to the execution of the man who had planned so carefully that of her husband. Once her cooperation had been assured, events had followed faithfully the course Max had set for them.

Al and Jo took another step upward. The man who stood with his back to them could only be de Gaulle. No one else wore that uniform. No one else took the salute. No one else stood so high.

There could be no point in delaying matters any longer. Max heard two distinct clicks as Al and Jo released their safety catches. Slowly they raised their revolvers. Curled around each trigger was a forefinger of white leather. The two motards prepared to take careful aim. During the several moments that followed, the roar of a tank regiment passing below the rostrum was no more than a kind of silence against the sound Max was waiting to hear.

A loose curtain framed the entrance onto the rostrum a few steps above. Its red cloth rippled as, behind it, two revolvers were brought to bear in perfect simultaneity on the pair of advancing motards. For Al and Jo the ripple was due only to the breeze. And perhaps that was all it was. But for Max and Coxy, the curtain nonetheless concealed, on either side, a member of de Gaulle's private bodyguard, dressed American-style in padded suits and hats. The "gorillas" were invisible to Al and Jo, but through the small holes made at eye-level in the curtain, there was no movement of the two motards that could escape them. Al and Jo had been covered even before they had drawn their revolvers at the foot of the stairs. The motards would kill the man they took to be de Gaulle, only to die themselves an instant later.

Silesia could not see the motards, but she knew they were there. She was watching the gorillas, and when their trigger fingers tightened, she hitched up her doctor's bag of instruments. Her manner, like her white coat, was professional, even surgical, as she listened in the wings for the shots that would call her onto the rostrum.

Morris was already out there. He stood behind the row of ministers, the row he had organized a short while before. He was peering at a notebook, learning by heart the spontaneous declaration that he would be dictating in a moment to representatives of the press. He repeated the practiced phrases in a rapid undertone. "He would have been proud to have known that he died in the service of the president. Selflessly he sacrificed . . ." Morris knew it had to be soon; he had seen the Minister's insidious movement across the carpet away from de Gaulle. But the shots had not yet come. Morris's stomach went suddenly hollow as he realized that it could be only a matter of moments before they did.

The Minister was wincing already. He had always been frightened by firearms, and in peacetime he found them even more alarming. He was still closer to de Gaulle than he would have liked. But it was having to salute that prevented him from going any farther. His protruding elbow added more than a foot to his breadth.

For some minutes a general unease had been taking hold of him. He was not in the habit of allowing himself to be planned for by somebody else. He had consented to the change of uniform simply to humor the wife of a condemned man. But the condemned man, too, had had a whim—a desire for equality between ministers and president requiring the salute and the same level of platform for each.

It struck the Minister as odd that husband and wife should thus have decided, simultaneously and independently of each other, on matters so closely connected. Not only that, they had decided in ways that were hardly in character. Never before had the self-effacing Madame de Gaulle asked a favor of the Minister. Never before had de Gaulle shown a wish to make more than a one-man team out of the government.

It was very strange. But the Minister realized it could only be strange if behind it there was a reason unknown to him. Aware that there was something he did not know, the Minister began to lose a little self-confidence. Even if the morning ended as it should, he thought, these last acts of de Gaulle and his wife would always puzzle him.

It was at this moment that the Minister felt a cool breeze from behind. Al and Jo, followed by Max and Coxy, had just brushed their way through the hangings at the foot of the staircase.

For a short while, there was no reaction from the Minister. Wholly absorbed in examining the odd conduct of de Gaulle and his wife, the Minister had even lost his fear of firearms. It came back with a vengeance when the air from behind fanned his theoretical doubts into a consuming terror.

He had more than a premonition of what was going to happen. He had a sure and certain knowledge of some unknown danger. Desperately he sought an answer.

He tried a glance first to the right, then to the left. He looked like a man caught on a hot day in a collar too tight for him. Though his head each time had hardly moved, he had seen that the curtain behind de Gaulle was closed.

The Minister sobbed. The shock almost brought him to his knees. He felt more than pure fear for his life. There was horror at the contrast between his own loneliness and abandonment and the vastness of the machinery mounted against him.

The revolvers behind were raised and ready to fire. But Al and Jo hesitated. Perhaps they were disturbed by the movements of the outline before them. But whatever its cause, their hesitation did not last long. They took yet another step upward. They were almost at point-blank range, and they were less than a second away from pulling the trigger.

The Minister swiveled round. His eyes and mouth opened wide. His hands flew above his head.

"Don't shoot!" he screamed.

The machinery had broken down.

A sudden stupor seized the participants. Morris knew there was nothing he could do. His was essentially a spectator's problem. It was the same for Silesia. Together they turned to the center of things, to Max.

But there, the Minister's reaction had brought momentary paralysis. Like Al, Max had a gun in his hand, and he was equally incapable of pulling the trigger. Al and Jo, for their part, were dumbfounded to discover how near they had come to bringing death to their chief. But where was de Gaulle? To find him meant stepping up onto the rostrum. After long moments of bewildered immobility, it was this that they drove themselves to do.

Behind the curtain, the gorillas' trigger fingers trembled. The Minister was too important a person for them to kill without orders. And they'd

been told to shoot Al and Jo only after the two motards had disposed of
the Minister. Yet here they were, Al and Jo, advancing onto the rostrum in
search of de Gaulle. The gorillas' dilemma reached an intensity at which it
could be resolved only by a reflex action. Which reflex was not a problem:
they had only one. It was the principle of their profession: "If in doubt,
shoot." The gorillas shot. Al and Jo fell back dead into the arms of Max
and Coxy as if all the time they had known they were there.

Their work completed, the gorillas hung back, depending on a signal
from Max. But it was from the opposite direction that the next move issued.

The Minister was coming back to life. He had half turned toward de
Gaulle. With his hand inside the jacket of his uniform, he was tugging
at a weapon concealed beneath his left shoulder. There was still time to
complete the work that Al and Jo had left unfinished.

But no one on the rostrum realized what he was doing. Though they had
heard the shots, they had no idea what had happened. They panicked. De
Gaulle even turned from reviewing a passing tank regiment. The Minister
was bent almost double as he desperately sought to extract his revolver from
its shoulder holster. But it was a maneuver to which he was not accustomed.
He was fumbling in his haste.

At last Max sprang up and slipped round behind him, shielding him
from the television and newsreel cameras. At the same time, with his heavy
gauntlet, he imprisoned the Minister's fumbling hand inside his jacket.

For a moment the Minister was powerless. He was leaning forward,
partly from Max's weight on his back and partly from his own belief that
the position would allow him to reach his weapon more easily.

But quite a different interpretation of the scene was possible. It occurred
to Max at the same time as it was voiced by Silesia.

"It's the shock!" she cried. "The Minister's been taken ill!"

It was the work of a moment for Max to take a lumbar puncture needle
from Silesia, to hold the thick material of the uniform aside and to drive
the long thin needle through the shirt deep into his chest, thrusting at
the heart. The Minister slipped through Max's arms to the carpet of the
rostrum.

He looked up at Silesia. Then, for the first time, it seemed, he recognized
the motard kneeling on the other side of him.

"So, Max," he whispered.

His body relaxed. Silesia got to her feet.

"Such a nice man, too," she said.

6. THE END

TWENTY-NINE

July the Sixteenth

It was Monday morning in Mincing Lane. This fact oppressed the office workers much as did the sun their less fortunate counterparts on the real plantations overseas. It was the extraordinary dullness of Monday that, curiously enough, provoked a degree of life that would not be found again until Friday. Only for the old-timers were jokes about Monday morning the worst part of the morning itself. For the others, just to name the day was enough to produce a smile.

Then there was, of course, old Mr. Palk, who was back from his holiday, as they all called it, and who looked about as fit as he could ever be expected to be.

"Did you have a swim for me, Mr. Palk?" asked a typist, her head on one side and laughing.

Mr. Palk smiled good-humoredly.

"As a matter of fact," he confessed, "I didn't swim at all."

"You went to the seaside and you didn't swim, Mr. Palk?" exclaimed another typist, rather more adventurous then her companion. "So tell us what you did do."

"Yes, tell us," echoed the first.

Mr. Palk tried to shrug the question off.

"Oh, go on, Mr. Palk," the typists chorused. "Be a sport. Go on."

Poor Mr. Palk could not understand their persistence. To him their apparent friendliness seemed barbed with a general Monday morning discontent.

"You know," he said, in a tone designed to persuade them to drop their cross-examination, "I was breathing. That's all I go to St. Anne's to do."

The typists looked at each other and giggled again.

"But where do you do your breathing?" they asked.

"Just in your old boardinghouse?" anticipated the first typist.

"Or in the dance-halls?" suggested the more adventurous one.

Mr. Palk felt himself being persecuted. He shook his head.

"Most of the time," he said, "I sit on one of the benches along the sea front. By now," he added, "I've almost got a bench of my own."

He tried to smile. But the typists had not finished with him yet.

"So you sit on your bench and you breathe," the second one concluded. "But what else do you do when you do that? Do you just sit?"

Mr. Palk began to wonder what past action of his there could have been to cause such vindictiveness. He felt that he didn't really want to reply this time.

"He sits," explained the first typist to her companion, "he stares out to sea and he dreams."

"Yes, he dreams," agreed the other with a laugh. "He dreams he hasn't got asthma."

With a cheery wave the two typists disappeared into their office.

Mr. Palk returned to his desk behind Mr. Cornwall and, though no one noticed, a large tear welled up from the corner of his eye and coursed its way sadly down his cheek.

1. Pseudonymous *Assassination!* co-author and ensuing libel-case defendant Robert Silman's 1959–60 Sorbonne student card.

2. The 1961–62 Sorbonne student restaurant card of Ian Young, co-author behind the Ben Abro pseudonym and co-defendant against Jacques Soustelle's charge of libel.

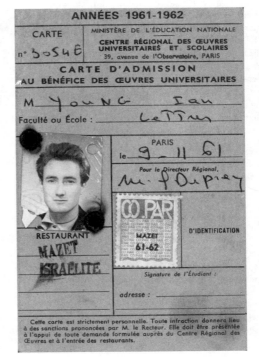

3. During the international libel trial over *Assassination!*, which stretched from November 1964 (through the near-toppling of Charles de Gaulle's administration in 1968) until the suit was dropped in early 1970, witnesses were asked to view this photograph and caption from the 2 March 1963 edition of *Paris Match*. The picture was taken at an executive meeting of the Conseil National de la Résistance (CNR) in Munich and shows (from left to right) "The Four of the Permanent Plot": George Bidault, Paul Gardy, Jacques Soustelle, and Antoine Argoud. The caption explains that in the aftermath of one assassination attempt and while another was being planned, these four men traveled from their places of exile and met to sign a document proving that there was no dissension among them. The caption quips that "Bidault, 'president of the CNR,' has completely adapted to his life in exile. He makes his bed and does his own shopping." Gardy, it says, "has a nostalgia for the army and cries every time he speaks of the Foreign Legion." Soustelle, eventual plaintiff in the libel lawsuit, is described as "the most secretive," a person who "never comes to meetings on time to avoid surprises." Last, Argoud, identified as a graduate from the École Polytechnique, is said to want "to be seen as the symbol of 'the lost soldiers.'" The caption closes with the sentence that made the photo spread so important in the trial: "The methods that they employ and that their associates use in France are those of all conspirators: mystery, fear, and assassination." (Translation by James D. Le Sueur)

JAMES D. LE SUEUR

Before the Jackal:
The International Uproar over *Assassination!*

Picture, if you will, Jacques Soustelle, the ex–French Resistance hero, ex–Gaullist minister, ex–governor general of Algeria, and Aztec scholar of considerable reputation, holding a glass of whiskey and staring into a camera's lens through his mysterious dark glasses. Soustelle raises his glass and toasts one of the most important dates in twentieth-century French history, 13 May 1958. Midway through the French-Algerian War (1954–62)—the extraordinarily violent war of independence that led to the decolonization of French Algeria—13 May 1958 marks the beginning of a civilian- and military-led coup d'état that eventually ended France's ill-fated Fourth Republic and returned the reclusive Charles de Gaulle to the helm of the French state. Flanked by some of France's most powerful men, Jacques Soustelle, with his gangsterlike persona captured by a photographer, radiates power.[1] As flamboyant as this image may seem today, its appearance in the French press had a dramatic effect on the metropolitan European popular imagination during the French-Algerian War because few observers could rule out the possibility that Soustelle was one of the masterminds behind de Gaulle's questionable (and many argued unconstitutional) return to power, the sole purpose of which (at least for Soustelle) was to keep Algeria French.

Now imagine that it is a few years later—near the end of the French-Algerian War—and Charles de Gaulle, the president of the newly created Fifth Republic, has been accused of "double-crossing" his May 1958 supporters by preparing the way for Algeria's independence. Soustelle and other powerful defenders of *Algérie française* (French Algeria) are known to have fled France and to be in hiding "somewhere in Europe," hiding from the mighty clutches of de Gaulle's secret police because—believing themselves to have been betrayed by de Gaulle—they have become his most implacable public enemies. In fact, so severe is the crisis that Soustelle and many other elite politicians and military officials have arrest warrants out on them. Then suddenly, in the midst of this political confusion and betrayal, on 22 August 1962, the world hears that would-be assassins Colonel Jean-Marie Bastien-Thiry and other members of a notorious paramilitary terrorist group known as the OAS (Organisation Armée Secrète), have botched a plot to murder de Gaulle and his wife at Petit-Clamart. And before Colonel Bastien-Thiry becomes the first soldier to be executed for treason during the Algerian conflict, he claims during his trial that he was acting on orders of the Conseil National de la Résistance (CNR), the exiled civilian political group of which Soustelle is one of four leaders and which is considered to be the direct political wing of the OAS.

Now imagine two young English students, Robert Silman and Ian Young, who are studying philosophy at the Sorbonne under Jean-François Lyotard, and who are listening in complete disbelief to the radio reports of the OAS's assassination attempt at Petit-Clamart. As unbelievable and as un-British as the OAS's actions appeared, they also caused Silman and Young to regard Soustelle and the other members of the CNR with uneasy awe. In fact, Silman and Young were so awe-inspired by the bravado of the terrorists' actions that they decided (long before *The Day of the Jackal* was penned by Frederick Forsyth in 1971) to capture the surreal quality of French politics in a political thriller, *July 14 Assassination*.[2] Recalling the powerful images of Soustelle during decolonization and his acrimonious break with de Gaulle over Algeria, they decided to cast the well-known, historical Soustelle as the central fictional character and mastermind behind the dark glasses. With a real-life and ready-made villain (Soustelle) in hand, this is a scenario we can all imagine.

Now imagine the unimaginable. It is the early 1960s and European and American audiences adore Ian Fleming's British secret agent, the very fictional hero whom Silman and Young want to dethrone: Bond, James Bond. In fact, Silman and Young loathe Bond so much that they will author a new fictional antihero's hero to do battle with the redoubtable real-life villain and political castaway, Jacques Soustelle. But in fueling the flames of fictional contempt for Bond, Silman and Young pushed the edge of the literary envelope. If disliking Ian Fleming's macho and flawlessly handsome character of James Bond were not already difficult enough to conceive of, imagine replacing Bond's hypnotic and dashing character with a dull, awkward, and asthmatic bureaucrat named Max Palk (yes, Palk, Max Palk!), who happens to be a physically quite unimpressive but nonetheless brilliant undercover British secret agent.

By the time Silman and Young had finished their pastiche of James Bond in 1963, they had coauthored a remarkable work of fiction that was truly on the cutting edge of a new genre of political thrillers, one that blurred the distinctions between real life and make-believe. *Assassination*'s story might have ended there, with the publication of a best-selling thriller nearly a decade before *The Day of the Jackal* came to press, or it could have started an important literary rebuttal to the Bond novels three decades before the awkward Austin Powers "shagged" his way into movie theaters in 1997 and 1999; however, in blurring the distinctions between fact and fiction, Silman and Young had come too close to the actual history of France at its nadir, immediately after the loss of French Algeria. As a result of adhering too closely to one of France's most notorious political figures during French decolonization, the revealing story of *Assassination* really begins after Jacques Soustelle reemerged from margins of exile in 1963 to file a libel suit against the creators of Max Palk, claiming that his reputation had been sullied *in fact* by the fiction of these aspiring anti–James Bond novelists.

The history of *Assassination* is thus a novel's history, a story of the mixing of fiction and history. It is the story of a historical process that began as history, metamorphosed into fiction, and ended as the history of forgotten fiction. But it is more importantly a unique vignette of French society and politics following what is widely considered the twentieth century's bloodiest war of decolonization. By navigating through a maze of stories and a myriad of (real) lives, the history and the story (keep in mind the difference) of *Assassination* will be woven through with fiction, peppered with tales of exile and intrigue. Yet the publishing and post-publishing history of *Assassination* remains fundamentally a true story about a work of fiction and fact, a story about what really happened—and did not happen; it is the *story* about how Jacques Soustelle—a real-life hero of the French Resistance, the last governor general of Algeria, and one of France's most powerful politicians in an epoch of gut-wrenching chaos—was "deceived" by the very man he helped put in power in 1958, President Charles de Gaulle.[3] More importantly it is about how Soustelle attempted to use a libel suit filed against the authors of the fictitious spy-thriller as a means to exculpate himself from his support for the terrorism of the OAS. Hence *Assassination*'s story underscores the tumultuous history of France after the French-Algerian War and, perhaps better than any other work (fiction or nonfiction), it reveals the depth of the passions that separated opponents and supporters of Algerian independence in France. But it is equally the story of two young, courageous, eager-to-debunk-Bond students who endeavored to create a work of fiction and who struggled to convince the British courts of the veracity of their quasi-fictitious portrayal of Soustelle. Although caught unaware by the claims of Soustelle, they continued to defend the factual basis of their novel because they realized how important it was not to allow Soustelle the opportunity to use it to distance himself from his connections to the OAS and French fascists. In short, the publishing history of *Assassination* is at once a defense against a libel, a pastiche of Bond, a matter of honor, and an important exposé on France's efforts to deal with the most powerful and dangerous terrorist organization in its history: the OAS.

French Algeria

Algeria was unique to France.[4] Of all the French overseas possessions acquired during the heyday of French colonialism in the nineteenth century, only Algeria was considered to be France itself. France conquered the North African territory on the other side of the Mediterranean in 1830 from the Ottoman Turks, whose occupation of Algeria dated from 1574. In 1834 Algeria became a French military colony. During the 1830s and 1840s, the primary resistance to the French occupation of Algeria was orchestrated by the Emir Abdelkader, an Algerian religious and political leader who was able to command a powerful Muslim army that successfully held off the French until 1847.

In 1848 Algeria was divided into three French provinces: Constantine, Algiers, and Oran. Algeria at that point became not just French territory, but French departments—in the same manner that Alaska and Hawaii are considered states in the United States of America, despite their geographic distance from the mainland. After Algeria was divided into three French provinces, many French and other European settlers began to move to Algeria. With the support of the French government, the *colons* (European settlers) expropriated most of the best land from the indigenous Muslim population of Arabs and Berbers (predominately Kabyles). Despite French claims of equality expressed in the so-called rights of man philosophy of French Republicanism, Muslims were treated as second-class citizens by the French, were given conditional citizenship, and faced wide-spread discrimination. Eventually Algerian nationalists, led by Messali Hadj in the 1920s and then by others, began to demand political parity for Algerians. In 1943 the Algerian nationalist Ferhat Abbas drafted the Algerian Manifesto, which proposed an autonomous and democratic Algeria that would maintain a federal relationship with France. Finally, frustrated by the unwillingness of the French authorities to come to the bargaining table, a small and newly created group of Algerian guerrillas known as the Front de Libération Nationale (FLN) launched a campaign of armed resistance against the French occupation of Algeria. This war—the French-Algerian War—lasted from

1 November 1954 to 18 March 1962. In the summer of 1962, almost all the approximately one million French settlers fled Algeria for France. The war's terrible legacy of violence, dislocation, and destruction continues to reverberate in France and Algeria to this day.

SOUSTELLE, DE GAULLE, AND THE DECOLONIZATION OF ALGERIA

Jacques Soustelle was one of France's leading post–World War II intellectual figures. He, like many of his colleagues on the political left, had emerged from the bitter years of WWII as a hero, a well-known leader of the French Resistance, and one of the few men who had rallied to de Gaulle's call for a self-imposed exile in London. Even before he joined de Gaulle's Free French government, Soustelle was well known in France for his intelligence. Born in 1912, Soustelle began his studies at the École Normale Supérieure, France's most elite college, at the age of seventeen. By the age of twenty, in 1932, he broke the ENS record with the highest grade in philosophy. At the age of twenty-three, he obtained his doctorate in ethnology from the Sorbonne. From 1932 to 1935, he conducted research in Mexico and returned to France as the nation's foremost Aztec scholar. He was subsequently given the prestigious post of assistant director of Paris's Musée de l'Homme in 1937. About the same time, he became one of three leaders of France's antifascist group, Comité de vigilance des intellectuels anti-fascistes (Antifascist Intellectuals' Vigilance Committee). During WWII, when he emerged as a close and trusted friend of de Gaulle, Soustelle became a leading member of the French Resistance. Soustelle was given the special responsibility by de Gaulle of creating the Comité des Français Libres (Committee of the Free French) and consolidating diplomatic ties with other governments and regions, mainly Mexico, South America, and the West Indies. After WWII, Soustelle's intellect and close association with de Gaulle placed him within an elite group of French intellectuals and politicians such as Raymond Aron and Pierre Mendès France. It therefore seemed natural that Soustelle would move into key political positions in the 1950s.

However, the smoothness of Soustelle's personal career did not at all resemble France's political landscape. Swept up in the current of Third World nationalist revolts against all European colonial governments, many of France's overseas territories were suddenly repudiating France's self-proclaimed right to rule over colonized peoples in Asia and Africa. The most immediate and important challenge to French colonial hegemony started in Indochina during WWII. By 1946 Ho Chi Minh had begun the process of decolonizing there, and after much political wrangling, on

14 January 1950, Ho Chi Minh stated that the Democratic Republic of Vietnam was the only legal government in Indochina. Indochina became the principal chess piece in Asia during the Cold War and eventually represented a unquestionable embarrassment for the French military. On 7 May 1954 the French army suffered a humiliating defeat at Dien Bien Phu that forced France to withdraw from Indochina. The French army swore it would never bow to defeat again and hoped for a chance to avenge its losses to anti-French nationalists. Coming on the heels of the French defeat at Dien Bien Phu, the FLN's revolutionary assault on the French government in Algeria in November 1954 provided the army and the real-life characters portrayed in *Assassination* with an opportunity to restore France's beleaguered reputation. Near the end of 1954, Soustelle stepped into the middle of this decolonization battleground when he announced that he would accept Pierre Mendès France's nomination for the post of governor general of Algeria.

Soustelle's fate as the governor general was not dissimilar to those who had preceded him in that office. The colonial lobby worked quickly to convert Soustelle to their cause of an eternal French Algeria. And, despite his initial humanism, Soustelle swiftly moved more to the right until he was eventually sucked into the quicksand world of the French colonists in Algeria. Soustelle's progressive move to the right became more apparent in 1955, after he viewed the site of the Philippeville massacre.[5] Philippeville convinced him that Algerian nationalists would rid the country of the French by any means and that reconciliation was improbable. The more violence against the French he saw, the more military violence he justified, and the more he assumed a pro-settler stance. His overzealousness precipitated the demise of political moderation and forced many moderate Muslims, who had formerly supported cooperation with the French, to part company with France.

While Soustelle continued to move to the socio-economic non-Socialist right, the Fourth Republic was on the point of collapsing. Guy Mollet became prime minister in 1956, and he replaced the position of governor general in Algeria with resident minister, substituting Robert Lacoste (a prominent Socialist) for Soustelle. Once out of office, Soustelle returned to his teaching post in France and picked up his pen in support of the colonialists' cause.

The crisis in France and Algeria reached a turning point in May 1958 following a conflict between Mollet in Paris and the military stationed in Algeria. Pierre Pflimlin, the leader of the Mouvement Républicain Populaire (MRP), tried to check the military's growing power by forming a new government in Paris, but his efforts were immediately jeopardized when a group of hard-line French colonists, the Vigilance Committee, tried to take control of Algeria. Even the military, however, was not comfortable with the radicalism of the *pieds noirs* (European settlers born in Algeria), so on 13 May Generals Jacques Massu and Raoul Salan created the so-called moderate and military-backed Committee of Public Safety in Algiers. In the face of these events, the far-away Parisian Parliament remained completely helpless and unable to gain control over the break-away colonists and the military in Algiers because there did not appear to be any loyal army units that could be sent in.

As ex–governor general and a pro-colonist intellectual, Soustelle watched these events unfolding in Algiers from Paris and realized that opportunities awaited him.[6] Aware of the potential danger Soustelle posed to the stability of the Fourth Republic, French officials placed him under house arrest, but when Soustelle heard that General Salan was in control in Algeria, he took this as his cue to perform a magical disappearing act. On 17 May Soustelle—who was supposedly confined to his apartment under careful police surveillance—miraculously reappeared in Algiers. He had given the police the slip by hiding in the trunk of his car, surfaced briefly in Geneva, and was piloted immediately to Algiers. Soustelle was given a hero's welcome in Algiers from the devoted settler population, many of whom apparently believed that he had come to take charge of the situation and side with the settlers against the French Parliament. A staunch Gaullist, however, Soustelle pressured the fractious General Salan to support de Gaulle's return to power. And, once again, de Gaulle (with the aid of Soustelle and the hard-liners in the military) would claim to be the savior of France and would reenter politics for the first time since 1946.

For his part, de Gaulle had been doing his own political maneuvering in France and understood how the events in Algeria would prompt his dramatic return to power. All eyes definitively turned to the mythic figure when, in Algiers, General Salan connected the settler-military coup to de Gaulle on 15 May by shouting *"Et Vive de Gaulle!"* after proclaiming his support for French Algeria. From that moment on, it was almost certain that de Gaulle would return as president. Not coincidentally, on the evening of 17 May, de Gaulle held his first press gathering in years. He stated confidently that he was prepared to take control of the French government. Such unconstitutional boldness horrified the majority of the Parliament's members who believed that France was being compromised by the dictatorial efforts of the military now forcing its will on a democratic state.[7] Finally a hesitant French Parliament caved in to the pressures and agreed that de Gaulle alone could impose control over the refractory military.

On 29 May, after the very real threat of a military strike from Algiers against Paris named "Operation Resurrection," de Gaulle began to form a new government. Under the direction of Michel Debré, France began to work out its new constitution, which was completed in August. De Gaulle and André Malraux formally presented it on 4 September 1958. And despite the anti-Gaullist socialist coalition (Union des forces démocratiques, UFD) formed by Pierre Mendès France and François Mitterrand to oppose de Gaulle's plans, the new constitution passed in a referendum by a large margin on 28 September. The Fifth Republic was well on its way, and the parliamentary elections of 23 and 30 November gave firm backing to a pro–de Gaulle government. In December de Gaulle was elected to the office of president. With the Fifth Republic in place, and now the president of France, de Gaulle entered the Elysée Palace on 8 January 1959. Michel Debré then moved to the Hôtel Matignon as prime minister of France.

The months from May 1958 to January 1959 were immensely important for France and Algeria. Everyone in France was preoccupied with the issue of decolonization, especially the French military commanders. Since the beginning of the French-Algerian War, military leaders had been seething from their very recent and humiliating loss in Indochina to the Vietminh. The loss of Indochina strengthened the military's commitment to keeping Algeria French, which in turn played well with the vast majority of French settlers in Algeria; however, the severity of the military's tactics used to control Algeria further divorced the remaining eight million Muslims from France. While it is true that Algerian nationalists, especially the FLN, suffered enormous losses during the infamous Battle of Algiers in 1957, the overzealous efforts of the French military to stamp out the rebellion rapidly extended to the systematic torture and "disappearing" of Algerians and, increasingly, their few European sympathizers. By the time the May crisis erupted, metropolitan France was beginning to waver on the Algerian question, the political machinery of France's Fourth Republic had come to a standstill, and many of France's leading intellectuals had become outspoken critics of continued colonial rule in Algeria. In short, May 1958 was indeed the critical breaking point in the war where those desirous of a French Algeria realized it would require a figure of mythical proportions such as de Gaulle to end the conflict in favor of French colonial interests.

For political power brokers like Soustelle, de Gaulle's return seemed to be the best way to ensure France's presence in Algeria. When de Gaulle gave his infamous "*Je vous ai compris!*" speech in Algiers as he raised his arms to form his victory V sign on 4 June 1958, Soustelle and Salan were content believing that he had understood the colonists' cries for a French Algeria. Since Generals Raoul Salan and Jacques Massu as well as Jacques Soustelle played critical roles in de Gaulle's return, they each expected de Gaulle to maintain the French status quo in Algeria. Unfortunately for Soustelle and the military engineers of the coup d'état, de Gaulle's future actions proved unpredictable.

By September 1958 a newly ratified Fifth Republic attempted to prevent further political chaos by weighing the scales heavily in favor of de Gaulle's presidential power, a move that won de Gaulle no friends among the French left. To keep the Fifth Republic from becoming victimized by the same forces that had ensured his return, de Gaulle swiftly removed any military officers from Algeria whom he suspected of being too sympathetic to the settler population. Even General Salan, who had shown his sympathies with Algiers, was reassigned to the prestigious but trivial post of the military governor of Paris. De Gaulle then filled Salan's place with air force General Maurice Challe. De Gaulle intentionally excluded Soustelle from any major position of power by giving him a minor post in the government as minister of Information.

On 16 September 1959, just over a year after he returned to power at the hand of the military and Soustelle, de Gaulle made it plain that he was fundamentally rethinking France's relationship with Algeria when he delivered his famous "self-determination" speech to the nation. In speaking of the self-determination of Algeria, de Gaulle clearly indicated that he would consider the question of independence and that he may push French public opinion toward this idea. Because of this, de Gaulle's caution with regard to his own troops in Algeria turned out to be well warranted. Within months of the self-determination speech, the extremist forces in Algiers began to move again against the government. This latest upsurge in extremist activity was triggered by an interview in which General Massu stated that the army could not understand (or support) de Gaulle's position on Algeria. Massu was quoted as having said—though he denied it—that de Gaulle had been the only one available during May 1958 and that the army had obviously made a mistake in choosing him. De Gaulle recalled Massu from Algeria less than a week later on 22 January and forbade him to participate in the making of Algerian policy. Reacting to Massu's recall, the French settlers put up barricades throughout Algiers on 24 January 1960. Amidst the chaos, a paramilitary organization led by two men, Pierre Lagaillarde and Joseph Ortiz, tried to take control of the city. Once again the government in Paris, this time with de Gaulle at the head, was at the mercy of the military in Algeria.

Fortunately the French government prevailed and the combined settler-military barricade revolt fizzled after a few days. Following the episode, Soustelle resigned from de Gaulle's cabinet in a fury. Despite the fact that he and de Gaulle had not been seeing eye-to-eye since the self-determination speech, Soustelle's resignation was important because it marked his first open political break with de Gaulle. Within months Soustelle began venting his frustration in the hotbed pro-colonialist group, the Vincennes Committee, whose membership included Georges Bidault, Robert Lacoste, Jean Dides, and Jean-Marie Le Pen (the controversial extreme-right-wing politician in France today), among many other prominent pro–French Algeria figures.

With de Gaulle's government facing opposition from both the right and the left, with tensions mounting because of Soustelle and General Salan leaving their posts in Paris, and with the French in Algeria fearing the prospect of Algerian autonomy, the army in Algeria once again mutinied against its commander in chief. In April 1961 a group of generals—Maurice Challe, Edmond Jouhaud, and Marie-André Zeller—were joined by Raoul Salan in a putsch against de Gaulle, which ended disastrously for them. During this critical show-down with the military, de Gaulle appeared on television in full military uniform and in his broadcast on television and radio he pleaded with the servicemen not to follow their renegade leaders in the mutiny against the French government. With great skill and grace and with the support of the anticolonialists within the army, de Gaulle succeeded, but his success had the unfortunate consequence of forcing his opposition underground.

Having quelled the putsch, de Gaulle went after its leaders. Those who were caught or who gave themselves up received stiff punishments. For example, two of France's highly decorated generals, Maurice Challe and André Zeller, were sentenced to fifteen years in prison. Others received punishments ranging from one to five years. Generals Jouhaud, Paul Gardy, and Salan, along with Colonels Joseph Broizart, Yves Godard, Charles Lacheroy, and Antoine Argoud, all moved beneath de Gaulle's police radar but were given the sentence of death in absentia. Many of them then went on to form one of the most notorious violent antigovernment terrorist groups in French history, the Organisation Armée Secrète.

The highly decorated ex–commander in chief General Raoul Salan took over leadership of the OAS. However, Salan was now a fugitive. In fact France was conducting an around-the-clock manhunt for the general, who continued to move throughout Europe. Meanwhile, by April 1961 General Gardy and Colonels Gardes, Argoud, Godard, Broizart, and Lacheroy decided to join the OAS in Algeria. At the same time, plans were underway to organize the OAS in France as an effort to expand the campaign of terror into metropolitan France.

The first real meeting of the OAS was held in mid-May 1961. Its purpose was to sabotage de Gaulle's efforts to remove French rule from Algeria. That month the OAS began a massive terrorist campaign and planted plastic explosives throughout Algiers and elsewhere in Algeria. By autumn Algiers and another major Algerian city, Oran, had firmly entrenched groups of OAS terrorists killing French and Muslims alike. Salan and Jouhaud (who oversaw the OAS in Oran) were becoming anxious with the OAS terrorist attacks, which they could no longer adequately control. During October 1961, the OAS killed more than 760 victims in Algeria.

As divisions began to widen between moderates and extremists in France and in Algeria, and as chaos descended on Algeria, Jacques Soustelle was placed under threat of arrest by the antiterrorist police. On 22 April Soustelle was ousted from the Gaullist party, Union pour la nouvelle République (UNR). Then he simply disappeared. On 3 November 1961 he surfaced briefly in Paris to hold a press conference. During this conference he declared that although the OAS was using murderous methods to oppose de Gaulle, de Gaulle would have to accept the OAS as a third force in Algeria. Soustelle stated that the OAS was there to stay, that it was a third force in Algeria, and that it was something to be reckoned with. What this meant, according to Soustelle, was that the OAS would have to be a member of the ongoing negotiations over the Algerian question between France and the FLN. Four hours after this conference, orders were given for Soustelle's arrest, but he had already secured safe passage into neighboring Belgium.

At about the same time as Soustelle's arrest warrant was signed, another anti-Gaullist faction set itself up in Madrid, calling itself the Central OAS Leadership. Among its leaders were Colonels Argoud and Lacheroy, as well as Pierre Lagaillarde. Shortly after this group surfaced in exile in order to maintain the war against de Gaulle's government, the OAS moved to mainland France from Algeria and began its campaign of domestic terrorism. A bomb meant for the French writer Jean-Paul Sartre missed its target when it was placed on the wrong floor of Sartre's apartment building. Another bomb meant for the Nobel Prize–winning author and de Gaulle's minister of culture, André Malraux, succeeded only in disfiguring a nearby four-year-old girl.

De Gaulle and the rest of France understood very well that the OAS had two principal aims: to render everyday political and civilian life in Algeria and France so chaotic that it would make independence impossible and to overthrow his metropolitan government. In this sense events concerning Algeria developed quickly. In March 1962 in Evian, Switzerland, the French government and the FLN representatives negotiated the Evian Accords and the terms of cease-fire. Aware of this, the OAS went on a murderous rampage throughout Algeria in an attempt to disrupt negotiations, and it decided to kill prominent Algerians and French citizens. For example—symbolically on the Ides of March—the well-known Algerian writer Mouloud Feraoun and five of his unfortunate colleagues were machine-gunned during the last planning session of the French educational institution known as the Centres Sociaux Éducatifs in Algeria.[8] Nevertheless, the Evian Accords were officially signed on 18 March, thus ending the war and outlining the provisions for the transfer of power. The cease-fire went into effect on 19 March 1962. On 5 July 1962 Algeria became independent.

The date of Algerian independence is crucial because it pinpoints almost to the day when the OAS transformed itself from a *pied noir*–based populist organization fighting within Algeria to prevent independence to an elite terrorist organization within metropolitan France plotting to overthrow the French government. But what is the connection between the reconstitution of the OAS as the Conseil National de Résistance (CNR) and the subsequent events relating to assassination attempts on de Gaulle?

De Gaulle made every effort to end the semi–civil war between the French government and the OAS and to restore order in France and Algeria. At the same time he supported a formal declaration of Algerian independence. In reaction to these moves by de Gaulle, George Bidault— along with Soustelle, Colonel Antoine Argoud, and General Paul Gardy— created a new group and recycled the name of the old Conseil National de Résistance. (The first CNR was founded by Bidault and others in 1943. It recognized General Charles de Gaulle as the leader of the Free French government in London and was the main body responsible for organizing the Resistance networks in wartime France.)

Bidault (caricatured as Boudin in the novel) was, like Soustelle, an extremely powerful and intelligent man. In 1925 he placed first in the *agrégation* (the most competitive exam in France for teachers) in history and geography at the Sorbonne. In the 1930s he served as editor in chief of the Christian Democratic paper *L'Aube* for which he also wrote a number of articles against Nazism and fascism. During WWII he volunteered for military service and was captured but then released in 1941. In that same year he founded the French Resistance movement Combat. From September 1945 to November 1945, Bidault served as the minister of Foreign Affairs under de Gaulle. He then became head of state and the president of the provisional government of France from June to November 1946. He was prime minister again from 1949 to 1950. Among other offices after WWII, he served as vice president of the Council and minister of National Defense. During the height of the French war in Indochina, Bidault served as minister of Foreign Affairs from January 1953 to June 1954. A devout Catholic, he founded a new party in France called Démocratie Chrétienne de France (Christian Democracy of France) during the French-Algerian War. After he broke publicly with de Gaulle over the Algerian question, he decided to found the second CNR in March 1962. On 15 July 1962 Bidault lost his parliamentary immunity, which he had held because he had also served continually as a deputy for the Loire department in the French National Assembly since 1945.

The other members of the new CNR, General Paul Gardy and Colonel Antoine Argoud, were two of the most respected French officers in Algeria during the war. General Gardy had been an important member of the French Resistance, had served in Indochina, and was a retired inspector general of the Foreign Legion. Colonel Argoud had served in Indochina and Algeria and, like his three colleagues, felt that de Gaulle had betrayed France and the military by allowing the abandonment of Algeria.

The decision by Bidault, Soustelle, Gardy, and Argoud to reuse the name of the CNR for their group was an obvious attempt to evoke the symbolism of the Resistance and to equate de Gaulle's abandonment of Algeria with Marshal Pétain's bowing to the Nazis. Hence the first goal of this reborn CNR was to oppose what Soustelle commonly referred to as the "Gaullist dictatorship."[9] As Bidault put it in *Resistance: The Political Autobiography of Georges Bidault*, published in English in 1967: "From my exile I sent out a message asking the people of France to vote against the surrender of Algeria and declaring the creation of a second National Council of the Resistance [CNR]." And he continues, "When I created the second [CNR], I did not worry about whether I would be understood right away by many, whether I would shock everybody, and whether I would be risking terrible difficulties and wild adventures. . . . I have never been popular with those who worship anyone who is in power, and I have been misunderstood by those who hypocritically pretend to see no evil, hear no evil and speak no evil of the men at the summit."[10] Meanwhile Soustelle continued to write polemical pieces against his former hero just as de Gaulle had done against his former hero, Marshal Pétain. The CNR also claimed that de Gaulle was destroying France's historic mission of bringing the glories of French civilization to needy North Africans.

On 3 July 1962 the CNR published a notice from the "Etat-Major Général des Forces Armées" declaring that de Gaulle had been condemned to death for treason by its "Military Tribune." According to the CNR, the order to kill de Gaulle was given by the "Military High Commander in metropolitan France through the directives of the Executive Commission of the CNR." The most famous assassination attempt on de Gaulle was at Petit-Clamart when Colonel Jean-Marie Bastien-Thiry ambushed de Gaulle's motorcade on 22 August 1962. A graduate of l'École Polytechnique and an air force missile designer, Bastien-Thiry had remained a staunch Gaullist until 1959. Later, after the OAS was liquidated by de Gaulle's special agents in Algeria (the *barbouzes*, "bearded ones"), responsible for tracking down OAS members, Bastien-Thiry became a primary organizer of the assassination efforts. Failing his attempt at Petit-Clamart, Bastien-Thiry was tried, convicted of treason, and executed by firing squad.

After Bastien-Thiry's failure, the OAS vowed to continue its efforts to assassinate de Gaulle; but once de Gaulle had suppressed the OAS in France, the CNR had to try to thwart de Gaulle from afar. It is somewhat difficult to determine the exact nature of Soustelle's involvement with the CNR during this period. We know, from the CNR's publications such as *Appel de la France* and from Soustelle himself, that he was one of the CNR leaders upon its founding. We also know from Antoine Argoud's writings that during the time Soustelle was a leader, the CNR was determined to launch an assault on the Fifth Republic and that the CNR saw the assassination of de Gaulle as essential. In his *La Décadence, l'imposture, et la tragédie*, published in 1974 (i.e., after the libel action had ended and after he was granted amnesty), Colonel Antoine Argoud stated: "Regardless of what has been said or written, the elimination of the head of state did not pose a moral problem for us. We were all convinced, Bidault the practicing Catholic, Soustelle the liberal, and myself, the *pied noir* of the group, that de Gaulle deserved capital punishment." And by no coincidence, Argoud referred to the missed attempt on de Gaulle's life by Bastien-Thiry as "a heroic act."[11] In other words, it becomes clear that with the birth of the CNR the OAS began to move from its highly active and destructive populist origins in Algeria (where, apparently, Soustelle played no role except that of supporter) to its secret elitist terrorist activities in France (where we have no knowledge of Soustelle's involvement or support) to its exile over the border where it plotted a new order based on the assassination of de Gaulle (and where, the evidence suggests, Soustelle played a primary role). And it is important to note that the CNR had condemned de Gaulle to death in July—more than a month before Bastien-Thiry's failed assassination at Petit-Clamart.

ENGLISH STUDENTS AND THE UN-BRITISH STORY

It was about the same time that Soustelle broke with de Gaulle over his Algerian policy that Robert Silman and Ian Young decided to pursue degrees in philosophy at the Sorbonne with Jean-François Lyotard. Silman and Young had been quite taken by the events in France while they were still in public school in England, and as they watched the events unfold during their years of study in Paris, they began to develop a political portrait of Soustelle and the other members of the CNR, who by now had become almost mythical in the international press. Reading and hearing about the generals' revolt (the unsuccessful April 1961 putsch) and of Soustelle's disappearance after the OAS fled to France from Algeria, Silman and Young scoured the journalistic landscape for traces of Bidault, Soustelle, Argoud, and Gardy's recreated CNR. At this point Silman and Young had every reason to believe that the CNR was synonymous with the OAS and that Soustelle was one of its leaders. Fascinated with France's political instability, which left the French government constantly on the verge of collapse and which forced French citizens to feel as if they were trapped on a civil-war seesaw, Silman and Young were struck by how un-British French politics appeared. Tottering on the brink of disaster, de Gaulle's government was ripe for a coup precisely because it lacked popular support; the right felt betrayed by de Gaulle's Algerian policy and the left was outraged by the unconstitutionality of de Gaulle's seizure of power. In short, for those willing to play political hardball, like Soustelle and the other exiled members of the CNR, Silman and Young believed that "it was possible to seize power in France because both left and right were opposed to de Gaulle and it was difficult to see where he could find support to resist a coup."[12]

They saw Soustelle as a mastermind, as a sort of evil political genius who was capable of toppling de Gaulle's government. Soustelle's real-life political performances laid the foundations for their fictional portrait of Soustelle as a devious antihero, one who was hiding somewhere in Europe from the grappling clutches of de Gaulle's infamous political police and who could be flushed out only by the mysterious Max Palk. The idea for the novel blossomed on the day that Bastien-Thiry ambushed de Gaulle's motorcade at Petit-Clamart. Silman and Young were on holiday in Burgundy with a couple of friends from England. From Silman and Young's point of view, this extremely complex and un-British story was ideal for fiction. It seemed clear to them that Soustelle was behind all of the political intrigue and that he should be the central character in the novel. The plot was plausible because if de Gaulle's government fell in real life, the CNR would certainly try to seize power in France. Hence, built around the historical situation of France at the time, their novel was endowed with a convincing plot and realistic characters. Presented with a plot, a motive, and a sympathetic villain, Silman and Young returned to Paris and began writing their novel of an OAS attempt to assassinate de Gaulle, which they titled *Assassination*.

With a few newspaper clippings, some of Soustelle's political tracts, and their own abundant imagination, the authors cast Soustelle in a fictional coup d'état against de Gaulle. Within months, Silman and Young had concocted a story about Soustelle and other desperadoes' thwarted effort to overturn the French government and assassinate Charles de Gaulle. This fictional coup d'état directed by Soustelle was very much informed by contemporary journalism and by public perceptions of Soustelle as the mastermind and antihero behind de Gaulle's return to power in 1958. According to Silman, the fictitious Soustelle was "a French amalgam of Henry Kissinger and Dr. Strangelove" (Silman interview). Silman and Young gave the novel an added spin by creating an authorial pseudonym, Ben Abro.

The authors had another motive in mind when they began to carve out their narrative; they wanted to create a new genre of writing and a new type of espionage hero in order to debunk the James Bond version of the British secret agent that had recently swept over the popular imagination. To confront the sleek, unrealistic, and macho James Bond–like characterization of an international spy, the coauthors offered a subtler, more self-effacing hero, Max Palk, a quiet desk-job type of a British secret agent who mysteriously disappears from his office to help the Paris chief of police, at that time Maurice Papon,[13] uncover the assassination attempt against General Charles de Gaulle.

The novel pits Jacques Soustelle as the humorless and charming antihero and mastermind against the shy and unimpressive Max Palk. Palk moves through a series of dangerous episodes in rapid succession, and is even saved by Soustelle from other fascists by a clever game of wits. Palk must go, as any rival to Bond would, undercover (and under bedcovers in one sexual encounter) to discover the conspiracy. Time after time, Palk escapes from peril (as only Max Palk or James Bond could) and is finally able to discover that the conspirators—led by none other than Jacques Soustelle, his associates, and one of de Gaulle's ministers—aim to assassinate the French president and take over the government as dictators. As any hero would, Palk must either spoil the OAS's plot to storm Paris or fail in his mission. Yet in an uncharacteristically James Bond fashion, the anonymity of Max Palk is preserved to the point that when he returns having accomplished his mission, he enters his office and is ridiculed by his secretaries. The satire of the James Bond character is given a finishing touch in the final scene of the book, which describes a tear trickling down Palk's face as he reseats himself in his dull, dusty, asthmatic, and forgotten office life in the city of London.

Silman and Young finished the novel in three months and sent the manuscript to publishers in England. They accepted an offer from Jonathan Cape because it was the original publisher of the James Bond series. Cape took a risk because—unlike today—the genre of the political novel was not a highly developed form. In fact, according to Silman, "Nobody at that time thought that the idea of writing a political novel using real characters was something that could take off in such a big way" (Silman interview). Young men in their early twenties, the authors thought their endeavor was "fun." They realized that there were legal dangers, but they did not believe that Soustelle would bother with them because, with a warrant out for his arrest and in political exile, he would be too busy to concern himself with anything as trivial as a thriller.

It should be noted here that *Assassination*, although at the cutting edge of historical political fiction, also fits into a wider literary and cinematic tradition. In fact, although *The Day of the Jackal* and *Assassination* were the two novels to treat the subject of the OAS's plots to eliminate Charles de Gaulle, the 1960s and 1970s witnessed the appearance of many other novels and films treating the French-Algerian conflict. The novels include Harry Whittington's *Guerrilla Girls* (1961), Maurice Edelman's *The Fratricides* (1963), Alan Williams's *Barbouze* (1963), Alan Sillitoe's *The William Posters Trilogy* (1965), Francis Fytton's *The Nation Within* (1967), and Con Sellers's *The Algerian Incident* (1970). The several feature films that must also be mentioned in this context are *The Day of the Jackal* (1973), directed by Fred Zinnemann, *Lost Command* (1966), directed by Mark Robinson and starring Anthony Quinn based on the novel *The Centurions* by Jean Lartéguy, *RAS* [*rien à signaler*], directed by Yves Boisset (1972), and finally *The Battle of Algiers* (1966), directed by Gillo Pontecorvo.[14]

The publisher was hopeful about the possibilities afforded by this new genre of historical fiction and especially liked *Assassination*'s ability to

blur the boundaries between history and fiction. On 20 February 1963
Tom Maschler, a director at Jonathan Cape, wrote Ben Abro: "I have just
finished reading your novel, *Assassination*, and would like to offer you my
congratulations. It is exciting and ingenious, and for the most part extremely
well written. Leaving aside the libel problems for the moment (and I don't
think they will be insuperable), I am delighted to tell you that we would like
to publish your book, subject to your making a few minor alterations."[15]
After taking legal advice, Jonathan Cape agreed to keep Soustelle's name
since he was portrayed as a *sympathetic* villain, and he was obviously a
prominent member of the OAS-CNR. However, Jonathan Cape's lawyers
thought the character of Bidault, a co-conspirator but minor participant in
the novel, was portrayed so unsympathetically that he might sue on personal
rather than political grounds. The authors therefore changed Bidault's name
to Boudin, which in French means pig's-blood sausage.

After making these revisions, the book was published on 1 July 1963 in
London by Jonathan Cape. Silman and Young were paid several thousand
pounds in advances, which was unusually high in those days for a first
novel.

Reviewers praised *Assassination* in England and the United States, trum-
peting the opaqueness that came from blending history and fiction. One
American reviewer wrote:

> There is, I repeat, much more fact than fiction behind *Assassina-
> tion!* Neither its British nor its American publishers knows just how
> much. . . . But the reader will find it as filled with suspense as anything
> ever written by Eric Ambler, Graham Green or James Bond [Ian
> Fleming]. This is not one to be put down until it is finished. . . .
>
> *Assassination!* has all the familiar ingredients of the fictional sus-
> pense-thriller, including a dab of sex—for once germane to the logic
> of the story. But in essence, it is a behind-the-scenes tale of what nearly
> happened to de Gaulle's France. And still could for that matter.[16]

The *Houston Chronicle* followed suit, writing that the novel was "one of
the most thrilling books of the year. Those who compile best-seller lists
should be considering whether to classify it as fiction or non-fiction."
The *Houston Chronicle* even offered this advice for reading the book:
"One adventure for the reader of 'Assassination' will be deciding where
truth ends and fiction begins. To add to the confusion, even the author's
name is kept secret."[17] The *Chicago Tribune* joined the reviewers' chorus,
titling Northwestern University history professor Richard Brace's review,
"Whodunit Masterpiece of Conspiracy in France."[18]

Even the advertising accentuated the confusion between history and
fiction and in doing so helped establish the conventions of a new genre.
The Morrow catalogue called *Assassination* its "Salesmen's choice. . . . The
most exciting, most salable thriller of the year," and lured book sellers with
this hook: "The original manuscript came over the transom. The author
is pseudonymous. Truth or fiction? We do not know, nor does the English
publisher. But we do know that it is the year's most exciting and most
topical thriller." Silman and Young were smart to publish the novel under
a pseudonym because this feature became one of the selling points of the
novel; the publishers insinuated that the author would be in danger if his
identity was revealed. And this insinuation of danger complemented one
reviewer's comment that the publishers had taken a "20–1 odds" policy
offered by Lloyd's of London against de Gaulle being assassinated before
the book was published, but that no one was prepared to insure the author![19]

THE LIBEL ACTION

This alleged policy by Lloyd's, however, could protect neither Silman and
Young nor the publishers from Soustelle's legal counsel, Lesser, Fairbank
& Co. On 10 April 1964 Jonathan Cape was accused of publishing a book
that was "utterly false, highly defamatory and most damaging" to Soustelle's
reputation. Claiming that Soustelle's precarious predicament of "political
asylum" had been compromised by such a libelous book, and that "our client
has no connection with any OAS organisation," Soustelle's solicitor asked
Jonathan Cape to "forthwith withdraw" *Assassination* from publication and
asked how the publishers were prepared to compensate Soustelle for such
"gross and unjustifiable libel" (Silman papers). Not surprisingly, this ended
references by the publisher to the blurring of fact and fiction. Jonathan Cape
now disavowed any claims that the book was factual, and five days later,
without reference to Silman and Young, its lawyers responded to Soustelle's
solicitor stating that the "book in question is quite clearly a work of fiction:
indeed of a rather fantastic nature." Furthermore, they continued, "We
are, of course, well aware that your Client is in political exile for reasons no
doubt very well known to him and to the French Government, and while
our Clients regret any offense which may have been caused we cannot
believe that your Client's reputation in some neutral country is likely to be
damaged by this obvious work of fiction, in English, of which the sales were
not large." On 17 April 1964 Graham C. Greene, who was codirector of
Jonathan Cape with Tom Maschler, advised Ben Abro that Jonathan Cape
had informed the American publisher of the letter from Soustelle's solicitor.
  Silman and Young were completely surprised by Soustelle's actions, and

on 19 April Robert Silman replied to Mr. Greene in a letter detailing that Soustelle's outrage was absurd in light of the mounting evidence of Soustelle's involvement in the OAS. Silman and Young were now under pressure to prove that their fiction was true, even though it was not clear what exactly was libelous about the book. Was Soustelle denouncing the book because it portrayed him as one of the leaders of the OAS? Or was Soustelle denouncing the book because it portrayed his organization, the OAS, in an unsympathetic light? In other words, was it a libel against Soustelle or a libel against the OAS? Pondering these questions, the authors promised to send Greene and Jonathan Cape's legal team documentation that would definitively link Soustelle to the OAS. Despite their anxieties, Silman and Young did not lose their sense of humor: "As regards the inferences drawn by Mr. Soustelle's solicitors," Silman wrote, "our book has portrayed Mr. Soustelle in a not unsympathetic light. He is shown to be an intelligent and sensitive individual who shies from violence and who tries to save the hero (Max Palk) from death. Our book could only be defamatory of Mr. Soustelle in the eyes of the OAS, but never in the eyes of the outside world. It is absurd to suppose that it could compromise his position in some neutral country" (Silman papers).

The publishers were not too concerned at this stage about the potential legal threat. On 4 May John C. Willey, the editor in chief at William Morrow, expressed his gratitude to Silman for his information concerning Soustelle's links to the OAS. Willey admitted that there was little he could do concerning the affair, which he likened to a "fishing expedition," and while praising the book's sales in the United States, he admitted that it would be "a blow" if anything happened to set back the U.S. paperback (Fawcett) edition. The same day Silman was notified that the U.K. paperback publisher (Mayflower) intended to proceed with its edition.

However, it became clear that it was no "fishing expedition" when on 12 November 1964 Soustelle made his move and filed libel suit in the English High Court of Justice Queen's Bench Division in *Soustelle v. Cape and Silman and Young*, 1964 S. No. 2346. In his "Statement of Claim," Soustelle, through his counsel, Colin Ross-Munro, argued that the novel made him out to be inter alia (i) "a man who was attempting with others to organize the assassination of the President of the French Republic namely General de Gaulle"; and (ii) "a man who was one of the heads of an illegal and violent terrorist organisation namely the said OAS." To support these charges, the "Statement of Claim" cited specific sections of the novel such as "in the said book at page 38 [29 of this edition], the OAS is described as a Fascist Organisation with no popular support but prepared to commit murder and treason in order to seize power." The "Statement of Claim" ended thus: "The plaintiff (Soustelle) has in consequence been seriously injured in character, credit and reputation and has been brought into public scandal, odium and contempt and has thereby suffered damages" (Silman papers).

Silman and Young felt that they had to prevent Soustelle from using the libel action as a means to disassociate himself and/or the OAS from the disrepute into which he/it had fallen and as a method of "castigating the French judicial system." They were determined that their "trivial novel" should not be used "for political gain." The book "was not a contribution to politics and suddenly it was being misused for a political purpose. We had a moral obligation to prevent this" (Silman interview). Silman and Young persuaded Jonathan Cape that there were good reasons not to give in to the legal pressures. They focused on two main issues. First, they cited newspapers and other publications to show that neither Soustelle nor the OAS had any reputation to protect. This strategy would have kept any possible damages to be paid for libel to a minimum. Second, they were prepared to prove that the so-called libel was *true* by going directly to the leaders in the OAS who knew Soustelle and who could testify to his involvement in the terrorist activities of the organization. This second strategy, if successful, would be enough to win their defense.

Jonathan Cape and Silman and Young were not yet convinced that Soustelle was really prepared to continue with his action. His reputation and that of the OAS were at an all-time low. General Salan, the leader of the OAS, had been arrested, tried, and convicted, thus reducing the OAS to a handful of fanatical fringe outlaws. French and world public opinion had turned definitively against the OAS. Hence Silman and Young believed that their mastermind was desperately scheming to use their novel as a shield against the political damage radiating from his ties to the OAS. Realizing that Soustelle's sympathies for the OAS were not going to win him points at home and that he had to synchronize his desire to distance himself from the OAS with his challenge from abroad to de Gaulle's power, Silman and Young saw that he was trying to use a lawsuit in England to restore his prestige in France. They believed that a strong defense would soon persuade him of the errors of this tactic.

They also believed Soustelle's paranoia against de Gaulle would not play well in the English courts. Soustelle had developed a violent antipathy for de Gaulle, which he made public. Soustelle remarked in *A New Road For France*, written in exile in 1963 and banned in France, "When the noise and shouting have died down and the tyrant's [de Gaulle's] banners of *grandeur* have disappeared, France will have to continue. It is difficult to

imagine the evil the present regime has had the time to accomplish. The
Gaullist regime is the expression of a declining society whose decadence it
reflects and at the same time precipitates."[20] But he did not stop there: "The
Gaullist regime can be defined as a hypocritical dictatorship."[21] And then:
"Few people outside France realize that our formerly democratic republic
has become a one-man, one-party autocracy thinly disguised under the veil
of a rubber-stamp Parliament. Even inside France, the brainwashing by the
State propaganda machine succeeds in obscuring the issues. The two pillars
of this authoritarian regime are the State-owned and State-run radio and
television network and the all-powerful and ever-present political police."[22]
Soustelle then claims to have been subjected to a most unusual "witch hunt"
and chased from one country to the next by de Gaulle's hoodlums:

> The truth is that this list of "undesirables" (read: the unworthy ones
> who dare deny the legitimacy of de Gaulle's regime and combat
> its policies) was compiled in Paris, and that "friendly pressure" was
> brought to bear on the neighboring countries to chase these exiles.
>   . . . Semi-officially, it is the secret agents, the kidnappers and the
> killers, commonly known as the *barbouzes* who are entrusted with
> the task of "neutralizing" by any and all means a certain number of
> persons, of which I am one. I can affirm, at the time of this writing,
> that I escaped by a hair's breath a few weeks ago from a plot to kidnap
> me, if possible, or else to liquidate me definitely. . . .
>   Ever since 1961, the spider's web with its center in Paris, has
> been spun little by little over the whole of Western Europe, with an
> efficiency and effrontery never equaled by the Gestapo or the OVRA.[23]

In other words, according to Soustelle, his current situation was the result
not of his own reactionary politics but of a vendetta that de Gaulle and
his lackeys had launched against him; his self-imposed and heroic exile was
necessitated by de Gaulle's totalitarian regime. De Gaulle's secret police
were engaged in a witch hunt in which he was a leading sorcerer. Thus
did Soustelle design his own drama, using his supposed persecution by de
Gaulle as the background and the case against Ben Abro as the foreground.
By having his case heard in the British courts he could simultaneously mock
de Gaulle's authoritarian judicial system and redeem himself in French
public opinion. At least that's how his plan might have worked had Silman
and Young not categorically refused to apologize.

As if to demonstrate that Soustelle was wanting to use the libel action
as a means to attack de Gaulle, Soustelle's solicitor, Uziel Hamilton, told
the press in November 1964 that he was anxious to have Soustelle appear

in the British courts and to have the case over with. Hamilton claimed that Soustelle's case could be helped if Soustelle appeared before the British courts but also admitted that this could pose a problem for the government of England. The British government could, however, deny Soustelle the right of entry as a fugitive.[24]

Unfortunately Silman and Young still had one major question unresolved. They did not know whether Soustelle's tactic was to disassociate himself from the OAS or to restore the reputation of the OAS. In public Soustelle was still writing in defense of the OAS: "We cannot pass over in silence the fact that most of the acts for which the OAS has been reproached were *defensive* in nature or in the form of reprisal." He continued, "What other way out was left to this people [the OAS] who had been given over completely to an arbitrary police rule?"[25] Or this statement: "From the time that these forces (the Gaullist regime) concentrated all their repressive means against the European population and no longer fought the enemy, the Organization [the OAS] had to take over the mission that the State had abandoned. Indeed, nothing can be explained or understood if one does not take into consideration the fundamental fact of this *reversal of alliances* by which the French government and the forces under its authority found themselves on the same side as the FLN terrorists against the French of Algeria."[26]

Before putting in their defense, Silman and Young tried to obtain "Further Particulars of the Facts and Matters Relied Upon" in Soustelle's claim, and on 7 April 1965, they received their reply. The "Further Particulars" gave an account of Soustelle's recent history: how he had "attacked" de Gaulle's policy "as he was entitled to do" at a press conference in Paris on 18 December 1961, how an arrest warrant was issued in France in 1962 charging him with "attacking the authority of the State," and how since December 1961 he had been living in political exile. As for the OAS, the reply seemed to go even further than the original "Statement of Claim:" "The OAS was and still is an illegal terrorist organisation with little or no popular support which believes in the use of violence and murder to achieve its political aims and has (inter alia) attempted to assassinate General de Gaulle." There was no mention of any link between Soustelle and the OAS or Soustelle and the CNR.

Silman and Young were still not quite sure of Soustelle's tactics. Was the description of the OAS the "ordinary meaning" or an "innuendo meaning"? That is, was this the real OAS or was this the OAS as libeled by Silman and Young? On 5 May they applied to the Queen's Bench Division to have the matter clarified. The "Amended Particulars" arrived on 18 May.

Here Soustelle's counsel agreed that the description of the OAS contained "innuendoes," and this was reinforced by a final added sentence, after the description of the OAS as an "illegal terrorist organisation" using "violence and murder" and attempting to "assassinate General de Gaulle," that turned everything on its head: "Alternatively a large number of people hold this belief" (Silman papers).

It seemed to Silman and Young that Soustelle was trying to have it both ways, at one and the same time distancing himself from the OAS and defending it. On 29 May 1965 the First (Jonathan Cape) and Second (Silman and Young) Defendants put in their "Defense," claiming: (i) that Soustelle was "at all material times one of the leaders of the CNR"; (ii) that "in or about the summer of 1962 the OAS came to be known as the CNR"; (iii) that "the objects of the OAS and the CNR were identical"; (iv) that Soustelle "supported the policy of the CNR and the OAS towards President de Gaulle, including the violent overthrow of his regime"; (v) that, following the assassination attempt on President de Gaulle at Petit-Clamart, the CNR had issued a communiqué stating that "President de Gaulle had been condemned to death for high treason"; (vi) that the CNR had been outlawed by the French Government on 11 September 1962; (vii) that Soustelle's own books were proof of his beliefs, and extracts from the clandestine publications of the OAS-CNR such as *Appel de la France*, *Bulletin d'Information*, *OAS Presse-Action*, *France Presse-Action*, and *Jeune Révolution* were proof of the murderous activities of the OAS-CNR; (viii) that if de Gaulle had been toppled by the OAS or the CNR, France would have been overtaken by a "military type" of government; and finally (ix) that they rejected Soustelle's claim that his so-called reputation had been damaged due to the novel (Silman papers).

Silman and Young hoped that by showing they were prepared to put in a strong defense, they would make Soustelle think twice about continuing his action. This did not happen. The legal steps progressed slowly but steadily. On 30 July they received a request for "Further and Better Particulars" about their defense, which demanded that they specify (i) "the dates during which it is alleged he (Soustelle) was one of the leaders of the CNR"; and (ii) "the facts in support of the allegation that he (Soustelle) was one of the leaders of the CNR." Silman and Young responded on 15 December 1965, stating (i) "From about the summer of 1962"; and (ii) "The Plaintiff (Soustelle) was a member of the Executive Committee of the CNR consisting of Monsieur Bidault, the Plaintiff, Colonel Argoud and General Gardy."

The core of the Soustelle's case became much clearer on 16 February 1966, when his lawyers filed their "Reply" to the "Defense." In Clause 2, "the Plaintiff (Soustelle) admits that between in or about the month of

November 1962 and in or about the month of March 1963, he was a member of the executive of a political organization known as the CNR. . . . The plaintiff denies that the CNR was part of or connected with or the successor of the OAS" (Silman papers). Accompanying the "Reply," Soustelle's lawyers also served a "Notice to Admit the Facts." Legally the defendants were given seven days to accept or reject Soustelle's account of the "Facts." There were several that Soustelle admitted to in this "Notice." The first two were banal, stating simply where the novel was published and that de Gaulle was and still is President of France. Points 3 and 4 were an unobjectionable definition of fascism:

> 3. That the Fascist Party's policy includes (inter alia) the abolition of a free press and individual freedom and the creation of a one-party state.
> 4. That a large section of right-minded members of the public abhor Fascists.

There was nothing untoward about this. Soustelle had already denied his fascist links in *A New Road for France*:

> The mania of these people [journalists] is to make me out to be a "Fascist," which they know pertinently well is a shameful lie. To this end, they invented stories of contacts and secret meetings I was supposed to have had in Italy and elsewhere with ex-Fascists. The principle is always the same:
> "Slander . . . slander . . ."[27]

What surprised Silman and Young was point 5:

> 5. That the OAS was a military terrorist organization with little or no popular support that believed in the use of violence and murder to achieve its political aims.

Suddenly the battleground had become clear. The old question of whether it was a libel against Soustelle or a libel against the OAS had been resolved. Soustelle, by his own "Notice to Admit the Facts," had denounced the OAS. It was now obvious that he was objecting to the novel because it had associated him with the OAS. The libel action was clearly intended to restore his own reputation at the expense of that of the OAS. Moreover, by simultaneously admitting he was a member of the CNR, Soustelle was claiming that the CNR was a different organization from the OAS. Silman and Young's defense was made simple: they had to prove that the OAS and the CNR were the same organization.

They had the documentary evidence on their side to prove that Soustelle's reputation was damaged before the novel appeared. First, there were ample OAS-CNR documents; second, published interviews with CNR members support Silman and Young's judgment that Soustelle was implicated as an executive member of the CNR; and third, the published books of the CNR members as well as unpublished CNR documents. All of this evidence showed that the CNR was the OAS and that it was plotting against de Gaulle.

To begin with, the CNR had several principal propaganda organs: *Appel de la France*, the journal of the CNR; *France Presse-Action*, the weekly bulletin of the Central Press Agency of the executive of the CNR and the metropolitan delegation of the OAS; and *OAS Presse-Action*, a weekly publication of the executive of the CNR and the metropolitan OAS. Two publications were printed under the direction of the CNR: *Jeune Révolution*, a periodical circulated to the young, and *Les Centurions*, a periodical circulated among the military. Within each of these publications, the CNR unequivocally threatened a coup d'état against de Gaulle led by the CNR, and a clear-cut chronology emerges from these documents: 9 April 1962, Georges Bidault announced the official constitution of the CNR ("Communication au peuple français relative à l'Ordonnance du 30 Mars, 1962"); 20 May 1962, Antoine Argoud took command of the OAS in metropolitan France ("Prise de commandement du colonel Antoine Argoud"). At this point, there was a formal recognition that the OAS and the CNR were struggling against the same objective: the abandonment of Algeria. Although the *OAS Presse-Action* changed its name to *France Presse-Action* between 27 June and 7 July 1962, other publications continued to use the CNR and OAS interchangeably. For example, the September 1962 *Appel de la France* still printed the OAS in bold letters on the final page of this issue. And in this issue of *Appel de la France*, the CNR restated its desire for a coup d'état and supported the methods of the OAS.

Additionally, the CNR (including Soustelle) was steady in its support for Bastien-Thiry. The 19 March 1963 edition of *Jeune Révolution* republished a quote from the recently executed Bastien-Thiry along with a quote from Bidault: "our martyrs did not choose to die. If they do die, it is because they want to live. . . ."[28] Not coincidentally, this very same edition of *Jeune Révolution* also printed a quote from the Commanding Officer of the "*OAS-Metro-Jeunes*" honoring Bastien-Thiry's sacrifice.

In an interview published in the 21–28 February 1963 edition of *Nouveau candide*, Georges Bidault expressed his uncompromising attitude vis-à-vis the CNR's desire to have de Gaulle "disappear." In his words, "I think that morally de Gaulle deserves to be killed." When asked if he still held to his description that the CNR was just the OAS plus an executive group and whether there was complete agreement among the executive members of the CNR, Bidault replied: "there is no problem between Soustelle and me, on the one hand, and the colonels and me, on the other." Importantly, in this interview Bidault stated that once de Gaulle was removed, "power would fall into our hands" and that Soustelle, Argoud, and Bidault had all agreed the use the name of the CNR for their movement because it shared the same objectives as the first CNR during WWII: the overthrow of a compromised regime.[29] Moreover, Soustelle (who was not one to shy away from making dramatic public statements) never publicly disavowed his support for any of the CNR's stated goals before *Assassination* was published.

Books by Bidault and Soustelle himself demonstrated, at the very least, that the CNR called for the overthrow of de Gaulle and that the CNR was engaged in such efforts. Neither of these books did anything to hide the intentions of the CNR. *Resistance: The Political Autobiography of Georges Bidault* was published in French in 1965 and in English in 1967. In it Bidault describes his encounters with [efforts against?] the Gaullist regime and his experiences in exile. Soustelle's *A New Road for France* appeared in French in 1963 and in English in 1965. Reviews were not favorable. Even usually moderately worded publications such as *Choice* did not abstain from harsh criticism of Soustelle's bitter diatribe against de Gaulle: "His book . . . excels in verbal violence: this is a reckless assault upon the present regime, the defenders of past political traditions, and the 'decadence' of today's France. . . . Fully half of the book is repetitious and savage."[30]

But all of this was hearsay evidence. Under British law, Silman and Young had to go to extraordinary lengths in order to prove that what they had written was in fact not mere fiction. Silman and Young were in an extremely difficult position: either they had to apologize publicly to Soustelle, which would have vindicated Soustelle's charges against the "Gaullist dictatorship," or they had to prove absolutely that the CNR was the OAS. To do the latter, they had to find members of the OAS-CNR willing to testify against Soustelle.

It was precisely at this crucial moment that the French philosopher Jean François Lyotard suggested that Silman and Young contact the young historian Pierre Vidal-Naquet. Pierre Vidal-Naquet had become a famous French intellectual during the French-Algerian War when he published *L'Affaire Audin*, a book that disclosed the scandalous murder of a young French mathematician and communist, Maurice Audin, by the French authorities in Algeria in 1957.[31] Although trained as a classical historian, Vidal-Naquet also published other influential books relating to the French-

Algerian War, and by the time of Silman and Young's troubles with Soustelle, Vidal-Naquet and Lyotard had proved themselves fierce opponents of Soustelle. Vidal-Naquet and Lyotard agreed with Silman and Young that Soustelle must not be permitted to use their novel to distance himself from his fascist political past. But how could Vidal-Naquet best help the authors of *Assassination* prove that Soustelle was a fascist?

Initially, Vidal-Naquet introduced the authors to policemen who had fought against the OAS. Then, through these policemen and their networks, Silman and Young made contact with "genuine shady characters," the people who had "actually worked to assassinate de Gaulle" (Silman interview). Navigating this dangerous network, they endeavored to confirm that Soustelle, Bidault, and Argoud were not only the leaders of the CNR but had been leaders of the OAS.

About the time that Silman and Young began to make their way into the lurid world of underground assassins and criminals, Argoud was illegally arrested in Germany by de Gaulle's secret police. Argoud, said to be one of the most intelligent officers in France, recounted in his *La Décadence, l'imposture, et la tragédie* that his second clandestine life lasted from 26 April 1961 to 25 February 1963. He admitted that "From the start [of hiding], I said that my decision was irrevocable. I would never give myself over to de Gaulle, the man who embodies all that I hate and distrust."[32] Argoud also disclosed that Bidault and Soustelle and their other comrades understood very well that de Gaulle posed a special problem for them, and there was no disagreement that de Gaulle had to be gotten rid of. Little wonder that de Gaulle's government decided to break international law by capturing Argoud in Germany, bringing him back over the French border, tying him up with rope and dropping him near the garbage cans at Notre Dame to be picked up by regular French police and arrested. When Soustelle and Bidault heard of Colonel Argoud's arrest, they immediately went on the run again. Bidault claimed that the only reason that kept de Gaulle's men from immediately snuffing out Argoud was the fact that the rivers in Germany were frozen over. For their own part, French officials never admitted that their agents had orchestrated Argoud's kidnapping.

The authors' refusal to offer an apology triggered the collapse of a joint defense with Jonathan Cape. Cape wanted out of the legal mess, whereas Silman and Young dug in their heels. Silman and Young were almost forced to settle because of a lack of resources. Jonathan Cape had nothing to gain in continuing to defend the libel action. The book had been withdrawn shortly after the case was opened; the costs were mounting. If they won the case against Soustelle it would cost them money, but if they lost it would cost them even more. For the publishers it was a no-win situation.

In January 1967 Jonathan Cape was presented with a way out. Soustelle's lawyer informed Cape and Silman and Young that Soustelle was willing to halt the process if they would pay the court costs and offer an apology that acknowledged that Soustelle was not a member of the OAS. Jonathan Cape agreed and told Silman and Young that if they wanted to continue their battle against Soustelle, they would be on their own. Facing severe financial considerations, and still without any firsthand evidence to prove that the OAS and the CNR were the same organization or that Soustelle was intimately involved in its machinations, Silman and Young were desperate enough to begin drafting a formal apology to Soustelle that gave away as little as possible. Then in February and March 1967, when their backs were against the wall, a miracle happened. In the 26–27 February issue of *Le Monde*, there was an interview with Soustelle in which he denied having any association with the OAS. On 1 March, Pierre Vidal-Naquet replied, writing, "as for his participation in the OAS, Mr. Jacques Soustelle is playing with words. . . . the CNR of Mr. Bidault . . . has acknowledged Soustelle's participation in the organization."[33] A few days later, Soustelle replied, "I do not know why Mr. Vidal-Naquet has decided to pick a fight with me."[34] The correspondence ended with Vidal-Naquet's letter on 9 March accusing Soustelle of playing word games. The letter closed, "I hope he dedicates himself to the study of the Aztecs rather than contemporary history since it is for the worst, for the Algerian people and our own, that he ever intervened."[35] As a consequence of this correspondence, Madame Fouri Argoud, the wife of the imprisoned colonel, contacted Vidal-Naquet, who put her in touch with Silman and Young. But what did the wife of the convicted leader of the OAS want?

As it happened, with her husband condemned for treason and locked away in a French prison, with little income and with children, Madame Argoud was willing to talk for a price. Silman and Young began a lengthy correspondence with Madame Argoud in which they asked her questions about her husband's involvement in the OAS, and she gave them the much-needed details. For example, she claimed that while she was with her husband, Colonel Argoud, in exile in Spain she saw plastic explosives being smuggled into France for terrorist purposes. It was in Madrid, she wrote to Silman, that she understood that her husband, who was an intelligent officer full of talent, had completely lost any notion of measure and reason. Furthermore, she told Silman that it was on 30 March 1962, following the putsch in Algiers and the collapse of the OAS in Madrid, that the CNR presented itself as a third way. In this same letter, Madame Argoud detailed how on 6 August 1962, while she and her husband were on vacation, Soustelle suddenly showed up on his way to Milan, and that Bidault, Soustelle, and Argoud traveled together as the heart of the CNR in August 1962. Even more damaging for Soustelle, Madame Argoud confessed that she had often talked with her husband about Soustelle and that while it was evident that Soustelle, Bidault, and Argoud were men with differences, they shared the same goal: to force an overthrow of the government and trigger a violent revolution (Silman papers).

Motivated by financial necessity and clearly for a price, Madame Argoud would testify that her husband had been meeting with Soustelle and that at these meetings Soustelle had indeed been plotting to assassinate Charles de Gaulle. With this confession, Madame Argoud suddenly became Silman and Young's star witness, and they tore up the apology their lawyers had just prepared. At this point Jonathan Cape (and Mayflower, who had recently been joined in the Defense) separated themselves from Silman and Young. The publishers' apologies remained on the record, but Jonathan Cape's would not be made public until Soustelle's case against Silman and Young was ended.[36] Everything that happened in the case following the British publishers' decision to apologize was between Soustelle and Silman and Young exclusively. The authors attempted to corroborate Madame Argoud's testimony by writing Colonel Argoud in prison. They tried to use Soustelle's "Notice to Admit the Facts" (which labeled the OAS as a violent fascist organization) to provoke Argoud into testifying against Soustelle, but their letters went unanswered.

However, Silman and Young did not pin all their hopes on convicted criminals or their penurious wives' testimonies. Indeed the authors also tried to enlist the support of reputable politicians, intellectuals, and military and civil authorities in France ranging from Pierre Mendès France to Raymond Aron to Paul Teitgen. Both Mendès France and Aron declined to give testimony against Soustelle but not for the same reasons. Mendès France responded in a letter on 27 October 1967, saying that he did not think he would be much help, but he did add that for most French people, "there really were no discernible differences" between the OAS and the CNR (Silman papers). In a second letter, Mendès France gave Silman the names of some people better able to provide more information on Soustelle since his exile. Raymond Aron's position was a bit different. In January 1968 Silman was able to persuade Aron to agree to respond to preliminary questions concerning Soustelle's politics, but in the end Aron decided not to testify against Soustelle because he thought France was already too divided and it was time to heal the wounds of the French-Algerian War.[37] Nevertheless, Silman and Young were able to assemble an impressive group of witnesses. For his part, Soustelle also enlisted the help of some high-profile witnesses. Without question though, Madame Argoud would be the star witness and her sworn testimony was as essential for Silman and Young's case as it was fatal for Soustelle's.

THE TESTIMONIES

For reasons of cost and convenience, both parties agreed that French witnesses should have their testimonies taken in Paris rather than during the court hearing in London. These testimonies are an extraordinary collection of documents—nothing similar exists in French history. They are cited and made available here for the first time. Because the use of a suit against a novel to restore one's name is unprecedented, large sections of the transcripts are reproduced here.[38] The testimonies show the depth of passions that the French-Algerian War ignited and the realization (by all involved) that the war would have consequences in contemporary French politics and society well beyond the independence of Algeria in 1962. But these testimonies also show something unique in the history of publishing. They demonstrate how a work of fiction was "tried" and used by both sides in the dispute to either damage or rehabilitate the career of one of the best-known and most powerful renegade intellectuals and politicians in twentieth-century French history. In other words, the following transcripts demonstrate that *Assassination*, as a work of fiction, was endowed with the unusual power to transform reality.

The legal testimonies were taken at the British Embassy in Paris and the results taken back to England for the British courts to adjudicate. Eric Edgar Young, the consul general in Paris (or his deputy John F. Taylor), was appointed special examiner in charge of overseeing the testimonies. Eleven witnesses were scheduled to testify. On Soustelle's behalf, Achille Perretti, General Marie-Joseph Pierre François Koenig, Gilbert Beaujolin, Dr. Leon Boutbien, and Jean-Louis Vigier would swear that they did not believe Soustelle was a member of the OAS. Against Soustelle, Pierre Vidal-Naquet, Madame Argoud, Daniel Mayer, Paul Teitgen, Paul-Marie de la Gorce, and Honoré Gevaudan would testify that they believed that he was an active member of the OAS-CNR.

During the questioning, the witnesses were asked to refer to passages in *Assassination* and to verify if the Soustelle described in the novel was the *real* Soustelle. Specifically, they were asked to compare the Soustelle they knew to the Soustelle found on pages 39 and 41 of the novel (pages 30–32 in the present edition). There were also other documents the witnesses were asked to verify and comment on. These items included a photograph of Soustelle with George Bidault, Antoine Argoud, and Paul Gardy at an executive meeting of the CNR in Munich in 1963. The photograph appeared in *Paris Match* on 2 March 1963 (see following page 182). Witnesses were also read selections from the interview with Georges Bidault that appeared in the 21–28 February 1963 issue of *Nouveau candide*. Other key documents consisted of various propaganda tracts of the OAS and the CNR as well as newspapers and other publications.

Achille Perretti and General Marie-Joseph Pierre François Koenig were the first to testify on Soustelle's behalf. Perretti and Koenig had formidable reputations. Both were heroes of the French Resistance, both were heavily decorated, both had distinguished careers, and both were staunch, well-known patriots. Colin Ross-Munro, Soustelle's attorney, began his substantive questioning by asking if Perretti had read the relevant passages of the novel. Ross-Munro followed this by asking him whether the fictional character resembled his friend, the real Jacques Soustelle:

> **Q.**47 Now, in those passages, Mr. Perretti, there is reference to a man called "Soustelle." Who do you think they were referring to when they talked of that man "Soustelle"?
> **A.** Dealing with matters relating to Algeria, it is difficult not to understand that it related to Jacques Soustelle. . . .
> **Q.**48 Mr. Perretti, as far as you are aware, has Mr. Soustelle ever taken part in a conspiracy to assassinate General de Gaulle?
> **A.** I cannot say naturally that he did not take part in anything. I can only say that knowing him as I do, I suppose that he did not do it and in any event I hope not.

After confirming that the fictional Soustelle was intended to represent the real Soustelle, Perretti insisted that the novel had marred the truth about his friend because, according to him, Soustelle was no fascist and could not have been represented as such. Perretti defended Soustelle based on his impressions of Soustelle's moral character in the past, but Perretti could offer no firm evidence to exculpate him from his fictional association with the OAS.

Perretti was cross-examined by the counsel for the defense, Brian Neill, who began by asking about the coup d'état of 1958 and the putsch of 1961. Neill's strategy with this first witness—and he used it throughout the testimonies—was to force the witness to admit that, according to popular opinion, the OAS was behind the putsch and other attempts to disrupt the government. This was a critical issue; it became a cornerstone of Silman and Young's defense because Neill hoped to prove that the novel was based on the general public's perception of Soustelle's connection to the OAS and was not a deliberate attempt by Silman and Young to libel him. Neill then asked Perretti about the relationship between the CNR and the OAS as it was reported in the press at the time. Perretti admitted that some newspapers made the connection between the CNR and the OAS and that there were allegations that the CNR was indeed behind the Petit-Clamart attack.

Later that day, General Marie-Joseph Pierre François Koenig was called to testify. At the time, Koenig was one of France's most decorated national heroes. He had been a member of the Free French government in London and was appointed the commander of the Free French forces in North Africa during WWII. General Koenig had been the French military representative on the staff of General Dwight Eisenhower, and he had commanded the Free French forces in Great Britain and inside France (the FFI). He spent four years as the commander of French Forces in Germany beginning in July 1945. Like Soustelle, General Koenig was a deputy in the French National Assembly and a member of the Rassemblement du Peuple Français (the RPF Party), of which Soustelle had been secretary general. From 1951 to 1959, he remained in the French Assembly but retired in 1960, near the end of the Algerian conflict. His testimony was important because he knew most of the central actors on the French side of the French-Algerian conflict. In fact, he had been a friend of de Gaulle since 1926 and of Soustelle since they first met in Algeria in 1943.

When General Koenig was asked by Soustelle's attorney, Ross-Munro, if he thought that the depiction of Jacques Soustelle in the novel was accurate and fair, he left no doubt:

> A. [108] When I read the book "July 14 Assassination" I was stupefied, horrified. If there was one thing that could not be held against Jacques Soustelle, it would be not only the murder of a man, let alone the murder of General de Gaulle. Jacques Soustelle was an intellectual. . . . But Soustelle was at the same time a man full of human feeling. Already before the war he was known to be a defender of the Rights of Man and no one who knew him could imagine that he could have taken part in a plot to murder a man of great importance any more than a man of humble status.

And when asked if the Soustelle he knew had ever supported fascists or been connected with the OAS, Koenig was even more animated: "Oh, my God.

Oh, my God. He was a very strong opponent of fascism" (A.110). Again, this was an important issue because in the novel Soustelle was portrayed as a fascist. When Koenig was cross-examined by Brian Neill, he spoke about Soustelle's career before 1961, but admitted that he could not accurately account for Soustelle's activities after he went into exile. And since this was the period in question, the general's ability to either hurt or aid Soustelle's case was minimal.

The first round of testimonies was completed. It certainly had not hurt Soustelle to have these two men with spotless reputations come to his aid, but their testimonies did not really damage Silman and Young's defense either. What the first two testimonies did accomplish was that they allowed both sides in the litigation to rehearse their arguments about the innocence or culpability of *Assassination* in damaging Soustelle's reputation and the relationship of popular opinion, history, and fiction. Furthermore, the first round of questioning had exposed a hole in Soustelle's case against the novel because he could not produce anyone actually present during the mysterious meetings of the CNR who could testify on his behalf, and for very good reason. The only ones who knew what was said—Gardy, Bidault, Argoud, and Soustelle—were either in prison or in exile.

Two and a half months later, the second round of testimonies was taken in Paris, from 29 January to 2 February. Nine witnesses were scheduled to testify. As before, the testimonies were taken in Paris in both French and English and then taken back to England to be examined by the British courts.[39]

On 29 January 1968 Gilbert Beaujolin, a highly decorated WWII military hero, a Gaullist, and a friend of Soustelle, was the first to testify in the second group. Like Soustelle's other character witnesses, Beaujolin was a hero of the French Resistance and a holder of many medals of honor. He had known Soustelle since the liberation of Paris in 1944. In addition, Beaujolin had been a founder of a "left-wing Gaullist party" called the Centre de la Réforme Républicaine in 1958. Although a friend of Soustelle he did admit that they did not have identical political views, especially over the Algerian question. The "Centre," he told Ross-Munro in questioning, "always supported the idea of the independence of Algeria and that of course applies to me as a member" (A.16). Ross-Munro questioned Beaujolin:

Q.17 Would it be fair to say that over Algeria, your political views differed considerably from those of Mr. Soustelle?
A. Certainly. My answer would certainly be yes, because Mr. Soustelle was still in favor of . . . "*Algérie française.*"

Beaujolin was then referred to the passages in the book and asked whether he believed that the character represented in the book was the same as Soustelle. Beaujolin replied coolly, "As far as I am concerned, there has never been any doubt in my mind that it was Jacques Soustelle referred to, otherwise I would not be here." And, a few questions later, Beaujolin comes to Soustelle's defense:

> **Q.22** To your knowledge, has Mr. Soustelle ever taken part in a conspiracy to murder General de Gaulle?
> **A.** To my knowledge, never.
> **Q.23** From your knowledge of Mr. Soustelle, has he ever had fascist views of politics?
> **A.** There again, to my knowledge, never. I consider him as an authentic antifascist and antiracist person.
> **Q.24** And why do you consider him an antifascist and antiracist person?
> **A.** I would say that it is public knowledge that this has been the case on all occasions, in his writings on such matters, which leaves no room for doubt.

Beaujolin concluded by stating emphatically that the Jacques Soustelle he knew could neither have tried to assassinate de Gaulle nor have been a leader of the OAS. Hence, for the third time, a character witness of Soustelle's came to his aid with an effort to preserve his antifascist image, which dated from the mid-1930s.

The following day, 30 January, Brian Neill cross-examined Gilbert Beaujolin. Beaujolin replied to Neill's initial questions and reaffirmed that he did not think that Soustelle was a leader of the OAS or had conspired to assassinate de Gaulle. Neill's line of questioning suggests that he first wanted to get Beaujolin to say that the CNR, created in 1962, was committed to overthrowing the French government. However, Beaujolin refused to take the bait and declined to answer the question. Neill then moved on to the issue of public opinion by repeating a question asked before about what "right-minded people" thought of the OAS. With much wit Beaujolin stated that being right-minded himself, he should be able to say what "right-minded people" thought at the time. The transcript continues:

> **Q.51** That is a very fair way of putting it, Mr. Beaujolin, but is it not right that all right-minded Frenchmen believed that the OAS was planning to overthrow President de Gaulle by violent means?
> **A.** I would say that all persons, even those not particularly informed

in political matters, know that the OAS had a programme which was to overthrow in France the legal Government of the Republic.

Q.52 And those people, that is all persons, even those not particularly informed, knew that that was the programme of the CNR, did they not?

A. I think these are very different matters, which does not mean that the CNR had not necessarily the same programme, but whilst the programme of the OAS was known to more or less everyone, that of the CNR was still to many people very vague and lacking in precision. I should perhaps add that this was the case for me.

Beaujolin's reply is important because it indicates that there was not a definite separation in the public mind between the OAS and CNR. Georges Bidault, the nominal head of the CNR, supported the claim when he observed in his autobiography that there were many actions taken in the name of the CNR which were not endorsed by its leaders. According to him, given the nature of the organization, the leaders of the CNR simply could not control what was done in its name. Therefore the public could not be expected to truly understand how the CNR related to the OAS, and this confusion would lead people to believe that they were the same organization. For example, Bidault claimed that he only learned that Salan had appointed him head of the OAS by reading an article in *L'Express*.[40] As Bidault stated: "I never received the letter which appointed me the head of the OAS and I therefore never gave orders in the OAS's name. Later, leaflets with the heading OAS-CNR were printed; but I have always regretted this was done and I gave instructions for it to be stopped which were never followed."[41] Regardless of Bidault's disclaimers about what he did not endorse, he and the other members of the CNR never described what types of actions they were taking to disrupt de Gaulle's government. And many of the testimonies suggested alternatives to Bidault's personal recollections.

The next day of the testimonies Neill asked Beaujolin if he knew that the assassination attempt on de Gaulle at Petit-Clamart was organized by some of the members of the CNR. After an objection by Ross-Munro, Beaujolin was shown the Manifesto of the CNR published in *Le Monde*. Beaujolin was also shown a statement by de Gaulle's minister of Justice, Roger Frey, in which Frey had claimed that the OAS and the CNR had the same goal— overthrowing the government. Beaujolin stated that he believed that the CNR was a "politically different organization" from the OAS. In reply to a question concerning Soustelle's connection to the CNR, Beaujolin added:

A.[64] Personally, I don't think that he [Soustelle] was a leader of the

CNR and that if he were I think that his aim would have been to carry out a programme politically and not by violent means.

The transcript continues with Neill pressing Beaujolin for answers:

Q.65 You see, you have described the CNR as an organization that was not recognized by the institutions of France. How could he [Soustelle] carry out the political programme?
A. I am basing what I am saying on the personal attitude of Jacques Soustelle, who, by accepting to stand for Parliament during the last general elections in a perfectly orthodox fashion, has shown that he intended pursuing his actions by legal means.
Q.66 You are not suggesting, are you, that he was attempting to pursue his programme by legal means in 1962?
A. I am not informed of the programme that Mr. Soustelle had in 1962. Nor of the manner in which he wanted to carry it out.

Late in the afternoon, Neill finished his cross-examination of Beaujolin. The witness had been careful not to implicate Soustelle in any antidemocratic activities. Yet, once again, the witness could not provide proof that Soustelle was not involved in an attempt to overthrow de Gaulle's "illegal" regime.

That same day, Ross-Munro reexamined the witness in an effort to drive home Soustelle's innocence and the separation of the politically-oriented CNR from the violent paramilitary organization, the OAS. Ross-Munro also wanted to demonstrate that the witness was for both Soustelle and Charles de Gaulle:

Q.82 Mr. Beaujolin, you have said in answer to Mr. Neill that you knew and heard that the OAS was trying to overthrow President de Gaulle by the use of violence. You have also said in answer to a question from Mr. Neill that you think there was a difference between the OAS and the CNR.
A. Yes.
Q.83 From the little that you know and have heard about the CNR do you think they wished to overthrow President de Gaulle by political means or by violent means?
A. I have always thought that the OAS intended applying its pro-gramme by violent means. With regard to the CNR, without having definite information on the subject, it is my belief that their pro-gramme was more of a political nature. Which does not preclude the fact that some of the members of the CNR may have wished a brutal overthrowing of the President of the Republic.

Q.84 But as far as Mr. Jacques Soustelle is concerned, did you think he wanted a brutal overthrow of the President of the Republic or the [over]throw of the Republic by political means?

A. If I am here today as witness for Jacques Soustelle it is because it is my sincere belief that Jacques Soustelle wished his programme to be put into effect through legal republican means. And that is how I interpret the fact that he recently stood for Parliament in the general elections.

Q.85 And the last question I would like to ask you is that Mr. Neill suggested that you were a Gaullist. Is it right that you are a supporter of General de Gaulle?

A. That is perfectly correct.

The next witness was Dr. Leon Boutbien. As with the previous witnesses for Soustelle, Boutbien's record was impressive. A medical doctor, he first met Jacques Soustelle in 1934 when they were students. In 1934 Boutbien, Soustelle, and Jacques Piette served as administrative secretaries on the Comité de vigilance des intellectuels anti-fascistes. During WWII Boutbien had been deported by the Germans to a concentration camp and condemned to death. After the war, he returned to France to serve as a deputy in the National Assembly from 1950 to 1955. He had been a member of the Socialist Party for more than thirty-three years.

As with Gilbert Beaujolin, Boutbien's replies to his first questioner, Ross-Munro, confirmed that Boutbien was a staunch defender of Soustelle's reputation. At bottom, he insisted that Soustelle could not have been a member of the OAS as he was portrayed in the novel. Boutbien was cross-examined by Neill. He was asked if he knew who took control of the OAS after Salan was arrested, and specifically if he knew that Colonel Argoud led the OAS after Salan. This question touched a nerve, and Boutbien charged that Argoud was "illegally fetched from Germany. He was kidnapped." Neill then asked Boutbien if he knew what the initials "CNR" stood for, to which Boutbien replied that that as a leader of the nation's French Resistance Association, he had published formal protests against the use of the CNR in connection with the "Algerian problem." Boutbien disagreed with the appropriation of the acronym CNR by the defenders of French Algeria, and he was obviously angered by the unwanted association of the French Resistance with the French-Algerian War. Neill asked about Petit-Clamart and then, in a very interesting part of the testimony, about the etymology of the word "reputation." Boutbien answered as follows:

A.[69] The Latin words *reputare* and *fama* are to some extent reputation; reputation is, in fact, the impression that one may have of someone whom he does not know. Etymologically, it does not mean that one knows a person. . . . There is nothing objective in this and someone's reputation cannot serve as a basis to what judgment one may have.

Q.70 And reputation will depend, for many people, to some extent at least, on what they read in articles in newspapers?

Ross-Munro objected and the transcript continues:

Q.71 Forget what Mr. Ross-Munro is saying. . . . Could you now answer the question in the Parisian context?

A. Reputations can be made and unmade; it depends on the means of information that one has at his disposal, and reputation is certainly not synonymous with truth.

A few questions later, after being shown the Bidault interview in *Nouveau candide* in which he stated that the OAS was committed to overthrowing de Gaulle, Neill asked the all-important question:

Q.81 Now it was the general view in France, was it not, in 1962–1963 among fair minded people that the OAS was committed to the overthrow of General de Gaulle?

A. Yes, of course. It was not only the case of the OAS. The OAS was not alone in wishing to replace General de Gaulle at the head of the government in 1963. There were others. The question was, what means were to be employed for this. . . .

Q.83 But the OAS was prepared to use violence?

A. That may well be but it does not concern me; I am not a member of the OAS.

Q.85 And the CNR was the body in control of the OAS after the summer 1962, was it not?

A. I think so. I would have to read this as you probably did in the press.

Once Boutbien acknowledged that the public perceived the CNR to be behind the operations of the OAS's terrorist campaigns, Neill then asked why he had, earlier in his testimony, referred to Paul Rivet, a known leader of the antifascist movement and the director of the Musée de l'Homme in Paris.[42] Neill knew that Boutbien was implying innocence by association by putting Soustelle in the company of one of France's best known antifascists. Neill continued to press the witness to get him to admit that a friendship with a known antifascist does not an antifascist make:

Q.93 But you were referring to Mr. Rivet, were you not, to show that it was unlikely that Mr. Soustelle would have expressed fascist views?

A. Yes.

Q.94 Did you know that Mr. Soustelle was connected politically with Argoud during the winter of 1962–1963?

A. No.

Q.95 Would that surprise you?

A. I am not here to evaluate that political position. I am asked if I consider him to be a fascist etymologically or not and I can say no.

Q.96 Why do you say that you are not here to evaluate his political opinion? You are here for that.

A. No, I am replying to this specific question put to me: do I consider him to be a fascist?

A few questions later, Neill showed Boutbien the *Paris Match* photograph that shows Jacques Soustelle, Colonel Antoine Argoud, Georges Bidault, and General Paul Gardy together in 1963. As the questions continued, it became clear that for Boutbien Soustelle's long-standing friendship with Rivet was proof enough that Soustelle was not fascist. The rest of Boutbien's testimony was inconclusive.

On 31 January Neill was finally able to bring forward the witnesses against Soustelle, beginning with Pierre Vidal-Naquet. As a historian of ancient Greece, Vidal-Naquet was a prominent French academic at the time, and as a leading French intellectual in the late 1950s and early 1960s, he had been a formidable opponent of the French-Algerian War. He had published extensively on Greek history and had written several important works about the French-Algerian War. During the French-Algerian War, he was on the editorial board of *Verité-Liberté*. He was the only witness to have been among the original signatories of the famous "Manifesto of the 121" in 1960, which supported draft evasion and for which he was suspended from his teaching post. By 1968 he was named sous-directeur of L'École des Hautes Études in Paris and professor of Ancient History. Testifying here against the real, exiled Soustelle and for the historical accuracy of the fictionalized character of Soustelle in *Assassination*, he brought with him the weight of his well-known and respected status as a professional historian. It was clearly Vidal-Naquet's intention to use this unique position to prove that Soustelle *became* a fascist during the French-Algerian War. Vidal-Naquet had good reason to dislike fascists: both of his parents had died in Nazi concentration camps. However, unlike the previous witnesses, Vidal-Naquet had never met Soustelle.

Near the beginning of his testimony, Vidal-Naquet admitted to Neill that he had followed Soustelle's career with great attention because he was the "personal enemy of fascist movements and of torture" (A.II).[43] For Vidal-Naquet, Soustelle's publications during the French-Algerian War and the fact that he did not discuss the violence and colonial injustices of the French state were telltale signs of an unflattering political stance. Vidal-Naquet cited numerous passages of Soustelle's books that supported Silman and Young's claims that Soustelle had indeed intended to overthrow de Gaulle. For example, referring to an interview Soustelle gave to the United Press International in November 1961, Vidal-Naquet noted:

A.[36] He says that the OAS is the expression of the people who do not want to die, and he means clearly by these people the French settlers in Algeria. . . .

As a professional historian would, Vidal-Naquet came armed with numerous documents printed by the OAS and the CNR copied from the holdings of the Bibliothèque Nationale. He argued that these documents demonstrated that Soustelle was linked directly to the leadership of the CNR. When asked by Neill if he believed that "sensible members of society" could have thought that Soustelle was "taking part in a conspiracy against General de Gaulle," Vidal-Naquet answered:

A.[112] None of the people I met at this time had the slightest doubts about this fact. I don't mean that Mr. Soustelle was himself preparing bombs, and I will say again that I am not a psychologist but an historian. . . . What I mean is that at that moment I thought, and many sensible people thought, that he was involved in a fascist plot against the Republic.

The transcript continues:

Q.113 What do you mean when you say fascist plot against the Republic? I suppose there are two kinds of plots, one involving very constitutional means and another kind of plot would involve the use of violence. Which kind do you have in mind?
A. I have the second one in mind.
Q.116 And what were the views of sensible people with regard to the effect on French institutions if the plot had succeeded?
A. If the plot had succeeded, there is no doubt that France would have been a fascist country.

To suggest that France would somehow become a fascist country if

Soustelle's alleged plot had been successful was undoubtedly a large argumentative stretch, but it was precisely the plot of *Assassination*. In short, Vidal-Naquet had so far done his best to present the characterization of Soustelle in the novel as not only accurate but *plausible*. Nevertheless, when Colin Ross-Munro cross-examined Vidal-Naquet on 31 January, he began asking a few routine questions (staying away from the question of fascism) but then asked how he had first come into contact with Robert Silman. Vidal-Naquet explained that they met sometime at the end of 1964 or the beginning of 1965 and that Silman had come to know him through Jean-François Lyotard. Ross-Munro tried to call in to question Vidal-Naquet's intentions by asking the following:

Q.146 Did Mr. Silman ever tell you about the sources of his information before he wrote this book "July 14 Assassination"?
A. I think he did not need to because I read the book and it is a detective novel; my impression—and that was confirmed by what he told me—is that he wrote this book according to what was France's general opinion of Mr. Soustelle at the time.
Q.149 So far as you are concerned, would it be correct to describe you as somebody who was a supporter of the FLN in Algeria?
A. I don't understand that word supporter.
Q.151 Somebody who sympathizes with the FLN in Algeria?
A. I will answer precisely. I sympathized with the efforts of Algeria to become independent.
Q.152 Would it also be right to say that the FLN hated Mr. Soustelle?
A. It would certainly be right.
Q.153 Would it be right to say that they tried to murder him in 1958 in Paris?
A. It is right.
Q.154 Did you approve or disapprove of that as far as the FLN is concerned?
A. I never approved nor made any statements about such acts. I have always publicly regretted that Mr. Soustelle was not tried before the Court. If I wanted him tried before the Court, I did not want him to be assassinated. That would be a contradiction.
Q.156 Would it be correct to describe you as a bitter political opponent of Mr. Soustelle?
A. I don't know if I am bitter, but I was certainly a political adversary of Mr. Soustelle. Bitter is a question of appreciation. . . .

Q.164 Would you agree that Mr. Soustelle has always had the repu-
tation for being against anti-Semitism?
A. I think I can agree with that but I will add that people can be
adversaries of anti-Semitism and be racists at the same time.
Q.165 Are you suggesting that Mr. Soustelle is a racist?
A. I am suggesting that during a period when he was governor general
of Algeria and specifically after August 1955 he behaved like a racist
and associated himself with people who were undoubtedly racists.
Q.166 When he was governor?
A. Yes and afterwards.
Q.167 And who were the racists that he associated himself with when
he was governor?
A. Alas, most of the French settlers in Algeria.
Q.168 Would it be correct to describe your politics, Mr. Vidal-Naquet,
as extreme left?
A. I would like to know what you mean by extreme left. If you mean
by extreme left the fellow travelers of the Communists, I would say
no.

During the rest of his long and antagonistic cross-examination, Ross-
Munro attempted to discredit the authenticity of the OAS documents. Vidal-
Naquet and Ross-Munro argued about Soustelle's connection to fascists,
the motives of the left in persecuting Soustelle, the perception among the
French public that the OAS and the CNR were one and the same, and whether
or not Soustelle was a member of the CNR on 22 August 1962—the day of
the botched assassination attempt at Petit-Clamart. All in all, Vidal-Naquet
was quite persuasive, and it was clear that the witness had enormous moral
contempt for Soustelle.

Following Ross-Munro's questions, Brian Neill briefly reexamined Vidal-
Naquet.

Q.282 What was your experience of the views of reasonable people as
to whether or not Mr. Soustelle was a supporter of fascism?
A. My experience of reasonable people I met at this time was that
Mr. Soustelle was looked upon as a fascist.

Immediately following his testimony, Vidal-Naquet gave testimony in
lieu of Madame Argoud because, unfortunately for Silman and Young,
Madame Argoud did not appear to testify. According to Silman, Madame
Argoud had received two phone calls from an "extraordinarily right-wing

individual" by the name of Jean La Hargue. La Hargue was the president of Secours Populaire pour l'Entraide et la Solidarité, an advocacy group set up to defend OAS members. As it happened, Silman and Young had been required by law to release their witnesses' names to Soustelle's lawyers. Shortly after Soustelle's counsel discovered that the chief witness against Soustelle was Madame Argoud—none other than the wife of Antoine Argoud, the man illegally fetched from Germany by de Gaulle's secret police, the notorious *barbouzes*—she claimed to have received two phone calls from La Hargue. During the first call, La Hargue allegedly told her that he had a dream in which "monsters were going to do her and her family harm" (Silman interview). Madame Argoud also claimed that she received an anonymous call that threatened to harm her children if she testified. At this point, she contacted Silman and said that she was still willing to testify but only if she were paid. Then the second call came from La Hargue who told her in no uncertain terms that she would be harmed if she testified. She immediately notified Silman that she was not going to appear. Silman recounted his reaction: "I was pretty pissed off. . . . In fact, I was so pissed off that it made me absolutely determined now not to apologize to Soustelle. Not only was this scum trying to wriggle out of his association with the OAS; not only was he condemning his old friends and therefore being doubly scum; but he was triply scum because he was using those same people [the OAS] and their scummy methods to try to wriggle out of being associated with them. I was totally outraged by what was going on. To my mind, it was only Soustelle and Soustelle's lawyers who could be behind Madame Argoud's nonappearance" (Silman interview).

Vidal-Naquet informed the court that Madame Argoud had been scheduled to appear but had decided not to because of a threat that her children would be kidnapped if she testified. However, and to Vidal-Naquet's surprise, not to mention to Silman and Young's, Ross-Munro had proof that Madame Argoud had first contacted La Hargue, not the other way around, as she had told Silman. She had asked La Hargue to forward a letter to Soustelle requesting that he stop his action against Silman. Ross-Munro had the letter read for the court: "If this case takes on a final form, I will not be able to avoid participating. This would be a disillusionment for the young man." It was clear, Vidal-Naquet agreed uncomfortably, that she was referring to Silman's disappointment. Yet, despite the fact that Madame Argoud's reference to "disillusionment" remained unclear, it was also plain that she had not been forthright in her conversations and correspondence with Vidal-Naquet or Silman.

Following this partial and unexpected discrediting of their star witness,

Silman and Young's next supporting witness, Daniel Mayer, took the stand on 31 January. A leading French political figure, Mayer was a former member of the first CNR and the former secretary general of the Socialist Party during and after WWII. He served as deputy from Paris in the National Assembly from 1945 to 1958, as the minister of Labor from 1946 to 1949, and as the minister for Ex-Servicemen and of Public Health in 1948. He became the president for the League of the Rights of Man in 1958. While serving with Soustelle in the London-based French Resistance, they became close friends. However, by 1968, that friendship had waned, a perfect example of how the political divisions of the French-Algerian conflict marred old friendships. He had come to testify against his onetime colleague in the Resistance, which it must be admitted was not a happy occurrence. But Mayer believed that his position as the president of the League of the Rights of Man obligated him to testify against Soustelle and not to allow Soustelle to exploit the case against *Assassination* in order to erase his questionable politics from the slate of public consciousness.

Mayer's testimony revealed the deep acrimony that existed not only between two onetime friends but also between two incompatible political philosophies. Mayer, like Vidal-Naquet, implicated Soustelle in the OAS:

Q.12 What was the opinion of right-minded thinking people in 1962–63 as to whether there was any connection between Mr. Soustelle and the OAS?
A. If I fall in the category of sensible people, it is quite certain that it appeared that there was a connection between the OAS and Mr. Soustelle, and that was probably the feeling that was held in public opinion.
Q.13 Among sensible people in 1962–1963, was there a link thought to exist between the OAS and the CNR?
A. I think I must make a distinction among sensible people. If we take sensible people on the extreme right wing, shall we say members of the CNR or the OAS, legally they must have known of such a distinction if such a distinction existed between the CNR and the OAS. . . . But it is quite certain that for public opinion and the whole of public opinion . . . I have no doubt that CNR and OAS [were] one and the same organization.

When Neill asked if he believed that right-minded people thought that the CNR aimed to overthrow French political institutions, Mayer replied unequivocally:

A.[17] There was no doubt, I think, that the result would have been an authoritarian form of government. . . . Fortunately this did not come to pass, but really there would have been an autocratic, authoritarian form of government, reactionary in the sense used by politicians, to suppress or considerably mutilate many of civil liberties. . . .

Mayer, thus, also confirmed Silman and Young's fictional hypothesis that the OAS-CNR really did pose a tremendous threat to the stability of France's Fifth Republic. This was probably not posturing on Mayer's part, for he probably did believe that if the OAS had assassinated de Gaulle as it planned, France's political institutions were not strong enough to withstand this fascist threat.

Ross-Munro began his cross-examination that afternoon by asking how Mayer met Silman and whether or not he had read *Assassination*. Mayer stated that Silman contacted him through the League of the Rights of Man and that he had not read the book. After Mayer read the pertinent passages, Ross-Munro asked him if he could prove that Soustelle had plotted to assassinate de Gaulle. Mayer replied:

A. [28] As we know, it is never the person who actually throws the bomb who becomes the foreign minister of the group who managed the attempt. There is a difference between the people who actually execute and the ones who benefit. So if you ask me: do you believe that Mr. Soustelle would have participated physically in an attempt on de Gaulle's life my answer would be no; but, secondly, if you ask me if I believe that in the circumstances in 1962–1963 politically he might have belonged to a group who would have benefited from a successful attempt of this kind, my answer would be yes.

At this point, the transcript shows a game of wits between Ross-Munro and Mayer, with Mayer insisting that he spoke for the man in the street's perception of the CNR and Ross-Munro calling on him to provide concrete proof connecting Soustelle to a plot against de Gaulle. Then, later in the questioning, Ross-Munro forced Mayer to concede that Soustelle had been a leading antifascist intellectual. But, as Vidal-Naquet did, Mayer alluded to a significant shift in Soustelle's beliefs following his tenure as governor general. After 1955, Mayer contended, the "traumatized" Soustelle moved even further to the right. At the very least, according to Mayer, Soustelle could no longer be considered a liberal. Ross-Munro tried to downplay the damage of Mayer's earlier responses to Neill. In particular, Ross-Munro attempted to question the notion of public opinion:

Q. 57 I put it to you that you are wrong when you say that in public opinion Mr. Bidault and Mr. Soustelle were the best known leaders of the OAS.

A. You have shed light on my earlier reply and I take note of this and I thank you for your judgment of my testimony.

Q.58 I would suggest to you, Mr. Mayer, that in public opinion the leader of the OAS was General Salan. . . .

A. Yes, also. My list was not an exhaustive one. I mentioned mainly the political figures who were the ones I knew best.

Q.59 I put it to you that in public opinion the leaders of the OAS or the main leaders of the OAS were people like General Salan, General Jouhaud, Colonel Godard, all they were known as the leaders in the OAS according to public opinion.

A. I do not agree. Those names were much less familiar to public opinion. The generals would have been considered to be executors not the politicians and indeed subsequent events proved this to be the case. Their names became really known at the time of their arrest or of their condemnation, but the name George Bidault was the name of a former president of the CNR, the real one, who had used the title for the purpose of preparing a putsch, and the name of Jacques Soustelle would be known since 1934. These names were much more present in public opinion than those of the executors or the accomplices.

Q.60 I put it to you, Mr. Mayer, that in the opinion of reasonable and right-minded people in France in 1962–1963 they did not associate Mr. Soustelle as a leader of the OAS but merely as a member of the CNR.

A. I was not aware that public opinion drew a distinction between the two; indeed I am convinced that for public opinion OAS and CNR was one and the same thing.

Q.61 I must also put to you as part of my case, Mr. Mayer, that public opinion of right-minded people in France at the time drew distinction between the OAS and the CNR.

A. This proves that there are two categories of right-minded and reasonable people.

Both Mayer and Ross-Munro realized the full import of public opinion and that the issue of public opinion was very often a gray area. Since neither of them actually cite public opinion polls, it is difficult to determine exactly what public opinion was. However, a number of newspapers very frequently blurred the distinctions between the OAS and the CNR. This fundamental ambiguity, as mentioned earlier, was due to the fact that even Bidault could

not keep tight control over the propaganda created in the name of the
CNR.

The next day, 1 February, Jean-Louis Vigier came to the stand on
Soustelle's behalf. At the time of his testimony, Vigier was a senator from
Paris. During WWII, he had been arrested by the Gestapo and condemned
to death but was freed during the Liberation. From 1945 to 1947, he
directed the French newspaper, *L'Époque*. From 1947 to 1959, he was a town
councilor from Paris, and from 1951 to 1958, he was a deputy in the National
Assembly. As a deputy, he was a member of the same party as Soustelle,
the Rassemblement du Peuple Français (RPF), until 1953, after which he
joined the extreme right-wing party known as the Independents. In 1959
he was elected to the Senate as a member of the Independent Republic
group. He was highly decorated, having been awarded a *Croix de Guerre*
with two bars and one star, a *Rosette de la Résistance*, a Military Cross, and
a Police Resistance medal, and was made a commander in the Legion of
Honor.

Being Soustelle's supporter, Vigier was first questioned by Colin Ross-
Munro about his affiliation with Soustelle. In the preliminary questions he
stated that he had known Soustelle since 1947. Next he was read the relevant
passages from *Assassination* and asked whether the Soustelle he knew could
have conspired to assassinate General de Gaulle. When asked whose name
came most easily to the public mind when the CNR was mentioned, Vigier
commented:

> A.[39] The only name that really comes to me is that of Bidault, and
> that is why one really can't take all this seriously because he is not the
> kind of man who could go to the end of his course. . . . It would have
> been necessary to assassinate General de Gaulle. . . . I am convinced
> that Georges Bidault would never dream of such a thing. . . . for one
> thing, he is a Christian. . . .
>
> Q.44 One more question: do you think it possible that Mr. Soustelle
> was a member or one of the leaders of the CNR?
> A. I do not know. As far as Bidault is concerned with the CNR, we
> have what Bidault said and wrote. He announced that he was setting
> the CNR up, he was probably acting on past memories and perhaps
> saw himself in the role of Liberator of Algeria just as, in the past, he
> had been Liberator of France, but about Soustelle all I can say is that
> Bidault said he was setting up the CNR. And so if the same had been
> true of Soustelle, I don't see why he would not have said the same
> thing himself and yet, judging from what Soustelle has written, he

has not said such a thing, and, in any case Soustelle, whom I have not seen for a number of years, I cannot answer the question. . . .

In short, while Vigier's intention was to free Soustelle from suspicion, his comments did not really aid Soustelle or condemn *Assassination*. In fact, they only reinforced the sense of confusion about who was in charge of the CNR and what Soustelle's exact relationship to the OAS was.

Later that day Algeria's former chief of police, Paul Teitgen, was called to testify against Soustelle. Teitgen was the son of Henri Teitgen (a prominent French politician) and was currently a *Maître des Requêtes* at the *Conseil d'Etat* (council of state) as well as the former vice president of the National Assembly. His brother had once been minister of Justice. During WWII Paul Teitgen was deported by the Gestapo to Dachau for his connections to the French Resistance. After WWII he was named a chevalier of the Legion of Honor, decorated with a *Croix de Guerre* and bar and a *Médaille de la Résistance*, and he had become a senior member of the civil service. Aside from holding the office of assistant prefect of Avallon, in 1956 he was chosen to be the man in charge of the police in Algeria during Jacques Soustelle's tenure as governor general. Teitgen's experiences in this position convinced him that Soustelle's leadership in Algeria posed a significant moral and legal threat to France. For example, Teitgen had come to Soustelle with reports of police criminal misconduct (especially the use of torture against Algerians) that Soustelle knowingly ignored.

Teitgen was first questioned by Brian Neill. Teitgen explained how he had resigned from his position in Algeria following a dispute with General Massu over Massu's defense of torture and the inexplicable "disappearance" of more than four thousand arrested Algerians. Ross-Munro objected to Teitgen's discussions of the torture of Algerians by French parachutists on the grounds that it was not relevant to the case at hand. Neill then proceeded to question Teitgen about his former friend, Colonel Argoud, and once again Ross-Munro objected that Teitgen's comments were inadmissible. The questioning continued. In the course of the questioning, Teitgen stated that he had also been in Algiers on 13 May 1958 and had been arrested by the paratroopers a few days later and "sent back to France by General Salan" (A.27). Neill moved to the issue of public opinion:

> Q.33 I want to ask you now about Mr. Soustelle and what the general view among sensible people was in France in 1962 and 1963 about him. After the arrest of General Salan in March, who did the general public believe to be the leader of the OAS?
> A. . . . at the time, when I no longer had any police responsibilities

through which I could and should of course have been informed personally, I can say that within the Conseil d'État, the senior Civil Service and the people whom I knew, the leaders of the OAS were those of the CNR: Salan, Argoud, Soustelle, Bidault. Those for public opinion were the names of the heads, the leaders, the brains of the organization. This is what the newspapers said and the clandestine publications which were sent to us, even in the Conseil d'État there were references to orders and decisions taken by the joint staff of the CNR and the OAS. This was the opinion generally held and in all honesty it was mine.

And the transcript continues with the issue of the state of public opinion vis-à-vis Soustelle and the OAS:

Q.38 What, in the public mind, was the aim of the OAS and the CNR in 1962 and 1963?
A. The aims of the CNR-OAS in public opinion, if I represent part of this public opinion, were, through the maintenance of Algeria under French dependence, the taking of power in France.
Q.39 What were the views of public opinion as the means which the CNR-OAS would use to achieve its aims?
A. It was fairly easy to form an opinion on what their methods might become. The CNR-OAS had already made use of their methods, which were murder, assassination, and bombs.
Q.40 Before the war Mr. Soustelle, it is common knowledge, was a member of the antifascist Committee. Where do you place Mr. Soustelle in the politics of 1962?
A. . . . I say regretfully, but I am convinced of this, that in 1962 the former member of the antifascist Committee became, after his spell of duty in Algeria, a fascist. His references to the earth, to blood, to the defense of the West, to the threat which he felt resulted from the danger of Communism for Europe and the whole free world and the necessity of having a strong army closely connected with academic circles, all this, if you make a political analysis, is the same as the themes which are bandied about under any dictatorship.
Q.45 Just two more questions: what was the general view as to the sort of effect on French institutions there would have been if the OAS-CNR had succeeded in obtaining power?
A. If OAS-CNR had taken power, for French opinion, and this is my opinion of which I am quite convinced, we would have had a fascist regime.

Teitgen's moral authority at the time in France was beyond reproach and he had made a convincing argument, as had Vidal-Naquet and Mayer, that at the time the novel was written France's government was balanced on the edge of a fascist precipice. Furthermore, Teitgen had made it sufficiently clear that even at the highest levels of French political circles and police intelligence, there was no firm understanding of the difference between the OAS and the CNR. And, if one is to take Georges Bidault at his own words, this confusion even appeared on the official propaganda of the CNR itself. In short, if Teitgen's testimony were used in England during the actual trial, Teitgen could explain how it was that the two young novelists had legitimately placed the real Soustelle in the heart of a nefarious OAS conspiracy.

When Teitgen was cross-examined by Ross-Munro, he was asked the standard questions such as when and how he was asked to testify. Teitgen replied that he had first been told about a novel written about Soustelle and the OAS. Once he heard about the novel's plot, the fate of the novel after it was published, and that when the authors wrote the book they believed that Soustelle had been a real-life "leader of the OAS," Teitgen agreed to give his name to Pierre Vidal-Naquet as a witness for the authors' defense. Vidal-Naquet then gave Teitgen's name to Silman and Young and their lawyer. Importantly, Teitgen recounted to Ross-Munro that he told Vidal-Naquet that he would testify to the fact that he honestly thought Soustelle had become a fascist. Through questioning, Teitgen also admitted that he and Vidal-Naquet became good friends in 1958, after the publication of Vidal-Naquet's book on the murder of Maurice Audin by the French authorities in Algiers. Furthermore, Teitgen acknowledged that he shared Vidal-Naquet's views on Algeria but pointed out that they had different political philosophies. The cross-examination was concluded for the day.

As Ross-Munro cross-examined Teitgen the next day, on 2 February, Teitgen was asked if he knew whether the publishers of the book had agreed to apologize to Soustelle and to pay damages. Then, in an attempt to confuse the witness, Ross-Munro asked if Teitgen knew that within the past year Silman and Young had been prepared to settle the claim against them and were prepared to say that Soustelle had never tried to attempt to assassinate General de Gaulle (Q.73). Teitgen responded that he could not provide evidence that linked Soustelle to an assassination attempt on de Gaulle, but Teitgen did call Soustelle's moral authority into question for failing to denounce the Petit-Clamart incident. Teitgen continued by citing Lieutenant Colonel Jean-Marie Bastien-Thiry's claim that he was operating under the authority of the CNR at Petit-Clamart.

Q.81 Did you know that, when Colonel Bastien-Thiry said he was acting under the CNR, he added that one of General de Gaulle's own ministers had taken part in the plot and had given information as to the time the General's car would be passing near Petit-Clamart?

A. It is correct that that was said also.

Q.82 And do you know that when the President of the Court asked Colonel Bastien-Thiry to name the minister he said that it was Mr. Valéry Giscard d'Estaing?

A.83 Yes, and the press mentioned this also.

Q.85 Did you know that Mr. Soustelle was not a member of the CNR on the 22nd of August 1962, the date of the Petit-Clamart attempt?

A. I did not read again the newspapers in order to prepare for coming to testify. On what date did Mr. Soustelle become a member of the CNR as an open organization I am not aware, but Soustelle from the very beginning was a member of the CNR and covered by his authority the rebellion against the government and the liberties of the Republic of France. When General de Gaulle was chief of the provisional government of the French Republic during the war, can one say that this was on the 18th of June 1940 or in 1945 when the country was liberated? I say that his moral authority began on the 18th of June 1940 and that is where the responsibilities lie. The members of the rebellion against the government and the liberties of France, even before the establishment of any organizations as such, have already shown their responsibilities by their attitude, by their authority, and, in some cases, by their revolt and that that is where the true responsibilities lie. I do not wish to go fully again into the proceedings against Bastien-Thiry. I am simply speaking as a citizen whose duty it is to state unambiguously his firm conviction relating to the moral responsibilities of the people who later became official members of the CNR and the OAS. It is merely in view of my conviction concerning their moral responsibility from the outset that I am here to be a witness for Mr. Silman.

Q.86 If we can leave aside for the moment your convictions and concentrate on the question of evidence, what evidence have you to support your statement that from the very beginning Mr. Soustelle was a member of the CNR?

A. This is important. I am not a member of the police and have no documents and no material proof. This is exactly as if, as a Christian, I were asked to provide material proof for the existence of Christ; it is exactly as if a judge or a barrister were called up to abandon their most intimate convictions.

Q.87 Have you any proof that Mr. Soustelle at any time took part, directly or indirectly, in an attempt to assassinate General de Gaulle?

A. That is also a profound conviction.

It became clear, through cross-examination, that Teitgen believed that Soustelle really was the mastermind behind Petit-Clamart but was unable to prove it. He even went further in his attack on Soustelle by claiming Soustelle had been a member of the extreme right in France since 1947 (A.100). And, when asked if he believed the OAS and CNR were the same organization, Teitgen insisted that this was the case since they both supported the idea of *Algérie française* and the overthrow of the government. Moreover, since OAS and CNR goals were the same, the CNR would employ violence as the OAS did.

A few hours later, the penultimate witness, Paul-Marie de la Gorce, testified against Soustelle. A writer and an author of several works on the French-Algerian War, including *The French Army: A Military-Political History*, de la Gorce was one of the first journalists to cover the "birth of the OAS" at the beginning of 1961 and was considered to be an expert on the history of the OAS (A.11). In addition, he served on the editorial board of *L'Express*, as an editor of *Jeune afrique*, and as a contributor to the leftist newspaper, *France observateur*. Since 1967, he occupied the post of technical counselor to the French Ministry of the Interior. After several questions concerning the authenticity of the OAS documents (mostly those that Vidal-Naquet introduced as evidence) and his activities as a journalist in Algeria during 1962, Neill focused on the leadership of the OAS. De la Gorce responded by explaining that he had heard an OAS clandestine radio broadcast after General Salan was captured that gave future control of OAS operations to General Gardy. Ross-Munro objected that this information was irrelevant, but Neill quickly moved to the issue of Soustelle's involvement:

Q.33 Now, in 1962 and 1963, what was the opinion of sensible fair-minded people generally with regard to Mr. Soustelle's political opinion?

A. In 1962–63, there was no doubt concerning the position of Mr. Soustelle concerning the political situation and concerning the events in Algeria because by then the general view was that he had left French territory. . . .

Q.34 What was the general opinion among sensible people about his attitude towards the OAS?

A. It is clear that as the OAS was a clandestine organization and its activities were clandestine . . . it is difficult to define exactly the responsibilities of each person in the organization. It is clear, however, that many people felt that Mr. Soustelle had relations with the OAS and responsibility regarding the political orientation of the organization. . . . [I]n a matter of opinion there is a fact, however, and that is that the observers were very impressed at the supposed contacts between Mr. Soustelle and the OAS when the *Nouveau candide* published a photograph showing Mr. Soustelle with Mr. Bidault, General Gardy and Colonel Argoud. . . .

Q.34 In the public mind among sensible people, was there any distinction between the OAS and the CNR?

A. No, except for dates. The CNR, as I said before, appeared somewhat later in the course of events, and many observers felt that this new name had been introduced partly because of the course of events in Algeria and the necessity of limiting the activities of the OAS after independence . . . and because the CNR, the word CNR, might awake in people's minds memories of the Resistance, and that thereby some confusion could be created which would attract goodwill on the basis of this ambiguity.

Q.36 As far as you are aware, in 1962 and 1963, did Mr. Soustelle ever attempt to lead the press to think that he had nothing to do with the CNR or the OAS?

A. I think Mr. Soustelle did what he could to shield himself from suspicion of having contacts and, possibly, responsibilities regarding the clandestine organizations. He certainly took a number of precautions in that respect but his attitude seems to leave in the minds of most people and journalists who were following the events closely the impression that he must have had, to a degree which it is impossible to assess, contact and perhaps responsibilities. . . .

Q.38 And also, what was the opinion as to the methods which the OAS and the CNR would use for the purpose of achieving their objective?

A. The opinion that one could have had on that was a direct consequence of the methods actually used by the OAS and the CNR in Algeria and Metropolitan France. For a long time I was a witness to such methods, particularly in Algeria: individual attacks on people, indiscriminate firings, indiscriminate attacks by mortar on civilian districts in Algiers, for instance, these are methods which the OAS and the CNR did actually use. . . .

As an expert witness, Paul-Marie de la Gorce was convincing. He knew the historical facts relevant to the history of the OAS and could state with confidence that there was in fact very little to distinguish the OAS from the CNR. And since it was known that Soustelle was a member of the CNR, it was not a very large step to argue that Soustelle's characterization in the novel could not be called a gross distortion. Ross-Munro understood how important this expert testimony could be as he began his cross-examination of de la Gorce. After a few questions about the history of the OAS and the differences between the OAS in Algeria and the OAS in France, Ross-Munro believed that he could derail the witness's assurances. Ross-Munro cleverly asked:

Q.51 In your book of the history of the OAS in Algeria, do you suggest that Mr. Jacques Soustelle was one of the leaders of the OAS in Algeria?
A. I do not think so, although I have not reread, quite honestly, my book which I wrote nearly six years ago, but in Algeria my feeling is that Mr. Soustelle's personal role was nil. Seen from Algiers, the journalists considered that the participation of important political figures such as George Bidault and Jacques Soustelle probably fitted in more in a metropolitan European framework about which it was more difficult for us to be informed.

Continuing his line of questioning, Ross-Munro pushed de la Gorce to explain why he had never claimed in his own historical writings that Soustelle was a leader of either the OAS or the CNR. Here Ross-Munro was very effective:

Q.54 Do I understand by that, Mr. de la Gorce, that you personally would never write something so defamatory as to call a man a leader of the OAS unless you had proper proof?

Evading the question, de la Gorce responded:

A. I think one should never say that someone has responsibilities in a clandestine organization guilty of criminal acts unless there is a very strong presumption such as the flight from French territory of a political figure benefiting from such broad consideration and often esteem as Mr. Soustelle.

Pushing the issue further, Ross-Munro continued:

Q.60 Have you ever suggested in writing that Mr. Soustelle had taken part in organizing an assassination attempt on General de Gaulle?

A. No.

In a barrage of ensuing questions, de la Gorce was forced to admit that as a journalist he had no proof connecting Soustelle's activities to the OAS. He was also obliged to concede that Soustelle could have been forced to flee France because he was being persecuted for having criticized de Gaulle's Algerian policy and out of fear that he would have been imprisoned without trial—as were many other de Gaulle opponents—for upwards of a year. But, returning to an issue raised by Daniel Mayer, de la Gorce insisted that a political figure of Soustelle's stature with nothing to hide would not have fled France like a criminal. This is probably a bit of an overstatement because there is little doubt that Soustelle's criticism of de Gaulle would have gotten him arrested. In fact there was a warrant out for Soustelle. Hence it is not entirely correct to suggest that Soustelle's leaving simply indicated guilt. And, with regard to Ross-Munro's claim that there were differences in public perceptions of the OAS and the CNR, de la Gorce responded:

> **A.** [84] I feel that, on the contrary, the position of the OAS and the CNR was entirely clear to everyone in France in 1962. These organizations were aiming at maintaining French presence in Algeria by use of force against the government which was attempting to bring peace to Algeria. The CNR was substituted for the OAS in my view because the OAS had lost the Algerian battle. . . . [I]n public opinion there was no distinction between the OAS and the CNR, except with regard to dates.

Concluding, Ross-Munro asked de la Gorce if he considered Soustelle to be sincere in his desire to maintain French Algeria. De la Gorce responded that he believed this to be the case and added ironically that he would "question the sincerity of no man engaged in a political endeavor and particularly that one" (A.101).

At this point in the testimonies it became clear to both sides that a large part of the case now rested on the ability to prove or disprove the authenticity of the internal OAS-CNR documents that linked Soustelle definitively to both organizations. Hence, when Honoré Gevaudan took the stand as the last witness on 2 February 1968, what he said was vital to the case. Why was he so crucial? At the time of his testimony, Gevaudan was Commissaire Divisionnaire at the Direction de la Police Judiciaire at the Sûreté Nationale (similar to the Scotland Yard). As a detective in 1962 he was responsible for state security and specialized in the repression of arson and arms trafficking. His work therefore focused on efforts to protect the security of the state, especially against organizations such as the

OAS. Appearing as a witness against Soustelle, he was first questioned by Brian Neill about police raids on OAS members. In particular, Gevaudan confirmed that during raids on the OAS the police had seized publications such as *Appel de la France*, *OAS Presse-Action*, and *France Presse-Action*—the very documents that connected Soustelle to the OAS. With Ross-Munro objecting, Gevaudan vouched for the authenticity of the documents. He also gave the specific case numbers to which these seized documents related, and he insisted that those introduced by Vidal-Naquet during his testimony were authentic pieces of OAS and CNR propaganda.[44] Neill then asked about the possibility of forgery in order to dismiss an accusation Ross-Munro had made suggesting that the CNR documents were forgeries. Gevaudan responded:

> A.[35] We have no knowledge of any forgery. . . . If I may add my personal impression, it is that the French Government is sufficiently attacked as it is by the press for it not to want to circulate further attacks in the form of forged documents.

After answering a few questions relating to other letters and publications found during arrests, Neill asked whether, as a member of the police, Gevaudan believed that the OAS and the CNR were the same entity. Gevaudan gave perhaps the most lucid analogy of the seven days of testimony:

> A.[65] The OAS and the CNR can be compared to a street which changes its name. The name changes but the paving does not change nor does the place which the street leads to.

And when Neill asked how the police viewed the CNR in 1962, Ross-Munro objected, forcing Neill to rephrase the question in the standard formula of how did "sensible people" view the CNR:

> A.[67] For everyone, as long as they were in good faith, the CNR was merely the OAS under a different name. No one thought for a second that the CNR was anything else than merely the continuation of the OAS, and indeed the leaders were the same and the missions were similar. But perhaps it became necessary to have a new name, to put on a fresh coat of paint, so to speak.

And how did the public view Soustelle's role in the CNR:

> Q.72 In addition to Georges Bidault, were there other names among those thought at the time, in general opinion, to be the leaders of the OAS and CNR?

A. During our operations after General Salan's arrest we discovered, by documents seized, that the CNR—which was a continuation of the OAS—was led by Georges Bidault and there were several documents that referred to an executive committee which had been set up and composed of Mr. Gardy, Mr. Soustelle and Colonel Argoud.

After a recess Neill continued his questioning of Gevaudan. This was immediately followed by Ross-Munro's cross-examination. The bulk of Ross-Munro's questions attempted to discredit Honoré Gevaudan's ability to evaluate the authenticity of the so-called OAS and CNR documents, especially signed documents. It was especially imperative for Ross-Munro to cast doubt on the authenticity of the CNR communiqué published in *Le Monde* on 10 October 1962. The communiqué not only condemned de Gaulle to death, but also had a swastika printed on it. Ross-Munro argued with a great deal of credibility that many people questioned the veracity of this document because it simply was not Soustelle's style to play off Nazi symbolism. In fact it was hardly the style of the other members of the CNR either. Gevaudan's obvious discomfort is recorded in his silence on this issue. A variety of questions followed, during which Ross-Munro tried to show that Gevaudan possessed no proof concerning Bastien-Thiry's claim that the CNR had ordered the assassination of de Gaulle at Petit-Clamart. Gevaudan was again forced to admit that he had "no proof and no fact" linking Soustelle to this organized assassination attempt (A.109). Still trying to discount the extant OAS and CNR documents, Ross-Munro continued to grill the witness:

> **Q.122** Did you know that rightly or wrongly it was suggested that the Gaullist government was forging documents in order to discredit the OAS and the CNR?
> **A.** I do not know what was said, but to discredit the OAS and the CNR it was certainly not necessary to forge any document.

A few minutes later, Gevaudan was reexamined by Brian Neill. With repeated objections by Ross-Munro, Neill asked the witness how many assassination attempts on de Gaulle had taken place after Petit-Clamart. Gevaudan replied that there were at least two, one at the École Militaire in February 1963 and then in Toulon in August 1964. Gevaudan also stated that there was a known link between the École Militaire affair and the CNR.

> **Q.145** Are you aware, Mr. Commissioner, of any link between the École Militaire Affair and the CNR?

A. Yes, from several sources. First of all, the searches which took place at the conspirators' homes and their own confessions.

OBJECTION: By Mr. Ross-Munro: And again if I can object on the grounds that what various people were arrested for the École Militaire Affair, that what they said in the absence of my client cannot possibly be evidence going to any of the issues in this case.

Q.144 You said you have found a link from several sources including the depositions and confessions. What was the link that you found in those confessions?
A. It was simply that according to the persons arrested, the attempt had been carried out under the CNR. I may add that this surprised no one.

Ross-Munro was given a second cross-examination period to ask further questions about the École Militaire assassination attempt, but Ross-Munro kept Gevaudan on the stand only for a few seconds. Honoré Gevaudan was the last witness to appear, thus concluding days of testimonies. It was hoped by both sides in the dispute that they now had enough convincing evidence to find a verdict in their favor.

FROM THE TESTIMONIES TO THE 1968 RIOTS

Following the testimonies, both sides wanted a quick resolution to the suit. This was especially crucial for Soustelle because by early 1968 he had already made it known that he intended to run for a parliamentary seat in Lyons by proxy in that year's election. Though in exile in Switzerland, he still had the legal right to run for Parliament. Before his candidacy could be validated, however, he had to return to France. If he returned to France, the charges still standing against him could be prosecuted, and they carried a ten-year sentence. A favorable ruling in the libel suit against Silman and Young would help smooth the path to the elections.

However, before the British courts had time to look over the testimonies, the political ground had begun to shift again in Paris. The lingering pain of the old wounds from the French-Algerian War gave way to a more urgent crisis that threatened de Gaulle's presidency: the student protests of 1968. Many in France believed that it was time to mend the divisions the war had created and that mending divisions would mean granting amnesty to those still in exile or in prison. Suddenly the student protests merged past and current political crises, and one thing was clear: de Gaulle's second honeymoon with the French people was over.

Silman and Young once again found themselves caught in the swift currents of surreal, un-British French politics. The first indications that something significant was afoot in France came from the new university in Nanterre. On 22 March, just a month and a half after the testimonies, what began as a student protest in opposition to de Gaulle's regime quickly moved to criticisms of the war in Vietnam, the university system, and the lack of student freedom. The movement spread to the Sorbonne in early May. This forced the French police to enter that site for the first time since the French Revolution. The police openly beat students as they moved to make arrests. For the next ten days, until 13 May (ten years to the day after the start of the coup in Algiers), the struggle remained student-led. Then, on 13 May, French workers reacted to the government's use of violence by uniting with the students.

On 13 May a universal strike paralyzed France, and the Gaullist regime teetered on the brink of complete collapse. When de Gaulle left Paris two weeks later on 29 May, most observers thought that he was going to relinquish his power. Little did the public realize that de Gaulle was visiting General Massu, whose French troops were stationed in West Germany. Many historians have traditionally claimed that General Massu agreed to support de Gaulle but offered one very important condition: de Gaulle would have to grant amnesty to everyone connected with the OAS. This, of course, meant that de Gaulle would have to agree to pardon a group of infamous people including Bidault, Soustelle, and Salan if he expected the army to help him in Paris.

What is more widely believed now is that George Pompidou, de Gaulle's prime minister in 1968, made a deal with Tixier-Vignancour—the right-wing politician who challenged de Gaulle in the 1965 presidential campaign—that provided for the release of the OAS people from prison and the return and amnesty of its leaders still in exile in exchange for Tixier-Vignancour's support of the Gaullists in the June 1968 parliamentary elections. De Gaulle agreed to this deal, and on 30 May, with the army firmly behind him, de Gaulle returned to Paris for a television address during which he accused the French Communist Party of instigating the revolt. After attacking the Communist Party, de Gaulle characterized the revolt as a choice between the forces of evil (Communism) and the benevolent forces of good (Gaullism). Within a day more than one million people took to the streets in support of de Gaulle. However short-lived his victory was (he resigned the following year), he had to make good on his promises: he had to allow Soustelle and the rest of his most bitter rivals to return to France unmolested and release those connected with the OAS from prison.

Two months later, on 23 July, Soustelle's eighty-year-old mother phoned her son in Italy to tell him that the French Parliament had just voted to grant him amnesty. Of his seven-year exile Soustelle wrote, "I have been a hunted man for the past seven years, a man without a country." Yet Soustelle added that de Gaulle's defeat was Soustelle's own vindication, in fact, France's vindication:

> De Gaulle's thunder apparently no longer impresses anyone. Besides, by this time, everyone knew that the monstrous and pitiless manhunt against me had no justification whatsoever, except in my staunch and outspoken opposition to the Gaullist regime, which is the right of every citizen in a true democracy.
>
> The events in France of last May and June have shaken the regime to its very roots. The movement for complete amnesty for all so-called "crimes" committed during the Algerian crisis, a movement led by such humanitarian leaders as Professor Jean la Hargue, could no longer be ignored, and so the amnesty was finally enacted into law. Previously, the Gaullists, with the help of the Communists, had either killed or watered down every bill presented in the National Assembly, but this time public opinion was too strong and the Gaullist majority had to accept the fact. So it is that as of July 23rd, all political prisoners, including General Raoul Salan, have been released from prison and political exiles such as myself are free once again to walk the soil of our native land. . . .
>
> All told, there is nothing I regret. For there is no price too high to be paid by a man, just to keep the right not to despise himself.[45]

After amnesty, Soustelle suddenly wanted to be rid of his case against Silman and Young. After all, the case could now become a political liability. Silman and Young, though, were determined to use the case to embarrass Soustelle and thwart his political comeback. Hence, when not long after the decree granting amnesty Colonel Argoud was released from prison, Silman and Young decided to make a trip to visit him. They wanted Argoud to testify against Soustelle. To get Argoud's testimony, Silman and Young would remind him that Soustelle had claimed that Argoud's OAS was a nefarious, fascistic "terrorist" organization. Silman and Young's letters to the imprisoned colonel had failed; could a personal visit change Argoud's mind?

When the two young authors finally found the ex-colonel walking in a field near his house in the country and indicated why they had come, Argoud "started screaming." In a furious state, Argoud said that it was "scum [*salaud*] like you who dragged us all into the mud." Then in a tirade, Argoud said that he had his own score to settle with both de Gaulle and Soustelle, and that when de Gaulle was dead he was going to "go to his grave and put a bomb on his tomb" (Silman interview).

Abandoning their hopes for Argoud, Silman and Young continued their efforts to win the case. In the meantime, Soustelle was beginning his new political career with a bid for a city council seat in Lyon (which he held from 1971 to 1977), and he planned to return as a deputy to the French National Assembly (where he sat from 1973 to 1978, proving how short-lived was the collective memory of the French). The case dragged on with no signs of resolution until one serendipitous afternoon in 1969 when Robert Silman's father, Louis Silman, was playing golf with an Israeli businessman. As they engaged in conversation, Louis Silman discovered that his friend, along with others, had been financing Soustelle's libel action against his own son. As the elder Silman soon learned, Soustelle had told his Zionist friends that the French Communist Party was behind Soustelle's persecution. (Soustelle was a well-known defender of Israel, and apparently Soustelle believed that the Communists had been behind the novel, and he convinced his financial backers of this as well.) Louis Silman explained that, contrary to what they had been told by Soustelle, the Israelis had been financing a case against a British Jew and not the French Communist Party. The Israelis decided it was time to broker a meeting between Soustelle and Silman and Young in order to put an end to the case.

Silman and Soustelle finally met at the beginning of 1970 (Young was not present). But this meeting with Soustelle forever changed Silman's vision of the onetime mastermind. Up until this time, despite a generalized disgust for the former political wheeler and dealer, Silman and Young maintained a profound respect for Soustelle as a "political animal." Yet, when they finally met, even his characteristic dark glasses (once symbolic of political savvy and power), which Soustelle still wore, could not hide the fact from Silman that they had been gravely mistaken to cast him as a dignified and intelligent politician, as the perfect antihero. Sitting across the table from Soustelle, a former political exile, Silman found him "pathetic." Just how pathetic was he? And how much had the young authors' image of Soustelle been altered by his actions throughout his case against them? According to Silman: "Here he [Soustelle] was, this pathetic, bronchitic old man, who really had nothing to say. It was a lethargic meeting. [I said], 'Will you stop the court case?' He said: 'Okay.'" Soustelle told Silman that he would drop the case and pay some of their defense costs.[46] But that was not quite all, Silman continues:

That was it, that was the end. Except for the Jonathan Cape apology, which had been agreed to back in 1967. The English papers published their apology as though I was also associated. I had to write letters saying that I had nothing to do with the Jonathan Cape apology. But it was pathetic; it all just ended as a somewhat pathetic event. My final view of Soustelle is of somebody who was actually a *pauvre type* [pathetic man]. Originally when I was at school in England in 1958, I had the image of the man in the boot of a car, escaping from his Paris apartment under the eyes of the police, turning up in Algiers to manage a coup d'état, getting General Salan to acknowledge de Gaulle, turning the coup in Algeria into a coup for the restoration of General de Gaulle. *That* image of *that* man who was the mastermind of that plot didn't exist. Yes, he did all that, but he could so easily have been stopped, and Teitgen was right. I mean the reason for the collapse of the Fourth Republic wasn't the skill of those people who brought about the Fifth Republic; it was the pathetic nature of politicians of the Fourth Republic and their refusal to take any action to stop it. I mean if you think about it, how wretchedly stupid of the police to let Soustelle get out of the country in the boot of his car! He's in his apartment; they know he's there; they know he's trying to get to Algiers; and they don't even bother to look at the cars as they come out to see what's in the boot. Preposterous! My image of Soustelle has gone full circle from a dynamic, controlling, mastermind figure, to somebody who doesn't control anything, who doesn't mastermind anything, who makes enormous errors and at the end of the day, was a *pauvre type, pauvre con* [pathetic bastard]. (Silman interview)

How could Silman and Young have been so mistaken about the validity of their awestruck and youthful impressions of Soustelle? How could they have confused the real Soustelle with the fictitious Soustelle? Perhaps the eight years of litigation had prepared the authors for this moment of disillusion when they would realize that they had thought too much of Soustelle. He was, after all, a man, not a myth. Nevertheless, it was certainly a great irony that in the course of that fateful meeting, the once mythical, dangerous, and energetic antihero of antiheroes, Jacques Soustelle, suddenly became a pathetic, weak man. Even more ironic is the fact that it took eight years for Silman and Young to discover that the Soustelle in the novel did not exist after all, that fiction really was fiction, that only the "reality of Soustelle existed." Or even more: that in the words of literary critic Tzvetan Todorov, "*all* literature escapes the category of true and false."[47]

But what was perhaps the cruelest irony of all was that Silman and Young's novel, which had been forgotten to history until now and which blended history with reality, helped create a whole new genre of historical fiction. Most notably, Frederick Forsyth's blockbuster *The Day of the Jackal* (London: Hutchinson, 1971; New York: Viking, 1971) was also a novel about an assassination attempt on de Gaulle. But, among other differences, the nationalities of the hero and the villain are reversed. While Ben Abro offers the asthmatic Londoner Max Palk as the fictional hero called to Paris to stop Soustelle's and his associates' plot to kill de Gaulle, Forsyth's nefarious English "Jackal" is called to France and contracted by a group of men (presumably Soustelle and company—though their names are wisely not used) to kill de Gaulle. It is Forsyth's French hero, Deputy Commissaire Claude Lebel, who successfully fends off the Jackal at the last moment. Forsyth had been a reporter for Reuters in Paris in 1963. It was that summer that *Assassination* made its debut and the summer that, as Forsyth himself has stated, he began to plan his master thriller. At the very least, it is a striking and fortuitous coincidence that *Day of the Jackal* was released the year after *Soustelle v. Cape and Silman and Young* was settled.

At the same time *Assassination* and the litigation surrounding it did nothing to stem the world's insatiable appetite for James Bond. Ian Fleming died in August 1964, but he authored no less than five Bond novels between 1962 and his death, including *The Man With a Golden Gun, Octopussy,* and *On Her Majesty's Secret Service.* The subsequent rash of Bond movies and the continuing popularity of James Bond seemed unstoppable. Could Silman and Young's Max Palk have rivaled Bond's popularity? Only you can be the judge of this.

Acknowledgments

There is no question in my mind that serendipity is the historian's greatest ally. Serendipity is, I think, the best way to explain how I came to play my own part in *Assassination*'s story. I first heard about this curious novel from the French historian Pierre Vidal-Naquet in the spring of 1994 while I was conducting an interview with him for my book *Uncivil War*, a study of intellectuals during the French-Algerian War. During that interview I asked Vidal-Naquet what he remembered of Jacques Soustelle, one of the key players during the decolonization of Algeria. Vidal-Naquet mentioned something I had never heard of before: a scandal involving a novel written about Soustelle. I made further inquiries, and there I was, a few weeks later, in London, looking through the cellar of Robert Silman's house for the documents that would eventually find their way into the preceding historical essay. Serendipity, therefore, deserves my first heartfelt thanks. But I owe many thanks to the countless people whose influence and presence can be seen throughout this work.

I am especially indebted to Pierre Vidal-Naquet for steering me toward *Assassination* and for the many hours he spent with me discussing the history of decolonization and intellectual life in contemporary France. Along with him, I must thank Robert Silman and Ian Young, or Ben Abro, for allowing me to work with them on the republication of this novel and for granting me the privilege to relive their unusual story with them. Robert's magnanimity, which included access to an important private collection of documents, will not be forgotten. Furthermore, both Robert and Ian provided invaluable information and comments to me over the several years I worked to unravel their story and the publication history of the novel. I sincerely appreciate their patience, kindness, and generosity.

In addition, the essay also benefited from the kind and thoughtful guidance of many colleagues who shared their comments and their time with me on this project. I am profoundly grateful to David L. Schalk, William B. Cohen, Alice L. Conklin, Philip Dine, Jon Cowans, Patricia M. E. Lorcin, Robert Soucy, William A. Cook, Lisa R. Manley, and Dorena Wright for their superb and insightful comments. I would also like to thank Loukia K. Sarroub for reading my drafts and for listening to my ceaseless ravings about Max Palk, Ben Abro, and the all-time classic anti–James Bond novel.

I assume, however, full responsibility for any errors or misinterpretations present in the essay.

The superb editorial board at the University of Nebraska Press deserves much of the credit for the republication of *Assassination*. It allowed me to pursue this project without restriction.

Finally, I would like to thank the various institutions whose financial and moral support allowed this project to reach fruition. The Georges Lurcy Foundation and the University of Chicago provided me with the means to stay in Paris to conduct research from 1993 to 1994. A generous grant from the Andrew W. Mellon Foundation provided the opportunity to write without interruption on this and another project from 1994 to 1995. And, finally, the University of La Verne proved invaluable with its ever appreciated assistance and support.

James D. Le Sueur
La Verne, California

Notes

1. This photograph appeared in *France observateur* on 2 July 1958 (page 11). It was one of many of Soustelle that I found in the papers of Robert Silman and Ian Young.

2. The novel was first published in the United Kingdom in July 1963 by Jonathan Cape as *July 14 Assassination*; in 1964, it was published under the same title in paperback by Mayflower Dell. In the United States, the novel was published in hardback by William Morrow in November 1963 under the authors' preferred title, *Assassination!*, and was subsequently published with this title in paperback by Fawcett in 1965. I will refer to the novel as *Assassination* throughout.

3. Following Soustelle's departure, the office of governor general was changed to resident minister. Robert Lacoste then became resident minister of Algeria.

4. There are several excellent works on the history of France's occupation of Algeria. For the best general histories of Algeria, see Charles-Robert Ageron, *Modern Algeria: A History from 1830 to the Present*, translated by Michael Brett (London: Hurst & Company, 1990) and John Ruedy, *Modern Algeria: The Origins and Development of a Nation* (Bloomington: Indiana University Press, 1992). For a more detailed account of intellectuals vis-à-vis the French Algerian War, see my *Uncivil War: Intellectuals and Identity Politics during the Decolonization of Algeria* (Philadelphia: University of Pennsylvania Press, 2001) and my introduction to Mouloud Feraoun's *Journal, 1955–1962: Reflections on the French-Algerian War*, edited by James D. Le Sueur, translated by Mary Ellen Wolf and Claude Fouialle (Lincoln: University of Nebraska Press, 2000). For other works dealing specifically with the French-Algerian War and the process of decolonization, see Geoffrey Adams, *The Call of Conscience: French Protestant Responses to the Algerian War, 1954–1962* (Waterloo, Ontario: Wilfrid Laurier University Press, 1998);

Anthony Clayton, *The Wars of French Decolonization* (London: Longman, 1994); Yves Courrière, *La guerre d'Algérie*, 2 vols. (Paris: Robert Laffont, 1990); Bernard Droz and Evelyne Lever, *Histoire de la guerre d'Algérie (1954–1962)* (Paris: Seuil, 1991); Martin Evans, *The Memory of Resistance: French Opposition to the Algerian War (1954–1962)* (New York: Berg, 1997); Frank Giles, *The Locust Years: The Story of the Fourth Republic, 1945–1958* (London: Secker & Warburg, 1991); Richard Joseph Golsan, ed., *The Papon Affair: Memory and Justice on Trial* (London: Routledge, 2000); Hervé Hamon, *Les Porteurs de valises: la résistance française à la guerre d'Algérie* (Paris: A. Michel, 1982); Alexander Harrison, *Challenging De Gaulle: The OAS and the Counterrevolution in Algeria, 1954–1962* (New York: Praeger, 1989); Alistair Horne, *A Savage War of Peace, Algeria 1954–1962* (New York: Penguin, 1987); Martha Crenshaw Hutchinson, *Revolutionary Terrorism: The FLN in Algeria, 1954–1962* (Stanford: Hoover Institute, 1978); Danièle Joly, *The French Communist Party and the Algerian War* (New York: St. Martin's, 1991); Jean-François Lyotard, *La Guerre des Algeriens: Écrits 1956–63* (Paris: Galilée, 1989); Robert Malley, *The Call From Algeria: Third Worldism, Revolution, and the Turn to Islam* (Berkeley: University of California Press, 1996); Rita Maran, *Torture: The Role of Ideology in the French-Algerian War* (New York: Praeger, 1989); Edgar O'Ballance, *The Algerian Insurrection, 1954–1962* (London: Faber, 1967); Pascal Ory and Jean-François Sirinelli, *Les Intellectuels en France, de l'Affaire Dreyfus à nos jours* (Paris: A. Colin, 1986); Peter Paret, *French Revolutionary Warfare from Indochina to Algeria: The Analysis of a Political and Military Doctrine* (New York: Praeger, 1964); Jean-Pierre Rioux, ed., *La Guerre d'Algérie et les Français* (Paris: Fayard, 1990); Jean-Pierre Rioux and Jean-François Sirinelli, *La guerre d'Algérie et les intellectuels français* (Paris: Complexe, 1991); David L. Schalk, *War and the Ivory Tower, Algeria and Vietnam* (New York: Oxford University Press, 1991), Harvey G. Simmons, *French Socialists in Search of a Role, 1956–1967* (Ithaca NY: Cornell University Press, 1970); Jean-François Sirinelli, *Intellectuels et passions françaises: Manifestes et pétitions au XXᵉ siècle* (Paris: Fayard, 1990); Paul Sorum, *Intellectuals and Decolonization in France* (Chapel Hill: University of North Carolina Press, 1977); Benjamin Stora, *Histoire de la guerre d'Algérie, 1954–1962* (Paris: La Découverte, 1993) and *La gangrène et l'oubli: La mémoire de la guerre d'Algérie* (Paris, La Découverte, 1992); John Talbott, *The War without a Name: France in Algeria, 1954–1962* (New York: Knopf, 1980); Pierre Vidal-Naquet, *Face à la raison d'État: un historien dans la guerre d'Algérie* (Paris: La Découverte, 1989) and *Torture: The Cancer of Democracy, France and Algeria, 1954–1962* (Baltimore: Penguin, 1963); and Nancy Wood, *The Vectors of Memory: Legacy of Trauma in Postwar Europe*

(London: Berg, 1999). Also see Ian Young, *The Private Life of Islam* (London: Allen Lane, Penguin, 1974; London: Pimlico-Random House, 1991). This striking account, by one of the authors of *Assassination*, depicts early post-independence Algeria inside a provincial hospital maternity unit.

5. On 20 August 1955 a group of FLN militants attacked the area in and around the small coastal town of Philippeville (present-day Skikda). Known as the Philippeville massacres, the attack on French civilians and Algerians suspected of collaboration represented a significant shift in the FLN's policy of not attacking the civilian population. The governor general's office estimated that 123 people were murdered, of which 71 were Europeans.

6. Soustelle's legitimate attempts to reenter politics by putting his name up for prime minister had been blocked by the leaders of the ruling parties who feared his aggressive pro-settler politics.

7. There was good reason for this belief because key members of the French military threatened to turn against Paris and take over the central government if its demands were not met. To show that they meant business, the French paratroopers took control of Corsica and threatened to continue the expedition northward to metropolitan France.

8. See James D. LeSueur, *Uncivil War*, 55–86, and the introduction to Mouloud Feraoun's *Journal, 1955–1962.*

9. It is worth pointing out that both the extreme right as well as the extreme left believed that they were being oppressed by the so-called Gaullist dictatorship.

10. Georges Bidault, *Resistance: The Political Autobiography of Georges Bidault*, trans. Marianne Sinclair (London: Weidenfeld & Nicolson, 1967), 276, 284.

11. Antoine Argoud, *La Décadence, l'imposture, et la tragédie* (Paris: Fayard, 1974), 314, 316 (my translation).

12. Robert Silman, interview by author, tape recording, London, 16 April 1994 (hereafter cited as Silman interview).

13. Maurice Papon's rather sympathetic depiction in the novel is particularly striking in the wake of the recent scandal over Papon's conviction for crimes against humanity for his involvement in the deportation of French Jews by the Vichy government during WWII. During his 1997 trial for his actions as a Vichy official, it was revealed that Papon had also lied about the police involvement in the equally infamous massacre of Algerians in Paris on 17 October 1961. On that night, the French police under Papon's direct command rounded up approximately twelve thousand Algerians and sent them to holding camps in the largest mass arrest since World War II.

In addition, several hundred were forced into the Palais des Sports, where dozens were tortured and killed. Throughout the Paris region, an estimated 230 to 250 were then murdered by the French police, their bodies tossed into the River Seine or buried in mass graves. At the time, Papon, and indeed most French officials, denied police involvement in the massacres, but evidence now substantiates the claims against the police and Papon. For further information, see Darius Sanai, "It was like unleashing a pack of rabid dogs," *The European* (London), 23 October 1997, and Jean-Luc Einaudi, *La Bataille de Paris: 17 October 1961* (Paris: Le Seuil, 1991).

14. For a more detailed account of these and other novels and films relating to the French-Algerian war, see Philip Dine's superb and unrivaled work, *Images of the Algerian War: French Fiction and Film, 1954–1992* (New York: Clavendon Press, 1994). See also Osman Benchérif, *The Image of Algeria in Anglo-American Writings 1785–1962* (Lanham MD: University Press of America, 1997); and Philip Dine, "Anglo-Saxon Literary and Filmic Representations of the French Army in Algeria," in Martin Alexander, Martin Evans, and John Keiger, eds., *The Algerian War and the French Army (1954–62)*, forthcoming. For *The Battle of Algiers* see Hugh Roberts, "The Image of the French Army in the Cinematic Representation of the Algerian War: The Revolutionary Politics of the Battle of Algiers," *The Journal of Algerian Studies* 2 (1997): 90–99.

15. Private papers of Robert Silman, London (hereafter cited as Silman papers).

16. Kenneth C. Crabbe, "The OAS against De Gaulle," review of *Assassination!*, by Ben Abro, *Augusta Chronicle* (Georgia), 17 November 1963.

17. Melvin Steakley, "Foiling Death Plot against De Gaulle—Fact or Fiction?" review of *Assassination!* by Ben Abro, *Houston Chronicle*, 24 November 1963.

18. Richard M. Brace, "Whodunit Masterpiece of Conspiracy in France," review of *Assassination!* by Ben Abro, *Chicago Tribune Magazine of Books*, 22 December 1963.

19. Mandrake, "20 to 1 at Lloyd's," review of *July 14 Assassination*, by Ben Abro, *Sunday Telegraph*, 2 June 1963.

20. Jacques Soustelle, *A New Road for France*, trans. Benjamin Protter (New York: Robert Speller & Sons, 1963), 11.

21. Soustelle, *A New Road For France*, 13.

22. Soustelle, *A New Road For France*, ix.

23. Soustelle, *A New Road For France*, 17–18. OVRA stands for Opera per la Vigilanza e la Repressione Antifascista, which was Mussolini's notorious political police created to combat antifascist activity in the 1930s.

24. *Evening Standard* (London), 7 November 1964.

25. Soustelle, *A New Road For France*, 71–72.

26. Soustelle, *A New Road For France*, 72.

27. Soustelle, *A New Road For France*, 21.

28. *Jeune Révolution*, 19 March 1963 (my translation).

29. *Nouveau candide* (Paris), 21–28 February 1963 (my translation).

30. Review of *A New Road for France* by Jacques Soustelle, trans. Benjamin Potter, *Choice* 3 (December 1966): 961–62.

31. Pierre Vidal-Naquet, *L'Affaire Audin* (Paris: Éditions de Minuit, 1958). The later edition, which also gives the history of the committee formed to investigate Audin's disappearance, is Pierre Vidal-Naquet, *L'Affaire Audin 1957–1978* (Paris: Éditions de Minuit, 1989). See also his *Mémoires*, 2 vols. (Paris: Éditions du Seuil, 1995–98).

32. Argoud, *La Décadence*, 295 (my translation).

33. Pierre Vidal-Naquet, "Une lettre de M. Vidal-Naquet," *Le Monde* (Paris), 1 March 1967 (my translation).

34. Jacques Soustelle, "Une lettre de Jacques Soustelle," *Le Monde* (Paris), 5–6 March 1967 (my translation).

35. Pierre Vidal-Naquet, "Jacques Soustelle et le 'CNR'," *Le Monde* (Paris), 9 March 1967 (my translation).

36. In June 1967, Mayflower Books apologized to Soustelle. To settle the case, Mayflower also agreed to pay an undisclosed sum to Soustelle as compensation and to cover his legal costs. When the settlement was reported in the *Evening News* (London), Silman and Young's solicitors immediately sent a letter indicating that they and Jonathan Cape were still joint defendants in the case against Soustelle. This was noted in the *Evening News* on 16 June 1967.

37. As it happens, Aron even signed a petition circulating in Paris in favor of granting Soustelle and Bidault amnesty.

38. The testimonies were recorded in both French and English but, to my knowledge, only the English transcript remains. Unfortunately, it is an English translation of French testimony, which is imperfect and requires some minor corrections. I have limited the corrections to a minimum and have intervened in the translations only when necessary. But I have made corrections in spelling, grammar, and capitalization. These transcripts are from the Silman papers.

39. Colin Ross-Munro represented the plaintiff (Soustelle) while Brian Neill represented Silman and Young, and Renée Stibbe, a prominent French lawyer and anitcolonial activist, also aided them in their defense. The testimonies were sworn before the vice-consul, Henry Norman Walmsley.

40. Bidault, *Resistance*, 277. On 31 May 1962 *L'Express* published the letter from the treasurer for the OAS that committed the transfer of one million "old" Francs to Bidault, who was to replace Salan.

41. Bidault, *Resistance*, 278.

42. Incidentally, Paul Rivet and Jacques Soustelle served as France's representatives to the United Nations where they defended the French-Algerian cause in 1957.

43. For more on Vidal-Naquet's criticisms of Soustelle's responsibility for torture in Algeria, see my "Torture and the Decolonization of French Algeria: Nationalism, Race, and Violence during Colonial Incarceration" in *Captive and Free: Colonial and Postcolonial Incarceration*, Graeme Harper, ed., forthcoming.

44. Especially the 20 August and 6 September 1962 issues of *Appel de la France* presented by Vidal-Naquet.

45. Jacques Soustelle, "Seven Years as a Wanted Man," *The Jerusalem Post*, 26 September 1968, 3.

46. When Silman and Young resolved the case with Soustelle, Jonathan Cape, which had drafted its apology to Soustelle back in 1967, formally settled the case with Soustelle in High Court on 4 May 1970 in London. Cape resolved to pay Soustelle an undisclosed amount to cover his court costs.

47. Tzvetan Todorov, *The Fantastic* (Ithaca NY: Cornell University Press, 1975), 83.

Biographies

JACQUES SOUSTELLE

Jacques Soustelle reentered France after he was granted amnesty in 1968. He returned to his academic position as a professor at the École des Hautes Études en Sciences Sociales in 1969. From 1971 to 1977 he was a member of the city council of Lyon. He was also elected to the French Parliament, where he remained as a deputy from 1973 to 1978. In 1970 he founded and became president of Progrès et Liberté (Progress and Liberty), a right-wing political movement. He represented France at the Council of Europe in 1973. Soustelle authored books on the archeology and anthropology of Mexico—including *L'Art du Mexique ancien* (Paris: Arthaud, 1966) and *Les Quatre Soleils* (Paris: Plon, 1967)—and continued to publish political works attacking de Gaulle—including *La Page n'est pas tournée* (Paris: La Table Ronde, 1965), *Vingt-huit ans de gaullisme* (Paris: La Table Ronde, 1968), and *Lettre ouverte aux victimes de la décolonisation* (Paris: Albin Michel, 1973). In 1983 he was elected to the Académie française. Soustelle died on 6 August 1990.

ROBERT SILMAN

Robert Silman completed a degree in philosophy at the Sorbonne, went on to become a doctor of medicine at the Middlesex Hospital, London University, and then earned a Ph.D. in neurobiology at St. Bartholomew's Hospital, London University. He has authored scores of research publications in major scientific research journals, principally on the role of the pituitary hormones ACTH and endorphin in human pregnancy and the pineal hormone melatonin in human reproduction. He became senior lecturer and honorary consultant at St. Bartholomew's and the Royal London School of Medicine and Dentistry, and was president and chief executive officer of a San Diego, California, research development company, which was created as a result of his research activities. He presides with Jean-Claude Carrière and Jean-Marie Cavada over the "Rencontres Internationales de l'Audiovisuel Scientifique," an annual awards ceremony in Paris honoring outstanding contributions in television and film to the arts and sciences.

Ian Young

After completing his philosophy degree at the Sorbonne, Ian Young qualified as a doctor in London. His training included an obstetric stint in Algeria described in *The Private Life of Islam* (London: Allen Lane The Penguin Press, 1974; London: Pimlico-Random House, 1991). He has worked as a doctor in London and Paris, and for the last fifteen years has codirected, with Charles Kreeger, the Lingua Medica translation and writing service at St. Bartholomew's Hospital in London.

James D. Le Sueur

James D. Le Sueur completed his B.A. at the University of Montana and then his Ph.D. in history at the University of Chicago in 1996. He is currently associate professor of history at the University of La Verne in southern California. He is author of *Uncivil War: Intellectuals and Identity Politics During the Decolonization of Algeria* (Philadelphia: University of Pennsylvania Press, 2001) and editor of the English translation of Mouloud Feraoun's *Journal, 1955–1962: Reflections on the French-Algerian War* (Lincoln: University of Nebraska Press, 2000), *The Decolonization Sourcebook* (London: Routledge, forthcoming), and *The Decolonization Reader* (London: Routledge, forthcoming). He is working on two new books: a comparative history of twentieth-century European decolonization and another work focusing on popular culture and postcolonial politics in contemporary France.